W9-DFX-595

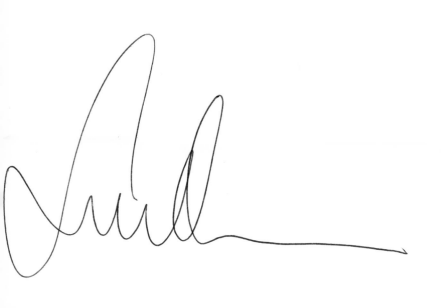

Past

THE SCHOOL for GOOD AND EVIL

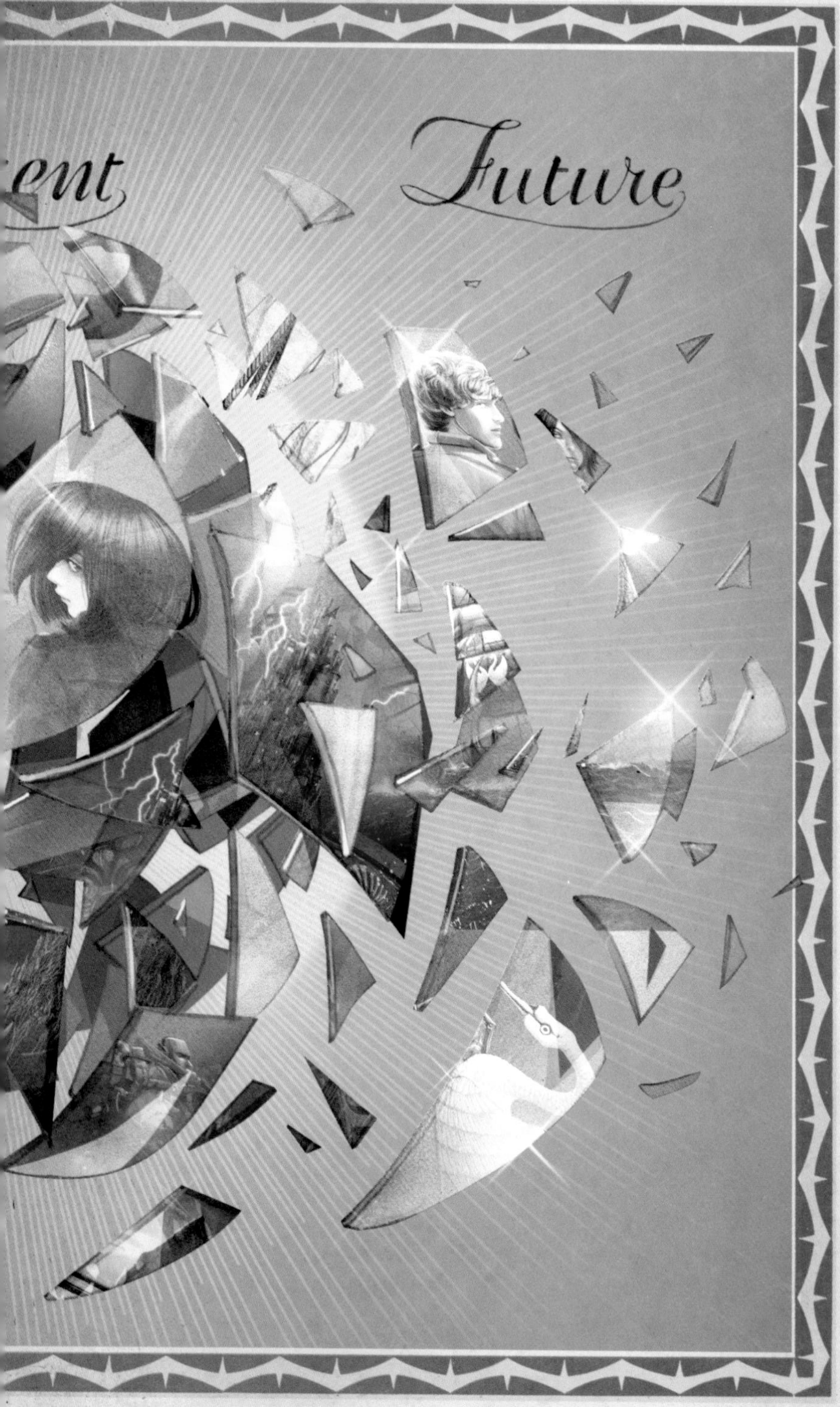
ent
Future

Soman Chainani

The SCHOOL for GOOD AND EVIL

THE CAMELOT YEARS

A CRYSTAL OF TIME

Illustrations by
Iacopo Bruno

HARPER
An Imprint of HarperCollinsPublishers

The School for Good and Evil #5: A Crystal of Time
Text copyright © 2019 by Soman Chainani
Illustrations copyright © 2019 by Iacopo Bruno
Library of Congress Control Number: 2018958691
ISBN 978-0-06-269517-8 (trade bdg.) — ISBN 978-0-06-288575-3 (int.)
ISBN 978-0-06-288641-5 (special edition) — ISBN 978-0-06-290697-7 (special edition)
ISBN 978-0-06-289559-2 (special edition) — ISBN 978-0-06-290764-6 (special edition)

Typography by Amy Ryan
19 20 21 22 23 PC/LSCH 10 9 8 7 6 5 4 3 2 1
❖
First Edition

For Uma and Kaveen

IN THE FOREST PRIMEVAL

A SCHOOL FOR GOOD AND EVIL

TWO TOWERS LIKE TWIN HEADS

ONE FOR THE PURE

ONE FOR THE WICKED

TRY TO ESCAPE YOU'LL ALWAYS FAIL

THE ONLY WAY OUT IS

THROUGH A FAIRY TALE

AGATHA

The Lady and the Snake

When the new King of Camelot intends to kill your true love, kidnap your best friend, and hunt you down like a dog . . . you better have a plan.

But Agatha had no plan.

She had no allies.

She had no place to hide.

So she ran.

She ran as far from Camelot as she could with no direction or destination, ripping through the Endless Woods, her black dress catching on nettles and branches as the sun rose and fell . . . She ran as the bag with a Dean's crystal ball swung and thumped against her ribs . . . She ran as WANTED posters with her face began appearing on trees, a warning that news traveled faster than her legs could carry her and that there was nowhere safe for her anymore . . .

By the second day, her feet blistered; her muscles throbbed, fed only by berries and apples and mushrooms she snatched along the way. She seemed to be going in circles: the smoky riverbanks of Mahadeva, the borders of Gillikin, then back to Mahadeva in the pale dawn. She couldn't think about a plan or shelter. She couldn't think about the present at all. Her thoughts were in the past: *Tedros in chains . . . sentenced to die . . . her friends imprisoned . . . Merlin dragged away unconscious . . . an Evil villain wearing Tedros' crown . . .*

She struggled through an assault of pink fog, searching for the path. Wasn't Gillikin the kingdom with the pink fog? Hadn't Yuba the Gnome taught them that at school? But she'd left Gillikin hours ago. How could she be there again? She needed to pay attention . . . she needed to think *forward* instead of backward . . . but now all she could see were clouds of pink fog taking the shape of the Snake . . . that masked, scale-covered boy who she'd been sure was dead . . . but a boy who she'd just seen alive . . .

By the time she came out of her thoughts, the fog was gone and it was nighttime. Somehow she'd ended up in the Stymph Forest, with no trace of a path. A storm swept in, slinging lightning through trees. She cowered under an overgrown toadstool.

Where should she go? Who could help her when everyone she trusted was locked in a dungeon? She'd always relied on her intuition, her ability to make a plan on the spot. But how could she think of a plan when she didn't even know who she was fighting?

I saw the Snake dead.

But then he wasn't . . .

And Rhian was still onstage . . .

So Rhian can't be the Snake.

The Snake is someone else.

They're working together.

The Lion and the Snake.

She thought of Sophie, who'd giddily accepted Rhian's ring, thinking she was marrying Tedros' knight. Sophie who believed she'd found love—*real* love that saw the Good in her—only to be taken hostage by a villain far more Evil than she.

At least Rhian wouldn't hurt Sophie. Not yet. He needed her.

What for, Agatha didn't know.

But Rhian would hurt Tedros.

Tedros, who'd heard Agatha tell Sophie last night that he'd been a failure as king. Tedros, who now doubted whether his own princess believed in him. Tedros, who'd lost his crown, his kingdom, his people, and was trapped in the hands of his enemy, who just yesterday he'd embraced like a brother. An enemy who now claimed to *be* his brother.

Agatha's stomach wrenched. She needed to hold Tedros

in her arms and tell him that she loved him. That she would never doubt him again. That she would trade her life for his if she could.

I'll save you, Agatha thought desperately. *Even if I have no plan and no one on my side.*

Until then, Tedros had to stay strong, no matter what Rhian and his men did to him. Tedros had to find a way to stay alive.

If he wasn't dead already.

In a flash, Agatha was running again, strobed by lightning as she slashed through the last of the Stymph Forest and then along Akgul's haunted beaches with ash for sand. Dovey's crystal ball weighed her down, pounding the same bruise in her flank again and again. She needed to rest . . . she hadn't slept in days . . . but her mind was spinning like a broken wheel . . .

Rhian pulled Excalibur from the stone.

That's why he's king.

Agatha ran faster.

But how?

The Lady of the Lake told Sophie that the Snake was king.

But Excalibur thought <u>Rhian</u> was king.

And Arthur told Tedros that <u>Tedros</u> was king.

Something's wrong.

<u>*Magically*</u> *wrong.*

Agatha held her breath, lost in a maze of thoughts. She needed help. She needed *answers*.

Muggy warmth turned to harsh wind and then to snow, the forest opening up in a sweep of tundra. In her sleepless haze, she wondered if she'd run through months and seasons. . . .

But now she could see the shadow of a castle in the distance, spires slicing through low-flying clouds.

Camelot?

After all this, instead of finding someone who could help her, had she run back to danger? Had she wasted all this time?

Tears rising, she backed away, turning to sprint again—

But she couldn't run anymore.

Her legs buckled and Agatha crumpled into soft snow, her black dress fanned around her like a bat's wings. Sleep came as hard and swift as a hammer.

She dreamed of a leaning tower stretched high into the clouds, built out of a thousand gold cages. Trapped in every cage was a friend or someone she loved—Merlin, Guinevere, Lancelot, Professor Dovey, Hester, Anadil, Dot, Kiko, Hort, her mother, Stefan, Professor Sader, Lady Lesso, and more— with all the cages teetering one over the other, and Sophie's and Tedros' cages at the very top, poised to come crashing down first. As the tower shook and swayed, Agatha threw herself against it to keep it from falling, her scrawny, gangly frame the only thing stopping her friends from dashing to their deaths. But just as she had the soaring column in hand, a shadow emerged atop the highest cage. . . .

Half-Lion. Half-Snake.

One by one, it threw cages off the tower.

Agatha woke with a start, sopped in sweat despite the snow. Raising her head, she saw the storm had passed, the castle ahead now clear in morning sun.

In front of it, two iron gates swung open and shut against

the rocks, the entrance to this white fortress that towered over a calm, gray lake.

Agatha's heart jumped.

Not Camelot.

Avalon.

Something inside her had steered her here.

To the one person who could give her answers.

Something inside her had a plan all along.

"Hello?" Agatha called out to the still waters.

Nothing happened.

"Lady of the Lake?" she tried again.

Not even a ripple.

Edginess fluttered in her chest. Once upon a time, the Lady of the Lake had been Good's greatest ally. That's why Agatha's soul had brought her here. To get help.

But Chaddick had come to the Lady of the Lake for help too.

He'd ended up dead.

Agatha looked up at the zigzagging staircase that ascended towards the circle of white towers. The last time she'd come to these shores, she'd been with Sophie, searching for Chaddick's body. Dark dregs of blood still stained the snow where they'd found Tedros' murdered knight, clutching a taunting message from the Snake.

Agatha had never seen the Snake's face. But the Lady of the Lake had seen it when she'd kissed him.

A kiss that had leeched the Lady's powers and betrayed King Tedros.

A kiss that had helped the Snake put a traitor on Tedros' throne.

Because that's what Rhian was. A filthy traitor, who'd pretended to be Tedros' knight when he was in league with the Snake the whole time.

Agatha turned back to the water. The Lady of the Lake had protected that Snake. And not just protected him: she'd fallen in *love* with him and lost her powers because of it. She'd thrown away a lifetime of duty. A sick feeling slid up Agatha's spine. The Lady of the Lake should have been immune to Evil's charms. But instead, she could no longer be trusted.

Agatha swallowed hard.

I shouldn't be here, she thought.

And yet . . . there was no one else to turn to. She had to take a chance.

"It's me, Agatha!" she bellowed. "Merlin's friend. He needs your help!"

Her voice echoed across the shore.

Then the lake shuddered.

Agatha leaned forward. She saw nothing except her own reflection in the silvery surface.

But then her face in the water began to change.

Little by little, Agatha's reflection morphed into a shriveled old hag's, with knots of white hair clinging to a bald head and spotted skin sagging off cheekbones. The hag loomed beneath the lake like a troll under a bridge, glaring up at Agatha with cold eyes. Her voice carried through the water, low and distorted—

"We made a *deal*. I *answered* Merlin's question," the Lady of the Lake seethed. "I let him ask me one thing—*one* thing—and in return, he would never come again. So now he tries to weasel out of our deal by sending *you*? Go. You're not welcome here."

"He didn't send me!" Agatha fought. "Merlin's a *prisoner*! There's a new king of Camelot named Rhian—he's trapped Tedros, Merlin, Professor Dovey, and all our friends in the dungeons. And Merlin's been hurt! He'll die if I don't save him! Tedros will too! Arthur's son. The *true* king."

There was no alarm or horror or even sympathy in the Lady's face. There was . . . nothing.

"Didn't you hear me? You have to help them!" Agatha begged. "You swore to protect the King—"

"And I *did* protect him," the Lady retorted. "I told you when you came here last. The green-masked boy had the blood of Arthur in his veins. And not just the blood of Arthur's son. The blood of Arthur's *eldest* son. I could smell it when I had my powers. I know the blood of the One True King." She paused, her face clouding. "He had powers too, this boy. Strong powers. He sensed my secret: that I've grown lonely here, protecting the kingdom, protecting Good, in this cold, watery grave . . . alone . . . always alone. He knew that I would trade my magic for love if only someone gave me the chance.

And he was offering me that chance. A chance Arthur never gave me. For a single kiss, the boy promised I could be free of this life . . . I could go with him to Camelot. I could have love. I could have someone to call my own, just like you. . . ." She glanced away from Agatha, hunching deeper. "I didn't know that giving up my powers would mean *this*. That I'd end an old crone, more alone than before. I didn't know his promise meant nothing." Her eyes sealed over. "But that is his right, of course. He is the king. And I serve the king."

"Except the king *isn't* the boy you kissed! *Rhian* is king! The boy they're calling the Lion," Agatha insisted. "That wasn't the boy who came here! The boy you kissed was the *Snake*. He kissed you to strip your magic and rob Good of your power. He kissed you to help the *Lion* become king. Don't you see? He *tricked* you! And now I need to know who that Snake is. Because if you can be tricked, so can Excalibur! And if Excalibur was tricked, then that's how an Evil villain ended up on Tedros' throne—"

The Lady of the Lake lurched towards Agatha, her decayed face just beneath the surface. "No one tricked me. The boy I kissed had Arthur's blood. The boy I kissed was the *king*. So if it was the 'Snake' I kissed, as you call him, then it is the Snake who rightly pulled Excalibur from the stone and now sits on the throne."

"But the Snake didn't pull Excalibur! That's what I'm trying to tell you!" Agatha hounded. "*Rhian* did! And I saw the Snake *there*! They're working together to con the people of the Woods. That's how they duped you and the sword—"

The Lady tore through the water. "I smelled his blood. I smelled a *king*," her voice resounded like thunder. "And even if I can be 'duped,' as you so boldly claim, Excalibur *cannot*. No one can outwit Good's most powerful weapon. Whoever pulled Excalibur from the stone is Arthur's blood heir. It was the same boy I protected. *He* is the rightful king . . . not the one you and Merlin defend."

She began to sink into the water.

"You can't go," Agatha gasped. "You can't let them die."

The Lady of the Lake paused, her skull shining underwater like a pearl. This time, when she looked up, the ice in her eyes had thawed. All Agatha saw was sadness.

"Whatever trouble Merlin and your friends have gotten into is their own doing. Their fates are in the hands of the Storian now," the Lady said softly. "I buried that boy Chaddick as you asked. I helped Merlin like he wanted. I have nothing left. So please . . . just go. I can't help you."

"Yes, you can," Agatha pleaded. "You're the only one who's seen the Snake's face. You're the only one who knows who he is. If you show me what the Snake looks like, I can find out where he and Rhian come from. I can prove to the people that they're liars! I can prove that Tedros belongs on the throne—"

"What's done is done," said the Lady of the Lake. "My loyalty is to the king."

She sank deeper—

"Would the true king hurt Merlin?" Agatha cried out. "Would Arthur's heir break his promise to you and leave you like *this*? You say Excalibur makes no mistakes, but *you* made Excalibur and *you* made a mistake. You know you did. Look at you! Please. Listen to me. Truth has become Lies and Lies the Truth. Good and Evil have become one and the same. A Lion and a Snake worked together to steal the crown. Even your sword can't tell what makes a king anymore. Somewhere inside you, you know I speak the Truth. The *real* Truth. All I'm asking for is the Snake's face. Tell me what the boy you kissed looks like. Give me the answer to my question and I'll never return. The same deal you made with Merlin. And I swear to you: this deal will be kept."

The Lady of the Lake locked eyes with Agatha. Deep in the water, the nymph treaded silently, tattered robes splayed like a dead jellyfish. Then she faded down into its depths and disappeared.

"*No*," Agatha whispered.

She dropped to her knees in the snow and put her face in her hands. She had no wizard, no Deans, no prince, no friends to rely on. She had nowhere to go. No one to turn to. And now Good's last hope had deserted her.

She thought of her prince lashed in chains. . . . She thought of Rhian clutching Sophie, his bride and prisoner. . . . She thought of the Snake, leering at her in the castle, like this was only the beginning. . . .

A burble came from the lake.

She peeked through her fingers to see a scroll of parchment floating towards her.

Heart throttling, Agatha snatched the scroll and pulled it open.

The Lady had given her an answer.

"But . . . but this is *impossible* . . . ," she blurted, looking back at the lake.

The silence only thickened.

She blinked back at the wet scroll: a bold, inked painting of a beautiful boy.

A boy Agatha knew.

She shook her head, baffled.

Because Agatha had asked the Lady of the Lake to draw the Snake's face. The Snake who'd kissed the Lady and left her to rot. The Snake who'd killed Agatha's friends and hidden behind a mask. The Snake who'd joined forces with Rhian and made him king.

Only the Lady of the Lake hadn't drawn the Snake's face at all.

She'd drawn Rhian's.

2

THE COVEN

Lionsmane

Hester, Anadil, and Dot sat shell-shocked in a stinking cell, flanked by fellow quest team members Beatrix, Reena, Hort, Willam, Bogden, Nicola, and Kiko. Just minutes ago, they'd been on the castle balcony for a Woods-wide celebration. Together with Tedros and Agatha, they'd presented the Snake's dead body to the people and basked in Camelot's victory over a vicious enemy.

Now they were in Camelot's prison, condemned as enemies themselves.

Hester waited for

someone to say something . . . for someone to take the lead. . . .

But that's what Agatha usually did. And Agatha wasn't here.

Through the cell wall, she could hear the muffled sounds of the ongoing ceremony, turned into King Rhian's coronation—

"From this day forward, you are rid of a king who closed his doors to you when you needed him," Rhian declared. *"A king who cowered while a Snake ravaged your kingdoms. A king who failed his father's test. From this day forward, you have a real king. King Arthur's true heir. We may be divided into Good and Evil, but we are one Woods. The fake king is punished. The forgotten people aren't forgotten anymore. The Lion is listening to you now!"*

"LION! LION! LION!" the chants echoed.

Hester felt her demon tattoo steam red on her neck. Next to her, Anadil and Dot tugged at the pastel dresses they'd been made to wear for the ceremony, along with their prissy, primped curls. Nicola tore off a strip of her dress to re-bandage a wound on Hort's shoulder that he'd gotten in battle against the Snake, while Hort kicked uselessly at the cell door. Beatrix and Reena were trying to light their fingerglows to no avail, and Anadil's three black rats kept poking heads out of her pocket, waiting for orders, before Anadil shoved them back down. In the corner, red-haired Willam and runty Bogden anxiously studied tarot cards, with Hester picking up their whispers: *"bad gifts"* . . . *"warned him"* . . . *"should have listened"* . . .

No one else spoke for a long while.

"Things could be worse," said Hester finally.

"How could it be *worse?*" Hort shrieked. "The boy we

thought was our savior and new best friend turned out to be the most Evil scum on the planet."

"We should have known. Anyone who likes Sophie is bound to be horrible," Kiko wisped.

"I'm not one to defend Sophie, but it isn't her fault," said Dot, failing to turn the ribbon in her hair to chocolate. "Rhian tricked her like he tricked all of us."

"Who says he tricked her?" said Reena. "Maybe she knew his plan all along. Maybe that's why she accepted his ring."

"To steal *Agatha's* place as queen? Even Sophie isn't that Evil," said Anadil.

"We just stood there instead of fighting back," said Nicola, despondent. "We should have done something—"

"It happened too fast!" said Hort. "One second the guards are parading the Snake's dead body and the next they're grabbing Tedros and slamming Merlin over the head."

"Did anyone see where they took them?" Dot asked.

"Or Guinevere?" said Reena.

"What about Agatha?" asked Bogden. "Last I saw, she was running through the crowd—"

"Maybe she escaped!" said Kiko.

"Or maybe she was beaten to death by that mob out there," said Anadil.

"Rather take her odds than be stuck in here," said Willam. "I've lived at Camelot most of my life. These dungeons are immune to magic spells. No one's ever gotten out."

"We don't have any friends left to *get* us out," said Hort.

"And given that we serve no use to Rhian anymore, he'll

probably cut off our heads by dinnertime," Beatrix scorned, turning to Hester. "So tell me, wise witch, how can things possibly be any worse?"

"We could have Tedros in our cell too," Hester replied. "That would be worse."

Anadil and Dot cracked up.

"*Hester*," a voice said.

They turned to see Professor Clarissa Dovey thrust her head through the bars of the next cell, her face clammy and pale.

"Tedros and Merlin might both be dead. The true King of Camelot and Good's greatest wizard," the Dean of Good rasped. "And instead of thinking about a plan to help them, you're making *jokes*?"

"Difference between Good and Evil. Evil knows how to look at the bright side," Anadil murmured.

"Not to be rude, Professor, but shouldn't you be the one thinking of a plan?" said Dot. "You're a Dean and we're technically still *students*."

"Hasn't been acting like a Dean," Hester groused. "Been in that cell the last ten minutes and didn't say a word."

"Because I've been trying to think of—" Dovey started, but Hester cut her off.

"I know fairy godmothers are used to waving away problems with pixie dust and magic wands, but magic isn't getting us out of this." Hester could feel her demon searing hotter, her frustration turned on the Dean. "After teaching at a school where Good always wins, maybe you're in denial that Evil actually won. Evil that's made itself look Good, which is *cheating* in my book. But win it did. And if you don't wake up and face the fact that we're fighting someone who doesn't play by your rules, then nothing you 'think' of is ever going to beat him."

"Especially without your broken crystal ball," Anadil seconded.

"Or broken wand," thirded Dot.

"Do you even have your Quest Map?" Hort asked Dovey.

"Probably broke that too," Anadil snorted.

"How dare you talk to her like that!" Beatrix blazed. "Professor Dovey has dedicated her *life* to her students. That's why she's in a cell to begin with. You know full well she's been ill—*gravely* ill—and that Merlin ordered her to stay at school when the Snake attacked Camelot. But still she came to protect us. All of us, Good *and* Evil. She's served the school for"—Beatrix glanced at Dovey's silver hair and deep wrinkles—"who knows how long, and you speak to her like she owes you something? Would you speak to Lady Lesso that way? Lady Lesso, who *died* to protect Professor Dovey? She would have expected you to trust her best friend. And to help her. So if you respected Evil's Dean, then you better respect Good's Dean too."

Quiet stretched over the cell.

"Come a long way from that Tedros-loving twit our first year," Dot whispered to Anadil.

"Shut up," Hester mumbled.

Professor Dovey, on the other hand, came alive at the mention of Lady Lesso's name. Tightening her bun, she pushed through her cell bars to get closer to her students. "Hester, it's natural to lash out when you feel helpless. All of us feel helpless right now. But listen to me. No matter how dark things seem, Rhian isn't Rafal. He's shown no evidence of sorcery, nor is he protected by an immortal spell like Rafal was. Rhian has only gotten this far because of *lies*. He lied to us about where he comes from. He lied to us about who he is. And I have no doubt he's lying about his claim to the crown."

"Yet he managed to pull Excalibur from the stone," Hester argued. "So either he's telling the truth about being King Arthur's son . . . or he's a sorcerer after all."

Professor Dovey resisted this. "Even with him pulling the sword, my instinct tells me he's neither Arthur's son nor the true king. I haven't proof, of course, but I believe there's a reason Rhian's file never crossed my desk or Lady Lesso's as a prospective student, when every child, Good *or* Evil, has a file at school. He claims he went to the Foxwood School for Boys, but that could be a lie, like all his other lies. And lies will only take him so far without skills, discipline, and training, all of which my students possess in spades. If we stick to a plan, we can stay one step ahead of him. So listen carefully. First off, Anadil, your rats will be our spies. Send one to find Merlin, the second to find Tedros, and the third to find Agatha wherever she may be—"

Anadil's rats sprang out of her pockets, elated to finally be useful, but Anadil squashed them down again. "Don't you think I thought of that already? You heard Willam. The dungeon is impenetrable. There's no way for them to— *Ow!*"

One of the rats had bitten her, and now all three were scampering through her fingers, sniffing and searching the cell walls, before they squeezed through three different cracks and disappeared.

"Rats always find a way. That's what makes them rats," said Professor Dovey, craning to see a crack in a wall that one of the rodents had squeezed into and spotting a golden gleam coming through. "Nicola, what do you see in that hole?"

Nicola pressed against the wall and put her eye to the crack. The first year probed at the hole with her thumbnail, feeling the mildewed stone crumble. Clearly the dungeons, like the rest of the run-down castle, hadn't been fortified or maintained. With the tip of her hair clip, Nicola pulled away more dirt and stone, which widened the hole a smidge bigger, more light spearing through.

"I see . . . sunlight . . . and the slope of a hill. . . ."

"Sunlight?" Hort scoffed. "Nic, I know they do things differently in Reader World, but in our world, dungeons are *below* ground."

"Is that one of the perks of having a boyfriend? Having him explain things to me I already know?" said Nicola acidly, squinting through the hole. "Dungeons might be below ground, but we're right up against the side of the hill. It's the only explanation for why I can see the castle." She scraped away more dirt with her clip. "I see people too. Lots of people packed uphill. They're looking up at the Blue Tower. Must be watching Rhian . . ."

The king's voice echoed louder through the hole.

"For as long as you've lived, you've served a pen. No one knows who controls this pen or what it wants and yet you worship it, praying it will write about you. But it never does. Thousands of years, it's ruled these Woods. What do you have to show for it? Each new story, it chooses someone else for glory. The educated. The children of that school. And leaves scraps for you, the hard-working, the invisible. You, the <u>real</u> stories of the Endless Woods."

The crew could hear the people buzzing.

"Never talked that much when he was with us," Dot mused.

"Give a boy a stage," Anadil quipped.

"Nicola, can you see the balcony where Rhian is?" Dovey asked.

Nicola shook her head.

Professor Dovey turned to Hester. "Have your demon chip at that hole. We need a view of the stage."

Hester frowned. "Maybe you can turn pumpkins into carriages, Professor, but if you think my demon can get us out by boring a tunnel through a wall—"

"I didn't say 'get us out.' I said 'chip at that hole.' But if you prefer to doubt me while we lose our chance at rescue, then by all means," Professor Dovey snapped.

Hester cursed under her breath as her demon tattoo swelled red on her neck, lifted clean off her skin, and flew towards the hole, jabbing its claws like pickaxes and garbling grunty gibberish: *"Babayagababayagababayaga!"*

"Careful," Hester mothered, "your claw is still wounded from Nottingham—"

She froze, catching a black blur of movement through the

hole. Her demon spotted it too and recoiled in fear . . . but it was already gone.

"What is it?" said Anadil.

Hester bent forward, inspecting the hole in the stone. "Looked like . . ."

But it couldn't have been, she thought.

The Snake's dead. Rhian killed him. We saw his body—

"Wait a second. Did you say *'rescue'*?" Dot said, twirling to Dovey. "First of all, you heard Willam: there's no way out of this prison. Second, even if there was and we summoned the League of Thirteen or anyone else, what would they do . . . *storm Camelot*? Rhian has guards. He has the whole Woods behind him. Who on the outside could possibly rescue us?"

"I never said it'd be someone on the outside," said Professor Dovey intently.

The whole crew looked at her.

"Sophie," said Hort.

"Rhian *needs* Sophie," Good's Dean explained. "Every King of Camelot needs a queen to consolidate his power, especially a king like Rhian who is so new to the people. Meanwhile, the Queen of Camelot is as vaunted a position as her counterpart. It's why Rhian took careful steps to ensure Sophie—a legend and beloved face across the Woods—would be *his* queen. As the people see it, the best of Good is marrying the best of Evil, which raises Rhian above the politics of Evers and Nevers and makes him a convincing leader to both. Plus, having Sophie as queen will calm any doubts about having a mysterious stranger as king. So now that that king has his ring on Sophie's finger, he will do everything he can to keep her loyalty . . . but in the end, she's still on *our* side."

"Not necessarily," said Reena. "The last time Sophie wore a boy's ring, it was Rafal's, and she sided with him against the whole school and nearly killed us all. And now you want us to trust the same girl?"

"This *isn't* the same girl," Professor Dovey challenged. "That's why Rhian handpicked her to be his queen. Because Sophie is the only person in the Woods who both Good and Evil claim as their own—at once the slayer of an Evil School Master and now Evil's new Dean. But we know where Sophie's true loyalties lie. None of you can argue that everything she's done on this quest has been to protect both her crew and Tedros' crown. She accepted Rhian's ring because besides being enamored with him, she thought he was Tedros' liege. She took Rhian's hand because of her love for her friends, not in spite of it. No matter what Sophie has to do to stay alive, we cannot doubt that love. Not when our own lives depend on her."

Beatrix frowned. "I still don't trust her."

"Me either," said Kiko.

"Join the club," said Anadil.

Professor Dovey ignored them. "Now for the rest of the plan. We'll wait for Anadil's rats to return with news of the others. Then, when the time comes, we'll send Sophie a message through that hole and establish a chain of communication. From there, we can plot our rescue," she said, checking on the quarter-sized breach that Hester's demon had managed to bash out of the wet, cracked stone. Rhian's speech amplified louder through it—

"*And let's not forget my future queen!*" he proclaimed.

The people sang back: "*Sophie! Sophie! Sophie!*"

"Can you see the stage yet, Nicola?" Professor Dovey pressured.

Nicola leaned forward, eye to the hole: "Almost. But it's so far uphill and we're on the wrong side of it."

Dovey turned to Hester. "Keep your demon digging. We need a view of that stage, no matter how remote."

"*Why?* You heard the girl," Hester pestered, wincing vicariously as her demon punched at the hole with its injured claw. "What good is a pea-sized rear view—"

"One of Rhian's pirate guards will likely check on us soon," Dovey continued. "Hort, given your father was a pirate, I'm assuming you might know these boys?"

"No one I'd call a friend," Hort punted, picking at his sock.

"Well, *try* to befriend them," Dovey urged.

"I'm not befriending a bunch of thugs," Hort shot back. "They're mercenaries. They're not *real* pirates."

"And are you a *real* Professor of History? If you were, you'd know that even mercenary pirates joined the Pirate Parley in helping King Arthur fight the Green Knight," Dovey rebutted. "Talk to these boys. Get as much information as you can."

Hort hesitated. "What kind of information?"

"*Any* information," the Dean pressed. "How they met Rhian or where Rhian really comes from or—"

Metal creaked and slammed in the distance.

The iron door.

Someone had entered the dungeons.

Bootsteps pounded on stone—

Two pirates in Camelot's armor dragged a boy's limp body past the cell, each gripping one of his outstretched arms. The boy resisted weakly, his eye blackened shut, his suit and shirt shredded, his bloodied body drained by whatever tortures they'd inflicted on him since they'd lashed him in chains onstage.

"Tedros?" Kiko croaked.

The prince raised his head, and seeing his friends, he swung towards them, gaping at the crew with his one open eye—

"Where's Agatha!" he gasped. "Where's my mother!"

The guards kicked his legs out from under him and yanked him down the corridor into pitch-dark shadows before dumping him into the cell at the very end.

But from Hester's vantage point, it seemed that the cell at hall's end had already been occupied, for as they flung Tedros into his cage, they let a prisoner out of it—three prisoners to be precise—who now slinked down the hall, unchained and free.

As these released captives moved out of the shadows, Hester, Anadil, and Dot pressed against the bars and came face-to-face with another coven of three. These haggard triplets glided past them in gray tunics with salt-and-pepper hair to their waists, rawboned limbs, and leathery, coppery skin; their necks and identical faces were long with high, simian foreheads; thin, ashy lips; and almond-shaped eyes. They smirked at Professor

Dovey before they followed the pirates out of the dungeons, the door slamming shut behind them.

"Who were those women?" Hester asked, swiveling to Dovey.

"The Mistral Sisters," said the Dean, grimly. "King Arthur's advisors who ran Camelot into the ground. Arthur appointed the Mistrals when Guinevere deserted him. After Arthur died, they had free rein over Camelot until Tedros came of age and put them in jail. Whatever reason Rhian has for freeing them, it can't be good news." She called down the hall. "Tedros, can you hear me!"

The echoes of Rhian's speech drowned out whatever response came back, if one came back at all.

"He's hurt," Dovey told the quest team. "We can't just leave him there. We need to help him!"

"How?" said Beatrix anxiously. "Anadil's rats are gone and we're trapped here. His cell is way at the other end of the—"

But now they heard the door to the dungeons open once more.

Soft footsteps padded down the staircase. A shadow elongated on the wall, then across their cell bars.

Into the rusty torchlight came a green-masked figure. His skintight suit of black eels hung in slashed ribbons, exposing his young, pale torso spattered with blood.

The entire crew flattened against the walls. So did Professor Dovey.

"But y-y-you're . . . *dead*!" Hort cried.

"We saw your body!" said Dot.

"Rhian *killed* you!" said Kiko.

The Snake's ice-blue eyes glared through his mask.

From behind his back, he produced one of Anadil's rats, the rodent writhing in his grip.

The Snake raised a finger and the scaly black scim covering his fingertip turned knife-sharp. The rat let out a terrible squeak—

"No!" Anadil screamed.

The Snake stabbed the rat in the heart and dropped it to the floor.

"My guards are searching for the two you sent to find Merlin and Agatha," he said in a crisp, deep voice as he walked away. "Next one I find, I'll kill one of you too."

He didn't look back. The iron door thudded behind him.

Anadil scrambled forward, reaching through the cell bars and scraping her rat into her hands . . . but it was too late.

She sobbed, clutching it against her chest as she curled into a corner.

Hort, Nicola, and Dot tried to comfort her, but she was crying so hard she started to shiver.

Only when Hester touched her did Anadil's wails slowly soften.

"She was so scared," Anadil sniffled, shearing off a patch of her dress and wrapping her rat's body in it. "She looked right at me, knowing she was going to die."

"She was a faithful henchman to the end," Hester soothed.

Anadil buried her head in her friend's shoulder.

"How did the Snake know the other rats were searching for Merlin and Agatha?" Hort blurted as if there was no more time to mourn.

"Forget that," said Nicola. "How is the Snake *alive*?"

Hester's stomach plunged.

"That thing I saw through the hole . . . I didn't think it could be . . . ," she said, watching her demon still hammering at the stone crack, undeterred by the Snake. She turned to the group. "It was a scim."

"So he was listening the whole *time*?" Beatrix said.

"That means he knows about everything!" said Hort, pointing at the hole. "No way can we send a message to Sophie. Scim's probably still out there, listening to us right now!"

Spooked, they turned to Professor Dovey, who was peering down the hall towards the staircase.

"What is it?" asked Hester.

"His voice," said Dovey. "It's the first time I've heard it. But it sounded . . . familiar."

The crew looked at each other blankly.

Then they tuned in to the king still booming from beyond: "*I grew up with nothing and now I'm your king. Sophie grew up a Reader and will now be your queen. We are just like you—*"

"Actually, he sounded a bit like Rhian," said Hester.

"A lot like Rhian," said Willam and Bogden at once.

"*Exactly* like Rhian," Professor Dovey concluded.

A crackling noise came from the wall.

Hester's demon had wedged loose another pebble-sized stone above the hole, opening it up further, before he'd exhausted all strength and collapsed back into his master's neck.

"I can see the stage now," said Nicola, putting her eye to the hole. "Just *barely* . . ."

"Good, we can mirrorspell it here. I can't do it from my cell, but Hester can," said Professor Dovey. "Hester, it's the charm I taught you after Sophie moved into the School Master's tower. The one that let you and me spy on her to make sure she wasn't voodoo hexing me or summoning the ghost of Rafal."

"Professor, how many times do we have to tell you, magic doesn't work inside the dungeons," Hester growled.

"*Inside* the dungeons," the Dean repeated.

Hester's eyes flared. This was why Dovey was a Dean and she was still a student. She should never have doubted her. Quickly, Hester hewed to the wall, slipped her fingertip through the tiny hole and into the summer heat. She felt her fingerglow activate and sizzle bright red. The first rule of magic is that it follows emotion and when it came to her hatred of Rhian, she had enough to light up all of Camelot.

"Should we really be doing this?" Kiko asked. "If the scim's out there—"

"How about I kill you, so you don't have to worry," Hester fired back.

Kiko pursed her lips.

She's right, though, Hester thought sourly. The scim could be outside the hole, listening . . . but they had to take the chance. A closer look at the stage would let them see Sophie with Rhian. It would let them see whose side Sophie was really on.

Quickly Hester lined up her eye to the hole, so she had a view of the stage, which looked like a matchbox from this far away. Even worse, just as Nicola said, she couldn't see the front of the stage—only a view from the side, with Rhian and Sophie's backs to her, high over the crowd.

Still, it would have to do.

Hester aimed her fingerglow directly at Rhian and Sophie. With half her mind, she focused on the stage angle she wanted to spy on; with the other half, she focused on the dank, dirty cell in front of her. . . .

"*Reflecta asimova*," she whispered.

At once, a two-dimensional projection appeared inside the prison cell, floating in the air like a screen. With colors muted, like a faded painting, the projection offered them a magnified view of what was happening on the Blue Tower balcony in real time. In this view, they could observe Rhian and Sophie close up, though only in profile.

"So a mirrorspell can let you see anything bigger from far away?" Hort said, wide-eyed. "Why didn't anyone show me this spell at school?"

"Because we all know how you would have used it," Professor Dovey scorched.

"Why aren't we watching them from the front?" Beatrix complained, studying Rhian and Sophie. "I can't see their faces—"

"The spell magnifies the angle I can see through the hole,"

said Hester testily. "And from here, I can only see the stage from the side."

In the projection, Rhian was still speaking to the guests, his tall, lean frame and blue-and-gold suit in shadow, while he held Sophie with one arm.

"Why doesn't she run?" said Nicola.

"Or shoot him with a spell?" said Willam.

"Or kick him in the marbles?" said Dot.

"Told you we couldn't trust her," Reena harped.

"No. That's not it," Hester countered. "Look closer."

The crew followed her gaze. Though they couldn't see Rhian's or Sophie's faces, they honed in on Sophie from behind, shuddering under Rhian's grip in her pink gown . . . Rhian's knuckles turning white as they dug into her . . . Excalibur clenched in his other hand, pressed against her spine . . .

"That dirty creep," Beatrix realized, turning to Dovey. "You said Rhian wants to keep Sophie loyal. How is sticking a sword in her going to do that?"

"Many a man has made his wife loyal at the point of a sword," the Dean said gravely.

Dot sighed. "Sophie really does have the worst taste in boys."

Indeed, only twenty minutes before, Sophie had leapt into Rhian's arms and kissed him, believing she was engaged to Tedros' new knight. Now that knight was Tedros' enemy and threatening to kill Sophie unless she played along with his charade.

But that wasn't all they could see from this vantage point.

There was someone else on the stage watching the coronation too.

Someone concealed inside the balcony, out of view of the crowd.

The Snake.

He stood there in his ripped, bloody suit of scims, watching the king speak.

"First, we need our princess to become a queen," Rhian proclaimed to the people, his voice amplified in the cell by the projection. "And as the future queen, it is Sophie's honor to plan the wedding. Not some pretentious royal spectacle of the past. But a wedding that brings us closer to you. A wedding for the people!"

"*Sophie! Sophie! Sophie!*" the crowd brayed.

Sophie squirmed in his grip, but Rhian shoved the sword harder against her.

"Sophie has a full week of parties and feasts and parades in store," he continued. "Followed by the wedding and crowning of your new queen!"

"*Queen Sophie! Queen Sophie!*" the masses anointed her.

Sophie's posture straightened, listening to the adoring crowd.

In a flash, she yanked away from Rhian, daring him to do something to her.

Rhian froze, still gripping her hard. Though his face was in shadow, Hester could see him watching Sophie.

Silence fell over the crowd. They sensed the tension.

Slowly, King Rhian looked back at the people. "It seems

our Sophie has a request," he said, even and serene. "A request she's been pressing upon me day and night and that I've been hesitant to grant, because I hoped the wedding would be *our* moment. But if there's one thing I know about being king: what my queen wants, my queen must get."

Rhian looked at his bride-to-be, a cold smile on his face.

"So the night of the wedding ceremony, at Princess Sophie's *insistence* . . . we will begin with the execution of the impostor king."

Sophie lurched back in shock, nearly slicing herself on Excalibur's blade.

"Which means a week from today . . . Tedros *dies*," Rhian finished, glaring straight at her.

Shrieks rang out from Camelot's people, who rushed forward in defense of Arthur's son, but they were stymied by citizens from dozens of other kingdoms, kingdoms once ignored by Tedros and now firmly behind the new king.

"*TRAITOR!*" one Camelot man screamed at Sophie.

"*TEDROS TRUSTED YOU!*" a Camelot woman shouted.

"*YOU'RE A WITCH!*" her child yelled at Sophie.

Sophie stared at them, speechless.

"Go now, my love," Rhian cooed, giving her a kiss on the cheek before guiding her into the hands of his armored guards. "You have a wedding to plan. And our people expect nothing less than *perfection*."

The last Hester saw of Sophie was her terrified face, locking eyes with her future husband, before the pirates pulled her into the castle.

As the crowd chanted Sophie's name and Rhian presided calmly at the balcony, everyone inside the dungeon cell was stunned silent.

"Was he telling the truth?" a voice echoed down the hall.

Tedros' voice.

"About Sophie wanting me dead?" the prince called out. "Was that the truth?"

No one answered him, because something else was happening onstage that the crew could see in the projection.

The Snake's body was changing.

Or rather . . . his clothes were.

Magically, the remaining scims rearranged into a slim-fitted suit, which turned gold-and-blue all at once: a perfect inverse of the suit that Rhian was wearing.

As soon as the Snake had conjured his new clothing, Rhian seemed to sense it, for the king glanced back at the masked boy, acknowledging his presence for the first time. The quest team now saw Rhian's tan, sharp-jawed face in full view, his hair glinting like a bronze helmet, his sea-green eyes running briefly over the Snake, who was still out of sight of the people. Rhian showed no surprise that his once mortal nemesis was alive or had magically changed his clothes or was wearing a suit that resembled his own.

Instead, Rhian offered the Snake the slightest hint of a smile.

The king turned back to the crowd. "The Storian never helps *you*. The *real* people. It helps the elite. It helps those who go to that school. How can it be the voice of the Woods, then? When it divides Good from Evil, rich from poor, educated from ordinary? That's what's made our Woods vulnerable to attack. That's what let a Snake slither into your kingdoms. That's what nearly killed you all. The pen. The rot starts with that *pen*."

The people murmured assent.

Rhian's eyes roamed the crowd. "You there, Ananya of Netherwood, daughter of Sisika of Netherwood." He pointed down at a thin, unkempt woman, stunned that the king knew her name. "For thirty years, you've slaved at your kingdom's stables, waking before dawn to groom horses for Netherwood's witch-queen. Horses you've loved and raised to ride in battle. Yet no pen tells your story. No one knows about what you've sacrificed, who you've loved, or what lessons you might offer—lessons more worthy than any puffed-up princess the Storian might choose."

Ananya blushed red as those around her gave her admiring looks.

"And you there, what about you?" said Rhian, pointing at a muscular man, flanked by three teenage boys with shaved heads. "Dimitrov of Maidenvale, whose three sons applied to the School for Good and were each denied, and yet all now serve as footmen for the young princes of Maidenvale. Day after day, you work to the bone, even though deep in your hearts you know these princes are no better than you. Even though you know that you deserved an equal chance at glory. Must you too die without your stories told? Must *all* of you die so ignored and forgotten?"

Dimitrov's eyes welled with tears while his sons put their arms around their father.

Hester could hear the murmurs building in the crowd, awed that someone with such great power was honoring people like them. That he was even seeing them at all.

"But what if there was a pen that told *your* stories?" Rhian offered. "A pen that wasn't controlled by mysterious magic, but by a man you trust. A pen that lived in plain sight instead of locked behind school gates. A pen made for a Lion."

He leaned forward. "The Storian doesn't care about you. I do. The Storian didn't save you from the Snake. I did. The Storian won't answer to the people. I will. Because I want to glorify all of you. And so will *my* pen."

"*Yes! Yes!*" cried the people.

"My pen will give voice to the voiceless. My pen will tell the truth. *Your* truth," the king announced.

"Please! Please!"

"The reign of the Storian is over!" Rhian bellowed. "A new pen rises. A new era begins!"

On cue, Hester and the crew watched as a sliver of the Snake's gold suit peeled off and floated over the balcony wall, out of view of the crowd. The golden strip reverted to a scaly black scim as it drifted higher into the air, still unseen. Then it descended over the mob and into sunlight towards King Rhian, magically morphing into a long, gold pen, knife-sharp at both ends.

The people gazed at it, enthralled.

"At last. A Pen for the People," Rhian called out, as the pen hovered over his outstretched hand. "Behold . . . *Lionsmane!*"

The masses exploded in their most passionate cheers yet. *"Lionsmane! Lionsmane!"*

Rhian pointed his finger and the pen soared into the sky over Camelot's castle and wrote in gold against the pure blue canvas like it was a blank page—

THE SNAKE IS DEAD.
A LION HAS RISEN.
THE ONE TRUE KING.

Dazzled, all citizens of the Woods, Good and Evil, kneeled before King Rhian. Dissenters from Camelot were forced to a knee by those around them.

The king raised his arms. "No more 'once upon a time.' The time is *now*. I want to hear your stories. And my men and I will seek them out, so that each day, my pen can write the *real* news of the Woods. Not tales of arrogant princes and witches fighting for power . . . but stories that spotlight *you*. Follow my pen and the Storian will no longer have a place in our world. Follow my pen and all of you will have a chance at glory!"

The whole of the Woods roared as Lionsmane ascended into the sky over Camelot, sparkling like a beacon.

"But Lionsmane alone is not enough to overcome the Storian and its legacy of lies," Rhian continued. "The Lion in the tale of *The Lion and the Snake* had an Eagle by his side to ensure that no Snake could ever find its way into his realm again. A Lion needs an Eagle to succeed: a liege to the king who can serve as his closest advisor. And today, I bring you this liege who will help me fight for a greater Woods. Someone you can trust as much as you trust me."

The crowd hushed in expectation.

From inside the balcony, the Snake started to move towards the stage, his green mask still in place, his back to Hester and the crew.

But just before he moved past an obscuring wall and into the view of the mob, the scims that made up the Snake's mask dispersed into the air, flying out of sight.

"I present to you . . . my Eagle . . . and the liege to your king . . . ," Rhian proclaimed. *"Sir Japeth!"*

Into the light walked the Snake, revealing his face to the throng, the gold of his suit kindling to shimmers in the sun.

Gasps came from the crowd.

"In that old, obsolete school, two just like us ruled over a pen. Two of the same blood who were at war with each other, Good and Evil," the king heralded, holding Japeth close beneath Lionsmane. "Now two of the same blood rule over a new pen. Not for Good. Not for Evil. But for the *people*."

The crowd erupted, singing the new liege's name: "Japeth! Japeth! Japeth!"

That's when the Snake turned and looked right into Hester's projection, revealing his face to the imprisoned crew, as if he knew they were watching him.

Taking in the Snake's beautiful, high-boned face for the first time, Hester's whole body went slack.

"What was that about staying one step ahead?" she breathed to Professor Dovey.

Good's Dean said nothing as Sir Japeth grinned back at all of them.

Then he turned and waved to the people alongside his identical twin brother, King Rhian . . .

The Lion and the Snake now lording over the Woods as one.

3

SOPHIE

Bonds of Blood

While the guards held her offstage, Sophie saw all of it.

The Snake becoming the Lion's liege.

Rhian's brother unmasked.

Lionsmane declaring war on the Storian.

The people of the Woods cheering on two frauds.

But Sophie's mind wasn't on King Rhian or his snake-eyed twin. Her mind was on someone else . . . the only person who mattered to her right now . . .

Agatha.

Even with Tedros set to die, at least she knew where he was. In the

dungeons. Still alive. And as long as he was alive, there was hope.

But the last she'd seen of Agatha was her best friend being hunted by guards through the crowd.

Did she escape?

Was she even alive?

Tears sprung to Sophie's eyes as she looked down at the diamond on her finger.

Once upon a time, she'd worn another ring . . . the ring of an Evil man who'd isolated her from her only real friend, just as she was now.

But that was different.

Back then, Sophie had wanted to be Evil.

Back then, Sophie had been a witch.

Marrying Rhian was supposed to be her redemption.

Marrying Rhian was supposed to be true love.

She'd thought he'd understood her. When she looked into his eyes, she'd seen someone pure, honest, and *Good*. Someone who acknowledged the shades of Evil in her heart and loved her for them like Agatha did.

He was gorgeous too, of course, but it wasn't his looks that made her take his ring. It was the way he looked at *her*. The same way Tedros looked at Agatha. As if he could only be complete by having her love.

Two by two and four best friends. It was the perfect ending. Teddy with Aggie, Sophie with Rhian.

But Agatha had warned her: *"If there's one thing I know, Sophie . . . it's that you and I don't get to have perfect endings."*

She'd been right, of course. Agatha was the only person Sophie ever truly loved. She'd taken for granted that she and Aggie would be in each other's lives forever. That their ending was safe.

But they were far away from that ending now . . . with no way back.

Four guards grabbed Sophie from behind and yanked her into the Blue Tower, their bodies reeking of onions and cider and sweat beneath their armor, their filthy nails digging into her shoulder before she finally flung out both arms and shoved them away.

"I wear the king's ring," Sophie seethed, smoothing her plunging pink dress. "So if you would like to retain your heads, I suggest you take your stultifying stench to the nearest baths and keep your grubby paws off me."

One of the guards doffed his helmet, revealing sunburnt Wesley, the teenage pirate who'd tormented her in Jaunt Jolie. "King gave us orders to take yer to the Map Room. Don't trust yer to git there on yer own, case you run like that wench Agatha did," he sneered, flashing a squalid set of teeth. "So either we walk yer nicely like we were doin' or we git you there a little less nice."

The three other guards removed their helmets and Sophie came face-to-face with the pirate Thiago, bloodred carvings around his eyes; a black boy with the name "Aran" tattooed in fire on his neck; and a supremely muscular girl with shorn dark hair, piercings in her cheeks, and a lecherous glare.

"Your choice, Whiskey Woo," growled the girl.

Sophie let them drag her.

As they goaded her through the Blue Tower rotunda, she saw a cadre of fifty workers, repainting columns with fresh Lion crests, refurbishing marble floors with Lion insignias in each tile, replacing the broken chandelier with one dangling a thousand tiny Lion heads, and switching out frayed blue chairs with spruced-up seats, the cushions embroidered with golden Lions. All remnants of King Arthur were similarly replaced, every tarnished bust and statue of the old king usurped with a buffed one of the new.

Sun sifted through the curtains, setting the circular foyer aglow, the light dancing off the new paint and polished gems. Sophie noticed three skeletal women with identical faces moving across the room in matching silk lavender robes. They handed each worker a satchel that clinked with coins, the three sisters gliding as one unit with imperious stiffness, as if they were the queens of the castle. The women saw Sophie watching them and gave her a simpering smile, bobbing together in a tight curtsy.

There was something off about them, Sophie thought. Not just their fake monkey grins and that bungled bow, like they were freak-show clones . . . but the fact that under those clean pastel robes, they weren't wearing any *shoes*. As the women continued to pay workers, Sophie peered at their grimy, bare feet that looked like they belonged to chimney sweeps, not ladies of Camelot.

No doubt about it. Something was *definitely* off.

"I thought Camelot had no money," Sophie said to the guards. "How are we paying for all this?"

"Beeba, say we cut her brain open, what we gonna find," Thiago asked the girl pirate.

"Worms," said Beeba.

"Rocks," countered Wesley.

"Cats," offered Aran.

The others looked at him. He didn't explain.

Nor did they answer Sophie's question. But as Sophie passed sitting rooms, bedchambers, a library, and solarium, each being renovated with Lion crests and carvings and emblems, it became clear that Camelot did have money. *Lots* of it. Where had the gold come from? And who were those three sisters acting like they owned the place? And how was this happening so soon? Rhian had barely become king and suddenly, the whole castle was being remade in his image? It didn't make any sense. Sophie saw more men shuffle by, carrying a giant portrait of Rhian in his crown and asking guards for directions to the "Hall of Kings" where they were supposed to hang it. One thing was for sure, Sophie thought, watching them veer towards the White Tower: all of this had to have been planned by the king long before today. . . .

Don't call him that. He isn't the king, she chastised herself.

But how did he pull Excalibur, then? a second voice asked.

Sophie had no response. At least not yet.

Through one window, she saw workers rebuilding the castle's drawbridge. Through another, she glimpsed gardeners reseeding grass and pulling in brilliant blue rosebushes, replacing the old dead ones, while over in the Gold Tower courtyard, workers painted gold Lions in the basin of each reflecting pool. A commotion disturbed the work and Sophie spotted a brown-skinned woman in a chef's uniform ushered out of the castle by pirate guards, along with her cooks, as a new young, strapping chef and his all-male staff were guided in to replace them.

"But the Silkima family has been cooking for Camelot for two hundred years!" the woman protested.

"And we thank you for your service," said a handsome guard with narrow eyes who was in a different uniform than the pirates—gilded and elaborate, suggesting he was of higher rank.

He looks familiar, Sophie thought.

But she couldn't study the boy's face any longer because she was being pulled into the Map Room now, which smelled clean and light, like a lily meadow—which wasn't what Map Rooms were supposed to smell like, since they were airless chambers, usually occupied by teams of unwashed knights.

Sophie looked up to see maps of the Woods' realms floating in the amber lamplight above a large, round table like severed balloons. As she peered closer, she saw these weren't old, brittle maps from King Arthur's reign . . . but the same magical Quest Maps that she and Agatha once encountered in the Snake's lair, featuring tiny figurines of her and her quest team, enabling the Snake to track their every move. Now all those figurines hovered over Camelot's tiny, three-dimensional castle, while their real-life counterparts festered in the dungeons below. But as she looked closer, Sophie noticed there was one labeled crew member on the map who wasn't near the castle at all . . . one who was breaking *away* from Camelot, slipping towards the kingdom border . . .

Agatha.

Sophie gasped.

She's alive.

Aggie's alive.

And if she was alive, that meant Agatha would do everything she could to free Tedros. Which meant Sophie and her best friend could work together to save Camelot's true king: Aggie from the outside, she from the inside.

But how? Tedros would die in a week. They didn't have any time. Plus, Rhian could track Aggie himself on this Quest Map anytime he wanted—

Sophie's eyes flared. *Quest Map!* She had her own! Her fingers clasped the gold vial attached to the chain around her neck, carrying the magical map given to each Dean. She tucked the vial deeper under her dress. As long as she had her own map, she could trace Agatha without Rhian knowing. And if she could trace her, maybe she could also send Agatha a message before the king's men found her. Hope flooded through her, drowning out fear—

But then Sophie noticed the rest of the room.

Five maids with white lace dresses that covered every inch of their skin and wide white bonnets on their heads were fanned around the table, silent and still like statues, their heads bowed so she couldn't see their faces, each holding a leather-bound book in her outstretched palms. Sophie moved closer, noticing that the books were labeled with the names of her and Rhian's wedding events.

BLESSING
PROCESSION
CIRCUS OF TALENTS
FEAST OF LIGHTS
WEDDING

She stared at a slim maid holding the book marked PROCESSION. The girl kept her head down. Sophie flipped through the book while the girl held it, the pages filled with sketches of carriage options and animal breeds and outfit possibilities that she and Rhian could use for the town parade, where the king and new queen would have a chance to meet the people up close. Would they ride in a glass carriage pulled by horses? On a gold-and-blue flying carpet? Or together atop an elephant? Sophie shifted to the maid with the CIRCUS OF TALENTS book and scanned through stage designs and curtain choices and decorations for a show where the best talents from the various kingdoms would perform for the betrothed couple . . . then she moved to the book branded FEAST OF LIGHTS and perused dozens of bouquets and linens and candelabras for a midnight dinner. . . .

All Sophie had to do was point a finger and pick from these

books, filled with everything she needed for the wedding of her dreams. A wedding bigger than life to a storybook prince. A wedding that had been her wish since she was a little girl.

But instead of joy, Sophie felt sick, thinking of the monster she was marrying.

That's the problem with wishes.

They need to be specific.

"King says yer to work till supper," Wesley ordered from the door.

He started to leave, then stopped.

"Oh. You've been asked to wear this at all times," he said, pointing at a white dress hung up on the back of the door, prim, ruffly, and even more modest than the maids'.

"Over my dead body," Sophie flamed.

Wesley smiled ominously. "We'll let the king know."

He left with his pirates, closing the door behind them.

Sophie waited a few seconds, then ran for the door—

It didn't budge.

They'd locked her in.

No windows either.

No way to send Agatha a message.

Sophie turned, realizing the maids were still there, posed like statues in their white dresses, faces hidden, as they clutched the wedding books.

"Do you speak?" Sophie snapped.

The maids stayed silent.

She smacked a book out of one of their hands.

"Say something!" she demanded.

The maid didn't.

Sophie snatched a book from the next maid and threw it against the wall, sending pages flying everywhere.

"Don't you get it? He's *not* Arthur's son! He's not the real king! And his brother is the *Snake*! The Snake that attacked kingdoms and *killed* people! Rhian pretended his brother was the enemy so he could look like a hero and become king! Now they're going to kill Tedros! They're going to kill the *true* king!"

Only one of the maids flinched.

"They're savages! They're *murderers*!" Sophie shouted.

None of them moved.

Furious, Sophie swiped more of the books and tore pages apart, ripping out the bindings. "We have to do something! We have to get out of here!" With a cry, she flung leather and parchment across the room, knocking the floating maps into walls—

Then she saw the Snake watching her.

He stood silently in the threshold of the open door, his gold-and-blue suit illuminated in the lamplight. Japeth had his brother Rhian's copper hair, only longer and wilder, as well as Rhian's sculpted face but paler, a cold milky-white, like he'd been sucked of blood.

"One book's missing," he said.

He tossed it on the table.

EXECUTION

Heart sinking, Sophie peeled it open to see an array of axes to choose from, followed by options for chopping blocks, each with a sketch of Tedros kneeling, his neck stretched over the block. There were even choices for baskets to catch his severed head.

Slowly Sophie looked back up at the Snake.

"I assume there'll be no more trouble about the dress," said Sir Japeth.

He turned to leave—

"You animal. You disgusting *scum*," Sophie hissed at the Snake's back. "You and your brother use smoke and mirrors to infiltrate Camelot and steal the real king's crown and you think you can get *away* with it?" Her blood boiled, the fury of a witch rekindling. "I don't know what you did to trick the Lady of the Lake or what Rhian did to trick Excalibur, but that's all it was. A *trick*. You can put my friends in jail. You can threaten me all you want. But people can only be fooled for so long. They'll see who you two are in the end. That you're a soulless, murdering creep and he's a *fraud*. A fraud whose throat I'll cut the second he shows his face—"

"Better get on with it, then," a voice said as Rhian entered, barechested in black breeches, his hair wet. He glared at Japeth. "I told you I'd handle her."

"And then you went for a bath," said Japeth, "while she refuses to wear *Mother*'s dress."

Sophie lost her breath. Not just because she had a storm of rage ready to unleash or because two brothers were dolling her up in their mother's clothes, but because she'd never seen Rhian without his shirt before. Now as she looked at him, she saw his chest was just as ghost white as Japeth, while Rhian's arms and face glowed a deep tan—the same tan that farmers in Gavaldon had after they wore shirts in the hot summer sun. Rhian saw her ogling him, and he gave her a cocked grin, as if he knew what she was thinking: even the tan had been part of the ruse to prevent anyone from seeing they were brothers, a ruse to make Rhian look like a golden Lion battling a cold-hearted Snake . . . when, in fact, the Lion and the Snake were perfect twins all along.

As Sophie stood there, taking in their matching smirks and sea-colored stares, she could feel a familiar fear—the same fear she'd felt when she kissed Rafal. No, this fear was sharper. She'd known who Rafal was. She'd chosen him for the wrong reasons. But she'd learned from her fairy tale. She'd fixed her mistakes . . . only to fall in love with an even worse villain. And this time, there wasn't one of him, but *two*.

"Wonder what kind of mother could raise *cowards* like you," Sophie snarled.

"Talk about my mother and I'll rip out your heart," the Snake spewed, launching for her—

Rhian held him back. "Last time. *I'll* handle her."

He pushed Japeth aside, leaving his brother stewing in the corner.

Rhian turned to Sophie, his eyes clear as glass.

"You think *we're* the cowards? You were the one who said Tedros was a bad king. In fact, during the carriage ride to recruit the armies, you said I could do better. That *you* could do better. And here you are, acting as if you stood by your dear 'Teddy' all along."

Sophie bared her teeth. "You set Tedros up. The Snake was your *brother*. You lied to me, you cockroach—"

"No," the king slashed, hardening. "I didn't lie. I never lied. Every single word has been the truth. I saved kingdoms from a 'Snake,' didn't I? I pulled Excalibur from its stone. I passed my father's test and for that, I am king, not that fool who *failed* his test again and again and again. Those are the *facts*. That speech I gave to the army in Camelot Hall: all of that was true too. It did take a Snake to bring forth the *real* Lion of Camelot. You loved me when I spoke those words then. You wanted to marry me—"

"I thought you were talking about *Tedros*!" Sophie screamed. "I thought he was the real Lion!"

"Another lie. In the carriage ride, I told you that Tedros had failed. That he'd lost the war for people's hearts. That a real Lion would have known how to win. You heard me, Sophie, even if you don't want to admit it. It's why you fell in love with me. And now that everything I said would happen has indeed happened, you act as if I'm a villain because it isn't exactly like you imagined. *That's* cowardly."

"I loved you because you pledged your loyalty to Tedros and Agatha!" Sophie fought. "I loved you because I thought you were a hero! Because you pretended to love me back!"

"Again. A lie. I never made such a pledge and I never said I loved you nor did you ask if I did," said the king, moving towards her. "I have my brother. I have the bond of blood, which is forever. Love, on the other hand, is a figment. Look what it did to my father, to Tedros, to *you*—it made you foggy-eyed fools. So, no, I don't love you, Sophie. You're my queen for a reason deeper than love. A reason that makes me willing to risk having you by my side, despite your sympathy for an impostor king. A reason that will bond us more than love."

"Bond? You think you and me can have a *bond*?" Sophie said, recoiling from him, knocking into a maid. "You're a two-faced lunatic. You had your brother *attack* people so you could ride in to save them. You put a sword to my spine, you imprisoned my friends—"

"They're still alive. Be thankful for that," said Rhian, cornering her. "But right now, you've wedded your loyalty to the wrong king and the wrong queen. You're blinded by friendship. Agatha and Tedros are not meant to rule the Woods. You and I are, and soon you will understand why."

Sophie tried to move, but he took her damp palm in his. "In the meantime, if you behave and as long as it's reasonable . . . ," he said, softening, "the maids and cooks will grant any requests you have."

"Then I request Tedros be freed," Sophie spat at him.

Rhian paused. "I said 'reasonable.'"

Sophie ripped her hand away. "If you are Arthur's son, as you say you are, then Tedros is your *brother*—"

"*Half*-brother," said the king coldly. "And who's to say that's true? Who's to say he's King Arthur's son at all?"

Sophie gaped at him. "You can't just mold the truth to fit your lies!"

"You think that Tedros shares *our* blood?" Japeth piped from the corner. "That whinging little tart? Unlikely. But maybe if you give Rhian an extra kiss tonight, he'll poison the boy instead of chopping off his head." He smiled at Sophie and flicked his tongue like a serpent.

"Enough, Japeth," Rhian groused.

Sophie could see one of the maids shivering in the corner, head bowed. "I told the maids what you've done," Sophie fumed. "They'll tell the rest of the castle. They'll tell *everyone*. That you're no king. And that he's no liege. That your brother's the Snake. All of them know—"

"Do they?" the Snake asked, raising a brow at his brother.

"Doubtful," said the Lion, turning to Sophie. "These were Agatha's chambermaids, so their loyalty to me was questionable to begin with. Instead of letting them loose in the Woods, I gave them the choice between a swift death and serving me and my brother. Provided they endured one slight modification."

Modification? Sophie couldn't see their faces, but the five maids appeared healthy. No missing limbs or marks on their skin.

But then she saw the Snake's eyes flash . . . that same insidious flash she'd witnessed whenever he'd done something especially Evil. . . .

Sophie looked closer at the maid nearest to her. And then she saw it. . . .

A long, thin scim sliding teasingly out of the maid's ear, eely scales glinting in the lamplight, before it wedged right back in.

Nausea coated Sophie's throat.

"Whatever you've told them fell upon deaf ears," said Rhian. "And given that Japeth promised to restore them to their original condition only once they prove their loyalty to the new king, I'd doubt they'd listen to you anyway."

He raised his finger towards the maids and the tip glowed bright gold. Responding to the signal, the maids quickly exited the room in a single-file line.

The same color as Tedros' glow, Sophie thought, gazing at Rhian's finger. *But how? Only students at the school have fingerglows and he was never a student there—*

As the last maid shuffled through the door, head down, the king suddenly barred her path. It was the maid Sophie had seen shaking in the corner.

"There was one maid whose ears we left alone, however. One who we *wanted* to hear every word," said Rhian, hand on the maid's neck. "One who required a different modification . . ."

He raised the maid's head.

Sophie froze.

It was Guinevere.

A scim curled around the once-queen's lips, sealing her mouth shut.

Guinevere gave Sophie a petrified stare, before Rhian guided her out with the others and closed the door.

Japeth's gold-and-blue clothes magically sloughed away,

returning to his shredded suit of black scims, his white chest showing through the holes. He stood next to his brother, their muscles rippling beneath the tawny lamps.

"She's a queen!" Sophie gasped, sick to her stomach. "She's Tedros' mother!"

"And she treated *our* mother poorly," said Japeth.

"So poorly it's only fitting she watches us treat her son poorly too," said Rhian. "Past is Present and Present is Past. The story goes round and round again. Didn't they teach you that lesson in school?"

Their eyes danced between blue and green.

Our mother, Sophie thought.

Who was their mother?

Agatha had mentioned something . . . something about her former steward who they'd buried in Sherwood Forest . . . What was her name?

Sophie looked at the two boys watching her, with their twin torsos and reptile smiles, the new King and Liege of Camelot, and suddenly she didn't care who their mother was. They'd jailed her friends, enslaved a real queen, and tricked her into being a false one. They'd forced her best friend to run and condemned Sophie to live as a stooge of the enemy. *Her*, the greatest witch in the Woods, who had nearly brought down the School for Good and Evil. Twice. And they thought she'd be their puppet?

"You forget that I'm Evil," Sophie said to Rhian, her rage replaced by a chilly calm. "I know how to kill. And I'll kill both of you without getting a spot of blood on my dress. So either you free me and my friends and return your crown to the *rightful* king or you'll die here with your brother, squealing like whatever's left of his slimy eel—"

Every last scim tore off Japeth and slammed Sophie against the wall, binding her like a fly in a web, her palms over her head, with another scim strangling her throat, one gagging her mouth, and two turning lethal sharp, poised to gouge out her eyes.

Wheezing in shock, Sophie saw Japeth leering at her, his scim-less, naked form concealed by the table.

"How about this as a compromise," said Rhian, posing against the wall next to Sophie's body. "Every time you behave badly, I'll kill one of your friends. But if you do as I say and act the perfect queen . . . well, then I won't kill them."

"Sounds like a fair deal to me," said the Snake.

"And besides, there are things we could do to you too," Rhian said, his lips at Sophie's ear. "Just ask the old wizard."

Sophie muffled into her gag, desperate to know what they'd done to Merlin.

"But I don't want to hurt you," the king went on. "I told you. There's a reason you're my queen. A reason why you belong here. A reason why you have this story all wrong. A reason why your blood and ours are so inextricably linked . . ."

Rhian raised his hand to the two sharp scims pointed at Sophie's pupils and took one of the scims into his hand. He twirled it on his fingertip like a tiny sword and stared right at his bound princess.

"Want to know what it is?"

His eyes sparkled dangerously.

Sophie screamed—

He stabbed the scim at her open palm and sliced across the flesh, opening up a shallow wound, which dripped small droplets of blood.

As Sophie watched in horror, the king cupped his hand beneath the wound and collected Sophie's blood like rainwater.

Then he smiled at her.

"Because you're the only person . . ."

He walked towards his brother.

". . . in all of the Woods . . ."

He stopped in front of Japeth.

". . . whose blood can do . . ."

He smeared Sophie's blood across his brother's chest.

". . . *this*."

For a moment, nothing happened.

Then Sophie jolted.

Her blood had started to magically disperse across Japeth's body in thin, shiny strands, branching and crisscrossing down his skin like a network of veins. The strands of blood deepened in color to a rich crimson and grew thicker, knotting into roped netting that sealed his body in. The ropes squeezed tighter, cutting into his skin like whips, deeper and deeper, until Japeth was corseted by Sophie's blood, his flesh stretched raw. He clenched his whole body in agony, his muscles striating as he tilted his head back, mouth open in a choked scream. Then, all at once, the ropes binding him turned from red to black. Scales spread across them like a rash, as the ropes began to undulate and move with soft shrieks like baby eels, replicating across the gaps in his chalky flesh, scim after scim after scim until at last . . . Japeth stared back at her, his suit of snakes as strong and new as the first time Sophie had seen it.

There was no doubting what she'd just witnessed.

Her blood had restored him.

Her blood had restored a monster.

Her blood.

Sophie went limp under her own binds.

The Map Room was silent.

"See you at supper," said the king.

He walked out the door.

The Snake followed his brother, but not before putting his mother's dress on the table and giving Sophie a last glare of warning.

As he walked out the door, the scims flew off Sophie with piercing shrieks and chased after Japeth, the door slamming shut behind them.

Sophie was alone.

She stood amongst the torn wedding books, her hand still seeping blood.

Her mouth trembled.

Her lungs felt like they were caving in.

It had to have been a trick.

Another lie.

It *had* to be.

And yet, she'd seen it with her very own eyes.

It wasn't a trick. It was real.

Sophie shook her head, tears rising.

How could something so hellish come from *her*?

She wanted this Snake dead in the worst possible way . . . and instead she'd restored him to *life*? After all she'd done to protect her friends from him? After all she'd done to change? And now she was the lifeblood of the worst kind of Evil?

Heat rushed to her face, a furnace of fear. A witch's scream filled up her lungs, clawing at her throat. A scream that would kill everyone in this castle and crumble it to ash. She opened her mouth to unleash—

Then . . . she held it in.

Slowly she let the scream slither back into the recesses of her heart.

"Past is Present and Present is Past."

That's what the new king said.

That's why he was always one step ahead: because he knew people's pasts . . .

And Sophie's past was Evil.

Evil that for so long had been her weapon.

Evil that was the only way she knew how to fight back.

But Rhian was too smart for that.

You can't beat Evil with Evil.

Maybe to win a battle, but not the war.

And no matter what, she would win this war. For Agatha. For Tedros. For her friends.

But to win, she needed answers. She needed to know who the Lion and the Snake *really* were. And why her blood had melded magically with theirs . . .

Until she found those answers, she'd have to bide her time.
She'd have to be smart. And she'd have to be careful.
Sophie gazed at the white dress on the table, her lips curling.
Oh, yes.
There were other ways to be a witch.

4

AGATHA

New Alliances

After leaving Avalon, Agatha planned to sneak into a neighboring kingdom and find food and a place to sleep. She needed time to think about the Lady of the Lake's strange drawing . . . time to stash a crystal ball that was weighing her down . . . time to plot her next moves. . . .

That all changed when she got to Gillikin.

It was past twilight when Agatha crossed into the Ever kingdom, home to the Emerald City of Oz. She'd snuck in on a wheelcart of visitors from Ginnymill who'd come traveling up the coast (Agatha stowed

herself under their luggage). By the time they reached the yellow brick road on the outskirts of Emerald City and dismounted in a market jammed with noisy tourists, the sky was dark enough for Agatha to slip out and blend into the crowd.

A week ago, Agatha had read reports of Gillikin plagued by the Snake's attacks—fairy-eating wasps, carriage bombs, and rogue nymphs—that paralyzed the kingdom. The Fairy Queen of Gillikin and the Wizard of Oz, once rivals vying for power, had been forced into a truce, both appealing to Tedros of Camelot for help. Now, with the Snake supposedly dead at Rhian's hands, Gillikin had pledged its alliance to Camelot's new king and its thoroughfares bustled once more, the people of the Woods no longer afraid to go about their lives.

Agatha had chosen to come to Gillikin for a few reasons: first, because it was the nearest Ever kingdom to Avalon and home to the invisible fairies who had once sheltered her from the School Master's zombies; and more importantly, because it was a melting pot of immigrants from all over the Woods, determined to find their way into Emerald City and win an audience with the wizard. Among such a motley mob, Agatha figured she was bound to suss out news of Camelot, as well as of Tedros and her friends. At the same time, with so many people clogging the yellow streets, clamoring for a coveted "green ticket" into Emerald City (either you won one by lottery or you scalped one from a dodgy vendor), Agatha assumed she'd go unnoticed.

Which turned out to be a mistake.

Everywhere she looked, there were WANTED posters in

different languages fixed to the market stalls, glowing in the torchlight—

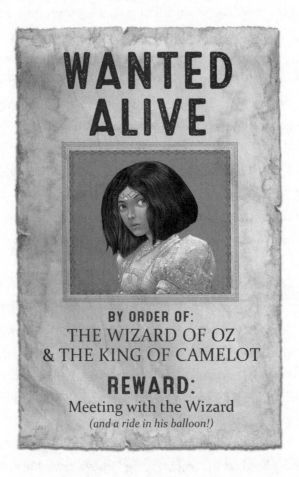

As the wizard only granted a few meetings a day, the search for Agatha had become a manic treasure hunt. Vendors hawked magical "Agatha-Vision" goggles to spot her, luminescent Lion lassos to capture her, Tedros voice boxes that emitted the prince's voice to bait her, faux-crystal balls to track her, even maps of Gillikin with notations where Agatha had supposedly been spotted.

"If I meet the wizard, I'm gonna ask him for a new leg," Agatha overheard a limping boy tell a scraggly vendor as he bought one of the maps. Agatha lingered behind the boy, six or seven years old, as he unfurled the parchment and scanned the tiny cartoon Agathas with witchy hair and gnashed teeth, dotted around the map. The boy looked up. "You *sure* you saw her?"

"Came and bought a map from me," said the vendor, smiling, "just like you."

"Then why didn't you catch her yourself?" the boy asked.

The vendor's smile flattened. "Uh, well, because I didn't have a Lion lasso like this one here!"

The boy peered at him skeptically . . . then started counting coins from his pocket.

Overhead, glittery floodlights scanned the crowds, projected by clouds of invisible fairies joining the hunt, the same fairies who'd once protected Agatha from Evil and now sought to deliver her back to it. The iridescent spotlights flushed across the market, about to light up her face—

Agatha dove behind a stall, crashing into a pine hedge and landing hard on the bag carrying Dovey's crystal ball. Cursing silently, she picked pine needles out of her chin, listening to the din of the market: the conversation in languages she didn't recognize . . . the sizzle of food carts selling "wizard" burgers (gold-dusted patties in green palm leaves) and "fairy" creams (hot buttermilk with sparkle-foam) . . . the sharp voice of a stall barker, drifting over the crowd: "*Step right up! Gilly's Ticket Hub! Best price on tickets in the Woods! Emerald City passes! Caves of Contempo tours! Fairy flights to Beauty and the Feast! Reservations available tonight! Step right up! Come to Gilly's!*"

As Agatha lumbered to her feet, she saw that the stall she'd crashed behind was selling both Wizard of Oz merchandise and King Rhian memorabilia in tribute to the new alliance, the shop packed with tourists waving bags of coins at the three vendors frantically dispensing Lion mugs, shirts, masks, bags, and candy.

"But I thought Agatha and Tedros were Good," said a young girl to her mother, who was jostling in the crowd, trying to buy a cheap gold pen that resembled the Storian. Only it wasn't meant to be the Storian, Agatha realized, because engraved in the gold surface was the word . . . LIONSMANE.

Lionsmane? Agatha peered closer at it. *What's that?*

"You used to tell me Agatha and Tedros' fairy tale every night before bed," the young girl was badgering her mother, "and they ended as king and queen, remember? That was their Ever After—"

"Well, turns out Agatha and Tedros were only *pretending* to be king and queen, while the real king was out here in the Woods," her mother assured. "King Rhian killed the Snake, while Tedros did nothing. King Rhian is the leader of Good now. And Sophie will be his queen."

"He's the leader of Evil too," rasped a black-cloaked hag near them, who was also waiting to buy one of the gold pens. "That's why he's marrying Sophie. To bring us all together.

Rhian is king of the *whole* Woods now. And Lionsmane will make sure you never hear a fake fairy tale like Agatha's again. King Rhian's pen is going to tell *real* stories." She grinned toothlessly at the little girl. "Might even write yours."

Rhian's pen? Agatha thought, bewildered.

The young girl blinked between her mother and the hag.

"But why does King Rhian have to kill Tedros?" she asked. "And why does he have to kill him at his wedding to Sophie?"

Agatha's stomach wrenched so hard she felt it in her throat.

Tedros killed at Rhian and Sophie's—

Impossible. They couldn't kill King Arthur's son at a royal wedding. It could never happen. Sophie would never *let* it happen. Sophie would protect Tedros . . . She'd plot against Rhian from inside the castle . . . She'd never marry that monster!

Agatha tensed. Or now that Sophie was about to be Queen of Camelot, worshipped by the entire Woods, would she suddenly turn back into—

Don't be stupid, Agatha scoffed. She'd seen Sophie's face when Rhian had trapped her at swordpoint. This wasn't the old Sophie, who'd betrayed her best friends for love. This time, they were all on the same team against a fake king.

A fake king who was planning to kill the real one.

Agatha expected to feel a rush of panic—

But instead a sense of calm came over her.

If she didn't find a way to get to Tedros, he would die in the worst possible way.

There was no time for helplessness.

Her prince needed her.

She slipped out from behind the stall, past the distracted vendors, and deftly stole a hooded shirt with Rhian's face on it as the crowd jostled for Lion merchandise. Pulling the hood low over her head, she wove her way through the wall of shoppers, the bag with Dovey's ball tight against her shoulder as she headed towards the blinking stall in the distance.

GILLY'S
TICKET HUB!

She passed more booths thronged with people buying phony Agatha hunting gear, while she hustled past, puffing out Rhian's face on her chest, pretending she was his biggest fan. She was approaching Gilly's now, the barker's voice growing louder: "*Step right up! Best tickets in tow*—"

Something collided with her.

Agatha looked up to see two hulking green hobgoblins in Agatha-Vision goggles, toting full bags of Lion souvenirs. They gaped at her through their goggles . . . then slowly lowered them.

"Gaboo Agatha gabber," said the first goblin.

"Gaboo *shamima* Agatha gabber," said the second goblin.

"No no Agatha gabber," Agatha said, pointing in the other direction. "Gaboo went that way."

The goblins narrowed their eyes.

Agatha pointed at Rhian on her shirt. "See. *King*. Ooooh."

The goblins looked at each other.

"Poot," said the first.

"Mah poot," said the second.

They dropped their bags and charged at her.

Facing five hundred pounds of rabid slime, Agatha plunged into the mob and shoved people in the goblins' way like shields but the goblins rammed past them, the two creatures reaching out with stubby arms and grabbing on to Dovey's bag—

Agatha spun around and overturned a vendor's cart of fake crystal balls in their path, the rubber balls parroting "*I see Agatha! I see Agatha!*" in off-synch yelps and tripping up the goblins and half the crowd. Panting in relief, Agatha slid behind a newsstand, watching the goblins flop all over the slippery balls, while a female vendor beat them mercilessly with her shoe.

Suddenly, Agatha noticed the headlines of the *Gillikin Gazette*, clipped to the front of the stall:

LION SETS EXECUTION FOR "KING" TEDROS; WEDDING FESTIVITIES BEGIN TOMORROW

Agatha leaned closer, reading the article's details about how Sophie handpicked the axe and executioner for Tedros' beheading (*a lie*, thought Agatha) . . . about King Rhian's new pen, Lionsmane, that was more trustworthy than the Storian . . .

An even bigger lie, Agatha scorned, remembering the cheap gold pens people were snapping up in the booth. The Storian told stories the Woods needed. The Storian kept the Woods *alive.* But if people were suddenly *doubting* the enchanted pen and favoring a fake one . . . then she wasn't just fighting Rhian. She was fighting the countless minds he'd corrupted too. How was she supposed to do that?

Only there was more in this Gillikin article, Agatha realized, reading on . . . this time about Rhian's brother, who'd supposedly been named the liege of the king . . .

Agatha studied a painting of this liege, included on the front page. Japeth, it said his name was—

Her eyes bulged.

Not just Rhian's brother.

Rhian's *twin.*

She thought back to the Lady of the Lake's drawing.

Now she understood everything.

It wasn't Rhian in the Snake's mask who the Lady had kissed. It was Japeth.

There were two of them all along.

One the Lion, one the Snake.

That's how they tricked both the Lady and Excalibur. They shared the same blood.

And yet, both the Lady and Excalibur believed that blood to be the blood of Arthur's heir.

But even if they were twins, wouldn't one of them have been born first? Agatha wondered. *Meaning only one of them is the true heir—*

Agatha shook her head. *What am I saying? Those two monsters can't possibly be Arthur's sons. They can't be Tedros' brothers.*

She could feel herself holding her breath . . .

Can they?

A shadow swept over her.

Agatha swiveled and saw the two goblins glowering at her, their bodies covered in welts.

The female vendor who'd beaten them was with the goblins too, staring at Agatha.

So were a hundred other people behind them, who clearly knew who she was.

"Oh. Hullo," Agatha said.

She dashed for her life, hurtling through the crowd, but more and more people ahead were hearing the cries of the people pursuing her and started chasing her too. Trapped on the yellow road between booths, there was nowhere for her to go—

Then she saw the stall next to her.

TAMIMA'S TADPOLES!
Best Frog Breeder in the Everlands

Tadpoles. She knew a spell about tadpoles. She'd learned it at school, reading Sophie's Evil textbooks . . .

Instantly, she veered towards the booth, diving under the fabric skirting the bottom of it and accosting the vendor, who was stewing a vat of the squiggling critters. Before the vendor could grasp what was happening, Agatha shoved her out of the way, snatched the tub of tadpoles with both hands, felt her fingerglow burn gold—

"*Pustula morphica!*" she gasped.

She dunked her face in.

When the goblins and other bounty hunters came rushing by, they couldn't find Agatha in the crowd—only a soggy girl covered in red boils, stumbling away from a tadpole booth.

A few moments later, itching at her red, oozing sores, this boil-covered girl shambled up to Gilly's Ticket Hub and its handsome young barker.

"Flight to Beauty and the Feast, please," she said.

The man jerked back in disgust.

"Forty silver pieces," he groused, reflexively touching his smooth cheek. "Or rather, forty silver pieces your pestilent fingers haven't *touched*."

"I don't have any silver," Agatha replied.

"Then give me whatever is in that bag," he said, eyeing Dovey's sack on her shoulder.

"Soiled diapers?" Agatha replied with a straight face.

The barker scowled. "Out of my sight before I call the Wizard Guard."

Agatha glanced over her shoulder and saw a commotion at the tadpole booth, the vendor pointing her way—

She whipped back to the barker.

"I could pay you with a good strong sneeze, though," she said coolly. "Feel one coming as a matter of fact. Right at your pretty little face."

The barker raised his eyes, taking in her pocked cheeks.

"Diseased hag. You want to fly? Be my guest," he sneered, shining a green-flamed torch into the sky, illuminating a cloud of invisible fairies, suddenly seeable in the green light.

"One look at you in Sherwood Forest and they'll put an arrow through your skull."

As the fairies soared down on the barker's command and scooped Agatha high into the sky, she grinned at him and the crowd of Agatha hunters rushing his booth.

"I'll take my chances," she said.

"YOU SHOULD HAVE come here straightaway instead of messing about in Fairyland," Robin Hood grouched, dabbing Agatha's boils with beer he'd soaked onto a napkin.

"It was too far to get here on foot and I wanted to find news of my friends," said Agatha, now itching with boils *and* beer. "Besides, last time I was here, you said Merry Men don't get involved in other kingdoms' affairs, and that's why you wouldn't help us fight the Snake. But now you *have* to help or Tedros will die in six days' time. You're my only hope—Lancelot is dead, Merlin's been captured, Professor Dovey and Guinevere too, and I don't know how to reach the League of Thirteen or if they're even still alive—"

"I knew that Rhian boy was a maggot," Robin growled, splashing beer all over his green coat. "Stuck to Tedros' bum like a flea: *'My king! My king!'* Saw right through him. Anyone that servile to a king is bound to be in it for himself." He tightened his brown cap, speared with a green feather. "Moment I heard the news I wasn't surprised in the least."

"Don't lie, you goat," snorted a ravishing black woman with

long, curly hair and a flowy blue dress, flitting around the bar at Marian's Arrow, rinsing wine cups and wiping down counters as moonlight streamed through the only window. "You told me you'd never met a 'sturdier chap' and that if you could, you'd steal Rhian from Tedros and induct him into the Merry Men."

"Always go countin' on Marian to tell us a'truth," a deep voice said.

Robin glanced over at twelve men of various shapes, sizes, and colors wearing brown caps like Robin's, each with a beer mug in hand, seated at tables in the otherwise deserted bar.

"First Robin brings a traitor into our ranks: that boy Kei who set the Snake free and killed three of our men," said a towering man with a big belly, "and now he wants to bring in an evil king too?"

"This is why Marian's Arrow is named after Marian and not him," a dark man jeered, bowing to the woman behind the bar.

"Hear! Hear!" the men resounded, banging their mugs.

"And this is why from now on, you can pay for your drinks in my bar like everyone else," Robin thrashed.

The Merry Men fell quiet.

"For the record, Marian's Arrow is *my* bar," Maid Marian said as she toweled a mug dry.

Robin ignored her, turning to Agatha. "King's guard won't step foot in Sherwood Forest. You'll be safe here," he said, inspecting her pustulous face, then slathering her with even more beer. "Stay with us as long as you please."

"*Stay?* Didn't you hear what I said? Rhian's going to kill Tedros!" Agatha shot back, her face itching more than ever. "He's captured everyone—Dot included, who freed *you* from jail and now needs you to do the same for her. I'm not staying here and neither are you. We need to attack the castle and rescue them!"

She heard the Merry Men murmur. A couple chuckles too.

Robin sighed. "Agatha, we're thieves, not soldiers. Might hate the nasty, scheming rat, but Rhian has the whole of the Woods behind him and royal guards in front of him. No one can rescue your friends now, no matter how much we love Dot. Just be thankful you escaped, even if you ended up a bit mangy-looking."

"She's lovely as she is, you shallow twit," Maid Marian snapped, marching towards him. "Won't be long before *you're* humpbacked and wrinkled like a prune, Robin. Who's going to take care of you then? All the young ladies you whistle at? And what in good heavens are you doing to the poor girl? If you're not going to help her, at least don't make things *worse*." She grabbed a red pepper shaker off a table, poured a handful of powder into her hand, and blew it straight into Agatha's face. Agatha hacked violently, shielding her eyes with her fingers . . . which probed at her soft cheeks.

The boils were gone.

Robin gaped at Marian. "How'd you know how to do that?"

"Forest Groups at school. I did your homework on 'Antidotes,'" said Marian.

Agatha wheezed, her throat filled with pepper. "You and I have a lot in common."

Marian's face fogged over. "No. Not anymore. I used to be like you. Willing to quest into the Woods and fight Evil like we were trained to do at school. But living in this Forest with Robin has changed me. Changed all of us. Turned us just as lazy and complacent as the fat cats Robin robs from."

Robin and his men glanced at each other and shrugged.

Agatha felt tears coming. "Don't you understand? Tedros is going to die. The *real* King of Camelot. King Arthur's *son*. We have to save him. Together. I can't do it alone."

Robin met her eyes, quiet for a moment.

Then he turned to his men.

"All I need is one more man to say yes," he spoke firmly. "If any of you wants to ride and take on the king, then we all ride as one. No man stays behind." Robin drew a deep breath. "All in favor of joining Agatha in the fight . . . raise a hand!"

The men surveyed each other.

No one lifted a finger.

Stunned, Agatha spun to Maid Marian, whose back was turned while she put away beer mugs in the cupboard, as if Robin's vote didn't apply to her.

Agatha launched to her feet, staring down Robin's men. "I get it. You came to Sherwood Forest to drink your booze and have your fun like overgrown boys. And sure, maybe you do raid the rich to give to the poor from time to time, believing it's all the Good you need to do to avoid real responsibility. But that's not what Good is. Good is about taking on Evil whenever it rises, no matter how inconvenient. Good is about stepping up to face the truth. And here's the truth: there is a fake king ruling the Woods and we in this room are the only ones who can stop him. Will it be dangerous? Yes. Will we risk our lives? Yes. But Good needs a hero and 'sorry, I have to finish my beer' isn't a reason to stay behind. Because if you turn a blind eye now, believing the 'Lion' and the 'Snake' are not your problem, I assure you it's only a matter of time before they will be." Heat rashed across her neck. "So I ask again. On behalf of King Tedros, your friend Dot, and the rest of my quest team who need you in order to stay alive, all those in favor of riding out to Camelot beside me and Robin . . ." She closed her eyes and said a silent prayer. ". . . Raise your hands now."

She opened her eyes.

No hands were raised.

None of the men could even look at her.

Agatha froze, her heart shrinking as small as a pea.

"I'll give you a horse so you can leave in the morning," said Robin Hood softly, avoiding eye contact too. "Ride on to someone who can help you."

Agatha glared at him, red-faced. "Don't you understand? There *isn't* anyone else."

She whirled to Marian for one last appeal—

But there was no one behind the bar, its namesake already gone.

WHILE THE MEN remained at Marian's, Agatha came back to Robin's treehouse, hoping to scrounge a few hours of rest before she left at first light.

But she couldn't sleep.

She stashed Dovey's bag in a corner and sat in the doorway, gazing out at the other treehouses, her legs dangling over the edge, brushed by bright purple lotus blossoms quivering in gusts. The wind upended the lanterns too, strung between the treehouses in a rainbow of colors, and forest fairies zipped about setting them right, their wings detonating red and blue like tiny jewels.

The last time Agatha was here, it had all felt so magical and safe, a protective bubble set off from the chaos of real life. But now the whole place felt callow. Insidious, even. Dark things were happening in the Woods and here in Sherwood Forest, purple lotuses luminesced and the houses still glowed bright, their doors wide open.

"*I used to be like you,*" Marian's voice echoed.

Then she'd come here to be with Robin. She'd come here for love. A love that had sealed her off from the world and made time stand still. Isn't that what true loves wanted in the end: to hide away in paradise?

After all, if she and Tedros had hidden away, they never would have had to lead Camelot. If she and Tedros had hidden away, he never would have heard her tell Sophie that he'd failed his quest as king.

They'd still have their Ever After.

They'd still have their perfect love.

Agatha let out a sigh.

No. That isn't love.

Love isn't locking yourselves in or hiding where everything is perfect.

Love is facing the world and its tests together, even if you fail them.

Suddenly, she felt the need to leave this place right now—to go back into the Woods, no matter how perilous—

But where would she go?

She was so used to taking care of things herself. That's what had made her set off on her quest to find the Snake after Tedros' coronation. She'd done it to help Tedros, of course. But she'd also done it because she trusted herself to solve problems: more than she trusted her prince or her best friend or anyone else.

Only this time, she *couldn't* work alone. Not with her prince a few days from execution and the whole Woods hunting her and Sophie under Rhian's thumb and the rest of her friends trapped in prison. If she tried to work alone, Tedros would die. That's why she'd come here. To forge new alliances. And instead, she'd leave even more alone than before.

The wind turned cold and she glanced back, hoping to find a blanket or quilt—

Something caught her eye in the corner.

A black coat, hanging amongst a sea of green ones in the closet.

As she moved towards it, she saw it was splotched with dried blood . . .

Lancelot's blood.

Tedros had worn the coat the night they'd come to Sherwood Forest to bury the knight along with Lady Gremlaine. He must have left it here when he'd changed clothes for their dinner at Beauty and the Feast . . .

Agatha clutched the coat in both hands and put it to her face, inhaling her prince's warm, minty scent. For a half-second, it made her feel calm.

Then it dawned on her.

This could be the last she ever had of him.

Her heart kickstarted, that helpless feeling returning—

Then her hands felt something stiff in the coat pocket.

Agatha reached in and pulled out a stack of letters, banded together. She flipped through the first few.

DEAR GRISELLA,

I KNEW THERE'D BE UNDUE ATTENTION ON ME AT SCHOOL, BUT THIS IS ABSURD. I'VE ONLY BEEN HERE A FEW DAYS AND I'M STILL TRYING TO GET MY BEARINGS, YET EVERY EVER AND NEVER IN THE PLACE KEEPS HOUNDING ME, ASKING ME ABOUT HOW I PULLED EXCALIBUR FROM THE STONE AND WHAT BEING KING OF CAMELOT FEELS LIKE AND WHY I'M AT SCHOOL WHEN I SHOULD BE RULING MY KINGDOM. I TELL THEM THE "OFFICIAL" STORY, OF COURSE—THAT MY FATHER WENT TO THE SCHOOL FOR GOOD AND I WANT TO HONOR HIS LEGACY . . . BUT THE NEVERS DON'T BELIEVE ME. AT LEAST THEY DON'T KNOW THE TRUTH—THAT THE PROVISORY COUNCIL ONLY

APPROVED MY CORONATION ON THE CONDITION THAT
I RECEIVE A FORMAL EDUCATION (AKA HAVE TIME TO
"GROW UP" BEFORE I RULE). BUT I DON'T INTEND TO TELL
PEOPLE THAT MY OWN STAFF WON'T LET ME BE KING
UNTIL I GRADUATE THIS PLACE. AND NOT ONLY GRADUATE,
BUT GRADUATE TOP OF THE CLASS AND WITH A SUITABLE
QUEEN-TO-BE PICKED OUT. I FEEL OVERWHELMED,
HONESTLY. I CAN BARELY CONCENTRATE ON MY CLASSES.
YESTERDAY, I BOTCHED PROFESSOR SADER'S QUIZ ON
THE HISTORY OF CAMELOT. THAT'S RIGHT: I FAILED A
TEST ON MY OWN KINGDOM—

DEAR GRISELLA,

THE DAYS AT SCHOOL ARE LONG AND DIFFICULT
(ESPECIALLY YUBA THE GNOME'S CLASS IN THE BLUE
FOREST—HE SWATS ME WITH HIS STAFF WHENEVER I MISS
AN ANSWER AND I MISS PLENTY). BUT YOUR LETTERS
FROM THE CASTLE HAVE GIVEN ME GREAT COMFORT AND
REMIND ME OF OUR LIVES AT SIR ECTOR'S BEFORE I WAS
KING, WHEN WE STARTED EACH DAY KNOWING EXACTLY
WHAT WAS EXPECTED OF US—

DEAR GRISELLA,

I'VE BEEN PICKED FOR THE TRIAL BY TALE! EVEN
THOUGH MY NEW FRIENDS LANCELOT AND GUINEVERE
BOTH PLACED AHEAD OF ME. GUINEVERE I CAN

UNDERSTAND (SHE'S BRILLIANT), BUT LANCELOT? HE'S GREAT FUN, BUT NOT THE SHARPEST SWORD IN THE ARMORY. NEEDLESS TO SAY, I'M FEELING THE SPIRIT OF COMPETITION MORE THAN EVER. IF THE NEW KING OF CAMELOT DOESN'T WIN THE TRIAL BY TALE, THE ROYAL ROT WILL BE RIDICULING ME ON THE FRONT PAGE FOR MONTHS. SPEAKING OF ROYALTY, IS EVERYTHING RUNNING SMOOTHLY AT THE CASTLE? I HAVEN'T HEARD FROM YOU IN WEEKS—

Agatha paged through more of them.

These weren't Tedros' letters. They were his *father's*.

King Arthur must have written them when he was a first year at the School for Good. But who was Grisella? And why did Tedros have his father's letters in his coat?

Then she noticed something stuck to the back of the last letter . . . a handwritten label . . .

And clipped to the label was a business card—

Agatha peered closer. *Camelot Beautiful*. That was the fund that Lady Gremlaine used to refurbish the castle, the one that never seemed to have any money, despite Agatha's relentless fundraising for it. Had Tedros kept the label for a reason? And what about the business card? The only Albemarle she knew was the spectacled woodpecker that tallied ranks at the School for Good and Evil, and he certainly wasn't a bank manager in Putsi . . .

Something rustled behind her and Agatha turned sharply. She dropped the letters in shock.

"Hello, my dear," said a tall woman in the doorway with wild, canary-yellow hair, an overabundance of makeup, and a leopard-print caftan billowing in the wind as she stepped off a hovering stymph into Robin's treehouse.

"Professor Anemone!" Agatha said, gaping at her former Beautification teacher as her bird-boned vehicle flew down to the ground below. "What are you doing he—"

Then she saw Maid Marian climbing into the treehouse behind her professor.

"Emma and I were classmates at school," Marian explained. "I sent her a crow the moment you came to Marian's Arrow. I knew Robin and his men wouldn't help you the way you needed. But the least I could do was find you someone who could."

Professor Anemone rushed forward and pulled Agatha into an embrace. "The faculty's been searching for you ever since we heard what happened. You have to understand: Clarissa kept us in the dark. Spent all her time cooped up in her office with her Quest Map and that crystal ball. She must have thought that if the teachers knew what was happening in the Woods, then the first years would find out something had gone wrong on your quests. She wouldn't have wanted them to worry or be distracted from their work. Always thinking of her students, even at her own expense . . . Her office is still locked no matter what spells we do on it and we can't get a hold of her Quest Map; that's why we couldn't find you. . . ."

Agatha teared up. She thought she'd been alone this whole time, when instead, her old teachers had been looking for her. For the briefest of moments, she felt safe again like she once had in their glass castle. "You don't know what we're up against, Professor. This is Evil like we've never seen. Evil that you don't teach in your classes. The Lion and the Snake are working together. They have the whole Woods on their side. And we have no one on ours."

"Yes, you do," said Professor Anemone, pulling away and staring hard at her charge. "You see, Clarissa might believe in sheltering students, but neither I nor the rest of the teachers do. Which means the king might have the whole Woods on his side, but you have something far stronger on yours. Something that has outlasted any king. Something that has always restored the balance between Good and Evil, even in the darkest of times. Something that was born to win this fight."

Agatha looked up at her.

Professor Anemone leaned in, her eyes glittering. "My dear Agatha . . . you have a *school*."

Sophie's Choice

Tedros imagined it was Rhian that they were beating.

That's how he'd survived the pirates.

Every stomping kick they'd given him, every brass-knuckled punch, every full-force blow gushing blood from his lip or eye, Tedros mentally redirected at the traitor who sat upon his throne. The friend who turned out to be his worst enemy. His loyal knight who turned out to be neither loyal nor a knight.

Now, curled up in his cell, Tedros could hear the scum's voice resounding down the hall, magically amplified by whatever hocus-pocus his friends were doing in their own cell.

Acid rage burnt his chest. It was like they were broadcasting Rhian's voice just to taunt him.

"Was he telling the truth?" he yelled.

Tedros' voice echoed into the hall.

"About Sophie wanting me dead? Was that the truth?"

He'd thought Sophie was on his side this time . . . that his friendship with her was finally real . . .

But he didn't know what was real anymore. Maybe Sophie had conspired with Rhian on all of this. Or maybe she'd been scammed by him too.

Tedros' face grew hotter.

He'd welcomed Rhian like a brother. Brought him into Camelot. Told him his secrets.

He'd practically handed the pig his crown.

Tedros could taste the anger now, foaming in his throat.

Agatha was right.

He'd been a bad king. Cowardly. Arrogant. Foolish.

When Agatha had told Sophie this last night, he'd been cut to the bone. Betrayed by the only girl he'd ever loved. It had made him doubt her the way she doubted him.

But in the end, she was right. She always was.

And now, in the most fitting of ironies, the same girl who called him a bad king was the sole person who could help him win back his throne.

Because Agatha was the only one who'd managed to escape Rhian's hands.

The pirates had revealed this by accident. They'd beaten him relentlessly, the gang of six reeking thugs, demanding to know where Agatha had fled. At first, his relief that she'd escaped numbed the pain of their blows. But then the relief wore off. *Where was she? Was she safe? Suppose they found her?* Riled by his silence, the pirates had only beaten him harder.

Tedros leaned against the dungeon wall, warm blood sliding down his abdomen. His raw, bruised back touched cold stone through the shreds in his shirt and he seized up. The throbbing was so intense his teeth chattered; he tasted a sharp edge in the bottom row where one of them had been chipped. He tried to think of Agatha's face to keep him conscious, but all he could conjure were the faces of those filthy punks as their boots bashed down. The pirates' assault had gone on for so long that at some point, it seemed disconnected from purpose. As if they were punishing him for his very existence.

Maybe Rhian had built his whole army on feelings like this. Feelings of people who thought because Tedros was born handsome and rich and a prince, he deserved to fall. To *suffer.*

But he could take all the suffering in the world if it meant Agatha would live.

To survive, his princess had to run as far as she could from

Camelot. She had to hide in the darkest part of the Woods where no one could find her.

But that wasn't Agatha. He knew her too well. She would come for her prince. No matter how much faith she'd lost in him.

The dungeons were quiet now, Rhian's voice no longer audible.

"How do we get out of here!" Tedros called to the others, enduring blinding pain in his rib. "How do we escape!"

No one in their cell responded.

"*Listen to me!*" he shouted.

But the strain had done him in. His mind softened like soggy pudding, unlocking from his surroundings. He pulled his knees into his chest, trying to relieve pressure on his rib, but his flank burned hotter, the scene distorting in the torch-haze on the wall. Tedros closed his eyes, heaving deep breaths. Only it made him feel more sealed in, like he was in an airless coffin. He could smell the old bones . . . "*Unbury Me,*" his father's voice whispered. . . .

Tedros wrenched out of his trance and opened his eyes—

Hester's demon stared back at him.

Tedros recoiled against the wall, blinking to make sure it was actually there.

The demon was the size of a shoebox with brick-red skin and long, curved horns, his beady eyes locked on the young prince.

The last time Tedros had been this close to Hester's demon, it had almost hacked him to pieces during a Trial by Tale.

"We thought this would work better than yelling across

the dungeon," said the demon.

Only it didn't speak in a demon's voice.

It spoke in Hester's.

Tedros stared at it. "Magic is impossible down here—"

"My demon isn't magic. My demon is *me*," said Hester's voice. "We need to talk before the pirates come back."

"Agatha's out there all on her own and you want to talk?" Tedros said, clutching his rib. "Use your little beast to get me out of this cell!"

"Good plan," the demon retorted, only with *Beatrix*'s voice. "You'd still be trapped at the iron door and when the pirates see you, they'll beat you worse than they already have."

"Tedros, did they break any bones?" Professor Dovey's voice called faintly through the demon, as if the Dean was too far from it for a proper connection. "Hester, can you see through your demon? How bad does he look—"

"Not bad enough, whatever it is," Hort's voice said, hijacking the demon. "He got us into this mess by fawning over Rhian like a lovedrunk *girl*."

"Oh, so being a 'girl' is an insult now?" Nicola's voice ripped, the demon suddenly looking animated in agreement.

"Look, if you're going to be my girlfriend, you have to accept I'm not some intellectual who always knows the right words to use," Hort's voice rebuffed.

"YOU'RE A HISTORY PROFESSOR!" Nicola's voice slapped.

"Whatever," Hort barged on. "You saw the way Tedros gave Rhian the run of his kingdom, letting him recruit the army and give speeches like he was king."

Tedros sat up queasily. "First of all, how is everyone talking through this *thing*, and second of all, do you think I *knew* what Rhian was planning?"

"To answer the first, Hester's demon is a gateway to her soul. And her soul recognizes her friends," the demon said with Anadil's voice. "Unlike your *sword*."

"And to answer the second, every boy you like ends up a bogey," Hort's voice jumped in, the demon trying to keep up like a ventriloquist. "First you were friends with Aric. Then you were friends with Filip. And now you canoodled with the devil himself!"

"I did not *canoodle* with anyone!" Tedros yelled at the demon. "And if any of us is cozying up to the devil, you're the one who's friends with *Sophie*!"

"Yeah, Sophie, the only person who can rescue us!" Hort's voice heckled.

"*Agatha's* the only person who can rescue us, you twit!" Tedros fired. "That's why we need to get out now, before she comes back and gets captured!"

"Can everyone shut up?" the demon snapped in Hester's voice. "Tedros, we need you to—"

"Put Hort back on," Tedros demanded. "After three years of Sophie using you as her personal bootlicker without giving you the slightest in return, now you think she's going to rescue us!"

"Just because *you* wouldn't help people who needed it when the Snake attacked doesn't mean *she* won't," Hort's voice thrashed.

"Idiot. Once she tastes a queen's life, she'll let us burn while she feasts on cake," Tedros slammed.

"Sophie doesn't eat cake," Hort sniffed.

"You think you know Sophie better than me?"

"When she rescues you from that cell, you're going to feel like a boob—"

"ANI'S RAT IS DEAD, THE SNAKE IS ALIVE, WE'RE IN A DUNGEON, AND WE'RE TALKING ABOUT SOPHIE! AND *CAKE*!" Hester's voice boomed, her demon swelling like a balloon. "WE HAVE QUES-TIONS FOR TEDROS, YES? GIVEN WHAT WE SAW ONSTAGE, OUR LIVES *DEPEND* ON THESE QUESTIONS, YES? SO IF ANYONE EVEN TRIES TO INTERRUPT ME, STARTING RIGHT NOW I'LL TEAR OUT YOUR TONGUE."

The dungeon went silent.

"The Snake is *alive*?" Tedros asked, ghost-faced.

Ten minutes later, Tedros stared back at the red imp, having learned about the Snake's reappearance, the birth of Lionsmane, and everything else Hester and the team had seen in the magical projection they'd conjured in their cell.

"So there's two of them? Rhian and this ... Jasper?" Tedros said.

"*Japeth*. The Snake. And that's how we think they tricked both the Lady and Excalibur. They're twins who share the same blood. The blood of your father, they say," the demon explained. "If we're going to bring them down, we need to know how that's possible."

"You're asking *me*?" Tedros snorted.

"Do you live your whole life with your head up your bum?" Hester's voice scorned. "*Think*, Tedros. Don't shut down what might be possible just because you don't like the idea of it. Can these two boys be your brothers?"

Tedros scowled. "My father had his faults. But he couldn't have bred two monsters. Good can't spawn Evil. Not like that. Besides, how do you know Rhian didn't pull Excalibur because I'd done all the work dislodging it? Maybe he just got lucky."

The demon groaned. "It's like trying to reason with a hedgehog."

"Oh, just let him die. If they *are* his brothers, it'll be survival of the fittest," said Anadil's voice. "Can't argue with nature."

"Speaking of nature, I have to use the toilet," said Dot's voice.

Professor Dovey's voice muffled something to Tedros through the demon, something about his father's "women"—

"I can't hear you," said Tedros, cramming deeper into a corner. "My body hurts, my head hurts. Are we done with the interrogation?"

"Are you done being a pea-brained fool?" Hester railed. "We're trying to help you!"

"By making me smear my own father?" Tedros challenged.

"Everyone needs to cool their milk," said Nicola's voice.

"Milk?" Kiko's voice peeped through the demon. "I see no milk."

"It's what my father used to say at his pub when it got too hot in the kitchen," said Nicola, calmly taking over the creature. "Tedros, what we're trying to ask is whether there's anything you can tell us about your father's past that makes Rhian and his brother's claim possible. Could your father have had other children? Without you knowing? We get that it's a difficult subject. We just want to keep you alive. And to do that, we need to know as much as you do."

There was something about the first year's voice, so lacking in pretense, that made Tedros let down his guard. Maybe it was because he barely knew the girl or that there was no judgment or conclusion in her question. All she was asking was for him to share the facts. He thought of Merlin, who often spoke to him the same way. Merlin, who was either in danger somewhere up there or . . . dead. Tedros' gut knotted. The wizard would have wanted him to answer Nicola honestly. Indeed, Merlin had been fond of the girl, even when Tedros hadn't been willing to give her a chance.

Tedros raised his eyes to the demon's. "I had a steward named Lady Gremlaine while I was king. She was my father's steward too, and they'd grown close before he met my mother. So close that I suspected something may have happened between them . . . Something that made my mother fire Lady Gremlaine from the castle soon after I was born." The prince swallowed. "Before Lady Gremlaine died, I asked her whether the Snake was her son. Whether he was her and my *father's* son. She never said yes. But . . ."

". . . she suggested it," Nicola's voice prodded, the demon looking almost gentle.

Tedros nodded, his throat constricting. "She said she'd

done something terrible. Before I was born." Sweat dripped down his forehead as he relived the moment in the attic, Lady Gremlaine clutching a bloody hammer, her hair wild, her eyes manic. "She said she'd done something my father never knew. But she'd fixed it. She'd made sure the child would never be found. He'd grow up never knowing who he was . . ."

Tedros' voice caught.

The demon was frozen still. For the first time no one spoke through it.

"So Rhian could be telling the truth," said Professor Dovey's voice finally, a remote whisper. "He could be the real king."

"The son of Lady Gremlaine and your father," Hester's voice agreed. "Japeth too."

Tedros sat up straighter. "We don't *know* that. Maybe there's an explanation. Maybe there's something she didn't tell me. I found letters between Lady Gremlaine and my father. In her house. Lots of them. Maybe they explain what she really meant. . . . We need to read those letters . . . I don't know where they are now—" His eyes glistened. "It can't be true. Rhian can't be my brother. He can't be the heir." He looked at the demon pleadingly. "Can he?"

"I don't know," said Hester, low and grim. "But if he is, then either your brother kills you or you kill him. This can't end any other way."

Suddenly they heard the dungeon door open.

Tedros squinted through the bars.

Voices and shadows stretched down the stairway at the end of the hall. The Snake glided into view first, followed by three pirates wielding trays slopped with gruel.

The pirates set down the gruel at the floor of the first two cells—the one with Tedros' crewmates and the one with Professor Dovey—and kicked the trays through the gaps along with dog bowls of water.

The Snake, meanwhile, walked straight towards Tedros' cell, his green mask flashing in the torchlight.

Panicked, Hester's demon flew upwards and Tedros watched it flail around, struggling to find a shadow on the ceiling to hide in. But with its red skin, the demon stuck out like an eyesore—

Then the Snake appeared through the cell bars.

Instantly, the green scims on his mask dispersed, revealing his face to Tedros for the first time.

Tedros gaped back at him, Rhian's ghostly twin, his lean body fitted in shiny black eels, the suit newly restored as if he'd never been wounded in battle at all. As if he was the strongest he'd ever been.

How?

The Snake seemed to sense what he was thinking and gave him a sly grin.

A shadow fluttered over their heads—

The Snake's eyes shot up, searching the top of Tedros' cell, his pupils scanning left and right. He raised a glowing fingertip, coated with scims, and flooded the ceiling with green light.

Tedros blanched, his stomach in his throat. . . .

But there was nothing on the ceiling except a slow-moving worm.

Japeth's eyes slid back down to Tedros, his fingerglow dissipating.

That's when Tedros noticed Hester's demon on the wall behind the Snake, crawling into the boy's shadow. Tedros quickly averted his eyes from the demon, his heart jumping hurdles.

The Snake gazed at Tedros' bashed-up face. "Not so pretty anymore, are you."

It was the way he said it that snapped Tedros to attention, the boy's tone dripping with disdain. He wasn't some masked creature anymore. He had a face. He was human now, this Snake. He could be defeated.

Tedros bared his teeth, glaring hard at the savage who'd killed Chaddick, killed Lancelot, and smeared his father's name. "We'll see what you look like when I ram my sword through your mouth."

"So strong you are," the Snake cooed. "Such a *man*." He reached out and caressed Tedros' cheek—

Tedros slapped his hand away so hard it struck the cell bars, the bone of the Snake's wrist cracking against metal. But the pale-faced boy didn't flinch. He just smirked at Tedros, relishing the silence.

Then he pulled the black dungeon key from his sleeve. "I wish I could say this was a social call, but I'm here on behalf of my brother. After she had supper with the king tonight, Princess Sophie was given permission by King Rhian to release one of you." He glanced down the hall and saw the rest of the crew poking their heads out of the cell at the other end, wide-eyed and listening. "That's right. One of you who will no longer live in the dungeons and instead be allowed to work in the castle as the princess's servant, under King Rhian's eye. One of you whose life will be spared . . ."

The Snake looked back at Tedros. ". . . for now."

Tedros bolted straight as an arrow. "She picked me."

In a flash, all doubts Tedros had about Sophie vanished. He should have never mistrusted her. Sophie didn't want him dead. She didn't want him to suffer. No matter how much they'd hurt each other in the past.

Because Sophie would do anything for Agatha. And Agatha would do anything for Tedros. Which meant Sophie would do anything to save Tedros' life, including finding a way to convince a usurping king to set his enemy free.

How had she done it? How had she gotten Rhian on her side?

He'd hear the story soon enough.

Tedros grinned at the Snake. "Get moving, scum. Princess's orders," he said. "Open the door."

The Snake didn't.

"Let me out," Tedros commanded, face reddening.

The Snake stayed still, the prison key glinting between his fingers.

"She picked *me*!" Tedros snarled, gripping the bars. "Let me out!"

Instead, the Snake just put his face to the prince's . . . and smiled.

The Dinner Game

Earlier that evening, the pirates Beeba and Aran brought Sophie down from the Map Room for dinner.

Rhian and Japeth were already halfway through their first course.

"It needs to be harsh. A warning," she heard Japeth saying in the refurbished Gold Tower dining room. "Lionsmane's first tale should instill fear."

"Lionsmane should give people *hope*," said Rhian's voice. "People like you and me who grew up without any."

"Mother is dead because she believed in hope," said his brother.

"And yet, Mother's death is the reason both of us are in this room," said Rhian.

As she neared the door, all Sophie heard was silence. Then—

"Supporters of Tedros are protesting tonight in Camelot Park," said Japeth. "We should ride in and kill them all. *That* should be Lionsmane's first tale."

"Killing protestors will lead to more protests," said Rhian. "That's not the story I want to tell."

"You weren't afraid of bloodshed when it got you the throne," said Japeth snidely.

"*I'm* king. I'll write the tales," said Rhian.

"It's *my* pen," Japeth retorted.

"It's your *scim*," said Rhian. "Look, I know it isn't easy. Serving as my liege. But there can only be one king, Japeth. I know why you've helped me. I know what you want. What *both* of us want. But to get it, I need the Woods on my side. I need to be a good king."

Japeth snorted. "Every good king ends up dead."

"You have to trust me," Rhian pressed. "The same way I trust you."

"I do trust you, brother," said Japeth, softening. "It's that devious little minx I don't trust. Suppose you start listening to her instead of me?"

Rhian snorted. "As likely as me growing horns. Speaking of the minx." He laid down his fork on his plate of rare, freckled deer meat and looked up coldly from the decadent table, his crown reflecting his blue-and-gold suit.

"I heard guards pounding on the Map Room door, Sophie. If you can't make it to dinner on time, then your friends in the dungeon won't get dinner at all—" He stopped.

Sophie stood beneath the new Lion-head chandelier, wearing the dress they'd left for her. Only she'd slashed the prim white frock in half, ruffled the bottom into three layers (short, shorter, shortest), hiked them high over her knees, and lined the seams of the dress with wet, globby beads, each filled with different colored ink. Crystal raindrops dangled from her ears; silver shadow burnished her eyelids; her lips were coated sparkly red; and she'd crowned her hair with origami stars, made from the parchment she'd ripped out of the wedding books. All in all, instead of the chastened princess the king might have expected after their encounter in the Map Room, Sophie had emerged looking both like a birthday cake and a girl jumping out of one.

The pirates with Sophie looked just as stunned as the king.

"Leave us," Rhian ordered them.

The moment they did, Japeth launched to his feet, his pale cheeks searing red. "That was our *mother's* dress."

"It still is," Sophie said. "And I doubt she would have appreciated you gussying up girls you've kidnapped in her old clothes. The real question is why you asked me to wear this dress at all. Is it to make me feel like you own me? Is it because I remind you of your dear departed mum? Or is it something else? Hmm . . . In any case, you told me what to wear. Not how to wear it." She gave a little shimmy, the light catching the colorful gobs on the dress like drops of a rainbow.

The Snake glared at her, scims sliding faster on his body. "You dirty *shrew.*"

Sophie took a step towards him. "Snakeskin is a specialty. Imagine what I could make out of your *suit*."

Japeth lunged towards her, but Sophie thrust out her palm—

"Ever wonder what map ink is made out of?" she asked calmly.

Japeth stopped midstride.

"Iron gall," said Sophie, green eyes shifting from the Snake to Rhian, who was still seated, watching her between tall candles in the Lion-themed centerpiece. "It's the only substance that can be dyed multiple colors and last for years without fading. Most maps are inked with iron gall, including yours in the Map Room. The ones you enchanted to track me and my friends. Do you know what else iron gall is used for?"

Neither twin answered.

"Oh, silly me, I learned about it in my Curses class at school and you boys didn't get *into* my school," said Sophie. "Iron gall is a blood poison. Ingest it and it brings instant death. But let's say I dab a touch on my skin. It would sap the nutrients from my blood, while keeping me alive, just barely, meaning any vampiric freak who might suddenly *need* my blood . . . well, they would get poisoned too. And it happens this entire dress—your *mother's* dress, as you point out—is now dotted in pearls of iron gall I extracted from your maps, using the most basic of first-year spells. Which means the slightest wrong move and—*poof!*—it'll smear onto my skin in just the right dose. And then my blood won't be very useful to you at all, will it? The perils of haute couture, I suppose." She fluffed the tail of her dress. "Now, darlings. What's for dinner?"

"Your *tongue*," said Japeth. Scims shot off his chest, turning knife-sharp, as they speared towards Sophie's face. Her eyes widened—

A whipcrack of gold light snapped over the eels, sending them whimpering back into the Snake's body.

Stunned, Japeth swung to his brother sitting next to him, whose gold fingerglow dimmed. Rhian didn't look at him, his lips twisted, as if suppressing a smile.

"She needs to be punished!" Japeth demanded.

Rhian tilted his head, taking in Sophie from a different angle. "You have to admit . . . the dress *does* look better."

Japeth was startled. Then his cheekbones hardened. "Careful, brother. Your horns are growing." Scims coated Japeth's face, re-forming his mask. He kicked over his chair, its pattern of Lions skidding across the floor. "Enjoy dinner with your *queen*," he seethed, striding out of the room. A scim shot off him and hissed at Sophie, before flying after its master.

Sophie's heart throttled as she listened to Japeth's footsteps fade.

He'll have his revenge, she thought. But for now, she had Rhian's undivided attention.

"A queen in the castle will take him some getting used to," said the king. "My brother isn't fond of—"

"Strong females?" said Sophie.

"All females," said Rhian. "Our mother left that dress for the bride of whichever of us married first. Japeth has no interest in a bride. But he is *very* attached to that dress." Rhian paused. "It isn't poisoned at all, is it?"

"Touch me and find out," Sophie replied.

"No need. I know a liar when I see one."

"Mirrors must be especially challenging, then."

"Maybe Japeth is right," said Rhian. "Maybe I should relieve you of that tongue."

"That would make us even," said Sophie.

"How's that?" said Rhian.

"With you missing your soul and all," said Sophie.

Silence spread over the hall, cold and thick. Through the wide bay windows, thunderclouds gathered over Camelot village in the valley.

"Are you going to sit down for dinner or would you like to eat from the horse trough?" the king asked.

"I'd like to make a deal," said Sophie.

Rhian laughed.

"I'm serious," Sophie said.

"You just threatened to poison my brother's blood and skin him of his suit and then brazenly insulted your king," said Rhian. "And now you want . . . a deal."

Sophie stepped fully into the light. "Let's be honest. We despise each other. Maybe we didn't before, when we were eating truffles at enchanted restaurants and kissing in the backs of carriages, but we do now. And yet, we need each other. You

need me to be your queen. I need you to spare my friends.
Would I rather watch you hacked into dog food? Yes. But in
every cloud there's a silver lining. Because I'll admit it: I was
bored as Dean of Evil. I know I'm an ogre for saying it, but I
don't care if little Drago is homesick or constipated or cheating
in Forest Groups. I don't care if abominable Agnieszka's warts
are contagious, roguish Rowan is kissing girls in the meat
locker, or dirty Mali snuck into the Groom Room pool and
peed in it. My fairy tale made me more beloved than Sleeping Beauty or Snow White or any of those other snoozy girls.
And what diva icon goddess uses her newfound fame to go . . .
teach? In theory the idea of devoting myself to a new genera-
tion sounded noble, but none of these students are nearly as
clever as I am and I was left feeling like a chanteuse playing
miles away from the main stage. I'm too young, too alluring,
too *adored* to be out of the spotlight. And now, through a series
of rather unfortunate events, voilà, I find myself poised to be
queen of the most powerful kingdom in the land. I know it's
not *right* for me to wear the crown. In fact, it's positively Evil,
especially when I'm taking my best friend's place. But will I be
a *good* queen? That's another question entirely. Attending state
dinners with exotic kings; negotiating treaties with cannibal
trolls; managing armies and alliances; preaching my vision for
a better Woods; opening hospitals and feeding the homeless
and comforting the poor—I'll do it all and do it well. That's
why you chose me as your queen. And because my blood has
the unfortunate property of keeping your brother alive . . . but

you don't need me as queen for that. You could have chained me up with my friends and bled me at will. No, I think you chose me as a queen because you know I'll be glorious at it."

Rhian parted his lips to speak, but Sophie barreled on.

"At first, I was going to come down and pretend I'd had a change of heart. That I still love you, no matter what you've done. But even *I'm* not a spry enough actress for that. The truth is, you pulled Excalibur from its stone. That makes you the king. Meanwhile, my friends are either in prison or on the run. So, I have two choices. Resist, knowing my friends will be hurt for it. Or . . . be as good a queen as I can and keep an open mind. Because I heard you say you want to be a good king. And to be a good king, you'll need a good queen. So here are the terms. You treat me and my friends well, and I'll be the queen you and Camelot need. Do we have a deal?"

Rhian picked at his teeth. "You're fond of the sound of your own voice. I can see why Tedros and every other boy dumped you."

Sophie went bright pink.

"Sit down," said the king.

This time she did.

A maid came in from the kitchen, carrying the next course: fish stew in a red broth. Sophie put a hand to her nose—it smelled like the goo Agatha's mother once made—but then she saw the maid carrying it was Guinevere, a scim still sealing her lips. Sophie tried to make eye contact, then caught Rhian watching her and she quickly tasted the stew.

"Mmmm," she said, trying not to gag.

"So you think that if you're a 'good' queen, I'll let your friends go," said Rhian.

Sophie looked up. "I never said that."

"And if they die?"

"Murdering my friends will only make people doubt our love and start asking questions. That's not how you're going to keep the Woods on your side," said Sophie, as Guinevere took her time refilling Rhian's cup, clearly eavesdropping. "That said, if I show you loyalty, I hope you'll show me loyalty in return."

"Define loyalty."

"Releasing my friends."

"That sounds a lot like letting them go."

"They can work in the castle. Under your supervision, of course. The same test you gave the maids."

Rhian raised a brow. "You really think I'd free a crew of enemies into my own castle?"

"You can't hold them in jail forever. Not if you want me to keep your secrets and play your loyal queen," said Sophie, well-rehearsed. "And better here in the castle than out in the Woods. Besides, if you and I can come to an agreement, then they'll come around too. They hated me in the beginning, just like they hate you." She gave him a practiced smile.

"And what of Tedros?" Rhian reclined, copper hair catching the light. "He's condemned to die. The people cheered for it. You think I'll 'release' him too?"

Guinevere's fingers shook on the pitcher, nearly spilling it.

Sophie's heart pumped faster as she looked up at Rhian, choosing her words carefully. What she said next could save Tedros' life.

"Do I think Tedros should die? No," she said. "Do I think he should die at our wedding? No. Do I think it's wrong? Yes. That said, you've announced your plans . . . and a king can't very well take back an execution, can he?"

Guinevere's eyes flew to Sophie.

"So you'll let Tedros die, then," said the king, skeptical.

Sophie met his gaze firmly. "If it means saving the rest of my friends, yes. I'm not Tedros' mother. I won't go to the ends of the earth to save him. And like you said . . . he *dumped* me."

A raw cry sounded in Guinevere's throat.

Sophie kicked her under the table. Guinevere's face changed.

"Since you apparently have nothing to do," Rhian said, glowering at the maid, "fetch the captain of the guard. I need to speak with him."

Guinevere was still searching Sophie's eyes—

"Shall we kill your son *tonight*?" Rhian spat at her.

Guinevere ran out.

Sophie probed at her soup, seeing her own face reflected. A drop of sweat plunked into the stew. Did Guinevere understand? If Tedros was going to survive, she needed his mother to do her part.

Sophie looked up at the king. "So . . . we have a deal? My friends working in the castle, I mean. I could use them for the wedding—"

Two more maids came out of the kitchens, carrying gruel lumped on brass trays as they headed towards the stairs.

"Hold," said Rhian.

The maids stopped.

"Those are for the dungeons?" he said.

The maids nodded.

"They can wait," said the king, turning to Sophie. "Like I had to wait for you."

The maids took the trays back into the kitchen.

Sophie stared at him.

The king smiled as he ate. "Don't like the soup?"

Sophie put her spoon down. "The last chef was better. As was the last king."

The king stopped smiling. "I proved I'm Arthur's true heir. I proved I'm the king. And still you side with that *fake*."

"King Arthur would never have a son like you," Sophie blazed. "And even if he did, there's a reason he kept you secret. He must have known how you and your brother would turn out."

Rhian's face went murder-red, his hand palming his metal cup as if he might throw it at her. Then slowly the color seeped out of his cheeks and he smiled.

"And here you thought we had a deal," he said.

Now it was Sophie who swallowed her fire.

If she wanted her friends released, she had to be smart.

She poked at her soup. "So, what did you do this afternoon?" she asked, a bit too brightly.

"Wesley and I went to the armory and realized there isn't

an axe sharp enough to cut off Tedros' head," said the king, mouth full. "So we considered how many swings it would take to sever through his neck with a dull axe and whether the crowd might cheer harder for that than a clean blow."

"Oh. That's nice," Sophie croaked, feeling ill. "Anything else?"

"Met with the Kingdom Council. A gathering of every leader in the Woods, conducted via spellcast. I assured them that as long as they support me as king, Camelot will protect their kingdoms, Good and Evil, just as I protected them from the Snake. And that I would never betray them, like Tedros did, when he helped that monster."

Sophie stiffened. "What?"

"I suggested it was Tedros who likely paid the Snake and his rebels," said Rhian, clear-eyed. "All those fundraisers his queen hosted . . . Where else could that gold have gone? Tedros must have thought that if he weakened the kingdoms around him, it would make him stronger. That's why he has to be executed, I told the Council. Because if he is lying about being Arthur's heir, then he could be lying about *everything*."

Sophie was speechless.

"Of course, I personally invited all members of the Kingdom Council to the wedding festivities, beginning with the Blessing tomorrow," Rhian went on. "Oh, almost forgot. I also proposed demolishing the School for Good and Evil, now that it no longer has its Deans or a School Master."

Sophie dropped her spoon.

"They voted me down, of course. They still believe in

that decrepit School. They still believe the Storian needs to be protected. The School and the Storian are the lifeblood of the Woods, they say." Rhian wiped his mouth with his hand, streaking red across it. "But I didn't go to that School. The Storian means nothing to me. And *I'm* King of the Woods."

His face changed, the cold sheen of his eyes cracking, and Sophie could see the smolder of resentments beneath.

"But the day will come when every kingdom in the Woods changes its tune. When every kingdom in the Woods believes in a King instead of a School, a Man instead of a Pen . . ." He stared right at Sophie, the outline of Lionsmane pulsing gold through his suit pocket like a heartbeat. "From that day, the One True King will rule forever."

"That day will never come," Sophie spat.

"Oh, it'll come sooner than you think," said Rhian. "Funny how a wedding can bring everyone together."

Sophie tensed in her chair. "If you think I'll be your good little queen while you lie like a devil and destroy the Woods—"

"You think I chose you because you'd be a 'good' queen?" Rhian chuckled. "That's not why I chose you. I didn't choose you at all." He leaned forward. "The *pen* chose you. The pen said you'd be my queen. Just like it said I'd be king. *That's* why you're here. The pen. Though I'm beginning to question its judgment."

"The pen?" Sophie said, confused. "Lionsmane? Or the Storian? *Which* pen?"

Rhian grinned back. "Which pen, indeed."

There was a twinkle in his eye, something sinister and yet

familiar, and a chill rippled up Sophie's spine. As if she had the whole story wrong yet again.

"It doesn't make sense. A pen can't 'choose' me as your queen," Sophie argued. "A pen can't see the future—"

"And yet here you are, just like it promised," said Rhian.

Sophie thought about something he'd said to his brother . . .

"I know how to get what you want. What we both want."

"What do you really want with Camelot?" Sophie pressed. "Why are you here?"

"You called, Your Highness?" a voice said, and a boy walked into the dining room wearing a gilded uniform, the same boy Sophie had seen evicting Chef Silkima and her staff from the castle.

Sophie tracked him as he gave her a cursory glance, his face square-jawed, his torso pumped with muscle. He had baby-smooth cheeks and narrow, hooded eyes. Sophie's first thought was that he was oppressively handsome. Her second thought was that he'd looked familiar when she'd noticed him in the garden, but now she was certain she'd seen him before.

"Yes, Kei," said Rhian, welcoming the boy into the dining room.

Kei. Sophie's stomach lurched. She'd spotted him with Dot at Beauty and the Feast, the magical restaurant in Sherwood Forest. Kei had been the newest member of the Merry Men. The traitor who'd broken into the Sheriff's prison and set the Snake free.

"Have your men found Agatha?" Rhian asked.

Sophie's whole body cramped.

"Not yet, sire," said Kei.

Sophie slumped in relief. She'd yet to find a way to send Agatha a message. All she knew from her Quest Map was that her best friend was still on the run. Inside Sophie's shoe, her toes curled around her gold vial, out of Rhian's sight.

"There is a map in the Map Room tracking Agatha's every move," the king said to his captain sourly. "How is it that you can't find her?"

"She's moving east from Sherwood Forest, but there's no sign of her on the ground. We've increased the size of the reward and recruited more mercenaries to track her, but it's as if she's traveling invisibly or by air."

"By *air*. Has she hitched herself to a kite?" Rhian mocked.

"If she's moving east, we think she's headed towards the School for Good and Evil," said Kei, unruffled.

The school! Of course! Sophie held in a smile. *Good girl, Aggie.*

"We've sent men to the school, but it appears to be surrounded by a protective shield," Kei continued. "We've lost several men trying to breach it."

Sophie snorted.

Rhian glanced in her direction and Sophie went mum.

"Find a way to beat the shield," Rhian ordered Kei. "Get your men inside that school."

"Yes, sire," said Kei.

Sophie's skin went cold. She needed to warn Agatha. *Does she still have Dovey's crystal ball?* If she did, maybe they could secretly communicate. Assuming Aggie could figure out how to use it, that is. Sophie had no idea how crystal balls worked. Plus, Dovey's seemed to have made the Dean gravely ill . . . Still, it might be their best hope. . . .

"One more thing," Rhian said to Kei. "Do you have what I asked for?"

Kei cleared his throat. "Yes, sire. Our men went from kingdom to kingdom, seeking stories worthy of Lionsmane," he said, pulling a scroll from his pocket.

"Go on, then," the king responded.

His captain peered at his scroll. "Sasan Sasanovich, a mechanic from Ooty, has invented the first portable cauldron out of dwarf-bone and demand is so high that there's a six-month waiting list. They're called 'Small-drons.'" Kei looked up.

"Small-drons," Rhian said, with the same tone he usually reserved for Tedros' name.

Kei went back to the scroll. "Dieter Dieter Cabbage Eater, the nephew of Peter Peter Pumpkin Eater, has been named assistant dumpling chef at Dumpy's Dumpling House. He will be in charge of all cabbage-based dumplings."

Kei glanced up. Rhian's expression hadn't changed. Kei spoke faster now: "Homina of Putsi chased down a burglar and tied him to a tree with her babushka. . . . A maiden named Luciana created an igloo from cheese rinds in Altazarra to house the homeless from milk monsoons. . . . Thalia of Elderberry came second in the Woods-wide Weightlifting Championships after bench-pressing a family of ogres. . . . A baby son was born to a woman in Budhava after six stillbirths and years of praying. . . . Then there is—"

"Stop," said Rhian.

Kei froze.

"That woman in Budhava," said Rhian. "What's her name?"

"Tsarina, Your Highness," said Kei.

The king paused a moment. Then he slipped open his suit jacket and Lionsmane floated out of his pocket. The golden pen twirled in the chandelier glow before it began to write in midair, gold dust trailing from its tip, as Rhian directed it with his finger.

Tsarina of Budhava has borne a son after six stillbirths. The Lion answered her prayers.

"Lionsmane's first tale," said Rhian, admiring his work.

Sophie guffawed. "*That*? That's your first fairy tale? First of all, that's not a tale at all. It's barely two lines. It's a blurb. A caption. A squawk into the night—"

"The shorter the story, the more likely people are to read it," the king said.

"—and second of all, you couldn't answer a prayer if you tried," Sophie spurned. "You had nothing to do with her son!"

"Says your pen, maybe," Rhian replied. "My pen says that Tsarina of Budhava didn't have a child until I happened to take the throne. Coincidence?"

Sophie boiled. "More lies. All you do is lie."

"Inspiring people is lying? Giving people hope is lying?" Rhian retorted. "In the telling of tales, it's the message that matters."

"And what's your message? That there's no Good and Evil anymore? That there's only you?" Sophie scoffed.

Rhian turned back to the golden words. "It's ready for the people—"

Suddenly, the pen reverted midair from gold to a scaly black scim and magically defaced Rhian's message with splotches of black ink:

"My brother is still upset with me, it seems," Rhian murmured.

"Japeth's right. It *is* weak," said Sophie, surprised she could ever side with the Snake. "No one will listen to your stories. Because even if a story *could* be that short, it has to have a moral. Everyone at the School for Good and Evil knows that.

The school you want to *demolish*. Maybe because it's the school *you* didn't get into."

"Anyone can poke holes in a story who doesn't have the wits to write their own," Rhian said defensively.

"Oh please. I or any one of my classmates could write a *real* fairy tale," Sophie flung back.

"You accuse me of being self-serving when you're nothing but an airheaded braggart," Rhian attacked. "You think you're so clever because you went to that school. You think you could be a real queen? About as likely as Japeth taking a bride. You couldn't do any *real* work if you tried. You're nothing but shiny hair and a fake smile. A no-trick pony."

"I'd be a better king than you. And you know it," Sophie flayed.

"Prove it, then," Rhian scorned. "Prove you can write this tale better than me."

"*Watch me*," Sophie hissed. She stabbed her fingerglow at Rhian's story and revised it in slashes of pink under Japeth's defacements.

Tsarina of Budhava couldn't have a child. Six times she tried and failed. She prayed harder. She prayed and prayed with all her soul. . . . And this time the Lion heard her. He blessed her with a son! Tsarina had learned the greatest lesson of all: "Only the Lion can save you."

"Takes a queen to do a king's job," said Sophie, frost-cold. "A 'king' in name only."

She looked back at Rhian and saw him peering at her intently.

Even the blackened pen seemed to be considering her.

Slowly, the pen magically erased its graffiti, leaving Sophie's corrected tale.

"Remember *Hansel and Gretel?*" Rhian said, gazing at her work. "Your pen says it's about two kids who escape a nasty witch . . . while my pen says it's about a witch who thinks herself so superior that she's duped into working against *herself.*"

Rhian turned his grin on Sophie.

"And so it is written," the king said to the pen.

Lionsmane coated back to gold, then thrust at Sophie's tale like a magic wand—

Instantly, the golden message shot through the bay windows and emblazoned high in the dark sky like a beacon.

Sophie watched villagers far in the distance emerge from their houses in the valley to read Lionsmane's new words, shining against the clouds.

What have I done? Sophie thought.

Rhian turned to his captain. "You're dismissed, Kei," he said as Lionsmane returned to the king's pocket. "I expect Agatha in my dungeon by this time tomorrow."

"Yes, sire," said Kei. As he left, he gave Sophie a shifty-eyed look. A look Sophie knew well. If she didn't know better, she'd think Rhian's captain had a crush on her . . .

It only made Sophie feel queasier, her eyes roving back to

Lionsmane's first story. She'd come to this dinner hoping to gain the upper hand over a villain. Instead, she'd been tricked into amplifying his lies.

She could see Rhian watching through the window as more of Camelot's villagers emerged from their houses. These were the same villagers who'd resisted the new king at the morning's coronation, vocally defending Tedros as the real heir. Now they huddled together and took in the Lion's tale, quietly reflecting on its words.

Rhian turned to Sophie, looking less a ruthless king and more an enamored teenager. It was the same way he'd looked at her when they first met. When he'd wanted something from her.

"So you want to be a *good* queen?" said the king cannily. "Then you'll be writing each and every one of my stories from now on." He studied her as if she was a jewel in his crown. "The pen chose you wisely after all."

Sophie's insides shriveled.

He was ordering her to write his lies.

To spread his Evil.

To be *his* Storian.

"And if I refuse?" she said, clutching at the side of her dress. "One drop of this iron gall on my skin and—"

"You already stained your wrist when you sat down for dinner," said Rhian, spearing a piece of squid in his soup. "And you're as healthy as can be."

Slowly Sophie looked down and saw the smear of blue on her skin; harmless ink she'd extracted from a quill in the Map

Room and dyed with magic.

"Your wizard friend refused to help me too," said the king. "Sent him on a little trip afterward. Don't think he'll be refusing me anymore."

Sophie's blood went cold.

In a single moment, she realized she'd been beaten.

Rhian was not like Rafal.

Rhian couldn't be wheedled and seduced. He couldn't be manipulated or charmed. Rafal had loved her. Rhian didn't care about her at all.

She'd come down to dinner thinking she had a hand to play, but now it turned out she didn't even know the game. For the first time in her life, she felt outmatched.

Rhian watched her with a trace of pity. "You called my story a lie, but it's already come true. Don't you see? Only I can save you."

She met his eyes, trying to hold his stare.

Rhian prowled forward, his elbows on the table. "*Say* it."

Sophie waited for the fight to swell inside of her . . . the witch to rear her head. . . . But this time nothing came. She looked down at the tablecloth.

"Only you can save me," she said softly.

She saw Rhian smile, a lion enjoying his kill.

"Well, now that we've made our *deal* . . . ," he said. "Shall we have cake?"

Sophie watched the candles in the Lion centerpiece melt wax onto their holders.

Cheap candles, she thought.

Another lie. Another bluff.

A dark flame kindled inside of her.

She still had a bluff to play of her own.

"You think I'm afraid of death? I've died before and that didn't stop me," she said, standing up. "So kill me. Let's see if that keeps the Woods on your side. Let's see if that makes them listen to your *pen*."

She swept past him, watching Rhian's face cloud, unprepared for her move—

"And what if I agree to your terms?" he asked.

Sophie paused, her back to him.

"One person from the dungeons that will serve as your steward, just as you asked," he said, sounding composed again. "Anyone you like. I'll free them to work in the castle. Under my supervision, of course. All you have to do is write Lionsmane's tales."

Sophie's heart beat faster.

"Who would you pick to be freed?" Rhian asked.

Sophie turned to him.

"Tedros included?" she asked.

Rhian stretched his biceps behind his head.

"Tedros included," he said decisively.

Sophie paused. Then she sat back down across from him.

"So I write your stories . . . and you let Tedros go," she repeated. "Those are the terms?"

"Correct."

Sophie watched Rhian.

Rhian watched her.

Now I know the game, she thought.

"Well, in that case . . . ," Sophie said innocently. "I choose Hort."

Rhian blinked.

Sophie stretched her arms behind her head and held his stunned glare.

It had been a test. A test to make her pick Tedros. A test to call her bluff and prove she could never be loyal. A test to make her his slave from this moment on.

A dirty little test he expected her to fail.

But you can't beat Evil with Evil.

Which meant now they had a deal.

She would write his stories. Hort would be freed.

Both would be her weapons in time.

Sophie smiled at the king, her emerald eyes aglow.

"I don't eat cake," she said. "But tonight I'll make an exception."

7

AGATHA

Agatha's Army

Straddling the spine of a stymph, her arms around her old Beautification professor, Agatha tried to see through the gaps in the canopy of branches as she flew high over the Endless Woods. Autumn was coming, leaves already losing their green.

It must be six o'clock in the morning, she thought, since it was still too dark to see the forest floor, but the sky overhead was starting to simmer with tones of gold and red.

A hand reached back holding a blue lollipop.

"Stole it just for you," said Professor Anemone. "It's illegal to take candy from Hansel's Haven, as you well know, but, given present circumstances, I think we all need to break a few rules."

Agatha lifted the lollipop from her teacher's hand into her mouth and tasted its familiar blueberry tartness. Her first year she'd gotten detention from Professor Anemone for stealing one of these lollipops off the candied classroom walls in Hansel's Haven (along with marshmallows, a hunk of gingerbread, and two bricks of fudge). Back then, she'd been the worst student at the School for Good and Evil. Now, three years later, she was returning to the school to lead it.

"Do they know what's happened?" Agatha asked, watching her teacher's lemon-yellow hair dance in the wind. "The new students, I mean."

"The Storian began its retelling of *The Lion and the Snake* before you and Sophie left on your quest. That's how we've stayed up-to-date on everything that's happened since Rhian took the throne."

"But can't we show the Storian's tale to the rest of the kingdoms?" Agatha asked, adjusting Dovey's bag on her arm, feeling Tedros' jacket that she'd taken from Robin's house cushioned around the crystal ball inside. "If we can make their rulers see that Rhian and the Snake are working together—"

"The Storian's tales reach other kingdoms only *after* The End is written, including your bookshops in Woods Beyond," said her teacher. "And even if we could bring the Kingdom

Council to the School Master's tower, the Storian won't allow anyone to look backwards in a fairy tale while it is writing one. Nor should we involve the Kingdom Council until we have clearer proof of Rhian's plot, since their allegiance is to the new king. That said, Professor Manley has been monitoring the pen's movements and our first years have been briefed on the story thus far."

"And they're trained to fight?" Agatha pressed.

"Fight? Goodness, no."

"But you said they're my army!"

"Agatha, they've been at school for less than a month. The Evergirls can barely produce passable smiles, the Nevers are hopeless with their Special Talents, and they've just had their fingerglows unlocked two days ago. There hasn't even been a Trial by Tale. They're certainly no army yet. But you'll whip them into shape."

"*Me?* You want *me* to train them?" Agatha blurted. "But I'm not a teacher! Sophie can bluff being a Dean because, well, she can bluff anything, but not me—"

"You'll love the new Everboys. Charming little foxes." Professor Anemone glanced back, her makeup dried out and cracking. "Especially the boys of Honor 52."

"Professor, I don't even know these students!"

"You know Camelot. You know the castle, you know its defenses, and most importantly, you know the false king who sits upon the throne," said Professor Anemone. "You are far better equipped than any of the teachers to lead our students in this fight. Besides, until you complete your quest, you're still an official student, and given the Storian is writing your tale, the teachers cannot interfere in it. Clarissa made that mistake and clearly paid the price."

Agatha shook her head. "But can the students even do basic spells? Will the Evers and Nevers work together? Have you told them what's at stake—"

"My dear, take advantage of the peace and quiet while you can," said her teacher, steadying the stymph at a cruising altitude. "There won't be much of either once we get to school."

Agatha exhaled through her nose. How could she relax until her friends were free? And how was she supposed to lead a school? A school full of students she'd never met? If she wasn't so overwhelmed, she'd appreciate the irony: Sophie had been thrust at the head of Camelot, where Agatha was supposed to be queen, and now Agatha was expected to command the School for Good and Evil, where Sophie was supposed to be Dean. Agatha's heart revved up, then sputtered, drained of adrenaline after her all-night visit to Sherwood Forest. She could feel her eyelids drooping . . . But with Dovey's crystal ball slung on her shoulder, weighing her down, she didn't dare fall asleep, for fear it would yank her overboard and drop her like a stone.

Clutching Dovey's bag tighter, Agatha scanned the landscape and spotted a golden castle ahead, thin spires clustered like organ pipes.

Foxwood, she remembered. The oldest Ever kingdom.

In front of the castle, the thick forest receded, giving way to Foxwood's outer vales, with rows of cottages surrounding a tree-lined square. The pavilion was mostly deserted this early in the morning, except for a baker setting up his cart in front of a stone fountain. Wrapped around the fountain, Agatha could make out colorful banners hand-drawn by the kingdom's children.

So Long, So Long, the Snake is Gone!

HAIL KING RHIAN, THE SNAKE SLAYER!

Long Live Queen Sophie!

As the stymph soared over increasingly lavish houses, closer to Foxwood castle, Agatha glimpsed three young kids in gold-foil Lion masks jousting with wooden swords as their father raked the yard of leaves. She'd seen the same thing in Gillikin: children idolizing the new King of Camelot as their hero. Disturbed, Agatha looked back up.

The stymph was about to smash right into the side of the king's castle.

"Professor!" Agatha shrieked—

Professor Anemone snored awake and in a single move shot a spray of sparks at her stymph, which jolted from its own slumber with a squawk, skimming the golden tower just in time.

The stymph reared in midair, panting hard, as Professor Anemone stroked its neck, trying to calm it down. "Seems we both fell asleep," she croaked as the stymph peeped sheepishly at his riders through eyeless sockets. "And no wonder, given the rumpus at school. Thankfully we'll be there soon enough."

"Rumpus" didn't sound good, Agatha thought, but right now she was worried they'd woken the Foxwood guard. If anyone spotted her, they'd surely alert Rhian. She peeked back towards the castle, about to urge Professor Anemone to get moving. Then her eyes widened—

"What's *that*?"

She'd been so busy looking down that she'd missed the giant message in gold, embedded in the lightening sky overhead.

"Lionsmane's first fairy tale," said Professor Anemone, still caressing the stymph. "You must have been deep in Sherwood Forest to miss it. Been up there nearly a full day now. Visible from any kingdom in the Woods."

"Lionsmane . . . You mean 'Rhian's pen'? The one he's pit against the Storian?" Agatha said, remembering the newspaper in Gillikin. She quickly read the message in the sky about a woman named Tsarina, blessed with a child after several stillbirths. "'Only the Lion can save you'? *That's* the moral of the story?"

Her teacher sighed. "The Storian spends weeks, months, often years crafting a tale for the purposes of bettering our world. And now a new pen arrives that replaces storytelling with a king's propaganda."

"A *fake* king and a *fake* pen," Agatha bristled. "Are people actually believing this? Is anyone fighting for the Stori . . ."

Her voice trailed off, because Rhian's fairy tale suddenly faded. Agatha and Professor Anemone exchanged anxious looks, as if their presence here was somehow responsible. But then a blast of light shot from the west, branding a new message in the sky, replacing the first one.

Citizens of the Woods! Revel in the tale of Hristo of Camelot, only 8 years old, who ran away from home and came to my castle, hoping to be my knight. Young Hristo's mother found and whipped the poor boy. Stay strong, Hristo! The day you turn 16, you have a place as my knight! A child who loves his king is a blessed child. Let that be a lesson to all.

"Now he's going after the youth," Professor Anemone realized, grim-faced. "Same thing Rafal tried when he took over both schools. Own the youth and you own the future."

Down below, Agatha could still see the kids' tiny figures swordplaying in their Lion masks. Only they'd stopped now and were gazing up at the Lion's second tale, along with their father. After a moment, the father's eyes swept towards Agatha and her teacher, perched atop their stymph.

"Let's go," said Agatha quickly.

The stymph propelled towards the rising sun.

Agatha looked back one last time at the Lion's new tale, her stomach screwing tighter. It wasn't just the Lion's message, smoothly glorifying himself as king . . . but it was how *familiar* the message was, its lies sounding like truths . . .

Ah. Now she remembered.

The Snake's pen.

The one he'd shown her and Sophie the first time they'd met.

His fake Storian that took real stories and contorted them into something darker and untrue.

His pen peeled off his own murderous body and now presented to the people as their guiding light.

His slimy, scaly strip of lies.

That was Lionsmane.

THE SCHOOL HAD taken no chances once Merlin and Professor Dovey had been captured. As the stymph descended, Agatha saw the two castles had been shielded in a protective, murky-green fog. A dove happened to get too close and the mist inhaled it like a living creature, then spewed it back out like a cannonball, pitching the shrieking bird fifty miles away. The stymph, meanwhile, passed through unscathed, though Agatha had to hold her nose to endure the fog, which smelled like rancid meat.

"One of Professor Manley's spells," Professor Anemone called back. "Not as secure as Lady Lesso's old shields, but it's kept out Rhian's men thus far. A few were caught snooping the past couple days. They must suspect you're on your way."

More than just suspicion, Agatha thought. If Rhian was the

Snake's brother, then that meant Rhian had the Snake's Quest Map. He could trace Agatha's every move.

In the meantime, all she could do was hope Manley's shield would hold.

Breaking through the fog, the first thing Agatha saw was the School Master's tower, perched in the middle of Halfway Bay between the clear lake bordering the School for Good and the thick blue moat around the School for Evil. A gang of stymphs was in the process of undoing the last scaffolding around the silver spire, revealing a dazzling statue of Sophie atop like a weathervane, along with ornate friezes in the tower's length depicting Sophie's most iconic moments. There were multiple floors within the tower, flaunting refurbished windows (through which Agatha could see walk-in closets, a dining room, a steam room and whirlpool), and a catwalk to the School for Evil, lit up with lights and a sign reading "SOPHIE'S WAY."

Professor Bilious Manley poked his pimpled, pear-shaped head out a window in Sophie's Tower and shot blasts of green light at the friezes and statue, trying to obliterate them—but every spell he did rebounded straight at him while a high-pitched alarm blared from Sophie's statue, sounding like a raven's shriek—

"*You have attempted an unauthorized redecoration of Dean Sophie's Tower,*" Sophie's voice boomed as a rebounding spell zapped Manley in the rump. "*Only an officially appointed School Master has authority here and you are not a School Master.*

Kindly vacate my premises."

Fuming, Manley stormed back into the tower, where Agatha glimpsed three wolves demolishing Sophie's interiors. But seconds after tearing down paintings and fixtures and lamps, they all floated straight back up.

"He's been battling that tower ever since he took over as Dean," Professor Anemone chortled as more repelling spells scalded Manley and his wolves. "I've learned never to underestimate that girl."

From inside the tower, Manley let out a primal scream.

It only made Agatha miss Sophie more.

The stymph landed on the south side of Halfway Bay in front of Good's castle. As Agatha dismounted, fairies swarmed her, smelling her hair and neck. Unlike the fairies that used to run the School for Good when she was a first year, this new fleet were of different shapes, sizes, colors, as if from a variety of lands, but they all seemed to know who she was.

As she followed Professor Anemone uphill, Agatha noticed the unusual quiet. She could hear her own clump-steps crackling on the Great Lawn's crisp grass, the spasm of fairy wings around her, the burps of water from the lake. Agatha peered across the bay and saw the same scene on Evil's shores as smooth blue slime lapped up and stained the sand. A lone guard wolf in a red soldier's jacket and a whip on his belt had fallen asleep on one of Sophie's new cabanas.

Professor Anemone opened the doors to Good's castle and Agatha silently trailed her through a long hall of mirrors. Agatha caught her reflection in the glass, grubby, windblown, and sleepless, her black gown ragged with holes. She looked worse than she did on her first day of school, when Evergirls had cornered her in this hall, thinking she was a witch, and she'd farted in their faces to escape. Smirking at the memory, Agatha followed her teacher, turning into the foyer—

"WELCOME HOME!"

A cheer exploded like a bomb, sending Agatha staggering backwards.

More than a hundred first years in the foyer whistled and hooted, while waving enchanted signs, with words popping off banners: "I STAND WITH AGATHA!"; "NEVER RHIAN!"; "JUSTICE FOR TEDROS!"

Agatha gawked at this new class of Evers, so fresh-faced and clean, with the girls in restyled pink pinafores and the boys in navy waistcoats, skinny ties, and tight beige breeches. Silver swan crests glittered over their hearts, branding them as first years, along with magical name tags that moved around their bodies to help Agatha see them from any sightline— "LAITHAN," "VALENTINA," "SACHIN," "ASTRID," "PRIYANKA," and more. Many looked close to her in age, especially the boys, so tall and princely with training swords on their waists . . . and yet, despite this, all of them seemed so *young*. As if they still held faith in the laws of Good and Evil. As if they'd yet to learn that the bubble of school could be so easily punctured. *I was like them once*, Agatha thought.

"QUEEN AGATHA! QUEEN AGATHA!" chanted the first years as they surrounded her like lemmings, crowding her between the foyer's four staircases: Valor and Honor to the

boys' towers, Purity and Charity to the girls'. Agatha looked up to see the teachers gathered on the Valor staircase—Princess Uma, who'd taught her Animal Communication; Professor Espada, who taught Swordplay; Yuba the Gnome, who'd led her Forest Group . . . It was the same scene that greeted Agatha on her own Welcoming day, only this time, there were two professors missing. Seven-foot nymphs with neon hair floated beneath the domed ceiling, sprinkling rose petals that caught in Agatha's dress and made her sneeze. Agatha tried to smile at the young Evers, singing her name and waving their signs and swords, but all she could think about was Professor Dovey and Professor August Sader, both absent from the top of the stairs. Without them, the school no longer felt warm or safe. It felt alien, vulnerable.

"GOOD IDLES AND EVIL WORKS," a voice boomed. "SOUNDS ABOUT RIGHT."

Agatha and the Evers swiveled to see the double doors at the rear of the foyer fly open. Castor the Dog stood inside the Theater of Tales, its two sides turned into a massive war room. More than a hundred Nevers in sleek black-leather uniforms toiled at various stations, littered with papers and notebooks and maps, while Evil teachers supervised.

"NICE TO SEE YOU'RE ALIVE," said Castor, glancing at Agatha, before baring sharp teeth at the Evers. "BUT WE AIN'T WON NOTHIN' YET."

THE FIRST YEARS were split into workstations based on their respective Forest Groups, with five Evers and five Nevers at each station. At the first station, Group #1 hovered over a pew that had been flipped over and turned into a long table, heaped with dozens of maps. Agatha shuffled over, feeling unsure how to take the lead, but luckily she didn't need to, because the students took the lead on their own.

"Couldn't find any current maps of Camelot Castle inside the Library of Virtue, but we did find this," said a beautiful, dark-skinned Everboy tagged BODHI, pointing to a crusty diagram inside a very old edition of *A Student's History of the Woods*. "According to this, the dungeon's at the base of Gold Tower, way underground. But since the castle is built on a hill, it looks like the dungeon might be against the *side* of that hill. If this map is still correct, that is." Bodhi looked up at Agatha. "That's where you can help us. Are the dungeons still there?"

Agatha tightened. "Um . . . not sure. I never saw them."

The whole team stared at her.

"But you were at Camelot for months," said an Everboy tagged LAITHAN, short and muscular, with chestnut hair and freckled skin.

"You were the *princess*," said Bodhi.

Agatha's neck rashed red. "Look, the dungeons are probably where they've always been, so let's assume this map is right—"

"That's what I say and these Good boys tell me I'm stupid,"

piped VALENTINA from the other end of the table. She had a high, black ponytail, pencil-thin eyebrows, and a breathy accent. "But I say jail must still be there and if jail is on side of hill, then we go to hill with shovels and *pew! pew! pew!* Tedrosito and your friends free."

Bodhi snorted with Laithan. "Valentina, first of all, this textbook is like a thousand years old and landmasses *move* over time."

"Excuse me, my family lives under a guanabana tree for a thousand years and guanabana tree is still there," said Valentina.

Laithan groaned. "Look, even if the dungeon *is* on the hill, there's no way to *pew! pew! pew!* because there's *guards*."

"Do you remember that fairy-tale *famoso* where the boy doesn't save his friends because he's afraid of guards?" Valentina asked.

"No," said Laithan, confused.

"Exactly," said Valentina.

"V, I know Nevers are supposed to defend each other in front of Evers, but we can't even *find* this hill," said a waifish Neverboy with dyed flame-red hair and the name AJA floating over his head. "I tried to locate the dungeons with heat vision and didn't see a thing."

"Heat vision?" Agatha asked.

"My villain talent," Aja clarified. "You know how Sophie's special talent was summoning Evil? Like when she summoned those ravens at the Circus of Talents? She wore that amazing snakeskin cape that she stitched herself . . . the one that turned her invisible . . . It's in the Exhibition of Evil now. I wish I could try it on, just to *feel* like her . . . Sorry, *huuuge* Sophie fan. Kept it low-key when she was Dean so she wouldn't think I'm a freak, but I know every word of her fairy tale and I dressed as her for Halloween with furs and boots and seriously, she'll be the best Queen of Camelot ever . . . like completely iconic . . ." Aja saw Agatha's frown. "Um. No offense."

"You were talking about heat vision," said Agatha tersely.

"Right. That's my villain talent: being able to sense bodies in darkness—even through hard objects. So I convinced Professor Sheeks to let me take a stymph to Camelot at night with one of the nymphs onboard, since stymphs hate villains and it would have eaten me without a guard from Good," Aja prattled. "We flew high above so Rhian's men on the towers couldn't see us. But if the dungeon is near the side of the hill, I should have been able to detect the bodies underground, and . . . I couldn't see a thing."

"Aja, no offense, but you can't even find the toilet in the middle of the night and I know that for a fact," said Valentina, giving Agatha a sordid glance. (Agatha pursed her lips.) "So just because you can't see the dungeon doesn't mean it isn't there."

"Honeybear, I placed top rank in Professor Sheeks' class six challenges in a row," Aja defended.

"Because your *real* talent is brownnosing teachers," said Valentina.

Agatha couldn't think with all this sniping, plus there was a strange stink wafting from Group #6 nearby. ("Smells like a skunk den on a Friday night!" she heard Princess Uma gasp.)

"What about mogrification?" Agatha asked. "Can't we turn into worms or scorpions and sneak into the castle and find the jail?"

"Magic doesn't work in dungeons," said Laithan, glancing at his teammates, and this time even the Evil ones agreed. He peered at Agatha. "You don't know that?"

"We're all in Yuba's Forest Group and he had that question on our first test. Seemed pretty basic," Bodhi piled on.

Agatha started to sweat. In times of stress, she always emerged the leader. But these kids were making her feel like an idiot. Fine, so she didn't know where the dungeons were; when she'd lived at Camelot, she'd been told the castle was impenetrable. Why would she go hunting for ways to invade it? And why should she remember every detail from a class three years ago? Especially when she was tired and anxious and focused on saving her friends' lives? Meanwhile, these amateurs were staring at her, so cocksure and poised, as if she had something to prove to *them*.

Agatha stood taller. "So we don't know exactly where the dungeon is. Let's address that," she said, the stink from Group #6 getting worse. "What about sneaking in as guards or maids and searching the castle? Or taking a cook hostage and demanding to know where the prisoners are being kept? What about sending a gift with a bunch of us hidden inside? Then boo, we attack!"

The young Evers and Nevers shifted uncomfortably.

"Those are really bad ideas," said Aja.

"For once I agree with Aja," said Valentina. "Rhian is very

smart. He'd suspect a bunch of lost-looking maids or a gift
with things whispering inside like a *chupacabra*."

"Plus, the Snake has a Quest Map," Bodhi said to Agatha.
"If you get anywhere near that castle, he'd know."

Agatha bristled, feeling even more defensive than before . . .
but deep down she knew they were right. Her plans were stupid. Yet there *was* no brilliant plan waiting for her to think of
it. There was no perfect secret entrance or dodgy gate or magical spell that would get them into Camelot undetected. And
even if there were, there was certainly no way to get Tedros,
Sophie, Dovey, and nine other prisoners *out*.

"I'll lock this in my office for you, dear," said Professor
Anemone, sidling up to her and slipping Dovey's bag off her
arm.

"No, I'll keep it with me," Agatha batted, holding it tight.
"Merlin ordered me not to let it out of my sight."

"Say no more," her teacher replied. "Ooh, I see you've met
the boys of Honor 52. Be strict with Bodhi and Laithan. Don't
let them flirt their way out of trouble. You're their commander
now."

"The teachers' commander too," said Princess Uma,
approaching. "We're here to help you. And my animals will
join the fight."

"As will the wolves and fairies," said Yuba the Gnome, wad-
dling up to them. "And don't forget the rest of the fourth years:
Ravan, Vex, and a few others are in the clinic, recovering from
the Battle of the Four Point, while the remainder of the class are
on their way back to school from their various quest sites. You

have a whole army at your service, Agatha. But my Forest Group just told me you've yet to decide on a plan. Think harder, my girl. Camelot isn't just your home; it's your *domain*. You know its weaknesses, along with the new king's. Somewhere inside you, you know how to rescue your friends. Somewhere inside, you have the plan. And now we need to hear it."

Heads poked up from workstations, all eyes on Camelot's princess. The theater went as quiet as a church on Halloween.

"The plan?" Agatha's voice came out a croak. She cleared her throat, hoping it would magically produce a strategy. "Yes. Um—"

"YOU SMELLY HOUSE APES!"

Everyone turned to see Castor kicking two boys' rumps at Station #6. "DOVEY'S IN PRISON, KING'S 'BOUT TO DIE, AND YOU'RE MAKIN' DUNGBOMBS!"

"Flaming dungbombs!" a puny blond named BERT pipped.

"Smell Missiles!" a fellow blond named BECKETT added. "The perfect weapon!"

"I'LL SHOW YOU THE PERFECT WEAPON!" Castor swiped a newspaper off the Group #6 table and thrashed both boys with it. "ONE MORE DUNGBOMB AND IT'S THE DOOM ROOM!"

"We're Evers!" Bert and Beckett protested.

"EVEN BETTER!" Castor barked, walloping them harder.

Noxious fumes spread out of control, sending groups ducking for cover. Agatha seized on the distraction and hustled to Group #6's table, where a boy and girl were poring over the newspapers Castor hadn't swiped, undeterred by Bert and Beckett's stink-plot.

These two look clever, Agatha thought. *Maybe they've found something I haven't.*

"Welcome to Forest Group #6," said a bald, ghostly Everboy named DEVAN with dark eyebrows and sculpted cheekbones. "Pleasure to be in your company, Princess Agatha. You are as regal and lovely as your fairy tale promised."

"She has a boyfriend, Devan," said a dark Nevergirl with ice-blue hair, matching eyes, and a choker strung with mini-skulls. Her name tag read LARALISA. She slipped her hand around Devan's waist. "And you're spoken for too, so don't lay it on too thick."

Agatha's eyes widened at the sight of an Ever and a Never so brazenly dating (Lady Lesso tried to murder Tedros and Sophie when they'd done it), but now Devan was pushing one of the newspapers towards her across the overturned pew.

"Take a look at today's *Camelot Courier*," he said.

Agatha scanned the front page—

IDENTITY OF SNAKE
STILL IN QUESTION
Castle Refuses to Comment on the Face Under the Mask

SNAKE'S BODY MISSING,
SAYS CRYPTKEEPER
Garden of Good & Evil Has No Reports of Snake's Burial

DOUBTS RAISED ABOUT
KING'S NEW LIEGE
Where Was Japeth When the Snake Was on the Loose?

Laralisa dropped another paper on top. "Now look at the *Royal Rot.*"

Agatha hunched over Camelot's colorful tabloid, known for its ludicrous conspiracy theories and outright lies.

CRYPTKEEPER DEBUNKED!
Snake's Burial Confirmed in Necro Ridge

JAPETH REVEALS
"My Brother Stopped Me from Fighting the Snake
—Rhian Wanted to Protect Me!"

COURIER OF LIES
80% OF STORIES PROVEN FALSE!

"The usual horsecrap," muttered Agatha. "But it doesn't matter. No one in Camelot will ever believe a word the *Rot* says, no matter what Rhian has them print."

"It's not the people of Camelot we're worried about," said Laralisa.

She slid a few more papers in front of Agatha.

THE NETHERWOOD VILLAIN DIGEST
CAMELOT DISPUTES CRYPTKEEPER!
Snake Buried in Necro Ridge!

THE MALABAR HILLS MIRROR
KING RHIAN VINDICATED
Snake's Body Verified in Secret Tomb!

THE PIFFLEPAFF POST
KEEPER OF LIES! Snake's Body Found in Garden of Good & Evil

"Rhian's fingerprints are all over this," said Laralisa. "He knows the *Courier* is onto him. So he's making sure the other kingdoms parrot his lies."

"And the other kingdoms go along with it because they trust anything Rhian says," Agatha realized. "In their eyes, he killed the Snake. He killed a deadly villain attacking their kingdoms. He *saved* them. The people of the Woods don't know it's a lie. They don't know he's playing them for fools. The Storian knows and we know."

"And the *Courier*'s getting close," said Laralisa. "But Rhian's discredited the Storian, he's discredited Tedros, he's discredited you, he's discredited the school, and now he's discrediting the *Courier*. Even if we did have proof to show the people that the Snake is still alive—and we *don't*—no one would listen to us."

"*Courier* might not even be around long enough to back us up," Devan noted, pulling open its pages. "They're on the run, printing in secret, and Rhian's men are hunting their reporters. And the more they're on the run, the more they're grasping at straws. Look at these headlines. It's like something out of the *Rot*."

MESSAGE IN BOTTLE FOUND: "SNAKE IS STILL ALIVE!"

MISTRAL SISTERS HIRED AS KING'S ADVISORS? SIGHTING THROUGH CASTLE WINDOW

PRINCESS SOPHIE SECRETLY TRADES FOR FRIEND'S RELEASE

Agatha quickly honed in on this last story.

Until now, the people of the Woods believed that Lionsmane was the pen of the King. Indeed, at his coronation, King Rhian made it clear that unlike the Storian, which was controlled by shadowy magic, his pen could be trusted. His pen would care about all people, rich or poor, young or old, Good or Evil—just like he cared about all people when he saved them from the Snake.

But according to an anonymous source, last night Princess Sophie and King Rhian struck an unusual deal over a dinner of fish soup and pistachio cake. The deal was this: Sophie would be the one to write Lionsmane's tales, not Rhian. And in return, Sophie's friend and former suitor, Hort of Bloodbrook, would be set free from the Camelot dungeons.

Our source offered no reason for this deal, but made it clear: it's the princess who is composing Lionsmane's words, not the king.

What does this mean? First, it means King Rhian lied about Lionsmane being his pen, since Sophie writes its tales. At the same time, Tedros loyalists have been hoping Sophie is secretly still on Tedros' side and working against the new king. But if Sophie is writing Lionsmane's messages, then those hopes are misguided and she is firmly behind the king's agenda.

Agatha's heart thumped harder.

On the one hand, the story couldn't be true. Sophie would never write Lionsmane's tales. She would never promote a phony king's propaganda. She would certainly never eat cake.

And yet, as much as she dreaded doing interviews with the *Courier* and its invasive reporters . . . the *Courier* never lied. And then there was that curious phrase—"a deal was struck"—which seemed to stand out on the page . . .

As the dung fumes cleared and Devan and Laralisa conferred with fellow group members ROWAN, DRAGO, and MALI, who had returned to the table, Agatha found herself wandering to the back of the theater. She gazed out into the Evers' foyer and its glass sundome overhead, Lionsmane's message about young Hristo glowing gold in the sky.

Agatha read the message again and again and again.

Until she was quite sure.

There was something off about it.

Not the story or language or tone . . . but *something*.

Something that told her the story in the *Courier* was true. That Sophie *had* written this message. That she was up to something, even if Agatha didn't know what it was yet.

The *Courier* had assumed the worst, of course. No one in their right mind would trust Sophie to risk herself for Tedros, a boy who'd rejected her again and again.

But Agatha trusted her.

Which meant that even with Sophie under a king's eye, facing mortal danger, and a pawn of the enemy, she was still fighting for her friends.

And here Agatha was, free and clear, with a school full of students ready to serve her, and nothing to show for it except sweaty palms and a nervous rash. Meanwhile, without direction, the groups around her seemed to be losing their way. Group #8's Evers and Nevers were having a loud row over whether they should kill or wound Rhian when they found him; Group #3 was debating whether Merlin was alive or dead; Group #7 battled with a hairy, three-eyed Never named BOSSAM, who insisted Rhian was a better king than Tedros; Group #4 heatedly argued over a diagram of Arthur's family tree . . .

Agatha felt even more useless watching these upstarts, so passionate and engaged, while she continued to flag, her body sleepy, hungry, and Dovey's infernal bag still on her arm, weighing her down—

Bag.

Agatha froze.

Something sparked inside her, like a torch in the night.

Lionsmane's message. Now she knew why it was off.

"When's the execution?" she asked, rushing back to Group #6.

Devan fidgeted. "Uh, you mean . . ."

"My boyfriend's execution. Yes. When is it?" Agatha pressed.

"Saturday," said Laralisa. "But the wedding festivities start today with the Blessing at Camelot's church."

"And the events are open to the public?" Agatha asked.

Devan looked at his girlfriend. "Um, as far as we kno—"

Agatha spun to the other groups. "Listen here!"

Students kept arguing at their stations.

Agatha's fingertip seared gold and she shot a comet through the hall. "I said *listen here.*"

Evers and Nevers lurched to attention.

"Tedros' execution will take place at Sophie and Rhian's wedding in less than a week," Agatha announced. "There'll be events leading up to the wedding. Forest Group #6, you'll be leaving to attend the Blessing shortly."

Devan, Laralisa, and the rest of their team gaped at each other.

"Um . . . what are we doing there?" Devan asked.

"While they're at the Blessing, Group #1, you'll go to the dungeons," Agatha continued.

Bodhi snorted. Laithan, Valentina, Aja, and the rest of their group looked equally incredulous.

"You just talked to us about how we don't know where the dungeons are," said Bodhi.

"Or how to get in," said Laithan.

"And they're not trained in combat yet," Professor Espada added.

"Nor in death traps," said Professor Manley, stalking into the theater.

"Nor in animal communication," said Princess Uma.

"Nor in talent manipulation," said Professor Sheeks.

"NOR IN BASIC COMMON SENSE," said Castor.

"How can they possibly go to the dungeons if they don't know where they are? How will they elude the guards?" Professor Anemone asked, wringing her hands.

"Magic," said Agatha.

"They've had two *days* of magic lessons," Manley scoffed.

"More than enough," Agatha replied.

Valentina raised her hand. "Excuse me, Miss Princess Agatha? Didn't you hear us before? Magic doesn't work in dungeons—"

"Which means we can't get to Tedros or Professor Dovey or anyone else," Aja agreed. "There's zero way for us to break in."

"You're not supposed to break in," Agatha answered calmly.

She smiled at the bewildered faces and held Professor Dovey's crystal ball tighter at her side . . .

"You're supposed to break them *out*."

Someday My Weasel Will Come

When Hort was a child, a pirate boy named Dabo used to bully him by roping him to a tree and putting things down his pants. Roaches, leeches, ants, cat poo, spiders, pee-filled snow, and once a stolen hawk egg, which the mother hawk came for, leaving Hort with ten stitches in his thigh.

But none of this compared to the sheer torture of having one of the Snake's slimy, sticky eels worm down his shirt, probing every inch of skin.

Hort stood stiffly in the corner of Sophie's bedroom, clad in a poofy, ill-fitting white tunic and matching harem

pants that he had to double-knot so they wouldn't fall down. He focused on the sounds of the bath running and Sophie's faint humming as the eel roamed over his chest. He tried not to scream.

His release from the dungeons had come with a price. A scim stuck to him like a parasite. A sliver of the Snake's body melded onto his own, spying on his every move—

"Hey!" Hort snarled, snatching the scim as it slithered into his pants. The eel hissed and stabbed his thumb, drawing a drop of blood, before it hopped up Hort's flank and neck and curled around his ear.

"Dirty little bugger," Hort murmured, sucking his thumb. He wanted to grab the little leech and smash it and grind it to a pulp, but he knew another scim would replace it. If he was lucky. More likely he'd be killed or thrown back in the dungeons.

Morning sun frayed through the window and Hort rubbed his eyes. He'd been freed from his cell last night by the Snake— who, upon hearing his brother had made a deal with Sophie to set Hort free, had taken it upon himself to do the freeing, for the sole purpose of tormenting Tedros into thinking it was the prince that Sophie had released. Then the Snake had dragged Hort out of the dungeons, slapped him with a surveilling scim, and whisked him straight to a servant's quarters the size of a closet, where he'd been locked in the dark. At dawn, Hort had been jolted awake by guards, fitted in this billowing uniform like a discount genie, and brought to the queen's chamber, sleepless and filthy, and told to wait for his new "Mistress" to emerge from her bath.

Why did Sophie pick me? he wondered now.

She could have picked anyone. Tedros. Hester. She could have picked Dovey. She could have picked the Dean.

Does she need me for something only I can do?

Is she sacrificing me so the others can live?

His blood pumped hotter.

Or . . . did she choose to save me first?

The scim moved and Hort remembered it was there. Only Sophie could make him forget about a monster on his ear.

He blushed hotter and sniffed his armpits. Blech. Maybe he could ask to use the bath after she was finished. He'd need to be quick. The Blessing was in less than an hour and as her new "steward," he'd been tasked with getting her ready, even though he had no idea what that meant.

Hort glanced around the vast room, suddenly ashimmer in sunlight. Everything looked freshly remodeled: the blue marble tiles with Lion emblems, the silk wallpaper textured with gold Lions, the flawless gem-crusted mirrors, and a clean white settee stitched with a gold Lion's head.

All that time playing Tedros' loyal knight, Hort snorted, thinking of Rhian's perfectly honed act. Almost made him feel sorry for Tedros.

Almost.

The scim started creeping down his neck again.

Hort could hear the bathwater draining. His thoughts turned to Sophie in the bath and he bit down on the inside of his cheek. He had a girlfriend now, who was pretty and smart and fun, and when you have a girlfriend, you're not supposed to think about other girls, especially girls in bathtubs and girls who you've obsessed about for three years. He tried to distract himself with details of the room but found his eyes moving to Sophie's bed . . . the silky, rumpled sheets . . . the tin of hazelnuts on the night table . . . the cup of tea and vial of untouched honey . . . the red lipstick on the edge of the cup . . .

The doors opened behind him and two young maids in white uniforms that matched the color of his own entered the queen's chamber, lugging heaps of garment bags. Hort hustled to help and saw each bag was branded with VON ZARACHIN FABRICS as he hauled them into his arms and laid them over the settee. He turned to the maids, but they were already shuffling back through the doors, heads down and faces hidden by their bonnets.

"Are those my dresses from Madame Clothilde? Thank *goodness*," Sophie said, sweeping out of the bathroom in a pink robe, a towel turbaned around her head, as she barely gave Hort a glance. "Madame Clothilde Von Zarachin is the *empress* of fashion in the Woods. All the best princesses are wearing her clothes. Madame Clothilde even designed Evelyn Sader's gown, you know, the one made out of those spying blue butterflies. Nearly killed us all our second year, but *c'est magnifique*, wasn't it? Last night I wrote Madame in a panic, begging her to send me something to wear for the Blessing, and given my new position, she naturally obliged. She warned it would be prohibitively expensive, but I told her Rhian would pay, whatever the cost. He and his brother have lost all right to clothe me after last night. Not just because the dress they gave me was gruesome (though I certainly made it more chic), but because it gave me *hives*, Hort. As soon as I got back to my room, it started burning my skin like it was made of fire ants. You know how allergic I am to cheap fabric. In any case, I got the dress off before it did any real damage and smoked it to a crisp." She watched the last shreds of it smolder in the fireplace. "No, no, no, I won't wear anything of their mother's ever again. They needn't even bring up the idea. Is that clear? *Hort?*"

She glared at Hort for the first time.

Hort blinked. "Um."

Only now he saw that Sophie wasn't glaring at him, but at the scim on his neck, as if her entire monologue had been delivered for its benefit. She fluttered over to the settee. "Now let's find something appropriate for *church*—"

Hort stepped in her path. "Sophie. What am I *doing* here?"

Sophie locked eyes with him. "First of all, it's 'Mistress' Sophie, since you are my steward now. Second, I don't know what you are 'doing' other than idling about in poor-fitting pajamas and smelling like a gorilla, but what you are *supposed* to be doing is helping me prepare for my first wedding event."

"Look, no one's here—get this thing off me—" Hort demanded, pointing at his scim.

"Help me open boxes . . . I'm going to be late . . . ," Sophie puffed.

"I don't care! Sophie, you need to—"

Sophie shot a pink spark past Hort's ear with her lit finger and the scim on his neck swiveled towards the door, just long enough for Sophie to mouth at Hort: "*IT CAN HEAR.*"

Hort swallowed.

"How about this?" Sophie said brightly, holding up a brilliant blue sari, stitched with peacock feathers. "It'll make the Blessing feel more *worldly*—"

Eight gold scims tore through it like arrows, ripping it to shreds.

Sophie and Hort spun to see Japeth enter in the gold-and-blue suit he'd worn at Rhian's coronation, before the eight gold scims circled back and fused into his suit. Rhian's twin had a black eye, gashes in his forehead and cheeks, and there were several rips in his shirt, bloody skin exposed underneath.

"*That* is what you will be wearing to the Blessing," he said to Sophie.

Sophie followed his eyes to the fireplace . . .

. . . where a prim, ruffled white frock lay over the cold coals.

Sophie recoiled in shock.

"That is what you will wear every day," said Japeth. "That is your **uniform**. And if you choose to desecrate my mother's dress again, I will desecrate *you* in precisely the same manner."

Sophie's eyes were still on the dress. "B-b-but I burnt it! To ashes, right there. There was nothing left . . . How can it be back . . ."

Meanwhile, Hort was gawking at Japeth, who looked like he'd been mauled by a tiger. Japeth returned a glare and morphed into his black Snake suit, the skintight scims revealing even more clearly the bloody rips in his armor.

"Protests to support Tedros," he explained. "Put up a fight, those dogs. Could have used the king's help, but he was too busy making deals to let prisoners free." He wiped blood from his lip. "Didn't matter in the end. There was nothing left of 'em." He peered down at his own battered body . . . then turned to Sophie, who was still gazing at the fireplace. Japeth's eyes sparked ominously.

"Like it never happened . . . ," he said.

He made a sharp move for the princess. Sophie saw him coming.

"Don't touch her!" Hort yelled, streaking for the Snake—

Japeth seized Sophie's palm and slit it open with a scim, before he smeared her hand over his chest and face in a single move.

Hort froze, shell-shocked.

The Snake quivered; he tilted his head back in pain, his jaw flexing, as Sophie's blood spread over his wounds and magically healed him, his face and body restored.

Hort swallowed a shriek.

"Now, then. How about a tea?" the Snake said, smiling at Sophie. "I'm making some for my brother. We're particular about our tea."

Sophie stared at him.

"It'll settle your nerves," said Japeth, reverting to his gold-and-blue suit, shiny and clean. His grin widened. "First wedding event and all."

"No thank you," Sophie rasped.

"Suit yourself," said Japeth. "Meet us in the Throne Room. You'll ride with us to the church."

His eyes flicked to Hort. "You too, steward."

Japeth strode out of the room and as he did, a last scim floated off his suit, dangled high in the air . . . and harpooned through Madame Clothilde's garment bags, up and down, right and left, zigging and zagging until they were shot through with holes. The scim moseyed after its master, the door closing softly behind it.

Silence filled the queen's chamber.

The eel on Hort's neck zipped over to the settee and found a garment bag that had slipped between cushions and stabbed it repeatedly, gurgling and grunting to itself.

Slowly, Hort turned to Sophie, who stood in the center of the room, her palm cut open, dripping blood onto her bathrobe.

He noticed a shallower cut on the same hand next to the open gash.

Japeth had done this to her before.

Hort's stomach curled.

What the hell?

How could her blood heal him?

What did I just see?

Sophie looked at him, lost and scared.

If she'd had a plan in getting him out, she'd lost faith in it.

Help, her eyes said.

Only Hort had no way to help. Not until she told him why she'd picked him over everyone else. Not until she told him what was going on.

Hort waited until the scim was well-distracted, continuing to tear up Sophie's new clothes. Carefully Hort raised his lit finger and wrote in tiny smoke letters that dissipated as they formed . . .

Sophie glanced over at the eel, stabbing and gurgling. Then she wrote Hort back.

At first he didn't understand.

But then he did.

Sophie had waited her whole life for love.

"*Someday my prince will come*," she'd wished.

She'd kissed a lot of frogs.

Some had tried to marry her. Some had tried to kill her.

But no one loved her. Not in the right way.

Except him.

And Sophie knew it.

She knew Hort loved her. That he would always love her, no matter what terrible things she'd done to him, no matter how many awful boys she'd snogged, no matter whether he had a beautiful, awesome girlfriend or not. She knew that even with his heart pledged to Nicola, Hort would help her. That if she could just get him out of jail, he'd never let *anything* happen to her.

And now here he was, sprung from the dungeons to join her in taking on a creep king and his bloodsucking liege.

That's why Sophie picked him.

To be her second. To be *her* liege in this fight.

Hort's muscles twitched.

No Agatha to show him up this time.

No Tedros to humiliate him.

No one but him.

Hort's fists sealed like rocks.

This was his chance to be a hero.

His one and only chance.

And he intended to take it.

As he accompanied Sophie through the Blue Tower hall, Hort slipped his hand in his pocket and felt the sticky nuts clumped together.

He'd stolen them while Sophie was changing in the bathroom. Two hazelnuts, which he'd smothered in honey and hidden in his big genie pants while his scim finished massacring Madame Clothilde's creations. He'd used a pebble coated in tree sap when he'd taken his revenge on Dabo, the pirate bully, but today, hazelnuts and honey would have to do. If all went according to plan, Rhian would be dead before the Blessing.

He glanced over at Sophie, but she wasn't looking at him, her hands folded in front of her prudish white dress, which she'd worn as Japeth commanded. Blood stained the bandage around her palm, getting redder by the second. Hort could tell she was still shaken by what the Snake had done to her: not because of her unsteady walk or her empty gaze or her poorly wrapped bandage . . . but because of her shoes. She'd worn flat, dull slippers with as much style as Agatha's clumps.

His hand grazed hers, which felt stone cold.

Hort wanted to comfort her . . . to tell her he had a plan . . . but his spying eel was around his ear again, back at attention.

Meanwhile, he could feel guilt gnawing at him, as if he was cheating on Nicola by being here with Sophie.

Don't be an idiot. Nicola would want him to do anything it took to save his friends. And it's not like he was trying to make Sophie his girlfriend. Those days were over. He had Nic now: a girl who loved him for who he was, unlike Sophie, who'd never thought he was good enough. Well, soon he'd have the last laugh. Because he was going to show Sophie he *was* good enough . . . Just in a strictly platonic way.

He saw a maid approaching, older than the ones in Sophie's room—

Hort startled.

Guinevere.

Her lips were sealed by a scim like the one on his ear. Which meant she too was under the king's eye.

But there was something else, Hort noticed. Something near *her* ear. Something tiny and purple tucked deep in her white hair that the scim on her mouth couldn't see . . . A flower. Tedros' mother never wore jewelry or makeup, let alone flowers in her hair, let alone while captive in a murderer's castle—

But by the time he could get a good look at it, Guinevere was already past them, giving Hort and Sophie only a cursory glance.

Hort refocused, hewing to Sophie's side as they neared the staircase at the end of the hall. Now wasn't the time to worry about Tedros' mother or what she was up to.

Rhian's waiting, he thought, nuts rubbing in his pocket. *You'll only get one chance.*

But as they neared the top of the staircase, Sophie paused over the banister.

Hort followed her eyes to the ground floor.

Rhian sat on King Arthur's throne, clutching a mug as he perused a large box of green marbles, holding up each one and peering into it like a spyglass. From overhead, Hort could see the copper gleam of his close-cut hair and a jagged scar across the top of his skull. Steam curled off Rhian's tea and rose over Arthur's gold throne, Camelot's crest carved into the back and Lion claws at the end of its arms. The throne occupied an elevated stage, leading down short steps to the rest of the Throne Room. Behind the king, blue sky framed him like a canvas through floor-to-ceiling glass, beyond which Hort could see a gold message in the sky from Rhian's phony pen, about a boy named Hristo who wanted to be Rhian's knight. At the king's feet lay a colossal rug, stretching down the steps, the fabric stitched like a painted tapestry, depicting the scene of . . .

Rhian's coronation, Hort realized, leaning over the rail.

In rococo hues of blue and gold, Rhian triumphantly pulled Excalibur from the stone, while Tedros, sewn with a gnarled body and ogre's face, was forced to his knees by guards. In the foreground, the people of Camelot cheered. Sophie was in the scene too, hands clasped, a loving smile on her face as she watched her new husband-to-be.

The scene looked so perfectly rendered, so real, that Hort had to remind himself that it hadn't happened that way at all.

He glanced at Sophie, who was staring listlessly at the rug, as if the lie might as well be the truth.

Hort scanned the room for Rhian's twin. The Snake was nowhere to be seen.

But Rhian wasn't alone.

Those three strange sisters that Hort had seen released from jail lurked at the base of the steps beneath the stage, cloaked in shadow. Two pirate guards in helmets and full armor stood on either side of them.

The sisters seemed tense, their bare feet twitching, as they watched Rhian gaze into each green marble in the box.

"These are the RSVPs to the wedding," he said. "Many rulers sent messages, showing me how excited their kingdoms are about their new king and queen." With a lit finger, he floated a handful of green marbles into the air, which cast smoky green projections of scenes from around the Woods: magic carpets departing in Shazabah from a station labeled "WEDDING TOURS," with mile-long lines of passengers waiting their turn; a beachside congregation in Ooty, where thousands gathered to watch Lionsmane's new tale glow against the northern lights; a fierce competition in Maidenvale to see who would represent the kingdom in the Circus of Talents; young Hristo's beaming classmates in Malabar Hills, holding a sign: "FRIENDS OF HRISTO, FUTURE KNIGHT."

"Every kingdom in the Endless Woods accepted the invitation," said Rhian. "Every single one."

Then he held up a red marble from the box.

"Except *this* one."

His eyes lowered to the three hags. "And its leader was kind enough to send a message too."

A projection leapt out of the ball in Rhian's hand, with a greasy, bearded man glaring daggers at the king.

Hort's and Sophie's eyes widened, recognizing him at once.

"I'm sorry to decline your invitation, Your Highness," the Sheriff of Nottingham said, "but as long as my daughter is in your dungeons, Camelot is an enemy of Nottingham." He loomed closer in the projection. "By the way, strange coincidence, isn't it, that the man who robbed my prison and freed the Snake is now the captain of your guard. Kei's his name, isn't it? Why would he want to go freeing the *Snake*? Hmm? One thing I do know: you robbed me . . . and soon I'll rob *you*."

The message flew back into the marble, which rolled out of Rhian's hand and clinked gently into the box.

The king looked at the three sisters. "You have one job. To keep the kingdoms on my side until the wedding. *All* the kingdoms. And you can't even do that."

The low-voiced sister cleared her throat. "Just release Dot and the problem will disappear. Sheriff won't cause trouble once she's free."

"I agree with Alpa," said the high-pitched one. "You don't need her. Dot's dumb as a slug. That's how we sprung Japeth out of prison. By using her."

"Bethna's right," the hissy third nodded. "Nip the problem in the bud. The girl's useless to you."

Rhian took a sip of tea. "I see. A leader of a kingdom threatens to attack me and you'd like to kindly return his daughter."

The three hags shifted on bony legs like egrets.

The king turned to a guard. "Send a team to kill the Sheriff. Make it look like supporters of Tedros did it." Then he gazed darkly at the sisters. "As for you, I'd think long and hard about what happens to advisors whose advice a king no longer takes. Get out."

The three hags sunk their heads and skittered from the room.

As they exited, Kei hustled in and blew past the pirate guards—

"Sire," he said. "Today's *Camelot Courier.*"

Rhian took it from his captain.

From the balcony, Hort could see the front page headline:

AGATHA SAFE AT
SCHOOL FOR GOOD AND EVIL
Leading a Rebel Army Against "King" Rhian

"A real captain would be *catching* Agatha instead of giving me old news," said the king. "Japeth's map already told me she'd made it to school. Lucky for you and your men, no one outside Camelot will believe it and you'll have her in my dungeons soon enou—" He saw Kei's expression. "What is it?"

Kei handed over two more newspapers.

THE NOTTINGHAM NEWS
AGATHA SAFE AT SCHOOL!
STIRRING A REBEL ARMY?

THE SHERWOOD FOREST REPORT
AGATHA LIVES! REAL QUEEN
OF CAMELOT LEADING ARMY
AGAINST RHIAN!

Loud cracks detonated behind him and Rhian turned to see a hawk rapping on the glass with its beak, a scroll in its talons and a royal collar around its neck. Then a collared crow flew up next to the hawk with its own scroll . . . then a fairy . . . then a hummingbird . . . then a winged monkey . . . all unfurling notes against the glass.

"Messages from your allies, sire," said the guard closest to the window. "They want to know if the Blessing will be secure, given rumors of a 'rebel army.'"

Rhian bared his teeth, turning on Kei. "Catch that witch *now*!"

"The magical barrier around the school is stronger than we thought," Kei defended. "We've recruited the best sorcerers from other kingdoms, trying to find one who can break through—"

But suddenly Hort wasn't listening anymore. He was staring at Rhian's tea mug, abandoned on the seat of the throne, directly under the balcony.

This was his chance.

As the scim curled around his right ear, Hort slowly slipped his hand into his left pocket, out of the eel's view.

Standing to Hort's left, Sophie felt his hand brush her hip. She glanced down and saw him draw two hazelnuts out of his pants, globbed in honey. Her eyes flew to Hort's. But he didn't look at her as he leaned across the railing on his right elbow, hung his left hand over the balcony . . . and smoothly released the clumped nuts.

They plunked deep into the mug of tea with the cleanest of splashes.

Sophie goggled at Hort, but the scim on Hort's ear had curled around, sensing something afoot, and Sophie quickly pretended to fix Hort's collar. "You know what? The king seems busy," she said to her steward, with a loaded look. "Let's go back to our chamber and let him enjoy his *tea*."

"Yes, mistress," Hort said, stifling a grin.

As they started walking, Hort could see Rhian still chastising Kei below.

"You got my brother out of prison, out of the Sheriff's enchanted sack, and now you can't break into a *school*?" the king seethed. "You and I are a team. We've been a team since the beginning. But if you're going to be the weak link, especially after I took you back—"

Kei reddened. "Rhian, I'm trying—"

The king lifted a finger and Lionsmane flew out of his pocket and lined up in front of Kei's brown eye, the pen's razor-tip caressing his pupil like a target.

"Try harder, captain," said the king, needling the pen even closer.

Kei's voice came out strangled. "Yes, sire."

"Guards!" Rhian called, summoning Lionsmane back into hand. "Bring me Sophie."

Spooked, Sophie sped her pace down the hall, but Hort's eel bolted off him and over the balcony, letting out a piercing shriek.

Rhian's eyes flicked to the second floor, where the black scim had blocked Sophie's path, pointing at the princess's head like an arrow.

A SHORT WHILE later, Sophie paced on the throne stage, gazing at her work, glowing hot pink in midair.

A pirate stood onstage, hand on his sword, his dark helmeted eyes moving warily between Hort and Sophie.

Sophie tapped her glowing pink fingertip to her lips, rereading her words—

Agatha has been caught! Another
traitor of Camelot, brought down by
the Lion. Do not believe other reports.

"Not quite right," Sophie murmured.

Hort studied her from one side of the stage steps, while Rhian watched her from the other.

Sophie turned to Rhian. "Are you sure this is wise? You said Lionsmane is supposed to rival the Storian. To 'inspire' and 'give hope.' Not be the king's mouthpiece."

"I choose the stories. You write them," said Rhian curtly.

"Plus, the Storian reports *facts*," Sophie argued. "So far Lionsmane's stories have been true, distorted as they are. But this is a lie that can be found out—"

"When your dear friend Agatha is being tortured in our dungeons, we can finish this conversation," said the king.

Sophie stiffened and went back to work.

Hort, meanwhile, had fantasies of bashing Rhian's head like a ripe pumpkin. Comparatively, Sophie was handling the situation quite well, he thought. He knew how much she cared about Agatha. Touting her own friend's demise couldn't be easy.

He glanced furtively at the mug of tea on Rhian's throne, growing cold.

He saw Sophie glance over at it too and meet his eyes for a half-second.

"Drat's your name, isn't it?" Rhian asked, sidling against Hort.

Hort wanted to knee the sleazy, lying scum in the crown

jewels or at least tell him to back the hell up, but he controlled himself.

"It's Hort, Your Highness. And thank you for generously allowing me to serve in your castle."

"Mmhmm," said Rhian. "Though you won't serve long if you keep smelling like a sewer. Do us all some good and learn to bathe. I'm not sure that's something they teach you in *fairy-tale* school."

Hort clenched his teeth. Rhian knew full well why he stank. He just wanted to bully Hort the way he'd bullied Tedros. It's why Rhian was pressed hard against him, so Hort could feel his biceps, bigger than his own. Hort himself had been jacked with muscle until he'd left on this quest, but he hadn't lifted weights in weeks and he'd started to whittle back down to a weasel's frame. It hadn't bothered him much, since Nicola liked the old, scrawny Hort she'd read about in books. But it bothered him now.

"Truth is, when Sophie chose you, I couldn't remember you at all," said Rhian. "Had to flip back through Sophie's fairy tale to see who you were. Easy to get you and Dot confused, since you're both deadweight. But you're the one who Sophie wanted free, so here you are . . . for now." The king turned to Hort, hardening to stone. "One wrong move and I'll carve out your heart."

Hort didn't give him the satisfaction of a response. He could see Sophie pretending to work, but he knew she was listening. The color had returned to her cheeks, as if her spirit had revived. As if she was brewing a plan . . . Her eyes darted back to the tea on the king's throne.

"Surprised she picked you," Rhian baited Hort. "From what I read, you're the boy she never wanted."

"Surprised you're still alive, Your Highness," said Hort.

"Oh, is that why she picked you? Because you're going to *kill* me?" Rhian attacked, eyes flashing.

Hort looked at him quizzically. "No, Your Highness. I meant that Willam and Bogden predicted you'd be dead by now. That you'd have an accident before the Blessing. Saw it in their tarot cards down in the dungeons. And they're never wrong."

"Don't be ridiculous, Hort," Sophie said, turning. "Those two couldn't predict a storm if they were in the middle of one." She peered at Hort intently, as if reading his mind, before looking at the king. "Bogden was my student and failed all of his classes and Willam is an altar boy who I once caught having a passionate conversation with a peony bush. If those two are 'seers,' then I'm the Bearded Lady of Hajira." She turned back to her work. "Oh yes, I see what's missing." She revised with her pink glow—

Celebrate! Rogue Agatha has been caught! Yet another enemy of Camelot, brought down by the Lion. Scoff at all other reports. There is only one army: the Lion's Army. And it is made of you: the people of the Woods! Live under the Lion and you will be safe forever.

"There. Ready to post," Sophie said, itching at her starchy white dress. "You know, the writing process is strangely fulfilling. Challenges every part of you." She picked Rhian's mug of tea off the throne, handed it to the guard onstage, and sank down onto the golden seat. "Even if it's in the service of pure *fiction*."

Hort tracked the mug in the guard's hands, waiting for Sophie to make her move . . . but instead, she reclined against the throne, looking increasingly at ease, as Rhian inspected her work. Lionsmane floated out of the king's pocket, the gold pen hovering next to him, waiting for him to approve Sophie's message.

Rhian kept rereading it.

"If you think you can do better, you're welcome to try," Sophie mused.

"Just seeing if you've hidden anything inside of it," the king growled. "You know . . . like a message to your friend and her 'rebel' army."

"Yes, that's me. The Sultaness of Subterfuge," Sophie wisped. "Slipping unbreakable codes into a king's propaganda."

Rhian ignored her, still studying her words.

To Hort's alarm, the king had forgotten about his tea entirely. With Rhian's back turned, Hort kept glaring at Sophie, who seemed to have forgotten about the tea too as she sat there smiling like a Cheshire cat. What was she doing? Why did she look so smug? She needed to get him to drink the tea! Hort's heart hammered. Should he offer Rhian the tea himself? How suspicious would that look! Sweat trickled down his cheek. He needed to settle down or his scim would sense something—

That's when Sophie rose and calmly took the mug back from the guard.

"Your tea is getting cold and I can't stand the smell," she said, walking it down to the king. "What did you make it with? Burnt leather and cow dung?"

Barely looking at her, Rhian swiped it and magically reheated the mug with his gold fingerglow, his eyes still vetting Sophie's message. . . .

"We're going to be late," Sophie said, firing a spell at the message, gilding it in gold, before she magically shot it through the window and into the sky, where it branded against the brilliant blue. "People will think I'm having cold feet."

Rhian frowned, still focused on the message. "Where's Japeth?"

"Licking his scales?" Sophie mused.

Rhian turned to the guard. "Fetch my brother, so we can ride with him." He took a last big swig of his tea.

Hort held his breath. He saw the clumped hazelnuts slide to the surface and straight into the king's throat—

Rhian choked instantly.

He dropped the teacup, which shattered and splashed as he grabbed his throat with a wheezing spasm.

It'd been the same choke that Hort had induced in Dabo with a tree-sapped pebble before the bully had managed to cough it out. But this time, Hort used two nuts. Rhian doubled over, hacking with all his might, but all that came out was a gasp.

For a brief, shining moment, he thought Rhian was going to die, just like he'd hoped. Sophie backed up at Hort's side, eyes widening, as if her nightmare was over—

But then Hort saw the guards running for the king.

Time for Plan B.

Hort's head swung to Sophie. She read his face.

Sophie sprinted in front of the guards and seized Rhian from behind, crushing his stomach with both arms, again and again, until the king coughed up the nuts with such force that they slammed a hole in the glass and flew out into the clean air.

Blue-faced, Rhian heaved for breath as Sophie thumped on his spine. He yanked away from her—

"You poisoned me . . . you witch!" he wheezed, spotting the crack in the window. "You put something . . . in my tea. . . ."

Sophie flashed that indignant look that Hort knew so well. "Poisoned you! And here I thought I saved your *life*!"

Doubled over, Rhian shook his head. "It was you—I know it was you—"

"Wouldn't the guard on the stage have seen it, then?" Sophie lashed. "Wouldn't my steward's slimy little *eel*?"

The king turned his head to the guard, who said nothing. Hort's scim gave a confused burble.

"If I wanted you dead, I'd have let you strangle yourself," Sophie hectored. "Instead, I rescued you. And you have the nerve to *accuse* me?"

Rhian searched her face. He glanced at Hort, who made

his move.

"Not to overstep my bounds, sire," said Sophie's steward, "but the real question is who *made* the tea."

Rhian eyed him narrowly. "Japeth brought it from the kitchens," he said, still rasping. He swiveled to a guard. "Ask him who made it. Whoever made the tea, bring them here and I'll rip out their throat—"

"*I* made it," said a voice.

Rhian, Hort, and Sophie raised their eyes.

Japeth posed in silhouette at the entrance to the Throne Room.

"And I made it exactly how you like it," he said.

"And you didn't notice something *in* it?" Rhian blasted. "Something big enough to kill me?"

Japeth's blue eyes chilled. "First you indulge that witch. Then you let a prisoner free. And now I'm trying to kill you with your tea."

"Accidents happen," his brother fumed. "Especially accidents that would make you king."

"That's right. Such a good sleuth," Japeth sneered. "Such a good *king*."

The two brothers glared daggers at each other.

"Think I'll skip this morning's festivities," said Japeth.

He exited the room, his boots clacking on tile.

A hot, wormy tension stayed behind.

Hort picked his moment.

One last move.

"See? Willam and Bogden were right," Hort whispered to Sophie, but loud enough for Rhian to hear. "They said the king would die before the Blessing!"

"Don't be an imp," Sophie scoffed, catching his drift. "First of all, the king didn't die. Second, it was a silly accident, and third, just because Willam and Bogden have had a few lucky guesses, doesn't mean they're harbingers of *doom*. Now go fetch the carriage. I'll bring Rhian—"

"Wait," said the king.

Hort and Sophie turned in perfect synch.

Rhian straightened, his shadow casting over them.

"Guards, bring Willam and Bogden from the dungeons," he ordered. "They'll ride with us too."

Sophie clasped her chest. "Willam and Bogden? Are you . . . *sure?*"

Rhian didn't answer, already stalking out of the hall.

Sophie hurried behind him, snapping at her steward to follow. And as she did, her eyes met Hort's for a sliver of a moment.

Not long enough for Rhian or a scim to notice.

But long enough for Hort to see Sophie wink at him, as if he'd earned his place at her side.

Hort blushed in his heart, chasing after his mistress.

At last, her Weasel had come.

9

Empress under the Boot

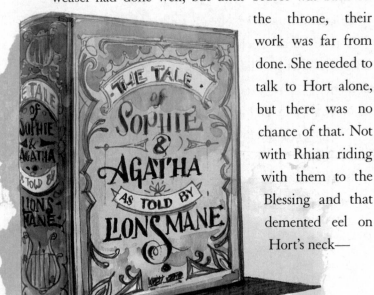

As Sophie followed Rhian, Hort trailing behind her, she could feel her heart rumbling like a drum. The weasel had done well, but until Tedros was back on the throne, their work was far from done. She needed to talk to Hort alone, but there was no chance of that. Not with Rhian riding with them to the Blessing and that demented eel on Hort's neck—

Sophie glimpsed the horses through the window, pulling the royal carriage up the drive.

Unless . . .

No time to think. She made her move, lurching back and grabbing on to Hort's sweaty hand, ignoring his stunned expression. She'd never held the weasel's hand before—who knew where that hand had been—but these were desperate times.

Tattooed Thiago held the door open for the king as the carriage arrived. "Wesley is fetching those boys from the dungeons as you ordered, sire," he said, armor glinting in the sunlight. "Will you need a second carriage?"

The king didn't break stride. "We'll all fit in one."

"Don't be ridiculous. A queen can't arrive at her first wedding event packed like a sardine. Hort and I can ride alone," Sophie scoffed, barreling past the king, dragging Hort like a scolded child, and throwing him into the carriage that hadn't fully stopped. She fumbled in behind him, grabbing on to his rump to steady herself, and smiled back at Rhian. "See you at the church!"

Pretending to lose her balance, she ripped Hort's scim off like a strip of hot wax and flung it out the carriage door—"Oh dear!" she gasped—before slamming the door shut.

"We have five seconds before he opens this door," Sophie intoned.

"Good news is I got Rhian and Japeth fighting," Hort said, breathless.

"Evil news: Rhian is still alive, Japeth is still his brother, and I'm still marrying a *monster*," said Sophie.

"Good: Agatha is safe at the School for Good and Evil," Hort contended.

"Evil: A team of sorcerers is on their way to her and I just lied to the entire Woods that she's been captured," said Sophie.

"Good: Willam and Bogden are about to be free—"

"Evil: Literally anyone else in that cell would have been more useful than those goons, your girlfriend included, and if the Blessing goes off as planned, that means we're three events from Tedros losing his *head*. If Agatha is building an army, then we need more time, Hort. We need to delay the Blessing, somehow!"

"Exactly," said Hort. "Why do you think I picked Willam and Bogden over everyone else?"

Sophie stared at him . . . then grinned with understanding.

The carriage door swung open—

Rhian glowered, his face in shadow.

Before Sophie could speak, a scim shot through the door and smashed into Hort, who let out a resounding shriek, sending the horses rearing.

A FEW MINUTES later, Willam and Bogden studied four tarot cards, laid out in Bogden's lap.

Neither Willam nor Bogden had time to bathe before being shoved next to Hort inside the carriage, which now reeked so badly of dungeon sweat that Sophie could hardly breathe.

Sitting beside Sophie, Rhian focused intensely on the two boys across from him. Meanwhile, Bogden and Willam kept giving Sophie anxious peeks as if they had no idea why they were here, but Sophie just smiled at Bogden reassuringly, the same way she did when she expected the beady-eyed stooge to do her bidding back at school.

"It's a yes-or-no question," the king said, his teeth clenched. "So let's have the answer. For the last time: Is my brother trying to kill me?"

Bogden looked at Willam, waiting for Willam to say something.

Willam looked at Bogden, waiting for Bogden to say something.

Say yes, Sophie thought, seeing Hort glare at them with the same message. *Just say yes. That's all we need.*

Bogden looked back at the cards. "Well, Tower and

Judgment side by side . . . that means there's bad blood between you and your brother. And the Empress card suggests a female involved . . ."

"Obviously," Rhian muttered, eyeing Sophie.

"Not her," Willam countered, fingering the Empress card. "Someone further back that made you and Japeth distrust each other. Add the Death card into all this . . . and there's, um, only one conclusion . . ." He and Bogden exchanged fretful glances.

"Well, what is it?" Rhian snapped.

Bogden gulped. "One of you will kill the other."

"Only there's no way to know who," Willam croaked.

Rhian looked startled for a moment, even a little . . . scared.

"So we should postpone the Blessing, then?" Sophie chimed, delighted by the boys' performance. "Can't possibly be worried about weddings with a *Snake* trying to kill you."

She knew she'd been too chipper, because Hort tensed his buttocks and Rhian gave her a suspicious look.

"I thought you didn't believe in all this," said the king. "I thought you said they were '*fools*.'"

Sophie went mum.

The king turned back to the two boys. "Should Sophie and I still get married?"

Willam quickly dealt new cards.

Say yes, Sophie prayed. *Or he'll know we put you up to this.*

"Hmm, the cards can't say if you 'should' marry Sophie," Willam replied, assessing his hand, "but they do say you *will*."

"Not on schedule, though," Bogden added.

"*Definitely* not on schedule," Willam concurred.

"See? We should postpone the Blessing at once," Sophie squawked, nearly hugging the two boys. "It's what we're *supposed* to do—"

"And tell me, will your friend Tedros be executed as planned?" Rhian said to the boys, ignoring his princess.

Bogden bit his lip as he fanned out a new hand on Willam's lap. . . .

"No," he rasped, clearly relieved.

"Mmm, I don't know if I agree, Bogs," said Willam, touching Bogden's arm. "Knight of Cups next to Death? I think it means someone will try to stop the execution. But to me, it's unclear whether they'll succeed."

The king's blue-green eyes flattened. "And who would this nameless avenger be?"

"Mmmm, can't say," said Willam, puffing at his red hair. "But you'll meet them soon, looks like. Near a holy place . . . with lots of people . . . and a priest . . ."

"A Blessing at a church, perhaps?" said the king witheringly.

"Oh dear, we should definitely postpone, then," Sophie pushed weakly, but she knew the boys had laid it on too thick, for Rhian was smirking now.

"Anything else you'd like to tell me about my *nemesis*?" he sneered.

Sensing tension, Bogden flung down new cards, but missed his own lap and scattered the whole deck over the carriage. "Oopsy-daisy—"

Willam scrambled and swiped a few cards from under

Rhian's boot. "Um, here we are. See, Magician, next to Hermit . . . Well, based on this, your enemy will be a . . ." He frowned. "Ghost?"

"But still mortal," Bogden prattled, pointing at a Death card.

"And Tower over Death means they can fly," Willam added.

"Or at least levitate," Bogden nodded.

"And it's a boy," said Willam.

"I see a girl," said Bogden.

"One or the other," Willam offered.

The carriage went quiet. Sophie's head was in her hands.

The king leaned back. "So a ghost that's mortal who flies near a church and is of dubious sex. That's who's going to try and stop me. Well done."

Sophie raised her head like a squirrel.

"You two really are as daft as Sophie promised," the king thrashed. "The second we return, you'll be thrown back in the dungeons." His eyes shot to Hort. "You too, since you vouched for these fruit flies. In the meantime, you three will be locked here during the Blessing. The smell of you alone is good reason to have you out of sight."

Rhian glowered at Sophie, daring her to protest, but she tried her best to look untroubled. Then she turned and stared out the window, her eyes welling.

Every time she thought she had a way out, she found the path sealed off, the maze closing in.

In the glass, she could see Rhian watching her in her

reflection as a tear slipped down her cheek. She didn't bother hiding it. It didn't matter. There was no plan now. She was back where she'd started.

The boys would return to jail.

The Blessing would continue.

Tedros would die.

Flying ghost or not.

THE BOYS IN the carriage were subdued the rest of the way, the king included. Sophie could see Rhian's lips pressed together, his eyes fixed on the Empress tarot card, which had never been retrieved from under his boot. Clearly his brother was still on his mind. Meanwhile, Hort kept glancing at Sophie, but she ignored him, while Willam and Bogden quietly reordered their cards. For a moment, it was so silent in the carriage that Sophie could hear the eel slithering around on Hort's skin.

Sophie gazed at the Empress, smiling so emptily from under the king's boot. A pawn in someone else's game.

That's me, Sophie thought. A pawn at a dead end.

What would Agatha do?

Agatha would find a way to fight back, even from a dead end. Agatha would never be a pawn.

Sophie's heart stirred, thinking of her best friend. *How long until Kei and his men get to school?* Without Lady Lesso or Dovey protecting the towers, surely they'd find their way in. Plus, Agatha had already escaped Rhian's clutches once—twice was asking too much, even for a girl who always seemed to land on her feet like a cat.

Speaking of which . . . *where was Reaper?* The last she'd seen of Agatha's hideous pet was in the castle before the battle against the Snake. Sophie's toes curled tighter around the vial hidden in her shoe. If she could only be alone: she could use her Quest Map and see if Agatha was safe or if Rhian's men had apprehended her . . .

A surging buzz drew her out of her head and Sophie flinched, knowing she was about to glimpse the crowds for the Blessing. Ironic, of course, since she'd spent her whole life coveting fame, but now felt allergic to all of it, eager to return to the castle. Alone in her bathtub, she could pretend this was a bad dream. That this wedding could never happen. That this lie would be found out. But it was outside the castle, in the presence of the people, that she knew she was wrong.

Because people can make a lie real.

The same way they make fairy tales real: by believing in them, by passing them on, by claiming them as their own.

That's why people needed the Storian to guide them. Because fairy tales were powerful things. Sophie knew this from experience. Try too hard to write your own instead of letting the pen write it . . . and bad things happen. That was the truth.

But it's easy to stop believing the truth.

It's as easy as deciding to believe in a Man over a Pen.

Thunder tremored outside and Sophie peeked through the window as thin black clouds unfurled like tentacles over the message in the sky about Agatha's capture. For a brief moment, she perked up, wondering if the clouds were due to more than just the weather. . . . But then the carriage veered sharply and now the people came into view.

The streets were crammed, five bodies deep, manic and unruly. A beautiful nymph with mint-green skin patterned with silver stars waved a sign: "ASK ME MY STORY, KING RHIAN!" while a hideous, furry creature held his own: "ME MUM'S A CAT, ME DAD'S A TROLL . . . WANT ME TALE? COME DOWN ME HOLE!" There was even a gnome with a fake moustache and hulking coat, clearly trying to disguise himself—

PICK ME!
PINKU OF GNOMELAND!
(I CAN'T PUT MY ADDRESS BECAUSE IT'S A SECRET)

Everywhere Sophie looked, ordinary citizens clamored for Lionsmane to tell their tales, as if the Storian no longer mattered, replaced by a pen that finally cared about *them*.

Rhian's promise had come true: a new pen had become the Woods' guiding light.

No longer could Sophie tell who was Good and who was

Evil like she'd used to. Before now, the tribes had stayed apart, identifiable not just by dress and decorum but also by their loathing for one another. That's why the two sides had worshipped the Storian. A pen that only told the tales of an elite few, but also made the rest of the Woods invested in the outcome. Because it kept score of who was winning and who was losing. Because it kept the two sides battling for glory.

That is, until Rhian had united them with a new pen.

A pen that didn't care if you went to a famous school.

A pen that gave everyone a chance at a fairy tale.

Now Evers and Nevers wore the same Lion masks and hats and shirts and waved cheap replicas of Lionsmane. Others flashed signs with the names of Tsarina and Hristo, newly minted stars in the Woods. A gang of teenagers, Good and Evil, hooted as they lit stacks of the *Camelot Courier* on fire: the one touting Agatha and her "Army." Nearby, a delegation from Budhava sang a "Hymn to the Lion," tossing roses at Rhian's window. Guards in Camelot uniforms patrolled the road, keeping the mob from the carriage, and a fleet of maids in white dresses and bonnets handed out books of *The Tale of Sophie and Agatha*, while the crowd flapped them at Sophie, trying to get her attention. These storybooks seemed to glow under the black storm clouds, with the lettering outlined in rubies and gold—

Sophie's eyes bulged.

Bewildered, she slid down her window and snatched one out of someone's hands, quickly pushing the window back up. She gaped at the cover.

THE TALE OF
SOPHIE & AGATHA
As Told by Lionsmane

Sophie flipped through and saw the entire fairy tale had been retold from Rhian's perspective, with beautifully drawn illustrations in blue and gold that resembled the rug in the Throne Room. The short storybook was scant in details, but offered the broad tale of a humble boy, growing up in a small house in Foxwood with his brother Japeth, the two of them watching from afar as the legend of Agatha and Sophie spread. Despite his allegiances to Good, Rhian always found himself rooting for Sophie, a girl he found bold and beautiful and clever, and against Agatha, a self-righteous know-it-all who'd betrayed her best friend and taken her prince. But in the end, it was Agatha who had the happy ending, claiming the throne of Camelot with Sophie's prince, while Sophie resigned herself to a future alone.

That is where everyone thought the story ended, including Rhian . . .

. . . until three shadowy women came to his house in the night and told Rhian the truth: that *he* was the real heir to Arthur and the One True King, destined to rule the Woods forever. And not only that, he'd been right about Sophie, the women revealed: it was she who deserved to be queen of Camelot, not Agatha. It was Sophie who deserved a prince. Only *he* was that prince, not Tedros. Agatha and Tedros, meanwhile, were fiendish usurpers who would bring shame to Arthur's kingdom and destroy the Woods. It was up to Rhian, as the rightful king, to stop them.

Rhian didn't believe any of this. But the women had more to tell.

Soon the day would come when Rhian must leave his old life behind, they said. On that day, the sword would return to a stone, waiting for the One True King to free it. And *he* was that One True King.

How could any of this be real? Rhian thought.

But just as the women promised, the day arrived when Excalibur returned to the stone.

Rhian couldn't rest until he knew if it was true . . . if he was really King Arthur's son . . . if he was the righteous ending to Sophie's story instead of Agatha or Tedros . . . if Excalibur had returned to the stone because of . . . *him.*

From there, the story proceeded as Sophie had lived through it, but refracted and distorted: Rhian as the "Lion" saving kingdoms from a deadly Snake . . . Tedros' jealousy growing towards the Lion . . . Agatha's jealousy growing towards Sophie . . . Sophie accepting Rhian's ring, uniting Evil and Good . . . Rhian freeing the sword from the stone. . . .

And now Sophie was on the last page, gazing at a painting of Tedros and Agatha beheaded bloodily as Sophie kissed Rhian, the two of them in their wedding clothes as Lionsmane glowed like a star above their heads. . . .

THE END.

Sophie's heartbeat jangled, her mouth dry.

She didn't know what was real about Rhian's story and what was lies. Everything had been twisted and spun, even the parts of her own tale, until she barely recognized herself. If the people of the Woods were reading this, then any last sympathies for Tedros and Agatha would be gone—along with any hope of convincing them they'd crowned the wrong king.

Stomach sinking, she raised her eyes and saw Hort, Willam, and Bogden gawking down at the book with the same expression, having clearly read along.

Slowly Sophie turned and looked at Rhian, who'd been watching her the whole time with a sly smirk. The carriage pulled up to the church, and the king clasped her palm gently, as if he no longer expected any resistance. Then he opened the door to a roar like thunder and he kissed Sophie's hand like he was her fairy-tale prince.

Blessing in Disguise

"If any of them move, kill them," Rhian ordered the scim on Hort's ear, leaving Hort, Willam, and Bogden trapped in the carriage with the sadistic eel. The second the door closed, Sophie could see the scim start slashing at the boys for sport and Hort fending it off with kicks and punches as the driver moved the carriage down the road and out of sight.

Rhian was guiding her towards the church now, past the pen of royal transports from other kingdoms, including crystal carriages, magic carpets, flying broomsticks, levitating ships, and a giant, slobbery toad. A cool wind blew through the darkening courtyard and Sophie hunched deeper into her white dress. She could feel Rhian puff his chest, posturing for the crowd outside, but their attentions suddenly seemed distracted, their eyes fixed overhead.

"What's happening?" Rhian murmured to Beeba, his pirate guard at the door, as he pulled Sophie into the church. Beeba hustled to find out.

Meanwhile, the leaders from other kingdoms rose from the pews as Rhian took the time to greet each one.

"You say you've caught Tedros' princess," spoke an imposing black-skinned elf with pointed ears, dressed in a ruby-and-diamond-jeweled tunic. "No truth to the stories of a 'rebel army,' then?"

"The only truth is that Agatha's whimpering in my dungeons as we speak," said Rhian.

"And you still think that she and Tedros were behind the Snake's attacks? That they were funding his thugs?" the elf asked. "It's a bold claim that you made to the Kingdom Council. I can't say that all of us believe it."

"The attacks have ceased, haven't they?" said Rhian briskly. "I'd think Agatha and Tedros being in my prison has something to do with it."

The elf scratched his ear, mulling this over. Sophie noticed a silver ring on his hand, carved with unreadable symbols.

"While we're on the subject of the Kingdom Council," Rhian probed, "have you given any further thought to my proposal?"

"No further thought is necessary. Lionsmane may be inspiring the people of the Woods, but the School for Good and Evil is our history," said the elf, his accent firm and crisp. "Dismantle the school and the Storian has no protection. It has no *purpose*. Its tales of the graduates of the school are the bedrock of the Woods. Its tales teach our world the lessons we need to learn and move our Woods forward, one story at a time. Your pen can't replace that, no matter how much people are taken with your message."

Rhian smiled. "And yet, what if Lionsmane wrote a story in the sky for all to see about the mighty Elf King of Ladelflop and how nobly he rules his people? A people who I hear were quite resentful that you didn't do more to stop the Snake's attacks? Perhaps I'll have your vote then."

The Elf King stared at Rhian. Then he smiled big white teeth and thumped him on the back. "Politics on your Blessing day, eh? Shouldn't you be introducing me to your lovely bride?"

"I only save her for allies," Rhian teased, and the Elf King laughed.

Smiling blandly behind them, Sophie found herself distracted by the church's facade, newly painted, and its lavish stained glass, depicting Rhian's slaying of the Snake with holy reverence. Stone airways painted with gold Lions beveled along the walls, cooling the hot summer drafts. A perilously old chaplain with a red nose and hairy ears waited at the altar, and behind him were two thrones, where the king and princess would sit while he gave the Blessing. To the left of the altar huddled the church choir in white uniforms and page-boy hats and to the right hung a cage of tweeting doves, which the priest would free into the Woods at ceremony's end.

Lucky little doves, Sophie thought.

Suddenly Beeba rushed forward and accosted Rhian as he greeted the King of Foxwood—

"Lionsmane, sire! Yer new message . . . i-i-it's *movin'* . . ."

Sophie's eyes widened.

"Impossible," Rhian snorted, releasing Sophie and prowling back through the church doors as Sophie hurried after him.

The moment she stepped outside, she saw the crowd's faces cocked towards the sky, watching Lionsmane's message about Agatha's capture. The letters seemed to be quivering against the black storm clouds.

"Definitely moving," Sophie wisped.

"Things move in the wind," said Rhian, unconcerned.

But the message began to quiver faster, faster, as if ungluing from the sky, a pink scar appearing behind each of the dislodged letters. Then all of a sudden, the gold letters lost their shape, melding into each other, one by one, until Lionsmane's message had collapsed into a single gold ball, swelling bigger, bigger, bigger, as big as the sun. . . .

Lightning ripped through the clouds. The ball detonated, splashing four letters in gold across the sky—

The gold and clouds dispersed, revealing clear morning blue.

Silence gripped the courtyard.

All down the road, thousands gaped upwards, wondering what they'd just seen, along with the visiting leaders, staring in shock through the church doors. Together, they looked at the king, but he was already dragging Sophie inside the church—

"You did something to that message!" Rhian hissed. "You corrupted it!"

"I did, did I? Just like I poisoned you in the Throne Room?" Sophie hissed back. "I've been here with you this whole time. When did I have time to conduct a matinee performance of 'Sorcery in the Sky'? It's obvious who did it. The same person who made your tea. The same person who chose to stay behind." She arched a brow. "I wonder why."

Rhian considered this, his eyes searching hers. . . . He turned to his pirate guard.

"Bring my brother here. *Now.*"

"Yes, sire," Beeba mumbled, rushing away.

Sophie, meanwhile, did her best to suppress a smile.

Because it wasn't Japeth who was responsible for what just happened.

It was her.

She'd snuck a code into Lionsmane's stories. The one about Young Hristo and the one about Agatha today.

A code only one person in the entire world could understand.

Rhian had searched her work for hidden messages and

she'd mocked him for it, insisting she couldn't possibly be capable of hiding a distress call right under his nose. . . .

But anyone who truly knew Sophie would have known better.

Because Sophie was capable of anything.

Not that she'd expected her hidden code to reach its target. It was a shot in the dark, a last-ditch Hail Mary, which is why she'd committed to Hort's nut-brained plan.

Yet in the end it was *her* plan that had worked.

Which meant that her friend had not only read her message . . .

But that help was on the way.

A dove zipped by—*"Agatha's been caught! Have you heard!"*

Sophie spun to see the cage near the altar emptied of its doves, which dispersed over the theater, tweeting in dignitaries' ears: *"We saw her captured!" "She cried for mercy!" "She's rotting in the dungeons!"*

Confused, Sophie looked up and saw Rhian's fingertip glowing behind his back, stealthily directing the birds as he greeted the Ice Giant of Frostplains.

"Agatha has no army!" "Don't believe the lies!" "She was alone when we caught her!" "Didn't even fight back!"

Rhian swished his finger and the doves blitzed out the church doors, spreading the king's lies into the crowd, distracting them from the message in the sky.

A dove crowed in Sophie's ear: *"Agatha's a traitor! Agatha's wicked—"*

Sophie slapped it away, launching it right into the face of a girl in a white dress. "Eep, sorry—"

"Excuse me, Your Majesty," said the girl, her head lowered, with a clipped accent and breathy tone. "I'm conductor of the Camelot Children's Choir and we'd hoped you might join us in singing a hymn of praise to the noble Lion."

Sophie scoffed. "A princess sing with the *choir*? Will the king tingle a timpani too? How absurd. I'll watch you and your friends suck up to the Lion from the comfort of my throne, thank yo—"

Her voice broke off, for the maiden had raised her head, revealing dark hair, pencil-thin eyebrows, and twinkling black eyes.

"My choir would really love to have you," said the girl.

Sophie followed her eyes to the group of teenagers in matching white uniforms and hats at the front of the church, gazing hard at her.

Help wasn't on the way.

It had already arrived.

As Rhian had a heated discussion with the Queen of Jaunt Jolie, Sophie squeezed his arm. "The choir would like me to sing with them—"

"Finally, the famous Sophie," cooed the queen, draped in a peacock-feather stole. She reached out her hand and Sophie noticed a silver ring with unreadable carvings, just like the one the Elf King of Ladelflop wore. "We were just talking about you."

"A pleasure," Sophie simpered, shaking her hand stiffly, before pivoting to Rhian. "Now about the choir—"

"The queen would like to meet with you," Rhian said. "But I told her your schedule has filled up."

"Whatever you say, darling. The choir is waiting—"

"I heard you the first time. Stay here and greet the guests," Rhian ordered.

Sophie's face fell.

"If my groom had spoken to me like that, I never would have made it to the altar," the queen mused to Sophie. "Indeed, your schedule only 'filled up' once I told the king that he's turned Camelot's new queen into a lapdog. No speech at the coronation, no presence at meetings, no comment on Tedros' capture or those of your friends, no mention by the king's pen. . . . It's as if you hardly exist."

The queen turned to Rhian. "Perhaps I'll take Sophie aside and discuss a queen's duties in private. Two queens often succeed in solving problems a king cannot."

Rhian glared back at her. "Now that I think about it, Sophie, your singing with the choir sounds like a good idea."

Sophie didn't need to ask twice. As she escaped, she saw Rhian whispering aggressively to the queen, his hand gripping her arm.

A moment later, Sophie gripped onto the choir conductor's arm. "Shall we rehearse in the priest's chambers?"

"Yes, Your Majesty," the conductor pipped, and her choir mates scurried after Sophie like chicks behind a swan.

Sophie listened to the patter of feet, a wicked grin spreading across her face.

The Queen of Jaunt Jolie was right.

It had taken two queens to solve this problem.

And now the king would pay the price.

THE PRIEST'S SANCTUM reeked of leather and vinegar, its mess of books and scrolls veiled by dust. Sophie locked the door and shoved a chair against it before she twirled to the choir.

"My babies. My poopsies. Come to save their Dean!" she cooed, hugging her first years, starting with the conductor. "Miss Valentina, *mi amor* . . . And hello, Aja."

"You remember my name?" squeaked the boy with dyed red hair.

"How could I not? You dressed like me for Halloween and wore the most *divine* boots. And Bodhi, Laithan, and Devan, my scrumptious Everboys. And lovely Laralisa, my cleverest witch. And my beloved Nevers, Drago and Rowan and dirty Mali—" Sophie frowned. "Um, who are those?"

In the corner of the room, a few kids in shirtsleeves and underpants were helping each other out a high window.

"The real choir," Devan answered. "Switched clothes with us because they're from Camelot and don't trust Rhian and think Tedros is king."

"Plus, you gave us gold," added the last choirboy, falling out the window with a yelp, coins trailing behind him.

Devan looked at Sophie. "Tried to tell them the *Courier*'s right: that the Snake is alive and that he's Rhian's twin and

that Agatha has a secret army . . . but even Tedros' biggest fans
didn't believe us."

"Would *you* believe it? It *sounds* ridiculous," said Sophie.
"But wait: tell me about Agatha! She's safe, isn't she? We have
to check the Quest Map. . . ." She reached for her shoe, but
Valentina grabbed her by the shoulders—

"*Señorita* Sophie, there's no time! Where is the royal carriage? The one that brought you here."

"Somewhere near the church—"

"Who's guarding it?" Bodhi asked, pulling a folded-up
cape from a bag.

"One of the Snake's scims. Hort, Bogden, and Willam are
there too," said Sophie. "They're trapped inside with it!"

"Five boys, one eel. We'll take those odds," said Bodhi, slipping the shimmery cape over him as he and Laithan swept
towards the window.

For a second, Sophie was distracted by the cape, which
looked familiar, but then she realized what they were saying.
"You're attacking the royal *carriage*?"

The two boys smiled as they straddled the window, Bodhi
hugging Laithan under his cloak. "More like reclaiming it,"
piped Bodhi. "For Tedros," chimed Laithan. They backflipped
off the ledge and disappeared like ghosts.

Sophie put a hand to her chest. "Who needs Tedros with
boys like that?"

A hard knock on the door—

Sophie and her students whipped their heads forward.

"The king wants to begin!" the priest's hoary voice called as Aja held the door shut.

"Coming!" said Valentina, spinning to Sophie. "We need to get you to school, *Señorita* Sophie. Here's the plan. You'll sing Budhava's hymn to the Lion with us—"

"Can we sing something else? I don't know that song," Sophie wisped.

"*Dios mío*, it doesn't matter if you know it! Just sing it!" Valentina snapped.

"And when we get to the phrase 'oh virile Lion' . . . *duck*," said Aja.

"*That's* the plan?" Sophie said, perplexed. "*Duck?*"

A scratching noise echoed overhead and Sophie looked up to see two kids in black masks scooting through a cramped stone airway. They lowered their masks, revealing blond Bert and blonder Beckett.

"*Definitely* duck," they said.

"Today, we bless young Rhian and Sophie as a reminder that despite all the festivities to come . . . marriage is first and foremost a spiritual union," spoke the old priest before a quiet audience. "There is no way to tell if a marriage is favored, of course. First, Arthur marries Guinevere in the throes of love, only to have that love be his downfall. Then, I planned to marry Arthur's eldest son, Tedros, to his own princess, only to discover Tedros isn't Arthur's eldest son at all. And now, a stranger from Foxwood and the Witch of Woods Beyond seek my blessing to be King and Queen of Camelot. So what do I know?" The priest hacked a laugh. "But no marriage can outwit the pen of fate. All we can do is let the story unfold. In time, the truth will be written, no matter how many lies someone might tell to obscure it. And the truth comes with an *army*."

Sophie could see Rhian glaring at the back of the priest's head as he perched in his throne on the elevated stage. The dignitaries seemed oblivious to the priest's message, but the king had heard it loud and clear: he may have expunged those loyal to Tedros from the castle, but he'd have no such ally in the church. Rhian sensed Sophie watching him and glanced over at her, ensconced with the choir. He gave her a baffled look, as if he knew he'd agreed to let her sing with them but couldn't remember why.

"Before I read from the Scroll of Pelagus, we'll begin with a hymn," said the priest, nodding at his singers. Sophie's students tilted their faces beneath their hats, so the priest wouldn't see his choir had been hijacked. "Ordinarily, Camelot's choir sings to exalt a sacred power that unites us all," the priest continued, dwarfed by a giant Lion head casting a glow on his altar, "but today, the choir has chosen to sing about our new king instead." Rhian's glare deepened behind him. "And in a further departure from the norm, the choir shall be joined by our new princess . . . I assume, as either a loving tribute to her husband-to-be, or a desire to show off her many talents."

All at once, the congregation turned towards Sophie, who was now the focus of more than two hundred royals, Good and Evil both. Sophie could see the gorgeous dark-skinned King of Pasha Dunes and his chic, bald-headed wife watching her; seated nearby was the Maharani of Mahadeva, dripping in jewels, with her three sons, while in front of them, the Queen of Jaunt Jolie looked anxious and chastened, far different from the bold woman who'd just confronted Rhian. All of their eyes were on Sophie.

She'd always dreamed of a moment like this: spotlit on a grand stage, an audience of luminaries, all of them knowing her name. . . .

Only in her dreams, she'd rehearsed.

Sophie stared at the sheet music in front of her.

OH HOLY LION
("BUDHAVA'S HYMN OF PRAISE")

She peeked at her first years—Aja, Devan, Laralisa, and more—their bodies tense, their pupils dilated. Only Valentina looked calm as she presided over the choir and gazed hard at Sophie as if to remind her of her cue. Sophie's heart thumped so hard she could feel it in her throat . . . not just because she hadn't a clue what would happen on that cue, but because she was about as good at reading music as she was at building cabinets, which is to say not at all.

Valentina raised her arms and brought them down, commencing the organist. Aja started two beats early, the rest of the choir two beats too late—

Glory be, oh holy Lion,
Glory be, our king!
His mercies shall endure,
Ever faithful, ever sure!

Sophie saw Rhian gaping like he'd been shot. Dignitaries rocked back in their seats. The church reverberated with the most strikingly awful sound imaginable, like a family of cats being dragged up a mountain. The worse they sounded, the more rattled Valentina looked, as if whatever plan was coming might be brought down by the singing before it, especially since Aja kept shimmying his hips either out of nerves or in an attempt to distract from the horror. Sophie, for her part, tried to dominate the chorus, but dirty Mali just kept wailing notes louder like a dying mountain goat. Devan, meanwhile, was cute as a button but had a voice like a sasquatch, and his girlfriend, Laralisa, unleashed a string of braying yelps like a broken jack-in-the-box. Worst of all, the stone walls and airways bounced the noise mercilessly, as if it was less a church and more some kind of echo-torture chamber. Mortified, Sophie held her sheet music higher over her face, so she couldn't see the crowd and they couldn't see her, but in her new sightline, she caught Bert and Beckett scooting like roaches through an airway overhead.

Sophie's eyes flicked back to Rhian, who hadn't noticed the masked spies, because he was already lurching out of his throne to stop this inferno.

Panicked, Sophie whirled to Valentina, who saw Rhian coming, and accelerated her conducting, waving her arms wildly, which led her charges to motormouth through the song like overfed chipmunks, the organist chasing to keep up, as the chorus barreled headlong into their cue.

> *Glory be, our king!*
> *Glory be, oh virile Lion—*

Sophie ducked.

CRACK! CRACK! CRACK! Flaming green-yellow bombs ripped through the theater like fireworks, sending the crowd diving under their pews. Devan and Laralisa tackled Sophie to the ground as sparks sprayed over them and the audience's screams filled the church. Shell-shocked, Sophie covered her ears, waiting for the next blast. . . .

Nothing happened.

Sophie raised her head. So did the spectators, their screams dissipating.

Then came the smell.

Like the fumes of a flaming dung heap . . . a stench so stultifying that the shrieks began again, this time with mortal urgency, as people fled the church in swarms—

"Come on!" Devan yelled at Sophie, dragging her towards the doors as Laralisa tried to clear a path for them, shoving gaudily dressed royals out of the way.

"Use your fingerglow!" Sophie barked, holding her nose.

"Our forest leader didn't teach us how yet!" said Laralisa,

headbutting a witch-queen aside. "We're behind the other group—"

A regally dressed cyclops sideswiped her as he stormed for the exit, flinging Laralisa backwards into the crowd.

"That one-eyed cretin!" Devan seethed, rushing to save her.

"What about me!" Sophie squeaked, trapped in the stampede.

The smell in the church was so putrid now that kings were fainting, queens masking their faces with capes, and princes shattering stained glass to escape with their princesses. Overhead, Sophie spotted Bert and Beckett lighting another dung missile.

I have to get out, she choked, hiking her dress collar over her nose. But the doors were still so far . . .

The Ice Giant of Frostplains thundered by, smacking people away and barreling towards the exit. Instantly Sophie started scurrying behind him like a mouse in the wake of an elephant, while the Giant swatted left and right, his huge, ice-blue hand flashing the same silver ring she'd seen on the Elf King and Queen of Jaunt Jolie. Through his legs, she spotted open doors and clear sky ahead—a comet streaked through the air outside, a helix of navy and pink, like a sailor's flare—

Did Bert and Beckett dungbomb the streets too?

Suddenly she glimpsed Bert and Beckett, using a rope to climb down a stone wall towards the doors, before the boys yelped and reversed direction as Aran, Wesley, and more pirate guards leapt onto the rope to chase them.

Sophie knew she should stay and help the boys; a real Dean

would protect her students, Evers and Nevers . . . but instead, she found herself scampering faster for the doors behind the giant, hiding in his shadow, so the pirates tracking Bert and Beckett wouldn't see her. She didn't bother feeling guilt over it. She wasn't Agatha, after all. She wasn't Good. Those boys needed to fend for themselves. That was the point of fairy tales. And she . . . well, she needed to get as far from Camelot as possible.

She was nearing the exit now, hugging closer to the giant's boots. If she could just slither out of this church, she could blend into the mob . . . she could disguise herself and find a way back to school . . . to Agatha. . . . The thought of seeing her best friend again made Sophie dump caution; she broke away from the giant and sprinted between his legs, elbowing people out of her path. She felt the heat of the sun flush across her skin and as she crashed through the doorway, she looked up into the heavenly white glare—

A hand snatched her backwards and she whirled to see Rhian in the doorway. "Stay with me!" he said, rattled. "We're under attack!"

Suddenly, loud bells jangled in the distance, frantic and high-pitched. . . .

Alarm bells.

Sophie and Rhian swiveled and saw Camelot shrouded by an alien fog, silver and glimmering, that obscured the entire castle. Behind the fog, they could hear shouts echo from the towers, resounding downhill, as the bells clattered wilder and faster.

"What's happening?" Sophie breathed.

"Intruders," said Rhian, clasping her wrist tighter. "They're at the castle too. . . . *Japeth*. He might still be there! He's alone . . . We have to help him—"

He yanked Sophie through the door, but it was mayhem outside, with dignitaries still fleeing the church now mixing with the hordes of citizens in the streets, who'd smelled the stink bombs and heard Camelot's alarms and joined the stampede like harrowed geese. At the same time, a heap of these spectators from far-flung kingdoms saw Rhian and Sophie emerge and flooded towards them, desperate to meet the new king and queen. Cornered, Rhian pulled Sophie back to the door, but that only got them caught deeper in the crush, like buoys in a storm.

But now Sophie saw someone streaking through the mob on horseback, smashing people aside. . . .

Japeth.

"The dungeons," he panted at his brother, his gold-and-blue suit sprayed with white rubble. "They've been breached—"

A cry tore through the sky overhead.

It wasn't human.

Rhian, Japeth, and Sophie raised their eyes.

A flock of stymphs ripped out of the fog, carrying Sophie's friends on their spines—Kiko, Reena, Beatrix, Dot, with fingerglows lit, leaning forward and firing spells at the king and his liege. Three stun spells hit Rhian in the chest, launching him through the open church doors, while another bludgeoned Japeth off his horse. Dot turned the ground beneath Japeth's feet to hot mocha, sending him plunging headfirst into the deep, steaming moat. Doves tweeted as Japeth flailed in boiling chocolate: *"Agatha's been caught!"* *"She's no match for the Lion!"* *"She's no match for his liege!"* *"Praise to King Rhian! Praise to Japet—"*

A red-skinned demon ate the doves.

Sophie wheeled and saw Hester and Anadil on a stymph, swooping towards her.

"Grab my hand!" Anadil ordered.

The pale witch reached out her palm as Hester steered their bird downwards, with Anadil's and Sophie's fingers about to touch—

A pirate dagger pierced Anadil's arm, hurled by Wesley as he surged out of the church. The witch lunged back in pain and her stymph bucked, throwing Anadil off its back.

"Ani!" Hester screamed. Her demon raced to save her friend, but Anadil was falling too fast, her arm outstretched and about to hit the ground first, the dagger in it sure to sever through—

A new stymph scooped under her and Bodhi and Laithan seized Anadil into their arms, swinging her up on their bird. The two boys were still in their choir uniforms, their faces and shirts spattered with black eel goo. More stymphs appeared in the fog behind them, carrying Sophie's friends. Two . . . then four . . . then five . . .

"Help me!" Sophie yelped, hope swelling. But these stymphs were too far into the fog for her to see the riders yet. She jumped and waved at them. "Please! Someone! *Anyone!*"

But now arrows were streaking towards these stymphs

as pirates galloped down from the castle on horseback, bows raised. Spooked, the stymphs veered away from Sophie, retreating into the fog. Beeba and Thiago rose upright onto their horses, balancing feet on the saddles, taking shots at Hester's and Kiko's and Anadil's heads, as Sophie's friends ducked and swerved, arrows soaring through the gaps in the stymphs' ribs.

"Help! Save me!" Sophie screeched at them, leaping uselessly at the stymphs as her friends tried to maneuver towards her.

More and more arrows flew as pirate guards poured out of the church, firing at the stymphs in the sky. Beatrix, Hester, Bodhi all tried to dodge and make one last dive for Sophie. But the onslaught was too much. Looking stricken, they had no choice but to flee en masse, away from the church, away from Camelot, and away from Sophie.

Sophie's heart plunged. She swiveled back to the castle, but the silvery fog was dissipating, with no more stymphs to reveal. Tears flooded her eyes. She'd been left behind. Just like she'd left Bert and Beckett, who were surely dead by now. She didn't know why she was crying. She deserved her fate. She deserved to be punished for her selfishness . . . punished for the bad deeds she couldn't help doing . . . punished for being herself. . . . That's why her story could never change, no matter what pen wrote it—

"Sophie!" a voice blared from above.

She raised her head to see a stymph throttling out of the fog through a hail of arrows, a shirtless boy reaching out his hand to grab her, his face veiled in mist, his hair white as snow. . . .

Rafal?

He ripped through the fog—

No.

Not Rafal.

Time seemed to slow, her heart pumping hot blood, as if it was the first time she'd ever seen this boy, even though she'd seen him a thousand times before. Only she'd seen him differently all those times . . . not like she was now . . . as a prince who'd patiently saved her again and again and again, until she finally had the sense to notice.

She thrust her hand into the sunlight as he flew down, his hair coated with white rubble, his face and pallid chest streaked in scim wounds, his fingers stretching out to clasp hers—

"Got you!" Hort said, starting to tow her onto his stymph.

Holding him tight, Sophie climbed towards him. . . .

But then she froze cold.

So did Hort, following her eyes.

So did the pirates, who lowered their bows in shock.

High over Camelot's castle, the dissipating fog had congealed into a giant bubble with a girl's face trapped inside of it, levitating like a ghost. The dark-haired girl was magnified as if reflected by curved glass. Behind her stood an army of students and teachers in the uniforms of Good and Evil, framed by a school crest on the wall. The girl gazed down at Sophie with big, glistening eyes.

"Agatha?" Sophie choked.

But her friend was already vanishing into the sky. "I couldn't free them all," Agatha rasped, pressing her hands against the fading bubble. "There's some left, Sophie. I don't know who. I tried to save them—I tried—"

"*Agatha!*" Sophie cried.

It was too late. Her best friend had disappeared.

Yet Agatha's voice seemed to linger, echoing in Sophie's head. . . .

There's some left.

There's some left.

There's some left.

She felt Hort shake off his daze and clutch her tighter. "Hurry! Get on!" he yelled, yanking her towards his stymph—

Only Sophie's face had changed, her body already pulling away from him. Hort's eyes widened, seeing what was about to happen, but Sophie moved too fast, wrenching her hand out of his.

"What are you doing!" Hort shrieked.

"I can't," Sophie breathed. "You heard Agatha. There's some left at the castle . . . they'll die if I leave them behind. . . ."

"We'll come back for them!" Hort retorted, seeing the pirates who'd been watching Agatha suddenly aim arrows at him once more. In front of the castle, Japeth was muscling out of Dot's chocolate swamp. "You have to come with me!" Hort thundered, nosing his stymph towards her. *"Now!"*

Sophie recoiled. "They're our friends, Hort. *My* friends."

"Don't be stupid! Get on!" Hort pleaded—

Sophie lit her fingerglow and shot his stymph in the tail-bone with a pink flare, sending the bird rocketing forward, just as arrows slashed for Hort's skull. Hort tried to veer back towards Sophie, but his bird ignored him and soared after the other stymphs, as if it knew its duty was to keep its rider safe. With an anguished cry, Hort looked back at Sophie, tears welling, while his stymph whisked him into the horizon without her. Pirates strung their bows one last time, but their arrows fell short, snapping against the church tower brick and showering wooden shards over the crowd.

Everything went quiet.

Sophie stood alone, rock still.

She'd given up a chance to be free.

To be with Agatha again.

To be safe at school.

So she could help people.

Her. Evil's once-queen.

She didn't even know who she was saving.

Or how many.

The real Sophie would be halfway to freedom by now.

The real Sophie would have saved *herself.*

A prickling dread snaked down her spine. Not just because she felt like a stranger in her own body.

But because someone was watching her.

She raised her head and saw Rhian in the church doorway, battered and bruised, his bluish eyes dead cold.

And then she knew.

He'd seen Agatha in the sky.

He'd seen her army.

He'd seen everything.

But he wasn't the only one.

Thousands of people from other kingdoms, including their leaders, stood downhill, their eyes pinned upwards on the clear air as the last flecks of Agatha and her army disappeared.

All at once, their eyes moved to the king, watching Rhian the way he was watching Sophie, as birds circled overhead, tweeting brightly into silence—

"Agatha's caught!" "She has no army!" "Did you hear?" "Praise the Lion! Praise the King!"

Friendship Lessons

As Agatha paced Merlin's Menagerie on the roof of the School for Good, she kept her eye on the sunset, waiting for the first sign of her friends.

She glanced back and saw the Good and Evil faculty silently fanned out behind her and the spying eyes of first years peeping through the frosted glass doors from inside the castle.

Agatha paced faster between the hedge sculptures from King Arthur's tale. She looked up again.

Still no stymphs.

What's taking them so long? she thought, shuffling past a leafy scene of Guinevere with baby Tedros.

She needed to know who'd escaped from the dungeons.

More importantly, she needed to know who hadn't—

She paced right into a hedge of Arthur pulling the sword from the stone, the rough shrubs slapping against her face.

Agatha sighed, remembering the moment when Tedros tried to pull a sword from the stone at his coronation. The moment that had precipitated everything that followed. And she still had no answer for why he'd failed and Rhian had succeeded.

She looked into the sky once more.

Nothing.

This time, however, she could see purple detonations of light over the school's North Gate, challenging the bubble of green fog around the school.

Rhian's men must be attacking Professor Manley's shield again.

She peered closer at the purple light. *Magic*, she thought. But Rhian's pirates couldn't do magic. So who was helping them?

On the shores of Halfway Bay, Professor Manley cast rays of green mist to reinforce the shield, while the school's wolf guards herded around the moat towards the North Gate, ready to fight Rhian's men if they got through.

It's only a matter of time, Agatha thought. How long until the shield gave way? A week? A few days? Rhian's men would show them no mercy. She needed to get the students and teachers out before the shield fell. Which meant they needed a new safe house . . . somewhere she and her army could hide. . . .

But first, Agatha needed her prince back.

She knew that she shouldn't be hoping for Tedros to have escaped over the others. That it wasn't Good in the slightest to root for someone else to have been left behind. But in times like these, even the purest of souls can't always be Good.

She leaned against the prickly green blade of Arthur's sword, out of sight of the teachers and first years.

This wasn't how it was supposed to go.

She was supposed to have *all* of her friends back, safe and sound. Sophie included.

But nothing ever went as it was supposed to.

At least not in her fairy tale.

A FEW HOURS earlier, Agatha stood at the window in Professor Sader's old office—now Hort's office—watching the stymphs fly off to Camelot, the students of Groups #1 and #6 on their backs. Little by little, the birds receded into the gold glare of Rhian's tale about Young Hristo, branded against the blue sky.

Agatha glanced down at the remaining first years, cramming in a quick lunch of turkey stew in the Clearing, their eyes pinned to the horizon, anxiously watching their classmates soar towards Rhian's kingdom.

"Nevers and Evers sitting together at lunch? Things have changed," Agatha marveled.

"Or maybe they've bonded over you sending their friends to *die*," Professor Manley's voice growled behind her.

Agatha turned to see the Good and Evil faculty standing around Hort's hopelessly messy desk, their faces tense with concern. Amidst the soggy books, ink-spattered scrolls, food crumbs, and strewn underpants lay Professor Dovey's gray bag, the outline of a sphere visible beneath the worn fabric.

"I agree with Bilious," said Princess Uma, arms folded over her pink gown. "You pull two groups of students into a corner, whisper with them like a pack of squirrels, and off they go into battle, with a plan you've yet to explain to anyone else."

"EVEN THOUGH WE'RE THE TEACHERS," Castor blistered.

"And even though one of the groups is *mine*," snapped Yuba the Gnome, thumping his white staff into the dirty floor.

"Look, the groups will reach Camelot soon. We don't have time to argue," said Agatha forcefully. "They wanted to go. They're not at this school to play it safe or be coddled. They're here to do what is *right*. And that means getting our friends out of Camelot. You *asked* me to lead them and I did. You asked me to come up with a plan and I did. And now, for this plan to work, I need your help."

"A PLAN NEEDS PLANNING," Castor savaged.

"A plan needs consultation," Yuba hectored.

"A plan needs time," Professor Anemone resounded.

"There was no time," Agatha bit back. "The Blessing is our chance to rescue our friends and I had to take it."

"So you send first years to die?" said Professor Sheeks

angrily. "Your fourth-year classmates in the clinic could have gone—*you* could have gone—"

"No, I couldn't. And neither could any other fourth year," Agatha retorted. "Rhian's brother has a map that tracks us. Just like Dovey's Quest Map. Rhian would see us coming. He can't see the first years."

Professor Sheeks went quiet.

"You think I wanted to send them into harm's way?" said Agatha. "I wish they could all be in class right now, with nothing to worry about except Snow Balls and ranking points. I wish they could be practicing their animal calls and weather spells and be immune to anything beyond the school gates. I wish *I* could be the one flying to Camelot. But wishes won't save my friends. For my plan to work, I needed them. And now I need you." She paused. "Well, it isn't really *my* plan. It's Sophie's."

The teachers stared at her.

"I found it in Lionsmane's message," Agatha explained, looking out the window at the gold words in the sky.

Citizens of the Woods! Revel in the tale of Hristo of Camelot, only 8 years old, who ran away from home and came to my castle, hoping to be my knight. Young Hristo's mother found and whipped the poor boy. Stay strong, Hristo! The day you turn 16, you have a place as my knight! A child who loves his king is a blessed child. Let that be a lesson to all.

"When we were in the theater, I read a news clip that claimed it wasn't Rhian writing Lionsmane's tales, but Sophie," said Agatha. "It seemed absurd at first, and yet something told me it was true. Because the more I read the message, the more it felt off . . . as if whoever had written it had picked their language very carefully. . . . Which meant if it *was* Sophie who'd written it, she'd chosen her words for a reason." Agatha smiled. "And then I saw it."

With her fingerglow, she drew circles in the air, marking up the message.

(C)itizens of the Woods! (R)evel in the tale of Hristo of Camelot, only 8 years old, who ran away from home and came to my castle, hoping to be my knight. (Y)oung Hristo's mother found and whipped the poor boy. (S)tay strong, Hristo! (T)he day you turn 16, you have a place as my knight! (A) child who loves his king is a blessed child. (L)et that be a lesson to all.

"First letter of each sentence," said Agatha. "C-R-Y-S-T-A-L. Sophie knows I have Professor Dovey's crystal ball. And she wants me to use it."

The faculty peered at her, unconvinced . . . except for Professor Manley, whose usually viperous expression had turned curious.

"Go on," he said.

"When Professor Dovey came to Camelot, she brought her crystal ball," Agatha explained. "It was making her ill, so Sophie and I kept it away from her, even though Merlin said I should return it. But I wasn't going to give Dovey back a ball that was hurting her. That's why I have it now." She glanced at the Dean's bag on the table. "Sophie knows the risks of using it, but she also knows it's the only way to save our friends. Because whatever its side effects, the ball *works*. When we were on our quest, Professor Dovey used it to communicate with us. I know that for a fact because I talked to her from Avalon. The crystal let her find students anywhere in the Woods. Which means we can use the crystal ball to find whoever is in Camelot's dungeons."

"No, we can't," said Yuba testily, waving his staff, "because anyone with sense knows you can't use magic in the dungeons—"

"The crystal ball can't get *in* the dungeons, but it can get our friends *out*," Agatha countered. "According to maps of Camelot, the dungeons are against the side of the hill. Meaning the crystal ball can find that exact spot on the hill, which is where our rescue team will break in."

"Where is this spot, then?" Professor Sheeks challenged, pointing a stubby finger at the ball. "Show it to us."

"I can't. At least not yet," said Agatha, her confident facade faltering for the first time. "Dovey told us the ball is broken; it can only be used for a short time each day before it cuts off the connection. We need to save that time for when our students make it to Camelot and send us the signal."

"And you know how to use the crystal?" Professor Anemone prodded skeptically.

"Well, um, now that you mention it . . . that's the other problem . . ." Agatha's throat bobbed. "I can't turn it on."

The room went silent.

"WHAT?" Castor blurted.

"It was glowing when I left Camelot . . . I thought that meant it was working . . . ," Agatha stammered. "But just now I took it in the bathroom and tried waving at it and shaking it and turning it upside down and nothing happens—"

Castor stalked towards her, baring his teeth. "YOU JUST SENT *MY* STUDENTS INTO A LION'S DEN, RELYING ON A CRYSTAL BALL *YOU CAN'T USE*?"

Agatha skirted around the desk. "You're teachers . . . You know how to use it. . . ."

"We *can't* use it, you head-dented twit!" Manley assailed, his baleful scowl returning. "No one can use it, except Clarissa! And we would have told you if you'd bothered to ask us before risking our students' lives!"

Agatha turned red as a rosebush. "I thought Merlin used it too!"

"You should 'think' less and *know* more!" Manley lashed. "To make a crystal ball, a seer takes a piece of a fairy godmother's soul and melds it with a piece of their own. That means every fairy godmother can only use the crystal made for her. To activate it, Clarissa would need to keep it still and look into its center at eye level. That is the *only* way it will work. If a fairy godmother wishes to give another access to her ball, then she can instruct the seer *at the time of its making* to have the crystal recognize a second person. If Merlin can use Clarissa's ball, then Clarissa chose him as her Second. No one else can make the ball work. *No one.* Unless, that is, Dovey happened to name one of us her Second *before she ever came to this school to teach.*"

Agatha couldn't believe what she was hearing. "B-b-but there has to be some other way—"

"Oh, really? Let's see," Manley mocked, practically foaming at the mouth. He ripped open Dovey's bag, dug past Tedros' jacket, and from its folds, pulled out a dusty orb the size of a coconut, blemished with scratches and a long, jagged crack in its blue-tinted glass. Manley held it up to eye level. "Look at that! It doesn't work! What about Uma? Can *you* make it work?" He shoved it in front of the princess. "Alas. No. Emma . . . ? No. Sheeba? No. Castor? Yuba? Aleksander? Rumi? No, no, and no. Like I said, completely, utterly *worthless*—" He thrust it at Agatha, clocking her in the nose—

The ball lit up.

Manley dropped it in shock, but Agatha caught it, raising the crystal towards her face. The sphere glowed wintry blue, like luminescent ice, as she gazed into its center, a silver mist brewing inside.

"Guess I should have tried holding it still," she breathed.

Teachers gathered around her, thunderstruck.

"Impossible," Manley croaked.

But now the mist was taking shape, snaking towards Agatha from the ball, as her sweaty palms left streaks on the glass.

"Dovey couldn't have named her as her Second!" Professor

Anemone sputtered. "The girl wasn't *born* when the ball was made!"

Slowly the mist inside the crystal congealed into a phantom face that pressed against the scratched-up glass, peering at Agatha through eyeless sockets. The phantom's face was foggy in texture and flickered every other second, as if suffering from a magical glitch, but the closer Agatha looked at the face, the more it seemed to shift between the features of Professor Dovey and the features of someone else familiar . . . someone who she couldn't quite pin down. . . .

Then it spoke, its low, metallic voice glitching too, so Agatha had to string together the words.

> *"Clear as crystal, hard as bone,*
> *My wisdom is Clarissa's and Clarissa's alone.*
>
> *But she named you her Second, so I'll speak to you too.*
> *So tell me, dear Second, whose life shall I cue?*
>
> *A friend or an enemy, any name I'll allow,*
> *Say it loud and I'll show you them now."*

Agatha opened her mouth to respond—

Suddenly, she felt the ball ripped out of her hands and the orb went dark.

"Wait," Yuba the Gnome mulled, the crystal hooked on the end of his staff. He dangled it in front of his brown, leathery face, studying its battered surface. "Clarissa is in Rhian's dungeons. He could know we have her ball. He could have forced her to teach him its secrets so he can lure Agatha to her doom." The gnome turned on his former student. "So how do we know it isn't the *king* who wants you to use the crystal? How do we know this isn't a *trap*?"

The faculty quietly considered this.

So did Agatha.

Then shadows rushed through the room, followed by a sunburst, and they all turned to see the sky changing out the window. Lionsmane's tale about Hristo was fading and in its place, a new message appeared.

Celebrate! Rogue Agatha has been caught! Yet another enemy of Camelot, brought down by the Lion. Scoff at all other reports. There is only one army: the Lion's Army. And it is made of you: the people of the Woods! Live under the Lion and you will be safe forever.

"Further proof he's trying to tempt Agatha out of hiding," Yuba said sternly. "By lying about her capture, he's daring her to show her face."

"But look . . . there it is again . . . ," said Agatha, highlighting the message with her glow. "First letter of every sentence. C-R-Y-S-T-A-L." She turned to Yuba. "It's Sophie. I'm sure of it."

"And I'm sure it's the king," the gnome refuted.

"I know Sophie." Agatha held firm. "I know my friend."

"We cannot risk our students' lives on a hunch, Agatha," Yuba attacked. "All logical evidence points to this crystal ball being a trap. As a student, you always gave Sophie the benefit of the doubt, privileging emotion over reason, while endangering both others and yourself. Sophie may be your best friend, but real friendship is about knowing the limits of that friendship, not foolishly believing it will always be there to save you. That is what got you in all this trouble to begin with. You blindly trusted Rhian as a friend and have paid the price. Rhian knows your instincts all too well. Follow them and you'll end up dead with your prince."

Agatha could see the teachers nodding, clearly siding with the gnome. Yuba shoved the crystal ball back in Dovey's bag—

Suddenly a row of fairies whizzed into the office, glowing around Princess Uma's head and unleashing a torrent of high-pitched jabber.

"They say Rhian's men are returning to the school gates," Uma recounted breathlessly. "And this time, they have a *sorcerer* with them."

"I'll reinforce the shield as best I can," Manley muttered as he headed for the door. He glanced back at Uma. "Find a way to turn those stymphs around before our students arrive in Camelot. Get them back here *now*." He gave Agatha an ireful look and left the office.

Professor Anemone corralled Uma. "Can you call the stymphs?"

"It's too late! They've surely reached Camelot by now!" said the princess.

"What if we send a crow, telling them to abandon plan?" Professor Espada proposed.

"Faster if we mogrify ourselves," said Professor Lukas.

"FASTER IF YOU RIDE ON MY BACK," Castor harrumphed. "LET'S BRING 'EM BACK OURSEL . . ."

His voice petered out. The faculty followed the dog's eyes to the window.

Agatha stood in front of it, burning a large circle into the glass with her fingerglow. Then she pulled the glass away, opening up a gaping hole.

"Never took her for a vandal," Professor Sheeks said.

Professor Anemone blinked overcurled lashes. "She's gone rogue!"

Agatha raised her lit finger to the hole in the glass, her chest filling up with emotion like a river after the rain. Then, pointing her fingertip like a wand, she shot her glow at Lionsmane's message, feeling all the anger, fear, and determination surge out of her body and into the sky. Over Camelot, black clouds gathered like tentacles around Lionsmane's message, moving to the beat of a low thunder. The clouds curled around the words as Agatha focused harder, directing the mist to weave around each letter like fingers pulling the strings of a violin. Then all at once, the letters began to quiver, each one trembling in the sky.

"How is she doing that?" Princess Uma rasped.

"First-year weather spell," said Professor Sheeks. "Yuba would have taught it to her himself."

"Don't be ridiculous," the gnome dismissed. "Elementary weather spells can't touch an enemy's magic!"

Agatha thrust her finger even harder at the sky, the letters shivering faster and faster. She could feel the weight of Lionsmane's message heavy under her hand, as if pushing a stone lid off a tomb. Clenching her teeth, she thought of Tedros, Sophie, Dovey, Merlin, and all her friends, summoning every last drop of resolve, her glow electrifying the veins down her whole palm . . . until at last, with a ferocious "*ummmpph*," she magically stripped the gold off the letters . . .

. . . revealing the pink imprint of the message beneath it, like a fresh scar.

The pink of whoever's magic had drafted the message in the first place.

A pink so bold and brash everyone knew who it belonged to.

"Elementary weather spells can't touch an enemy's magic," said Agatha, gazing at the remnants of Sophie's glow, "unless the magic isn't an *enemy's* at all."

In the glass, she could see the teachers goggling at her: Manley, too, from the stairwell outside the office doors.

Agatha stabbed out her hand and shot a spell that collapsed Lionsmane's message into a golden ball, swelling and detonating it like a rival sun—

She watched the word burn against the sky.

Too much, she thought.

But she couldn't help herself.

She had to send a message to that fraud on Tedros' throne . . . to the Snake at his side . . . to every last dupe that was following him. . . .

And most of all to Sophie.

To tell her that she'd broken her code.

That help was on the way.

Agatha walked up to Yuba, yanked Dovey's bag from his grubby little hands, and strode out of the office. "Shall we get back to saving people?" She glared back with fire. "Or does anyone else want to teach me lessons about *friendship*?"

Teachers peeked at each other . . . then scampered to follow.

The gnome included.

THEY DID IT in the Library of Virtue, on the highest floor of Honor Tower, so Agatha could have a clear view of the Woods through the library's windows.

She stood facing the glass, with the crystal ball placed on a lectern in front of her. Behind her, the teachers watched, along with the hushed first years, who huddled against a wall painted with the school crest, their eyes on Agatha too.

Agatha insisted the first years be present, despite the teachers' misgivings. They deserved to be part of this. They *wanted* to be part of this. Their classmates' lives were on the line. If she could bring Groups #1 and #6 home safely, she'd earn the remaining kids' trust as their leader. And she needed that trust for the war to come.

Over Halfway Bay, fairies flew Manley up to the School Master's tower, so he could reinforce his shield against Rhian's men from a closer distance. All the while, Agatha watched the sky beyond the tower, waiting for the signal from Camelot. The library was quiet around her, the only sound the labored breathing of the new librarian, a withered gray-whiskered goat, who stamped books so listlessly that Agatha wondered if he might die before he got through his pile. Nor did he show the faintest curiosity as to why the whole school had herded into his library to stare at a crystal ball. He continued to stamp—*fump, fump, fump*—the slow pace clashing with Agatha's restless heartbeat as she pinned her eyes to the empty sky, her breath shallowing, a sense of doom crawling up her throat. . . .

Then a tiny flare appeared far away: a crisscrossing navy-and-pink helix, like an accidental firework.

Agatha exhaled. "Bodhi's and Laithan's glows. They made it through Camelot's gates without being seen."

"They're safe!" cheered a lively, dark-haired girl labeled PRIYANKA.

First years broke out in applause—

"Premature," Professor Anemone clipped anxiously. "Now comes the real danger. Bodhi and Laithan have to sneak onto the Gold Tower hill and wait for Agatha's bubble to appear, so she can show them the precise spot on the hill where they can break into the dungeons. Agatha, meanwhile, has to use the crystal ball to find this spot. And *quickly*. Every second Bodhi and Laithan spend on the castle grounds waiting for Agatha is a second too many."

The students hushed again.

Agatha focused on the crystal ball.

Nothing happened.

"Look directly into its center," Princess Uma urged.

"Don't blink," Professor Sheeks nagged.

"I know," Agatha gritted.

But still, the ball didn't work.

Bodhi and Laithan were looking for her bubble on the hill at this very moment. . . . They were counting on her to appear. . . .

In the crystal's reflection, she could see students creeping towards her from behind, trying to get a closer look—

"BE STILL, PEONS!" Castor boomed.

"Shhh!" Professor Anemone hissed.

Agatha took a deep breath and closed her eyes.

Be still.

Be still.

Be still.

She couldn't remember how to be still. She couldn't remember the last time she *was* still.

Then a memory surfaced.

Her and Sophie by a lake in Gavaldon . . . a breeze rippling the surface, their bodies intertwined on the shore . . . their breaths synched, the silence endless . . . two best friends, basking in a sunset, wishing it would last forever. . . .

Agatha opened her eyes.

The crystal glowed blue.

Strands of silver curled towards her and the phantom appeared.

> *"Clear as crystal, hard as bone,*
> *My wisdom is Clarissa's and Clarissa's alone.*
>
> *But she named you her Second, so I'll speak to you too.*
> *So tell me, dear Second, whose life shall I cue?*
>
> *A friend or an enemy, any name I'll allow,*
> *Say it loud and I'll show you them now."*

"Show me Tedros," she ordered.

"*As you wish,*" the crystal replied.

The silver phantom dispersed into mist and reassembled, depicting a scene within the ball—

Tedros bursting into the Theater of Tales, a rose in one hand, a sword in his other, as he fenced playfully against handsome Everboys, all the while grinning at girls in the audience.

"That isn't 'now,'" Agatha said, dismayed. "That's his first day of school! That was years ago!"

The crystal ball glitched, the scene stuttering and breaking apart into a thousand tiny crystal orbs within the larger one, each little bauble replaying the same clip of Tedros fencing the boys. Then a storm of blue lightning shot through the orb, rejoining the mini-crystals into a new scene. . . . Tedros as a young child, hiding under the bed in that strange guest room Agatha once saw in Camelot's White Tower, the prince giggling to himself as fairies zoomed through looking for him. . . .

The crystal glitched harder, faster—

This time it showed *two* Tedroses running together through the Woods, both shirtless and bloody . . . then Tedros as a baby, playing with Merlin's hat . . . then Tedros with Agatha underwater, peering into the crystal with her like she was now. . . .

"There is something very wrong with that ball," Yuba murmured.

"Dovey said it was broken, but not like this," Agatha fretted, grabbing the ball with both hands. Without her help, Bodhi and Laithan would be stranded at Rhian's castle. The crystal *had* to work. "Show me Tedros the way he is!" she spewed. "Not as a child, not as a student, but as he is now!"

The ball detonated with lightning and showed Tedros kissing Sophie in a sapphire cave.

"Stupid *ball*!" Agatha shouted, upending it like an hourglass.

Only now it was showing an eagle flying over a bloodred lake.

"Show me Tedros, you piece of crap! The real Tedros!" She rattled it with both hands like a cheap maraca—

Something seemed to lock into place.

Now inside the crystal's frame, a silver bubble roved over lush green grass, sun-kissed on a golden afternoon. As the bubble coasted uphill, the grass trembling in its breeze, Agatha could see the edges of a familiar tower overhead, armored guards manning the catwalks with crossbows.

"Wait. This is it," she breathed. "This is Camelot."

The bubble slowed, then stopped on a patch of grass halfway up the hill before zeroing in, close enough for Agatha to see ants skittering across the green blades.

"The crystal is telling us this is where Tedros is. His dungeon is under that grass!" Agatha said, emotion straining her voice. She was a layer of dirt away from seeing her prince again. "That's where they have to do it! That's where Bodhi and Laithan have to break in!"

For a moment, the Library was overtaken by silence.

Castor's voice interrupted it.

"IF THEY SHOW UP."

Agatha's thought exactly.

Where were they?

The pink-and-blue flare meant they'd safely entered Camelot's gates. They were supposed to sneak onto the Gold Tower hill and wait for her. The hill was small. It should have been easy to scan the grass and see her bubble the moment it appeared. . . .

Her heart stopped.

Had Bodhi and Laithan been captured by Rhian's pirate guards? Had her plan to keep them unseen failed? Were they hurt or worse, still . . .

What was she thinking! Letting first years go on a daredevil mission that had the slimmest chance of succeeding? Were her friends' lives worth killing innocent kids? Would Tedros,

Sophie, and Dovey want students dying for them?

This is a mistake, she thought. She was so caught up in try-ing to save Camelot's future that she'd borrowed against the school's. She had to correct course. She'd order the crystal to show her Bodhi and Laithan. Wherever they were, she'd find a way to get them out. Even if it meant losing Tedros. Even if it meant losing everyone else.

She glared into the ball. "Show me Bo—"

A handsome face thrust into the crystal's frame, spattered with black goo, a shimmery cape held over his head like a shield.

"Sorry," Bodhi panted, his breath shaking the bubble. "Couldn't see your bubble in the sunlight. Plus, Sophie's old snakeskin cape is a nightmare to handle. Thin, slippery, and just the worst. To stay invisible, we had to shuffle under it like one of those dragon puppets. And Laithan has a big behind."

"I take that as a compliment," whispered goo-covered Lai-than, squeezing in under the cape. "In fairness to my behind, we planned for two of us, not three, so that made things worse."

"Three?" Agatha said, mystified.

"Hiya," said a new goo-splotched face, crowding under the cape.

"*Hort?*" Agatha blurted.

"So I'm sitting in the carriage with Willam and Bogden fending off one of the Snake's eels," said the weasel, "and then what do you know, here come two of my former students, raid-ing the royal carriage like wild men and stunning the driver with a pretty mediocre spell but giving me just enough time to beat that scim to a puddle, and bang on, we're off and rolling to Camelot. Boys said they're supposed to invade the dungeons alone—that Sophie's old cape wouldn't fit three of us—but no way was I gonna let two first years go without me. I'm a *professor*. Oh, and Bogden and Willam wanted to come, but those boys are better as lookouts, if you know what I mean."

"Bogden and Willam?" said Agatha, even more baffled now.

"They stashed the carriage in the Woods near the castle and are waiting there, in case we can't use the stymphs to escape," said Bodhi. "No clouds today, so stymphs can't hide overhead or the guards on the towers would see them. Have no idea where they've flown to. We'll try signaling them once we free the prisoners, but no guarantee they'll pick us up."

"A real crystal ball? Sooo cool," said Laithan, poking at the bubble and distorting it. He searched the frame. "Is Priyanka watching? Tell her I say hi."

"Professor Anemone is watching, and you should be focusing on your vital mission instead of peacocking for girls!" the Beautification teacher scorched.

Laithan cleared his throat. "Um, the dungeons are . . . here?"

"Right where you're standing," Agatha confirmed.

Bunched under the snakeskin, the three boys barraged the ground with their lit fingerglows, burning holes in the grass. Hort's magic burrowed far faster than the first years', searing through dirt like the sun melting ice, until he hit a solid gray wall. He gave it a kick, hearing a hollow sound and saw specks crumble, as if the wall was exceptionally old or not very sturdy. Then he silently cued the boys and they renewed their glows' assault.

Suddenly a gust of wind swept in, blowing the snakeskin off them. The boys' outlines brightened in Agatha's frame. They weren't invisible anymore. Agatha saw a guard on the tower turn—

Hort snatched the cape back down, shielding them once more. "Holy frogballs. Did they see us?"

"I don't know," said Agatha. "Just *hurry.*"

The boys shot their lit fingers harder at the dungeon wall, but this time, Bodhi and Laithan's glow just spurted weak sparks.

"New boys never last long," Princess Uma lamented.

"Easily drained," Professor Sheeks concurred.

Hort glowered at Bodhi and Laithan as he redoubled his glow strength. "And you wanted to do this *alone?*"

There was another problem now too.

"Hort?" Agatha rasped.

"What."

"My connection's weakening."

Hort looked up into the frame and saw what she was seeing: the image in the bubble turning translucent.

"Oh, for Hook's sake," Hort growled.

He redirected his glow onto himself and, with a choked scream, exploded out of his clothes, morphing into a giant man-wolf, nearly evicting the two boys out from under the cape with his girth, before hugging them back under his furred torso like a lion protecting his cubs. Then with the snakeskin hung tight around them, Hort raised two hairy fists and slammed the wall, once, twice, three times, the last with a roar—

The wall caved in.

Two boys and a man-wolf tumbled down in an implosion of brick, dirt, and grass as Agatha watched, bug-eyed, hearing the confused shouts of distant guards through the crystal and then the clatter of alarm bells. Black dust swirled inside the crystal ball like a storm, obscuring everything behind it; Agatha pressed her nose to the glass, while teachers and students crowded in behind her, desperate to see if the boys survived.

Little by little, the dust cleared, revealing three walls of a dark prison cell, a ray of sunlight piercing through like a saber. Hort, Bodhi, and Laithan lay facedown in the rubble, groaning as they stirred.

But that's not who Agatha was looking at.

Agatha was watching a sallow, glassy-eyed boy, covered in blood and bruises, slowly rise from a crouch into the sunlight, like he was lost in a dream.

"Agatha?"

Tears came to his princess's eyes. "Tedros, listen to me. Everything I said that night before the battle . . . everything I said to Sophie . . . I was lost in a moment. I was scared and frustrated. It's not how I feel about you—"

"You came for me. That's all that matters," Tedros said, choked up with emotion. "I didn't think there was a way. But you found one. Of course you found one. You're *you*. And now you're here . . ." He cocked his head. "Along with a lot of other people. Um, I see Yuba . . . and Castor and . . . are you at *school*?"

"For now," said Agatha quickly. "And soon you will be too. You're hurt and the teachers can heal you."

"Do I look as bad as I feel?" Tedros asked.

"Still handsomer than Rhian," said Agatha.

"Good answer. And Sophie?"

"A group of first years is distracting Rhian long enough to free her. There'll be plenty of time for us to talk once you're here at school. You need to get out now, Tedros. You and Dovey and all the others."

But Tedros just gazed at her like they had all the time in the world. Agatha, too, felt herself falling into Tedros' eyes, as if there was no barrier between them at all.

"Um . . . guys?"

Tedros turned to the man-wolf, head raised on the floor.

Hort pointed with his paw. "They're coming."

All of a sudden, Agatha saw shadows rushing in from every side of the crystal, converging on the dungeons.

"Free the rest!" Tedros cried at Hort, who bounded with the prince down the hall towards the other cells. Bodhi and Laithan lumbered up from the floor, limping after them, but Hort flung them backwards—"Call the stymphs, you fool!"

Bodhi spun around, firing navy flares through the sinkhole into the sky, past pirate guards who were starting to leap down from the hill into the dungeons. More dirt and rubble clouded Agatha's ball, obscuring her view. She could see Laithan repelling guards with stun spells, but his glow wasn't strong enough to stop them. A pirate charged forward and tackled him, wrestling the muscly first year into a headlock, blocking Agatha's sightline completely.

Meanwhile, the bubble inside her crystal had faded two shades lighter. She could hardly see anything anymore, her connection about to break.

Hort's roars echoed down the hall, along with the sound of crashing metal. Disconnected voices rose in the chaos—

"This way!" Tedros yelled.

"Nicola, look behind you!" shouted Professor Dovey.

"Get off me, you brute!" Kiko screamed.

The cry of shrieking stymphs drowned them out.

More debris exploded through the dungeons, flooding Agatha's crystal. The crystal glitched again and the dust morphed to silver shimmer, slowly re-forming the phantom mask. . . .

"I can't see them anymore," Agatha gasped.

"The stymphs came too late," Princess Uma said, ashen. "They won't get everyone out."

"They have to," Agatha panicked. "If we leave anyone behind, Rhian will kill them!"

"WE NEED TO GO NOW!" Castor blasted, lurching for the doors. "WE HAVE TO HELP THEM—"

"You'll never get there in time," Yuba said.

Castor stopped in his tracks.

The library went quiet, students and teachers alike.

Agatha took a deep breath and looked up at her army.

"Maybe we won't get to them," she said. "But I know some-one who will."

Professor Anemone read her face. "You're overestimat-ing her goodness, Agatha. She'll save herself, no matter what it costs. It doesn't matter who's still left. She'll be on the first stymph to school."

Agatha didn't listen. She'd learned her lesson too many times: friendship can't be explained. Not a friendship like hers. Some bonds are too deep for others to ever understand.

She looked back at the crystal as the silver phantom inside prowled towards her, fading quickly, with just enough power for one last wish. . . .

"Show me Sophie," Agatha commanded.

BACK ON THE rooftop, Agatha leaned against the leafy sculp-ture of King Arthur, still thinking about his son.

He wouldn't be one of those left behind.

He'd find a way back to her.

Like she always found a way back to him.

Someone's voice ripped her from her trance: *"They're here!"*

Agatha leapt out from behind the hedge, her eyes on the sky.

Stymphs soared towards the school from the Woods,

smoothly penetrating Manley's green fog, as their young riders began to come into view against the red-hot sunset.

First years burst through the roof door behind Agatha, cheering their return, the teachers joining in. *"THEY'RE SAVED!" "WE WON!" "LONG LIVE TEDROS!" "LONG LIVE THE SCHOOL!"*

Agatha was too busy counting the stymphs' riders—

Hester . . . Anadil . . . Dot . . .

Beatrix . . . Reena . . . Kiko . . .

Bodhi . . . Laithan . . . Devan . . .

More bony birds tore through the fog, more riders on their backs.

Ten . . . eleven . . . twelve, Agatha counted, as her army's cheers amplified.

Two more stymphs, two riders on each.

Fifteen . . .

Sixteen . . .

The birds stopped coming.

Agatha waited, as the first wave of stymphs landed on the Great Lawn below, Hester and Dot dismounting, helping Anadil, who was soaked in blood.

Instantly, teachers and students rushed back into the castle and down onto the lawn to help her, along with others landing nearby: Bert . . . Beckett . . . Laralisa . . .

Agatha stayed on the roof, searching the fog for more stymphs.

The sky stayed clear.

Seven short.

They were seven people short.

Seven who only Sophie could save now.

Agatha welled with tears, realizing who'd been left behind—

CRACK!

The sound ricocheted across the school grounds like a stone through glass.

Agatha looked out and saw Professor Manley screaming violently at her from the School Master's window . . . students and teachers fleeing into the castle from the lawn . . . wolves covered in blood at the North Gate. . . .

Agatha raised her eyes to a hole in the green shield . . . to the steel and boots coming through. . . .

She backed up and started running.

No time to mourn the missing.

Not now.

Because while she was breaking into Rhian's castle . . .

Rhian's men had broken into *hers*.

12

Lucky Seven

Beneath the cold, murky water, Tedros finally felt clean. He let his arms and legs splay out, floating like seaweed beneath the algae-green surface. The biting chill numbed his sore muscles and froze out his thoughts. As long as he stayed underwater, he didn't have to face what was above it.

But he could only hold his breath for so long.

Each time he came up, long enough to inhale, he heard a snippet of conversation.

"If I'd been picked to wear Sophie's cape instead of those *boys*, we would have escaped—"

Tedros went back under.

"The tarot cards said a flying ghost would be at the church and Agatha's bubble looked *just* like a flying ghost—"

Back under.

"If we'd only made a run for it when I told us to—"

Back under.

Tedros' skin screamed with cold, his heart pumping madly. His breaths grew shallower and shallower . . . his brain shut down like a closing door. . . . He could see King Arthur's statue above the mold-colored surface, refracted and hazy, a stone Excalibur clasped in his folded hands. But now Arthur was bending towards the water, leering through empty sockets, which crawled with maggots and worms. Tedros dog-paddled backwards, but his father chased him, the statue coming alive, as if the king had at last learned who had carved out his eyes . . . as if he'd discovered his son's cowardly betrayal. . . . Flailing backwards, Tedros slammed against a wall, out of breath, flattened like a starfish as his father came swimming, his sword pointed at Tedros' heart—

"*Unbury Me*," the king commanded.

Tedros crashed through the surface of the pool, spraying water and heaving for breath.

Valentina and Aja lounged against the marble wall of King's Cove, drenched by Tedros' splash. Behind them, King Arthur's statue stood eyeless and still.

"Why is he swimming in a dirty *piscina*?" said Valentina.

"Boys are a mystery," said Aja, wringing out his devil-red hair.

"You *are* a boy," said Valentina.

"Then why didn't Agatha pick me to wear Sophie's cape?" Aja puffed. "She knew I loved that cape and instead she let Bodhi and Laithan wear it—"

"Oh, give up on that damn cape, will you!" a new voice said.

Tedros turned to see Willam and Bogden against the opposite wall, both in muddy, grass-stained shirts.

"We've been here for hours with no food or water or anything and all you can talk about is a cape!" said Bogden. "You should be worrying about getting out of here before we die!"

"Then stop all this jabbering and help us *find* a way out," said Professor Dovey's voice.

Tedros swiveled to see the Dean and Nicola at the stone door to King's Cove; Nicola was picking the lock with her hairpin while Dovey tried shooting spells repeatedly across the molding of the door, only to see the spells extinguish midair.

"There *is* no way out," Tedros groused, climbing out of the pool and letting the cove's muggy air thaw his torso as he slumped against the wall near Valentina. "Dad put a shield against magic in this room to get rid of the fairies after Merlin left. Plus, why do you think they moved us here now that the dungeons are smashed in? It's called King's Cove for a reason: Dad built it as a safe room, in case the castle got invaded. Nothing can penetrate it. We're as trapped here as we were there."

"At least it's the only room in the castle Rhian hasn't remade into a tribute to himself," said Willam.

Tedros looked at him.

"We saw when they took us upstairs," Bogden explained. "It's all gold Lions and Rhian busts and shirtless statues of him looking buff."

"Not that I'm complaining," said Willam airily. "Been around Camelot my whole life and the castle looks so much better than it did before"—he saw Tedros glowering—"in a gaudy, low-class sort of way."

Tedros raked a hand through his salt-coated hair. "Probably left this room alone since no one will see it. Everything that pig does is for show."

He rubbed at the bruises on his muscled stomach and chest . . . then noticed Aja, Valentina, Willam, and Bogden watching him intently.

"What?" Tedros said.

"Nothing," all four chorused, looking away.

Tedros put his shirt back on.

Meanwhile, Dovey and Nicola had resumed their assault on the door. Dovey's green gown shed beetle wings while she stood on tiptoes and shot sparks out of her fingertip, trying to find a weakness in the magic shield. Beneath her, Nicola's tongue stuck out in concentration as she crouched in a squat, picking deeper in the lock.

"I *lived* in this castle. Don't you think I'd know if there was a way out?" Tedros hounded.

"Weren't you also the one who said Good never gives up? That Good always *wins*?" Nicola bit back.

"When did I say that?" Tedros scoffed.

"Right before you and Sophie went into the Trial by Tale your first year," she said. "Check your fairy tale."

Tedros frowned.

"Should have seen her in class," Dovey murmured.

But now Tedros was thinking about that moment when he and Sophie went into the Trial together. At the time, he'd thought that the Trial was the biggest test he'd ever face . . . that Sophie was his true love . . . that Good would always win. . . .

Maybe I do need to check my fairy tale, he thought. Because while living it, he could never see it clearly.

The Trial was hardly a test at all, compared to what he faced now.

Nor did Sophie turn out to be his true love.

And Good didn't always win.

In fact, it might never win again.

Panic rippled in his chest, as if the numb chill had worn off, his feelings rushing back. Agatha had come to save him. She'd given him a chance to fight for his crown. And somehow in the chaos, he'd gotten caught. Again.

Forget being king, Tedros thought. *You can't even get rescued right.*

He should be at school. He should be at her side, plotting his revenge on Rhian. He should be leading the war to take back the throne.

Bogden sniffled. "We were so close. Willam and I had the royal carriage. We took the horses into the Woods, but we didn't know how to get to school. Then I remembered Princess

Uma taught my Forest Group to speak Horse, so I told the horses to take us to school. . . ." He cried harder. "They took us back to Rhian instead."

"Horses are so disloyal," Willam sighed, patting Bogden's head.

"What exactly did you say to the horses?" asked Nicola skeptically, still working the lock.

Bogden mimicked a few grunts and a spirited neigh. "That means 'go to school.'"

"That means 'poo on my foot,'" said Nicola.

Bogden bit his lip.

"Explains a lot," Willam mumbled.

Professor Dovey let out a pained gasp and Tedros turned to see her fingertip smoking, the skin raw. "Whatever shield Arthur put in place has had enough of me testing it," she said, sitting wearily on a marble bench next to the pool. All of them looked terrible, but Dovey looked especially feeble, as if she'd never fully recovered from whatever her crystal ball had done to her. She let out a long sigh. "It seems Tedros is right about the room's defenses."

A second later, Nicola's hair clip broke in the lock.

Aja and Valentina, meanwhile, were at the edge of the pool, poking at the rotten water with one of Valentina's boots.

The sum of all this dithering made Tedros snap from his own stupor. Here he was, judging his teammates, when he wasn't doing *anything* to help them. Meanwhile, Agatha had escaped, Agatha had gotten to school, Agatha had come to save him, Agatha had done everything, everything, everything.

Had he done anything for *her*? Or anyone else? That's why he was in this room to begin with. That's why he'd lost his crown. Because he'd been so whiny, so self-involved, so entitled that he'd never stood up and done what a king was supposed to do: *lead*.

Tedros took to his feet. "Listen, we can't use magic to get out of here, but maybe we can use something else."

"Didn't we just agree that there's no way out of this room?" the Dean muttered.

"Then let's *make* a way out," Tedros resolved. "Does anyone have any talents?"

Professor Dovey sat straighter, suddenly alert. "Good thinking, Tedros! Aja and Valentina. You two are Nevers. What are you practicing in Professor Sheeks' class?"

"I can climb guanabana trees," said Valentina.

"Your *villain* talent, you goose," Dovey snapped. "The one you practice in school!"

"That *is* the one I practice in school," Valentina repeated.

Dovey pursed her lips, then turned to Aja.

"Heat vision," said the flame-haired boy. "I can see through solid objects."

"Can you see through this wall?" Tedros said eagerly.

Aja locked on the wall and its big marble bricks, each the size of a small window. "I see . . . a black pond . . . Sophie, looking so chic in white furs and a babushka, lost in thought as she feeds the ducks . . . probably coming up with a plan to save us. . . ."

"We're in a *basement*," Tedros growled. "There's no *ponds* at the castle, let alone a 'black' one. And when I saw Agatha in her crystal ball, she told me your friends were rescuing Sophie from the church. She's safe at school by now."

Aja tossed his hair. "I see what I see."

"And you've never gotten one thing right. Not one!" Valentina sniped. "Maybe you should find another talent. Like kissing Sophie's behind."

"Anyone else have a talent?" Professor Dovey pressed.

"Fortune-telling," said Bogden.

"Mine too," said Willam, pulling out tarot cards.

Tedros remembered their prophecy about gifts. . . . The two boys had warned him to be wary of them. . . . and it was Rhian's "gift" to Tedros that had let Rhian pull Excalibur from the stone and steal Tedros' crown. . . .

Tedros looked at the two boys with new interest. "Ask your cards if we'll get out of this room."

Bogden dealt a hand. "Says yes."

"And soon," said Willam.

Tedros' eyes lit up. "Ask the cards how we do it! Ask them how we get out of King's Cove!"

Bogden and Willam looked at the cards . . . then at each other . . . then at Tedros. . . .

"Potatoes," the boys said.

Everyone in the room stared.

"*Potatoes?*" Tedros repeated.

"Clearly they speak Tarot as well as they speak Horse," said Professor Dovey. "What about you, Nicola?"

"Readers don't come with talents," Tedros griped, watching her search the walls for loose bricks.

Nicola glanced at him. "Yet your girlfriend's a Reader and done far more to help us than you have."

Tedros made a face . . . then perked up. "She's right. Agatha freed our friends by using Dovey's crystal ball from a thousand miles away. She figured something out. Surely we can figure something out too."

"Crystal ball? Agatha used *my* crystal ball?" Dovey chortled. "How ridiculous."

"Ridiculous or not, it worked, didn't it?" said Tedros.

"No, I mean, she *couldn't* have used my ball," said the Dean. "No one can use my crystal ball besides me. I didn't name a Second when I had it made. The ball would never answer to her."

"Well, I saw her inside it," Tedros pointed out.

"Me too," said Valentina.

"Could have been any crystal ball—" Dovey started.

"Let's hope so, because this one was broken," Aja puffed. "Kept glitching and it only lasted a few minutes."

Dovey's face dropped. "But . . . but . . . Agatha *can't* know how to use my ball! It's impossible. Because if she does, then she's in *grave* danger! That crystal ball nearly killed me! It isn't working. Not the way it's supposed to. She must have taken it from me when I came to Camelot! I have to speak to her—I have to tell her never to use it again—"

"Well, you can't tell her anything until we get out of here!"

Tedros said, venting his new fears for Agatha back at the Dean.

"There's only one way out of King's Cove," Nicola piped up.

Everyone turned to the first year, who stood in front of a hole in the wall, struggling under the weight of the big brick she'd extracted from it.

"We can squeeze through there?" Tedros said excitedly.

"No. There's another layer of wall behind it," Nicola clipped. "The only way out of King's Cove is to wait for someone to open that door and we hit them with this brick and make a run for it."

"That sounds about as promising as '*potatoes*,'" Tedros snorted, shooting a glare at Willam and Bogden.

"Well, what's your idea, then?" Bogden attacked.

"Yeah, what's your talent other than taking off your shirt and bullying kids at school?" Willam harped.

"Bullying kids at *school*?" Tedros said, boggled.

"Don't play the altar boy," said Willam, cheeks searing pink. "My brother told me everything."

"I don't even know who your brother is—" said Tedros.

Nicola dropped her brick on the ground with a thud. "No one cares about what happened at school or your history of sibling abuse. We're condemned to die in a basement and ambushing whoever opens that door is our only chance. Surprise them before they surprise us."

"Oh please. No one's coming," Aja groaned, back to making waves in the pool with Valentina, using Valentina's boot. "They're gonna let us starve."

"Well, everyone except Tedros," said Valentina, poking harder at the pool. "They're still going to cut off his head."

"Thank you for the reminder. Is now really the time to be studying the properties of water?" Tedros barked, red-faced.

"We're keeping *el ratón* away," Valentina explained.

"*Ratón?* What's a *ratón?*" said Tedros.

Aja and Valentina pointed at the end of her boot. "That."

Tedros leaned closer and saw a fuzzy black cloud squirming in the middle of the pool. "A rat? Nevers are scared of rats?"

"Valentina and I are from Hamelin," said Aja.

"Like Pied-Piper-of-Hamelin Hamelin," said Valentina.

"Like the Hamelin-that-had-so-many-rats-it-gave-its-children-to-a-rat-catching-musician Hamelin," said Aja.

"Wait, that isn't just any rat," Professor Dovey blurted, lurching up from her bench. "That's *Anadil's* rat!"

Tedros met Dovey's eyes. Instantly the prince and the Dean dropped down and started pushing at the water from opposite sides, trying to bring the rat to the edge. Nicola, Willam, and Bogden joined in, the two boys cooing things like "Here, little ratty!" and "Swim, little pup!" while the rat floundered, choking and spitting, as everyone's currents competed, keeping the rat stuck in the center of the pool, before Tedros had enough and leapt in the water with his clothes on and seized the rat in his fist.

He flung the thankful rodent onto the tiled floor. Splayed on its side, the rat sucked in air with hyper squeaks, regurgitating water again and again, until it took a last deep breath . . .

. . . and puked out a small purple ball.

Dovey retrieved the ball as Tedros climbed out of the water and dripped over her shoulder, the rat still panting at their feet.

The Dean saw Nicola and the others crowd in and she held out her hand—

"Give Tedros and me a moment."

She yanked the prince behind Arthur's statue.

"The less they know, the better. Otherwise Rhian can torture them for information," she whispered. "Look."

She held up the purple ball, revealing a crumple of velvet embroidered with silver stars.

"*Merlin*," said Tedros, unfurling the velvet with his fingers. "It's from his cape—"

He froze. Because there was something else.

Something tucked inside the fabric.

A lock of long white hair.

Merlin's hair.

Tedros paled. "Is he alive?" he rasped, swiveling to the rat.

But the vermin had already raced around Arthur's statue and dived back into the fetid pool. Between his father's stone legs, Tedros watched the rat streak to the bottom of the water and disappear through a crack in the wall.

"So we know it found Merlin. We just don't know where or in what condition," the prince said.

He heard a loud noise from the other side of the room, like a stone dropping, and the clatter of footsteps, the first years surely up to something. He turned to check on them—

"Maybe we do know," said the Dean.

Tedros saw Dovey holding the lock of hair up to the light of a torch.

"What is it?" said the prince.

"Look closer," said the Dean.

Tedros moved behind her, focusing on the clump of long white hair.

Only it wasn't all white, Tedros realized.

Because the more he looked at it, from every angle, the more Merlin's hair seemed to change in color as it progressed along each strand: from thin, stark white at one end to a robust, sturdy brown at the other.

Tedros furrowed his brows. "Merlin's like a thousand years old. His hair is all white. But this hair looks like his at the top . . . only the further down the hair you go, the more it looks like it belongs to someone . . ."

"*Younger,*" said Dovey.

The prince met her eyes. "How can hair be old and young at the same time?" he asked, taking the lock from the Dean. But as he did, his palm brushed across Merlin's hair and a glittery sheen cascaded off it onto Professor Dovey's hand.

All of a sudden, the spots and veins of her hand seemed to lighten . . . the wrinkles visibly shallowed . . .

"Huh?" Tedros marveled.

But Professor Dovey was still gazing at the lock of hair. "I think I know where he is, Tedros. I think I know where Rhian's kept Merlin—"

A burlap sack slammed over Dovey's head.

"Head-choppin' time!" a snaggle-toothed pirate snarled,

yanking the Dean backwards. "Execution's been moved up!"

Tedros spun to see Nicola, the first years, and Willam and Bogden already gagged, with sacks dumped over their heads by armored pirates.

"B-b-but it's me you want! Not them!" Tedros spluttered. "It's me who's supposed to die!"

"Plans have changed," said a smooth voice.

Tedros turned—

Japeth posed in the doorway. He wore his shiny suit of snakes and carried a last burlap sack in his hand.

"Now it's *all* of you," he said.

Scims shot off him and grabbed hold of Tedros, sweeping the sack over his head.

As the eels ripped him forward, Tedros inhaled a whiff of what once filled the sack . . . the sack now dragging him and his friends out of King's Cove and to the executioner's axe. . . .

Potatoes.

It smelled like potatoes.

13

Sometimes the Story Leads You

"**H**ow many men!" Agatha cried, sprinting through the pink breezeway.

"I lost count at twenty!" Dot panted, behind her.

"They got through the shield . . . I saw some kind of purple light attacking it . . . ," Agatha called back, the bag with Dovey's crystal ball pounding against her shoulder. "But *how*? Rhian's thugs can't do magic!"

"Maybe they learned a spell!"

"Only students who went to the school can do spells!

And those pirates didn't go to the school!"

"I can't run and talk at the same time!" Dot wheezed.

Agatha glanced back at Dot and the twenty first years herding behind her through Good's glass tunnel towards Honor Tower. Against the darkening sky, the new students shuffled like spooked sheep, whispering anxiously, their eyes wide, their feet pattering high over the Great Lawn.

Out of the corner of her eye, Agatha saw movement through the other colorful glass breezeways that connected the towers of the School for Good: Hester and Professor Anemone leading a group of first years through the blue breezeway to Valor Tower, Hort and Anadil guiding their first years along the yellow tunnel to Purity, and Yuba and Beatrix's group using the peach passage to Charity. Meanwhile, on the roof over the crisscrossing breezeways, Agatha glimpsed Castor booting first years along. . . .

Agatha knew Rhian's men were searching for her. To throw them off, she and the teachers had divided up the students into Forest Groups, with each group taking a different route to the same place. The one and only place in the school they would all be safe. If they could get there alive, that is.

"Who are those men?" she heard Priyanka ask.

"Camelot guards," said a hairy, three-eyed Never tagged Bossam.

"They don't *look* like Camelot guards," said Priyanka.

Agatha tracked their stares through the pink glass to the dirt-caked, dead-eyed pirates in silver chainmail as they came into view, stepping over slaughtered wolf bodies and creeping towards the castle behind their captain, wielding swords and bows and clubs. If the pirates looked straight up, they'd see Agatha and her charges in the tunnel. They needed to get out of this breezeway now—

"Wait!" Dot yipped, pulling to a halt.

"We don't have *time* to wait!" said Agatha.

"No, look," Dot said, hands against the glass. "It's *Kei*."

Agatha glanced down at Tedros' former guard leading the pirates, sword in hand as he skulked up the hill towards Good's castle doors, a second man at his side. Neither Kei nor his lieutenant seemed in a rush, nor did any of the thugs fanned out behind them, as if they didn't need to chase Agatha at all. As if they were waiting for her to come to them. Their movements unsettled her. Agatha peered closer.

"Kei was the one who took me on a date to Beauty and the Feast," Dot said softly. "He was my first kiss. . . ."

"That guy kissed *you*?" said Bossam. Priyanka kicked him.

"Only so he could put something in my drink and steal my keys," Dot sniffled. "That's how the Snake got out of Daddy's jail. He better hope we don't come face-to-face or I'll—" She saw Agatha gazing downwards. "I know. Soooo handsome, right?"

But Agatha wasn't looking at Kei.

She was looking at his lieutenant. A short, big-bellied man in a brown robe, with a red beard and even redder face, who appeared less like a pirate and more like Santa Claus' surly brother. A sleek glass orb floated over his open palm and he and Kei were studying it like a compass as they walked. Purple light filled the glass orb . . . the same purple light that Agatha had seen attacking Manley's shield. . . .

"That's a crystal ball," said Dot. "Smaller than Dovey's. Means it's newer." She glanced at the bag on Agatha's arm. "Old ones are like cinder blocks."

Agatha had the bruises to prove it.

"Thought only fairy godmothers can use crystal balls," Priyanka said.

"Fairy godfathers too," Bossam corrected, blinking his third eye. "Must be a strong one if he got through Professor Manley's shield."

"But what's the captain of Camelot's guard doing with a crystal *ball*?" Priyanka asked.

"Can't see the inside from here," said Agatha, squinting hard.

"We can if I mirrorspell it," Dot said quickly. "I watched Hester do it in the dungeons—"

Her fingertip glowed and she pressed it against the glass, before closing her eyes to summon the right emotion. *"Reflecta asimova!"*

From her finger spewed a puff of purple fog that formed a two-dimensional projection, floating in the breezeway above the group's heads.

"This is a close-up of what they're seeing inside the ball," said Dot.

Agatha watched as the purple mist swirled in the projection, half-heartedly forming various scenes: a castle . . . a bridge . . . a forest . . . before it finally seemed to settle on one: a tunnel . . . with bodies packed inside . . .

The image sharpened, revealing a group of boys and girls in crisp uniforms, swan emblems on their chests . . . led by a tall, pale girl with big bug eyes and helmet-cut hair. . . .

A girl who was gazing up at a projection of the very same scene.

Agatha's heart stopped.

"They're seeing . . . *us*," she breathed.

Rhian's men hadn't gone looking for her because they didn't need to. The crystal ball told them exactly where she was.

Slowly Agatha and the group looked down through the glass.

Down on the ground, Kei and his companion slowly looked up.

Arrows launched from the pirates' bows, spinning towards Agatha and the students. They came too fast. No time to run. She thrust out her arms and uselessly shielded her group as the arrows hit—

They rebounded off the glass, clinking and chiming with different tones like a strummed harp. The arrows halted mid-air, suddenly glowing the same pink as the breezeway glass, the castle's defenses activated. Then they magically turned around and whizzed back down, impaling several of the pirates, while Kei and the others ducked for cover.

Two of the arrows stayed back, however, hovering over the field, as if calculating their target. . . .

Crouched on the ground, the fairy godfather swished his palm over his crystal, kindling a purple bonfire inside it. The orb shuddered above his hand, the storm inside burning hotter, hotter. Then it shot like a cannonball at Agatha's breezeway, poised to obliterate it like a bomb.

The last two arrows waited a beat as if to make no mistake. . . .

Then they flew with a vengeance, one ripping through the fairy godfather's heart, the other through the lit crystal ball, shattering it into a thousand pieces.

The robed man's eyes bulged with shock. Then he fell forward, his corpse landing hard in the glowing wreckage of glass.

First years blinked through the breezeway.

"Didn't see that in his ball, did he?" Dot puffed.

"Come on!" Agatha gasped, pushing the group forward—

She spotted Kei rising from the ground, jaw clenched, as he swiped a bloodstained bow from beneath a dead pirate . . . then a fragment of glass from the broken crystal ball, alive with purple glow. . . .

He aimed it right at Agatha.

Kei unleashed the glass shard, which speared through the breezeway like a bullet, grazing Agatha's ear and blasting out the other glass wall.

For a moment, everything went quiet.

Then a slow cracking sound filled the tunnel.

Agatha looked up at the breezeway walls, splintering like a frozen pond hit by the sun.

"Run!" she screamed.

The breezeway imploded around her as students dashed for their lives, hurdling over the breaking glass and diving for the Honor Tower landing. Agatha and Dot chased behind the first years, but they were a step too late. The floor exploded beneath their feet and they went plunging off the tower, along with Priyanka and Bossam. Agatha felt the cool night wind as she fell past the other breezeways, Dovey's bag on her arm dropping her like an anchor. Her hands flailed for Dot and the others as if she could somehow save them—

Then a big, hairy paw slapped Agatha hard, knocking her backwards.

For a moment, she thought she must be hallucinating, but now she was batted into wide, open jaws, and she landed on a wet tongue alongside Dot, who looked just as dazed. Agatha poked her head between sharp teeth and peeked up at Castor's long snout and bloodshot eyes as he balanced atop the blue breezeway, with Priyanka and Bossam squired in his paw. A gob of drool splashed on Agatha's cheek.

Down below, pirates began stringing their bows, while Kei raced into the School for Good, Agatha tracking him through the castle's glass. Kei bounded up the spiral staircase, his boots skipping steps.

"Castor, he's coming!" Agatha cried.

Instantly, the dog was on the move, leaping between breezeways towards the roof, clamping Agatha and Dot in his hot, rancid mouth—

An arrow struck Castor in the buttock and he roared in

pain, nearly spewing Agatha and Dot out into the air, but the two girls held on by the tips of his teeth as Castor dove off the last breezeway, his claw catching onto the rooftop. Agatha saw Castor's legs dangling over the edge and she thrust out her arms, pulling him up, before an arrow almost decapitated her and she dove back under his tongue. With a last surge, Castor threw himself forward, sliding onto the roof, and a moment later, he was on his feet again, weaving through the hedge sculptures of Merlin's Menagerie, as Priyanka and Bossam yanked the arrow out of his rump.

Agatha could feel Castor's heartbeat in his throat as she and Dot lit their fingerglows and magically erased the blood he was dripping, so it wouldn't leave a trail. It would take Kei another minute to make it to the roof, but Castor's pace was slowing, his leg limping as he hustled past hedge scenes of King Arthur crowned . . . Arthur and Guinevere married . . . their son's birth . . . until he turned a corner to the final one: the Lady of the Lake rising from a pond to bestow Excalibur on the king. Agatha knew the sculpture well: not just because of her own history with the Lady and the sword, but because the pond was a secret portal to Halfway Bridge. A portal she'd used often in her time at school. Now, as Castor lumbered towards it, Agatha glimpsed Yuba and Beatrix on the shore of the pond, frantically herding a few last first years into the water's portal. The students vanished beneath the surface in a blast of white light, before the gnome and fourth year jumped in themselves.

Agatha heard the door to the rooftop slam open behind the hedge . . . the rush of Kei's bootsteps . . .

But Castor was already in midair, flopping towards the water, its portal gleaming with magic—

Rhian's captain turned the corner a few seconds later.

With his sword, Kei probed at a boy's blue tie caught on a hedge, a girl's pink slipper under a bush, a spot of blood on the stone floor. His narrow eyes scanned the horizon . . . the moonlit hedges . . . the rippling pond . . . But there were no signs of life, except the shadow of a cloud moving across Halfway Bridge.

If only he'd looked closer at that shadow, he would have found what he was looking for—

A dog hobbling into the School for Evil, the last of his tail slithering into the castle like a snake.

"You can put us down now," said Agatha.

"Not until we get there," Castor garbled, girls in his mouth.

He clamped his teeth harder on her and Dot and clutched the first years tighter as he limped through the School for Evil, still leaking blood.

"You're as stubborn as your brother," Agatha sighed.

"My brother is a *prat*," said Castor, pulling the girls out and fixing them with a stare. "First Dovey fires him. Then he goes to Camelot and Tedros fires him. I wrote him telling him to come here to Evil. That we could rejoin heads and work together. Never heard from him again. Probably working for Rhian now. Sucks up to whoever will have him, my brother. Doesn't realize I'm the only one who will always be there."

There was a sadness in Castor's voice that surprised Agatha. Castor and Pollux may have tried to kill each other at times, but Castor loved his brother to the end. Who knew that she and a dog could have so much in common, Agatha thought wryly. Her relationship with Sophie wasn't so different.

"Poor thing," Dot said, turning a passing roach to chocolate.

For a moment, Agatha thought Dot was talking about Castor . . . then saw her watching Bossam, who had fainted in the dog's paw, as if the stress of the chase had been too much for him.

Meanwhile, Priyanka was staring wide-eyed at her new surroundings.

"If I'd known Evil would be like this, I wouldn't have been so Good," Priyanka marveled.

"You should see my room," said Bossam, stirring.

"No, thanks," said Priyanka curtly.

Castor snorted.

Indeed, this was Agatha's first look inside Dean Sophie's School for Evil: its black onyx floors, chandeliers with S-shaped crystals, walls of violet vines, bouquets of black roses, and floating lanterns that flooded the foyer with purple light. Black marble columns broadcasted magical replays from Sophie's fairy tale—Sophie winning the Circus of Talents, Sophie fighting the Trial by Tale as a boy, Sophie destroying the School Master's ring—while the floor tiles lit up bright purple as Castor stepped on them, with Sophie appearing in each one in different high-fashion ensembles, posing, giggling, blowing bubbles as if the entire castle was an advertisement for herself. The walls of the foyer, meanwhile, had been repainted with murals of Sophie looking windswept and ravishing, each labeled with a different motto.

THE FUTURE IS EVIL

LOOK GOOD . . . BE BAD

EVERS WANT TO BE HEROES; NEVERS WANT TO BE LEGENDS

INSIDE EVERY WITCH . . . IS A QUEEN

"Not sure this is what Lady Lesso had in mind when she made Sophie Dean," Dot quipped.

"Where is everyone?" Bossam asked, surveying the empty halls.

"At the meeting point," said Agatha.

"Or dead," Castor muttered.

Priyanka and Bossam paled.

Agatha knew Castor was in pain, that he was just being sour, but his words hung in the air as he limped towards the spiral staircases, leading up to Evil's dormitory towers. For a while, the only sounds in the whole castle were the dog's lagging footsteps, Bossam's and Priyanka's whispering, and Dot's chomping on chocolate carcasses of whatever insect or rodent crossed her path.

Agatha thought of those left behind at Camelot: Tedros . . . Nicola . . . Professor Dovey . . . Sophie . . . What would happen to them? Were they still alive? She stifled the panic just as it began. *Don't think about it.* Not when an entire class of first years was counting on her to keep them safe. She had to trust that Sophie would protect her friends at Camelot the way she was protecting Sophie's students at school.

Castor climbed the Malice staircase, laboring harder and harder.

"Look, my old room!" said Dot as they passed Malice Room 66.

"Everyone wanted that room since your coven lived there," Bossam pointed out. "It's famous."

"*Really?*" said Dot, agog. "Wish Daddy knew that."

"As soon as we get outside, keep your heads down and be quiet," Castor commanded, approaching the end of the hall. "Pirates see any of us and we're *all* dead."

Dot frowned. "But won't they see us when we jump into the—"

"Quiet starts now," Castor snarled.

He pulled open a door and they slipped onto a catwalk high over Evil's sludgy moat. Castor's body stayed flat to the ground as he prowled forward, the stone rails concealing him from the pirates down below. Agatha could see the red-and-gold lights of a sign, SOPHIE'S WAY, blinking over the walk that connected the School for Evil to the School Master's tower. As they proceeded, the sign shined a red spotlight on each of their faces, before blinking green and moving to the next, magically vetting them. Ahead, the silver spire loomed in shadow as Castor inched closer.

Pirates' shouts echoed below—

"No one inna Good towers!"

"Imma tear up the Evil school, then!"

"Bet they're cowerin' inna Blue Forest like mole rats!"

Castor slid across the catwalk floor on his stomach, approaching the School Master's window, ten feet over their heads. From this angle, Agatha couldn't see anyone inside the tower.

Castor paused beneath the window, breathing hard.

"It's a big jump, Castor. And you're hurt," Agatha whispered. "Can you make it? Without them seeing us?"

Castor gritted his teeth. "We'll find out."

Holding his breath, he sprung onto his paws and vaulted off the catwalk. His wounded leg buckled, pulling his jump short. His head grazed the wall and his stomach scraped hard across the windowsill, forcing a bellow of pain that nearly blew the girls off the dog's tongue, before Castor lunged up and dragged his legs over the edge into the tower, landing face-first on a plush white carpet.

"Yeh hear 'at?" a pirate yelled below.

"Hear what?"

"The dog, yeh fool! Heard 'im o'er there!"

Castor's fist opened, dropping Priyanka and Bossam. His mouth slackened, letting Agatha and Dot slide out in a spurt of drool. Then he gurgled a last moan of pain—"Tell my brother he can have the body"—and he passed out cold.

"Still breathing," Agatha heard Yuba say.

Flat on her back, she smeared drool out of her eyes and saw the entire first-year class crammed inside the School Master's tower, now Dean Sophie's lavish chamber, where they safely crouched beneath the window line so they wouldn't be spotted by the pirates below. Everywhere she looked there were students: jammed into Sophie's closet between shoe racks, peeking out from the mirrored bathroom, blinking owlishly from under the bed. In the corner, the Storian painted in its open book, its silver tip glancing back at Agatha before scribbling again, as if trying to keep up with the story.

Meanwhile, the teachers huddled around Castor.

"Arrow wound in the muscle," Yuba said to the others.

"Is he okay?" Agatha asked urgently, tossing Dovey's bag aside.

"Lost a lot of blood to get you here," said Princess Uma, tying her shawl around Castor's back leg to staunch the wound. "But he'll recover. Let him rest for now."

"*Rest?*" Agatha scoffed. "Pirates are trying to *kill* us. Call the stymphs! We'll fly somewhere safe—"

"And where's *that?*" said a familiar voice.

Agatha turned to Hester, spotlit beneath the glittery aquarium in Sophie's ceiling next to Hort, Anadil, Beatrix, Reena, and Kiko, all still caked in rubble from Camelot's dungeons.

"Every kingdom is on Rhian's side," Hester argued. "Where can we hide a whole *school?*"

"Plus, the Snake's Quest Map is tracking us," Anadil added, her arm bandaged.

"We don't even have enough stymphs to get us all out of here," said Hort.

"And even if we did, the pirates have arrows to shoot us down," Kiko pointed out.

"We're trapped," said Beatrix.

Agatha shook her head. "But . . . but . . ."

"Most of the wolves are dead, Agatha," said Professor Manley. "Rest probably escaped through the hole in my shield. That sorcerer must have helped the pirates break through; crystal balls can find weakness in any magic."

"Even more reason for us to get out of here, before another sorcerer comes," Agatha insisted.

"I sent the fairies to look for help in the Woods. Someone who can rescue us," Princess Uma advised. "In the meantime, the castle will defend itself against intruders. Our best hope is to hide here until they leave."

"And if they *don't*?" Agatha countered. "We can't just wait while monsters invade our school!"

"The only way to the tower is Sophie's catwalk, which is charmed to attack trespassers. Even if Rhian's men try to break in here, we're safe," Professor Anemone said, pulling pillows off Sophie's gold-veiled bed and laying them under Castor's head. "For now, the smart move is *no* move."

"If I know Sophie, she's at Camelot, doing everything she can to rescue our friends. She'd want me to do the same for her students, not sit around and hope we don't die!" Agatha challenged. "What if we mogrify and make a run for it?"

"First years haven't even *learned* mogrification," Professor Sheeks argued, "let alone how to control it under stress—"

"Or what if some of us distract the pirates while the rest of you run?" Agatha hounded, her voice shallowing. "Or what if we use a spell . . . any spell . . . There has to be something we can do!"

"Agatha," said Yuba sharply. "Remember the first lesson of Surviving Fairy Tales. *Survive.* I know you want to keep our students safe. But Emma and Uma are right: there is no move to make. Not yet." Agatha's eyes followed the gnome's to the Storian in the corner, halted over the open storybook and its painting of this very scene: the School Master's tower . . . the children hiding inside . . . the pirates down below. . . . The pen stayed completely still, a gleam at its tip, as if watching Agatha the way she was watching it. "You're like all the best heroes, Agatha. You think you lead your story," said Yuba. "You think you control your own fate. That the pen follows in your wake. But that's not always the truth. Sometimes the story leads *you.*"

Agatha resisted. "Defeating Evil means fighting for Good. Defeating Evil means *action*. You told me not to use the crystal ball. You told me not to send first years to Camelot. But that's how we saved people!"

"At what cost?" said Yuba. "Those left may be in even greater danger than before."

Agatha felt her stomach hollow. The gnome had spoken her

biggest fear: that in her effort to save Tedros and her friends, she'd ensured their doom. She turned to Hester, Hort, and the others who'd returned, waiting for them to reassure her. To tell her she'd done well. But they said nothing, their faces solemn, as if this was a question with no right answer.

Once upon a time, there'd been Good and Evil.

Now they lived in the in-between.

"I say we fight these thugs," said another familiar voice.

Agatha turned to Ravan, Mona, and Vex stuffed into a corner, along with other fourth years she hadn't seen since the Four Point, each of them bandaged and bruised.

"Ever since our quests, we've been trapped in the infirmary, with nothing to do but read books, search for clues about the Snake, and watch first years do *our* job," Ravan grouched, a book under his arm. "This is our school and we have to defend it."

"If you fight, we're fighting too," said Bodhi, crouched with Laithan and the first-year Evers.

"Us too," said Laralisa with the Nevers. "Between all of us, we have numbers on our side."

"So did the wolves," Hort retorted. "I'm not a coward, but I know pirates and they fight dirty. Everything about them is dirty. And Rhian has my girlfriend and Sophie and Dovey and Tedros. I know we need to save them. But we also can't rush out of here and die a stupid death. Because then they're really doomed."

The tower went quiet.

Agatha could see the mix of fear and courage in her school-mates' eyes, all of them locked on her as their leader.

She instinctively looked at Hester.

"This is your decision, Agatha," the witch said. "You're Queen of the Castle, here or Camelot or anywhere else. We trust you."

"All of us do," said Anadil.

Kiko and Reena nodded. "Me too," said Beatrix.

Hort crossed his arms.

They glowered at him.

"Okay, fine. I'll do what she says," Hort grumped, "as long as she doesn't kiss my new girlfriend like she kissed Sophie."

"Priorities," Dot wisped.

Agatha was lost in thought, gazing at her quest crew, depending on her as their leader . . . at her injured classmates, itching to go into battle . . . at the teachers, who were looking at her for directions the way she once looked at them . . . at the first years who would risk their lives on her command. . . .

She'd always been a fighter.

That's who she was.

But Good isn't about who you are. Her best friend had taught her that lesson once upon a time. Good is about what you *do*.

She took a deep breath and looked at her army.

"We wait," she said.

Everyone heaved a sigh of relief.

As they went back to whispering amongst themselves,

Agatha suddenly heard scratching from the corner. . . .

The Storian was drawing again, amending its painting of the tower.

Strange, she thought. Nothing in the scene had changed.

She crawled over to the Storian's table and slid up the wall, out of view from the window, so she could see what the pen was drawing.

The painting was the same as it was before: Agatha, the teachers, her friends, and the students hiding in the tower, while down below the pirates searched the shore. But the Storian was adding something else now. . . .

A blast of gold in the sky.

The beginnings of a new message from Lionsmane.

High over the Endless Woods.

Even stranger, Agatha thought, peeking out the window at the clear sky with no message from Rhian's pen in sight. *Why would the Storian draw something that isn't there?*

Agatha gazed at the night's blank canvas, listening to the pen behind her, presumably filling in the fictional message. It didn't make sense. The Storian recorded history. It didn't invent things. She felt herself tighten, doubting the pen for the very first time—

Then a flash of gold lit up the sky.

A message from Lionsmane.

Just like the Storian promised.

Sometimes the story leads you, the gnome had said.

As the light settled over the Woods, Agatha read Rhian's

new tale in the sky, praying it was still by Sophie's hand, praying she'd snuck another code into it—

She stumbled back in shock.

She read the message again.

"Agatha?" a voice said. "What is it?"

She turned to see her whole army quietly staring at her.

Agatha bared her teeth like a lion.

"We need to get to Camelot," she said. *"Now."*

He Lies, She Lies

Sophie stood at the edge of a black pond, swathed in white furs, a babushka wrapped over her hair, as she sprinkled sunflower seeds to a family of ducks.

In the dusty water, the dark sky reflected as if it was a scene in a crystal ball, the three-quarter moon tinged with red like a severed head. The crack of a hammer made her shudder and she looked up at the workers build-ing a stage on the Gold Tower hill, directly over the imploded hole exposing the dun-geons. Aran paced the stage, a dag-ger on his belt, his coal-black eyes fixed on Sophie through his helmet. Two maids flooded the stage with buckets of soapy water and scrubbed the wooden planks, siphoning the dirt into the grass, where it ran downhill, collecting in the pool at Sophie's feet.

Overhead, a new message from Lionsmane gleamed in the sky.

Due to the attack on the Blessing
by Tedros' allies, Tedros' execution
has been moved up.

The similarity of this attack to the
Snake's suggests Tedros and his allies
were in league with the Snake all
along, sabotaging your realms to make
himself stronger. The sooner he is
dead, the safer our Woods will be.

The Kingdom Council will witness
the execution at dawn and the traitor's
head will be mounted on Camelot's
gates for the world to see.

Sophie could feel herself holding her breath. It was the first message Rhian had written without her help.

Part of her wanted to admire Rhian. The boldness of his lies. The ambition of his Evil.

But she couldn't admire him. At least not until *his* head was mounted on that gate.

Wind blew through the holes in the fur that she'd salvaged from Madame Von Zarachin's scim-ravaged box and magically mended as best she could. A short while ago, she'd been about to get on Hort's stymph and escape this place. Holding Hort's hand, she'd tasted freedom. She'd looked into the eyes of a boy who cared about her, the *real* her, warts and all. She'd glimpsed what happiness could look like in a different life, a different story. . . .

But her story wasn't about happiness anymore.

It wasn't about her at all.

That's why she'd stayed behind.

Under her furs, the white dress itched at her skin, more urgently this time, grabbing her out of her thoughts.

Midnight had long come and gone.

In a few hours, Tedros would be dead. Along with Professor Dovey and five more students and friends.

How do you stop an execution?

How do you stop an axe from coming down?

She didn't even know where the prisoners were being kept, with Rhian sealing her under Aran's supervision while he met with the Kingdom Council inside the castle. The rulers of the Woods had descended upon Camelot for a week-long royal wedding, along with their servants and flunkies, packing every last inn and guesthouse, and now less than a day after they'd been dungbombed out of a church, they would gather for the beheading of King Arthur's son. Until now, they'd mostly sided with Rhian over Tedros, believing their new king to be a Snake-slaying saint. But Agatha's appearance in the sky had changed all that. Sophie had seen the rulers' faces outside the church, looking at Rhian with new doubt, new questions. He'd lied to them about her best friend's capture. He'd lied to the entire Woods. *What else had he lied about?* they must be wondering. . . . Surely this was why the Council had convened a meeting.

She glanced back at the castle, where she'd seen the leaders stream in before sunset, grim-faced and muttering to one another. There'd been no sign of them since.

Sophie's heart hummed faster. She had to tell them the truth about Rhian. About the Snake. About everything. They'd never have believed her before, these other rulers. Not after everything Rhian had done to save their kingdoms. But they might believe her now. She just needed to find a way to speak to them. . . .

The pond rippled as footsteps crackled in the grass behind her, a pale, copper-haired boy appearing in the water's reflection.

"*Crystal*," said Japeth, barechested in black breeches, his face and body scalded from Dot's boiling chocolate. "The first letters in your tales spelled out the word. That's how you communicated with Agatha about a crystal ball. Clever, I must say."

Sophie said nothing, watching the workers lay down an ornate block of dark wood, with a divot for a prisoner's head.

"When the Mistrals told us we were Arthur's sons, I didn't believe them," said Japeth. "It took a pen to convince me. A pen that showed Rhian and me the future. A future with *you*. You would be queen to one of us; your blood would keep the other from dying. Keep you at our sides and we'd be invincible. That's the future the pen promised." His cold breath shivered her neck. "Of course you're thinking: *Which* pen? Lionsmane can't see the future. So it must be the Storian. Except neither my brother nor I ever went to your precious school. So which pen could it be? That's the part you have to figure out, Clever Little Cat. Just like my brother had to figure out that girls can't be trusted, even his shiny new queen. He thought if he kept some of your friends alive, you'd fall in line. But now he sees what I've been telling him all along. The only way to keep a queen loyal is to keep her at the blade of fear. To *destroy* everything she loves. You think cleverness can save you. Despair cures cleverness. Pain cures cleverness. That's why your friends will *all* die now. My brother made the mistake of thinking you could be reasoned with, but he's learned his lesson. . . ." His lips touched her ear. "You can no more reason with a girl than you can with a Snake."

Sophie spun, glaring into his hateful blue eyes. "You think Agatha will let you kill Tedros? You think the school won't come for their Dean? They'll *all* come."

The Snake smiled. "We're *counting* on it." He flicked his tongue at her mouth—

Sophie punched him in the head, gashing open his temple with the diamond of Rhian's ring, sending blood spilling down his brother's blistered cheek.

Instantly Japeth seized her wrist and for a second, she

thought he was going to snap it like a stick. Sophie wrenched away, terrified—

But then she felt a familiar stab of pain and she turned to see her palm dribbling blood, a scim wiggling back into Japeth's suit . . .

. . . and the skin of his face and chest perfectly restored.

He backed away, grinning, as a black horse sprinted towards him, and he turned and swung onto it. Behind him, twenty pirates in black shirts, black breeches, and black balaclavas rode their own black horses, carrying swords, spears, and clubs. Japeth morphed into his black Snake's suit and looked up at Aran. "Take her to the castle. My brother's orders." Japeth lowered his gaze to Sophie. "The Kingdom Council would like to see her."

Sophie's eyes widened as the Snake and his pirates galloped down the hill and out the castle gates, nothing more than dark shadows against the night.

"King'll call when he wants ya," said Aran, bringing Sophie and her bandaged palm to the double doors of the Blue Ballroom.

A maid scurried over and whispered in Aran's ear. Something about the Map Room.

"Don't move a inch or I'll cut yer in half," Aran ordered, following the maid. He reached back and ripped Sophie's coat off her. "And this ain't part of your uniform."

Sophie knew better than to argue. But as soon as he was gone, she tiptoed up to the door of the ballroom and cracked it open, just wide enough to get a peek inside.

A hundred leaders were gathered in the castle's biggest hall, seated at a constellation of round tables that looked like moons orbiting Rhian's throne, gleaming on an elevated dais in the center of the room. As the king presided in a clean blue-and-gold suit, Excalibur on his waist, Sophie noticed that each ruler had magically emblazoned their name on the placard in front of them, the names blinking and quivering like moving pictures: THE SULTAN OF SHAZABAH . . . THE QUEEN OF RAJASHAH . . . THE KING OF MERRIMAN . . . THE GRAND VIZIER OF KYRGIOS . . . The ballroom, meanwhile, had been completely overhauled from the stale, crumbly space Sophie remembered: the walls and columns now retiled in mosaics of blue, the floor embellished with a gold Lion crest, and the ceiling fitted with a colossal blue-glass Lion's head that reflected the king's throne below.

"So you're admitting Agatha's capture was a lie?" said the King of Foxwood, gaping at Rhian.

"In Ooty, liars have all their clothes taken away and they must earn them back, one truth at a time," drawled an eight-armed female dwarf, sitting high on cushions. She was close enough to the door that Sophie could see she was wearing the same silver ring with carvings that she'd noticed on the Queen of Jaunt Jolie and the Elf King of Ladelflop at the church.

"Tedros may have been a coward, but he didn't lie," growled

the Wolf King of Bloodbrook, also flaunting a silver ring.

"Except about being king," said Rhian stonily.

"How can we be sure?" said the Princess of Altazarra, curvy and milk-smooth. "Tedros went to the School for Good like me, where you're taught *not* to lie. Clearly you went to a school whose standards were not as exacting."

"If you lied to us about Agatha's capture, then you could be lying to us about many things," said the horned King of Akgul. "This is why we want to talk to Sophie."

"And you will. I don't expect you to take my word, given what's happened. Not until I explain myself. In the meantime, I've sent my brother to fetch her," said Rhian, his eyes moving to the door. Sophie dodged so he wouldn't see her spying. The king turned back to his audience. "But now it's my turn to speak."

"We want to talk to Sophie *first*," demanded the Minister of the Murmuring Mountains.

"She'll tell us the truth!" the Queen of Mahadeva agreed.

"Camelot's own *Courier* suggests that Tedros is still the true king, not you," said the old, graceful Queen of Maidenvale, seated directly below Rhian. "There was no reason to believe them before, but your lies about Agatha give me pause. Indeed, there's even talk that you've kidnapped Sophie and that she still supports Tedros' claim to the throne. Until Sophie vouches for you and gives us proof that *you're* the king, how can we trust you—"

A sword shot through the air and impaled her table.

"*That* is the proof," Rhian thundered, his face reflected in

Excalibur's steel. "I pulled the sword. I passed my father's test. Tedros *failed*. He usurped the throne that belonged to me by right. And usurpers are beheaded by Camelot law. By all of your kingdoms' laws. As are traitors. I didn't hear your support for Tedros when he turned his back on your kingdoms while a Snake tore them apart. I didn't hear your support for Tedros when I was saving your children from being *hanged*."

The room fell silent. Sophie saw Rhian watching the Queen of Jaunt Jolie, the intended audience of his last line. The queen had lost the defiance she'd showed in the church, her head bowed, her throat bobbing. Sophie thought of the way Rhian had gripped the queen's arm, hissing into her ear. Whatever he'd said had made its mark.

"I lied about Agatha's capture because I hoped to have her in my dungeons before the people knew otherwise," Rhian declared to the Council. "Now that they know Agatha and her friends are free, they sense a threat to Camelot's new king. And that gives Agatha power. Power that endangers not only my kingdom, but all of yours too. So yes, I lied. I lied to *protect* you. But I can't protect those who are not loyal to me in return. And you cannot be loyal if you continue to wear those *rings*."

Leaders glanced down at the carved pieces of silver on their hands.

"Each of you wears a ring that pledges your kingdom's faith to the Storian and to the school that harbors it," said Rhian. "A ring that bonds you to the school and that pen. A ring that has been passed down in your kingdoms since the beginning of time. A ring that now puts you in danger. And I am telling you: if you want my protection, those rings must be *destroyed*."

Leaders murmured, a mix of amused chuckles and snorts. Sophie could see red rising in Rhian's cheeks.

"King Rhian, we've advised you repeatedly," said the Elf King of Ladelflop, "these rings keep the Storian alive—"

"Those rings are your *enemy*," Rhian assailed, standing from his throne. "As long as Agatha is free, she fights under the banner of that ring. She fights under the banner of the Storian and the school. She is a scheming terrorist. A rebel leader who will do anything to put her feckless boyfriend back on the throne, including attacking your kingdoms. Wear that ring and you are aligned against me. Wear that ring and you are as much my enemy as Agatha and her army."

The leaders looked skeptically at one another.

"You are right, King Rhian. Excalibur would not move from the stone for you unless the throne is yours," said the Empress of Putsi, wrapped in goose feathers. "I believe you are the true king and Tedros is a false one. No one can deny that. It is why we did not oppose your decision to punish him and his princess. But to imply Agatha is a 'terrorist' . . . that is a bridge too far."

"Especially considering *you're* the proven liar," said the Duke of Hamelin. "King Arthur once wore the same ring you want us to destroy. Then the Mistrals became his advisors and it was said that he destroyed his ring at their urging. That he destroyed Camelot's ring forever. It is why Tedros never wore it and why you never took possession of it. Arthur died an ignoble death. Burning his ring brought him nothing."

"Because he was too weak to recognize the enemy—" Rhian pounced.

"Or because he listened to voices like yours," the Duke lambasted. "Why should we believe you over thousands of years of tradition? Why should we believe you over a school that has taught our own children or a princess who is a hero in these Woods? Agatha may have colluded with a usurper, wittingly or not, but she is trained in the ways of Good. And the first rule of Good is that it defends, not attacks."

Rhian raised a brow. "Really?"

He thrust a glowing fingertip at the doors, which swung open, and a sparrow, a hawk, and an eagle flew in, each wearing the royal collar of a kingdom messenger and carrying a scroll in their talons or beaks. The birds dropped their messages to their patron leaders.

"A break-in at my castle," the King of Foxwood blurted, reading his scroll.

"Fairy nests set on fire in Gillikin," gasped the Fairy Queen, reading hers.

"My son has been wounded," said the Ice Giant of Frostplains, looking up from his scroll. "He says he escaped. They were masked men in black. Like the Snake."

"The Snake is dead," Rhian retorted. "But those who conspired with him are not. This is the work of Agatha and her school. She will do anything to dampen support for the real king, including disrupting the wedding and sabotaging your realms while you are all gathered here. Are you willing to see your kingdoms ripped apart again? After *I* put them back together?"

The gall of his lies made Sophie gasp. These were Japeth's attacks. She'd seen him ride off with his men. He'd attacked the Woods to help his brother win the throne and now he was attacking the Woods again to keep him there. And the sheer lunacy of the idea that it was her best friend behind it—

"Agatha? Attacking Gillikin? Attacking Foxwood? Two *Ever* kingdoms?" said the Ooty Queen, as if reading Sophie's thoughts.

"Except Agatha was spotted causing chaos in my kingdom just days ago," the Fairy Queen of Gillikin countered. "If fairy nests were burned tonight, it could very well be her doing."

"And I saw young boys in black masks at the church," added the Ice Giant of Frostplains. "The ones that set off the bombs. They could have been students from the school."

"Princess Agatha protects kingdoms; she doesn't hurt them," the Princess of Altazarra pooh-poohed. "All of us know her fairy tale!"

"The *Storian*'s version," the King of Foxwood piped in.

"The only version! The *true* version!" the Duke of Hamelin spouted.

"Sophie is Agatha's best friend," the Sultan of Shazabah cut in. "We need to hear from Camelot's future queen!"

"Hear! Hear!" piped the other leaders at his table.

This is my chance, Sophie thought, about to throttle in and expose Rhian—to scream the truth and save herself and her friends—

But then the King of Foxwood stood up. "My castle is being *attacked*! And all of you are worried about hearing from a Reader instead of trusting the king who saved *your* kingdoms!" He turned to Rhian. "You need to stop these terrorists at once!"

"Like you did the Snake!" the Fairy Queen pleaded.

"The rebels are moving east, my hawk tells me," said the Ice Giant of Frostplains, the bird perched on his shoulder. "They'll attack the Four Point kingdoms next. Then . . . who knows?"

The room went quiet.

No one was defending Agatha anymore.

Like a school of fish, Sophie thought. How quickly they turned.

"I'll commit my royal guard," the Queen of Mahadeva announced. "They'll find these rebels."

"My men will join yours," said the Minister of the Murmuring Mountains.

"I don't trust Never guards in my kingdom," said the King of Foxwood.

"Or mine," said the Fairy Queen of Gillikin. "And by the time you send word to your guards, the rebels will have sacked a dozen more realms. They know we're all here for the wedding. Our kingdoms are vulnerable and they're moving too fast for us to send alerts or mount a defense. We need King Rhian and his men to ride out at once."

Ripples of assent swept across the room, until all eyes were on the king.

"You want me to stop Agatha's attacks?" he said, reclining

in his throne. "You want me to risk my life and my knights? Well, then, I expect you to show me loyalty in return."

His fingertip glowed and a small blue fire appeared in front of each leader's face, flickering in midair.

Rhian's eyes smoldered with the reflection of a hundred flames. "Burn your rings," he commanded. "Burn your rings and pledge your faith to me over Agatha and her school. To me over the Storian. Then I'll help you."

The leaders froze, their eyes wide.

Rhian's gaze deepened. "All those who want my protection . . . burn them *now*."

Sophie's heart stopped.

The rulers scanned the room.

For a moment, none of them moved.

Then the King of Foxwood slipped off his silver ring and put it into the blue flame.

The ring melted—*crackle! whish! pop!*—and burst into a puff of white-silver smoke.

The Fairy Queen of Gillikin and the Frostplains King both glanced at each other. Neither took off their ring.

But the Queen of Jaunt Jolie did.

She slipped it into her fire.

Crackle! Whish! Pop!

Then a plume of white.

No one else followed.

The flames cooled and vanished.

"Two rings," Rhian said, toying with each word.

He turned to his guards. "Send men to protect Foxwood

and Jaunt Jolie from further attacks," he said, before looking back at the Council. "The rest of you are on your *own*."

Relieved, Sophie leaned against the door, thankful most of the rulers had resisted the king . . . only to see Rhian staring right at her, as if he'd known she was there all along. He swished his lit finger and the doors swept open before she could move back. She tumbled forward and crashed into the ballroom, landing hard on the marble floor.

Slowly she raised her eyes to the entirety of the Kingdom Council peering down at her.

"My love," Rhian cooed.

Sophie rose to her feet, the white dress burning at her skin more than ever.

"The Council has a few questions for you before today's execution," said the king. "Perhaps you can help them come to their senses."

Two guards subtly moved in behind Sophie. Beeba and Thiago. She could see their hands on their swords. A threat.

Sophie turned to the leaders, cool and composed.

"At your service," she said.

The Fairy Queen of Gillikin stood up. "Is Agatha our enemy?"

"Is the school behind these attacks?" asked the Ice Giant of Frostplains, rising too.

"Must Tedros die?" asked the Ooty Queen, standing on her cushions.

Sophie could see the fear in their faces. In all the leaders' faces. The tension in the room was so thick it squeezed at her throat, sealing her voice in.

All she had to say was one word.

No.

The pirates would kill her, but it would be too late. The Woods would know the monster that was on the throne. Tedros and her friends would be saved. Rhian would be thrown to the wolves.

Sophie took in the dead green glass of the king's eyes, the sneer of his lips. It was the same way Japeth had looked at her when he told her his brother would no longer play nice. Not after she'd used Lionsmane's messages to reach Agatha. But even so, Rhian still needed her. Her reassurance would make the rest of these leaders dance to his tune. Bringing her here was a risk, of course. But Rhian was betting on the fact that Sophie always did what was best for herself. That she'd stand behind him to stay alive. That her own life was more valuable to her than telling the truth.

Sophie glared back at him.

He'd miscalculated.

Rhian realized what she was about to do.

He launched to his feet, his face turning the color of Japeth's. Sophie opened her mouth to answer the Council—

Then she saw something.

At a table in the back, near the window. A man, dressed in a brown coat and hood, his face in shadow. He was playing with the silver ring on his hand, reflecting the moonlight, so it would catch Sophie's attention.

She saw the name on his placard.

Sophie's heart blasted like a cannon shot.

The hooded man gave her a sharp move of his head, telling her in no uncertain terms how to answer the leaders' questions.

Sophie searched the whites of his eyes, gleaming through the darkness under his hood.

She turned back to her questioners.

"*Yes*," she said. "Agatha is your enemy. The school is behind these attacks. Tedros must die."

The crowd thrummed like a shaken beehive.

Rhian gaped at Sophie from the throne.

Suddenly Aran accosted him, clutching a large scroll of parchment—

Sophie didn't wait to see what it was about. With Rhian distracted, she rushed into the room, heading straight for where she'd glimpsed the hooded man. But she couldn't see him anymore with the leaders crowded around tables, frantically conversing and pointing at their rings, their voices rising. Behind her, Rhian and Aran argued over a map—the Snake's Quest Map—except from this angle, it looked like all the figurines on it were . . . gone?

I must be seeing it wrong, Sophie thought.

But then she caught Rhian looking up, searching for her—

Sophie ducked along the rims of the tables in a squat, scooting towards the back of the room. She could see leaders streaming out the doors, asking maids to call their transports, while others remained in heated debate. She spotted the Ice Giant of Frostplains and the Queen of Gillikin together in the corner, conjuring a magical fire before burning their rings at the same time. *Crackle! Whish! Pop!*

"Sophie!" the Queen of Jaunt Jolie called, hurrying towards her.

Sophie dove under a table, crawling through a maze of legs and chairs, past jeweled boots and regal hems, hearing the sounds of voices and crackling fires and dozens more rings burning and popping, until she slid under the very last table and came out the other end, precisely where the hooded man had been sitting—

Only he wasn't there anymore.

All that was left of him was his royal placard, his name blinking and swirling on the front.

Sophie crumbled into his chair, her heart shrinking. Had she imagined him? Had she lied to the rulers for no reason? And lost her chance to save herself and her friends? Had she just ensured Tedros' death? She took the placard into her shaking palms.

That's when she saw it.

On the back of the card.

In tiny magical letters that evaporated as she read them.

MAKE HIM THINK YOU'RE ON HIS SIDE

Sophie looked up. Rhian was striding towards her, pirates flanking him.

Stealthily, she turned the card over, seeing the name of the man who had left the message in a forest-green script.

The King of Merriman

The last word morphed as it disappeared, winking like a changeling fairy. . . .

Merriman.
Merri man.
Merry men.

15

One True King

"Tedros will die unless we stop the execution," said Agatha, standing in the shadows of the School Master's window, Lionsmane's message glowing in the sky behind her. "And if he dies, the Woods belongs to Rhian. The Woods belongs to a madman. *Two* madmen. Our world is at stake. We can't let them win. Not without giving Tedros a chance to fight for his throne."

She took a deep breath. "But first we need to get out of this tower without Rhian's men seeing us."

Her army stared

back at her, packed like sardines into Dean Sophie's chamber.

"If Rhian plans to execute Tedros at dawn, then the other captives are in danger too, Clarissa included," Professor Manley said, eyeing his fellow teachers. "Agatha's right. We have to make a move."

Professor Anemone swallowed. "How many men are still down there?"

Agatha inched to the side of the window, between crouching first years, and peeked through. Some of Rhian's men roamed the grounds in front of the schools, hacking through lily beds with their swords, while the red and yellow flowers snared and strangled them. Through the glass of Good's castle, Agatha saw others prowling Hansel's Haven, smashing the candied halls, which belched sticky sugar in defense, gluing them to walls like flies in a web. There were more pirates skulking around the School for Evil, lighting smoke bombs in the corridors to snuff out their prey, only to have the bombs rebound and blast them off balconies. Alarms screeched from both castles as more magical safeguards activated, thwarting the guards' advance.

But for every man foiled by the school's defenses, there were ten more sliding through the hole in the shield over the North Gate, armed with weapons and brandishing lit torches against the dark.

"Agatha?" Professor Anemone pushed.

Agatha turned to her troops. "They're everywhere." She shoved down her panic. "We need to think. There *has* to be a way into the Woods without them seeing us."

"What would Clarissa do?" Princess Uma asked the teachers.

"She'd use every spell in her book to blast these goons," Manley spat. "Come on, Sheeba, Emma, all of you. We'll fight them ourselves." He made a move to stand up, but blue fire-bolts shot across the chamber, electrifying him and knocking him to the ground.

Agatha froze. "What in the—"

Then she saw where the firebolts had come from.

The Storian, pulsing with spidery blue static, over its open storybook.

"Teachers can't interfere in a fairy tale, Bilious," said Professor Sheeks, helping her trembling colleague sit up. "We can shield the school. We can fight alongside our students. But we can't do the job for them. Clarissa made that mistake and look where she is."

Wiping sweat from his face, Manley still looked shaken. But not as shaken as the first years, who now realized they were on their own.

The fourth years, meanwhile, were undaunted.

"What if me and Vex sneak out?" Ravan postured, a book in one bandaged hand, while his pointy-eared friend, leg in a cast, kept sniffing Sophie's scented candles. "We can mogrify and escape before they notice a thing."

"You're injured, first of all," said Hester. "And if they catch you leaving, that means the rest of us are dead meat. Otherwise Ani and I would have gone a long time ago."

"Me too, obviously," Dot pipped.

"And even if Hester and I could go, Rhian would see us coming on his map," said Anadil.

"Not if we switch swan emblems," said Bossam, pointing at the glittering silver crest on his black uniform. "If you guys wear these, the Map will think you're us and won't track you."

"Our emblems don't come off, you three-eyed monkey. Castor told us at the Welcoming. Look," Bodhi snapped, unbuttoning his shirt and disrobing, only to see the swan crest magically move and tattoo on his tan chest. "It's on our bodies at all times. That's the point of it. Right, Priyanka?" He flexed his muscles and Priyanka blushed.

"I could get it off if I tried," Bossam puled, giving Priyanka a wounded look.

"Just like you said you could find Priyanka during the Glass Coffin challenge, when Yuba turned all the girls into identical princesses?" Bodhi jeered. "Guess who found her instead."

"Lucky guess," Bossam sniffed. "And I'm not a monkey."

"No one's switching emblems and no one's leaving on their own," said Princess Uma firmly. "We have to stick together. The way lions do when they're attacked. No one left behind. That's our only chance to beat the pirates and save Tedros."

"There's more than two hundred of us," Hort pointed out helplessly. "Is there a spell to hide that many people? Maybe teachers can't interfere, but that doesn't mean you can't give us ideas."

"Invisibility can only be conferred by snakeskin," said Yuba, turning to Bodhi and Laithan. "Where's Sophie's cape? That won't cover more than a few of you, but the right few might be able to save Tedros and the rest."

Bodhi frowned at Laithan. His friend's shoulders sagged. "Lost it on our flight back," Laithan mumbled.

"What about Transmutation?" Priyanka asked. "The spell Yuba used to make all the girls look the same during the Glass Coffin challenge. We could transmute into pirates!"

"Highly advanced hex," the gnome replied. "Even fourth years would struggle to perform it, let alone first years, and besides, the spell only lasts a minute."

"We know weather spells, though," Devan proposed, gesturing to his classmates. "We could conjure a tornado and sweep us all to Camelot?"

"And kill half the Woods in the process," Professor Manley murmured, still convulsing slightly.

"What about the Flowerground train?" asked Beatrix.

"We'd have to get to the *ground* to call it," said Anadil.

Agatha tried to stay engaged, but all she could think of was Tedros being dragged onto a wooden stage . . . thrashing against the guards . . . his head slammed on a block as the axe swung down. . . . Fear suffocated her like a hood. Her friends and teachers could flail for ideas all they wanted, but there was no way out of here. There were pirates occupying every corner of the school. And even if they could get past them, they'd never make it to Camelot in time. It was at least a day's journey away and Tedros would die in *hours*—

"Agatha," said Hester.

Maybe I should go, Agatha thought. *Alone. Before anyone can stop me.*

She'd turn into a dove and fly out of here without Rhian's men spotting her. She could get to Camelot easily . . . though it wouldn't solve the problem of Rhian tracking her. . . . Even so, she trusted herself when it counted. And she knew Camelot better than anyone here. Still, stopping Tedros' execution on her own seemed like a fool's game. Too many things could go wrong and the stakes were too high—

"*Agatha*," Hester barked.

She raised her eyes and saw Hester looking at her. Along with everybody else.

No, not looking at her.

Looking *past* her.

She glanced down and saw the Storian paused over the story-book, its painting of the scene complete. The pen hadn't added anything new to the scene since it drew Lionsmane's message. But there was something different about the pen now. . . .

It was *glowing*.

An urgent orange-gold, the same color of Agatha's finger-glow.

As she leaned in, though, she saw it wasn't the whole pen that was glowing, but the carving along its side: an inscription in a deep, flowing script that ran unbroken from tip to tip. . . .

She didn't know the language, but the pen pulsed brighter while Agatha gazed at it, as if it *wanted* her to know. Then, very deliberately, as if aware that it had Agatha's attention, the Storian pointed at the storybook and a tiny circle of orange glow spooled from its tip like a smoke ring. Agatha stooped lower, watching the glowing circle drift around the painting like a spotlight, roving across the lurking pirates on the ground . . . then up the School Master's tower and through the window . . . past the huddling first years . . . and settling on the fourth years in the corner.

No . . . not all the fourth years, Agatha realized, peering closer.

One fourth year.

And it wasn't her.

Instead, the pen had picked a brown boy with long, matted hair, a bushy unibrow, and a surly scowl.

The glowing spotlight honed tighter on the boy, zeroing in on his bandaged hand . . . something *in* his bandaged hand. . . .

Agatha turned. "Ravan," she said, whip-sharp. "Give me that book."

Ravan gawked at her.

"*Now!*" Agatha hissed.

Startled, Ravan tossed it to her like a hot stone. "It's not mine! It's a library book! It was the only one with pictures instead of words! Mona made us search for clues about Rhian while we recovered—"

"Don't blame me, you illiterate fool!" his green-skinned friend berated. "Who carries a library book when running from murderers! No wonder you were so slow!"

"Tried to toss it along the way but the book bit me!" Ravan defended.

Agatha was already kneeling as she lit up the cover with her glowing fingertip, teachers hovering over her.

The History of the Storian
AUGUST A. SADER

Just seeing her old History professor's name calmed Agatha's heart. August Sader had never led her astray. Even after his death. If the Storian had pointed her to the book, then there was something she needed in its pages. Something she needed to win this fairy tale. She just had to find what it was.

She pulled open the cover and saw that like all of Professor Sader's books, the pages didn't have words. Instead, each page was streaked with a pattern of embossed dots in a rainbow of colors, small as pinheads. As a blind seer, Professor Sader couldn't write history. But he could *see* it and he wanted his readers to do the same.

"Is there a reason we're reading a crackpot's theory while pirates ravage our school?" Professor Manley growled.

"If it wasn't for August Sader, we wouldn't *have* a school," Professor Anemone chided.

"Bilious is right, Emma," Princess Uma added meekly. "As much as I loved August, his theory about the Storian has no proof. . . ."

Agatha tuned them out, thumbing through pages, but the

book was as thick as her fist. Where was she supposed to start reading when all the pages looked exactly the same?

Then, out of the corner of her eye, she saw the Storian glow brighter in midair.

Without thinking, Agatha turned a page, keeping her eye on the pen.

The Storian pulsed brighter.

Agatha turned more pages.

The Storian pulsed even brighter.

Agatha flipped through the book, faster and faster, the Storian glowing hotter, hotter, like the last flare of a sunset, its light ballooning through the entire tower. Agatha surged to the next page—

The Storian went dim.

She flipped back to the page before.

"This one," she breathed.

Far below, she heard the pirates. *"Light inna School Master's tower! Someone's inside!"*

Another answered: *"How we gonna git up there?"*

Inside the tower, teachers and students exchanged petrified looks.

Agatha was already running her fingertips across the dots on the page—

"*'Chapter 15: One True King,'*" spoke Professor Sader's voice.

Agatha swept her hand across the next line of dots and a ghostly three-dimensional scene melted into view atop the page: a living diorama, the colors gauzy, like one of Professor Sader's old paintings. Agatha could see the whole school crowding in to watch a vision of the Storian, twirling over the book.

"*From the very beginning of the Endless Woods, the Storian has been its lifeblood,*" Sader's voice narrated. "*As long as the Storian writes new tales, the sun will keep rising over the Woods, for it is these lessons of Good and Evil that move our world forward. But just as the Pen keeps Man alive, so too does Man keep the Pen alive. Each ruler wears a ring that pledges his or her loyalty to the Storian, carrying the same inscription as the pen's. A hundred founding realms in the Endless Woods. A hundred rulers. A hundred rings. As long as the rulers continue to wear these rings, the Storian will continue to write.*"

The scene zoomed in on the inscription, gleaming in the pen's steel.

"*For many years, the bond between Man and Pen was peaceful,*" Sader continued. "*But then rulers began to question what the inscription in their rings meant. It is not a known language of any kingdom. The inscription appears nowhere else. So the best scholars of the Woods studied the symbols and offered their own readings.*"

Over the book, the phantoms of three wizened old men appeared, their beards to the floor, holding hands in the School Master's tower. . . .

"*First, there were the Three Seers who brought the Storian to the School for Good and Evil for protection, believing only a School Master could prevent the pen from corruption by either side. These Seers testified the inscription was a simple edict:* 'THE PEN IS MAN'S TRUE KING.' *As such, the Storian was the Woods'* one true master, entrusted with preserving the balance. Man existed purely to serve the pen and should live humbly under its rule."

The scene atop the book changed: now a grisly war, soldiers of Good and Evil spilling each other's blood. . . .

"This theory held for hundreds of years until a King of Netherwood insisted his scholars had decoded the carving to mean precisely the opposite: 'MAN IS THE PEN'S TRUE KING.' According to these scholars, the Storian needed a master. The Woods needed a master. This, in turn, set off a series of wars between kingdoms, each vying to claim the Storian, only to see those victorious suffer a grisly fate. . . ."

Agatha watched as ruler after ruler triumphantly climbed the tower and seized the pen, only to be stabbed through the heart by it and pitched into the moat below.

"But then came the Sader line of seers, my ancestors, who proposed their own reading of the Storian's inscription."

Once more, the scene depicted the pen's strange symbols . . . only now they were shape-shifting into readable letters . . .

"WHEN MAN BECOMES PEN, THE ONE TRUE KING WILL RULE."

Agatha studied these words. She could hear pirates outside and harsh scrapes against the School Master's tower, like hooks or arrows hitting stone. Students moved away from the window, but Agatha kept her focus on the book—

"Leaders clashed over the meaning of the Sader Theory. Was the Storian encouraging Man to fight the Pen? Or was it ordering Man to bow to the Pen as King? The Sader Theory, then, only *added fuel to the fire that divided the Woods: Who controls our stories? Man or Pen?"*

The letters on the phantom Storian reverted to the unusual symbols.

"This battle raged for centuries until a new School Master, the Evil half of two twin brothers who presided over the School for Good and Evil, made a startling discovery. . . ."

The scene zoomed in on the inscription, revealing etchings *within* the carvings.

"Each symbol of the Storian's inscription was a mosaic of squares, and inside each square: a swan. One hundred swans in total, fifty of them white, fifty of them black, representing a hundred Ever and Never kingdoms in the Endless Woods. Taken together, the inscription included every known realm, Good and Evil, the entirety of our world reflected in the pen's steel."

A silver ring appeared over the book, the same inscription carved in its surface.

"In light of this, I proposed a new theory," said Sader. *"'When Man Becomes Pen' didn't mean that one should reign supreme, but that Man and Pen existed in perfect balance. Neither could erase the other. Neither could manipulate fate. Neither could force the outcome of a story. They had to share power for the Woods to survive. At last, the debate was settled. Who controls our stories: Man or Pen? The answer was: both."*

The silver rings multiplied in midair.

"The ring that each ruler wore, then, was an oath of loyalty to the Pen. As long as the rulers wore these rings, Man and Pen

would stay in balance, just like Good and Evil. But if Man were to forsake the Pen and deny its place . . . if all the rulers were to burn their rings and instead swear loyalty to a king of their own . . ."

The rings burned up in a burst of flames—

". . . then the balance would be gone. The Storian would lose its powers and this king would claim them. A king who would become the new Storian."

Out of the ashes, a human form rose, holding a new pen.

A pen glowing gold.

"This king, the One True King, would no longer be bound by the balance. He could use his pen like a sword of fate. Every word he'd write would come to life. With his power, he could bring peace and wealth and happiness to the Woods without limit. Or he could kill his enemies, enslave the kingdoms, and control every soul in the Woods like a puppetmaster does a puppet."

The shadow of the king grew, bigger, bigger, and in this shadow, a new scene played: three scrawny hags atop wooden boxes, preaching to passersby in the square.

"My theory was widely dismissed, likely because no one wanted to entertain the thought of a single Man possessing so much power. To reject my theory was to keep the rings and the balance of Man and Pen intact. And yet, there were some ardent believers: most significantly, the Mistral Sisters of Camelot, who King Arthur brought in as his advisors before his death. Other proponents included Evelyn Sader, former Dean of the School for Girls; Rebesham Hook, grandson of Captain Hook; and Queen Yuzuru of Foxwood, who believed she was the One True King. But in the

end, the solidarity of the Woods prevailed, their rings uniting them in trust of the sacred pen . . ."

The mist over the book began to dissipate.

". . . for now."

The chapter went dark.

So did Agatha's fingerglow.

Eyes met around the room, Evers and Nevers trying to decipher what they'd just heard. The whole school seemed to draw a collective breath.

"There's a catwalk to the tower!" a pirate shouted outside. *"Lookie!"*

"Get to the catwalk!" Kei commanded.

Pirate roars echoed over a low rattle of thunder.

"They found us," Kiko peeped, glancing at her scared friends and teachers.

Agatha leaned across the windowsill to get a look, but Hort snagged her back.

"That's how my dad died," he glared. "Doing something stupid."

"I don't get it. Storian knows we're in trouble. That's why it sent us to that book," Anadil muttered, rubbing her bandaged arm. "How did *any* of that help us?"

Agatha had the same question.

"I told you it's all malarkey," Professor Manley harrumphed. "No one knows what that inscription says. No one has the slightest clue. Just a bunch of guesses to suit those making them."

Except Agatha was considering the Storian now, its carvings still glowing as it hovered over the painting of this very scene . . . "Dot, what's that spell you used in the breezeway? The one that zoomed into the crystal ball—"

"Mirrorspell? That's *my* spell," Hester swiped, crawling towards Agatha, already anticipating what she was going to ask next.

"Show me the inscription," Agatha told her.

Hester pointed her glowing fingertip at the Storian and immediately a two-dimensional projection floated over the floor, magnifying the mysterious script.

On their knees, students and teachers gathered closer, gazing at the enlarged symbols . . . at a hundred tiny squares buried inside them like seeds . . . and inside every square, a black or white swan. . . .

"Just like the book said," Agatha pointed out. "Can't *all* be malarkey, then."

Only she noticed something.

Something different about the inscription from the way it looked in the book.

There were empty squares in it.

Two of them, to be precise.

Two blank boxes, where a swan should be, the glow in the carving darkened in those spots like missing teeth.

Suddenly there was a sharp noise and Agatha's eyes shifted further down the inscription.

A white swan had gone up in flames. It crumpled like burning metal—*crackle, whish, pop!*—

Then it vanished. Just like the two others.

Only now another swan was on fire. A black one.

Then five more swans . . . no, ten more . . . no, more than that, combusting too fast for Agatha to count—*crackle, whish, pop!*—as they disappeared from the Storian's steel.

"What's happening?" Professor Anemone said nervously.

It can only mean one thing, Agatha thought.

"They're burning their rings," she said. "The leaders are burning their rings."

Her heart pumped harder.

Everything Rhian had done . . .

Saving kingdoms from the Snake.

Picking Sophie as his queen.

Telling lies with Lionsmane.

He'd had a bigger plan all along.

"Camelot isn't what he wants," she said, hearing her voice tighten. "Rhian wants the Storian. To destroy it. To *become* it. To rule as the One True King."

"Horsecrap," Professor Manley scorched. "We told you there's no proof!"

"Then why did the Storian lead us to that book?" Agatha said intensely. "This is what it wanted us to see. Leaders are burning their rings. Something's happened. Something that's making them swear loyalty to Rhian over the Storian. Over the school. And it's that loyalty that keeps the Storian *alive*. If all of them burn their rings . . . if that carving disappears . . . then Rhian will control the Woods. Professor Sader's theory was *right*. That's why the Storian's doing more than just recording our fairy tale this time: it's jumping ahead . . . warning us of dangers . . . guiding us to clues. . . . Don't you see? The Storian needs our help. The Storian is *asking* us for help."

Professor Manley fell quiet. So did the other teachers.

"For a Man to possess the Pen's magic . . . even Rafal never managed that," said Professor Anemone, distressed.

"Rhian would be invincible," said Hort.

"More than that," Agatha warned. "You heard Sader. The One True King takes the Storian's powers. But under Man's control, those powers are unchecked. Rhian will be able to use Lionsmane to write whatever he wants . . . and *it will come true.* Imagine if everything Lionsmane writes could become real. If everything Rhian *wishes* could become real. You think he's going to give everyone in the Woods a sack of gold and a pony? No, he wants the Storian's powers for a reason. I don't know what that reason is yet, but I know it's nothing good. Not that we'll be around to see it happen. He can write that I've been eaten by wolves and wolves will come to devour me. He can write that the School has fallen and it will crumble to dust. He can destroy kingdoms. He can bring people back from the dead. All with the stroke of his pen. Rhian will have control over every soul in the Woods. He'll have control over *all* stories, past and present. Our world will be at his mercy. *Forever.*"

No one spoke as Hester's projection fizzled. Even the night air outside had gone silent, except for a misting rain, as if the pirates were listening too.

"Kiss my arse! All of you!" a voice yipped.

Everyone turned to hairy, three-eyed Bossam in the corner,

holding up his silver swan emblem, detached from his uniform.

"Knew I could do it!" he boasted. "Castor's strategies for training henchmen. You know, the ones we used in the Golden Goose challenge. Step 1: Command. Told the swans we're gonna die unless they helped us and if we die, they die too." He threw a dirty look at Bodhi and grinned at Priyanka. "Came right off."

Castor craned his head up, stirring. "Madman trying to control souls, whole Woods about to die, and you're diddling with your clothes."

The sound of pen scratching against paper cut through the tower—

Agatha spun to see the Storian writing again . . . adding to the same painting she'd thought was finished. . . .

This time, it was painting something on Sophie's Way, the catwalk between Evil and the School Master's tower.

The pen drew in slashes of lines, filling in slowly.

Rain misting over the catwalk.

And through the rain . . .

A shadow, Agatha realized.

Coming towards their tower.

Tall, hulking, with a black hat pulled low over the face.

It was carrying something over its shoulder.

Her stomach clamped.

"Pirate," she said.

Instantly students sprung up from the floor, backing away from the window—

Agatha turned and saw the shadow in real life, skulking

across the catwalk towards the School Master's tower.

With the rain pummeling harder, veiling his face under his black hat, she still couldn't see which pirate he was. Nor could she see what he was toting over his shoulder. He wore all black instead of silver chainmail, his leather coat flapping in the wind. *He must be of higher rank*, Agatha thought. *Like Kei.* The pirate moved with no hurry, his right leg slowed by a clear limp, his tall black boots snapping against stone.

Castor surged forward to attack, but the Storian shot a fire-bolt past his head and teachers grabbed him back. First years shielded behind them.

"The alarm on the catwalk," Professor Anemone rasped. "It'll catch him!"

On cue, red light beamed off the Sophie's Way sign, scanning the man's face.

The light turned green and let him pass.

"Or not," said Hort.

"Must have tricked it—" said Reena.

"This is ridiculous. We're not a bunch of geese about to be turned into a pie," Hester blazed. "There's one of him and a whole school of us." She turned to Anadil.

"Ready?"

"Even with one arm," Anadil replied coolly.

Hester's demon exploded off her neck like a firebomb, engorging with blood as it scudded through the window and slammed the pirate in the face. With a flying leap, Hester and Anadil dove out the window and tackled the thug to the catwalk.

"Wait for me!" Dot called, hurrying after them and hopping over the windowsill, only to trip onto the catwalk with a shriek.

Behind her, students gawked as Hester and Anadil wrestled the pirate.

"What are we waiting for!" Agatha snapped at them. *"Charge!"*

Her army let out a roar and throttled through the window to help their friends. As they besieged the villain with kicks and punches and amateur stun spells, Dot pushed through the crowd, knocking first years aside, determined to rejoin her coven and do her part. She jostled her way to the pirate, finger glowing, prepared to turn his clothes to chocolate licorice that would bind him like ropes—

She saw his face and screamed.

"STOP!"

The attack ceased, everyone spinning to Dot, confused.

All except Agatha, who now saw the pirate's bloodied, bruised face in the moonlight.

The pirate who wasn't a pirate at all.

"Daddy?" Dot gasped.

Curled up on the stone, the Sheriff of Nottingham squinted up at her, his wild hair coated with rain, his beard dripping blood, his right eye swelling. "I *really* don't like your friends," he snarled.

"What are you *doing* here?" Dot asked as she, Hester, and Anadil sheepishly helped him up, the Sheriff giving the latter two a hateful look.

His face contorted with pain as he ignored his daughter and looked right at Agatha. "If you want to save your boyfriend, we have to go *now*."

Agatha's chest tightened again, her eyes darting off the catwalk towards the castle. "Go where? There's no way out . . . there's pirates . . . they're coming . . ."

Except they *weren't* coming, she realized.

Because she didn't see any pirates at all.

Not on the catwalk. Not in the School for Evil. Not in the School for Good.

Every last pirate. Gone.

It's a trap, she thought.

"No time to faff around, Agatha," the Sheriff growled. "Rhian ain't just killing your boyfriend. He's killing all of 'em, Dovey included."

It hit Agatha like a kick to the stomach. She saw teachers pale around her. Hort too, scared for Nicola.

"Bring your best fighters," the Sheriff ordered, turning to leave. "Young ones and teachers stay behind to protect the school."

Agatha couldn't breathe. "B-b-but I told you! There's no way to get us out of here safely! Even if we could, there's no way to get us to Camelot in time—"

"Yes there is," said the Sheriff, turning back to her.

He raised his arm and held up a familiar gray sack, its ripped pieces stitched together, something squirming inside. His bloodied lips curled into a grin.

"Same way I took care of all those *pirates*."

16

What Makes Your Heart Beat?

I know where Merlin is.

He meant for me to find that clump of hair he sent with Anadil's rat. He knew I'd understand.

But what I know will come to nothing unless I tell someone.

Someone who can find Merlin if Tedros and I die. Someone out of Rhian's clutches.

I must tell them before the axe falls. But who? And *how*?

As soon as we're shoved out of King's Cove, these moldy sacks jammed over our heads, all I'm left with is my sense of smell and sound. I feel myself kicked up a staircase, my limbs knocking against the other captives. I recognize Tedros' solid arms and clasp his sweating hand before we're pulled apart. Bogden hushes Willam's whimpers; Valentina's and Aja's high-heeled boots clatter out of rhythm; Nicola's breaths start and stop, a sign that she's deep in thought. Soon my gown scrapes smooth marble walls, beetle wings rustling as they fall, and my knees buckle as I lurch onto a landing, my body drained from all it has endured. A minty breeze blows in, along with the scent of hyacinths. We must be passing the veranda in the Blue Tower, over the garden where the hyacinths grow. Yes, I hear the songbirds now, the ones outside the queen's bedroom, where Agatha let me rest when I came to Camelot.

But these senses aren't all I have to guide me.

There is a sixth sense that only fairy godmothers have.

A sense that churns my blood and makes my palms tingle.

A sense that a story is barreling towards an end that isn't meant to be, and the only thing that can steer the story right is a fairy godmother's intervention.

It is this sense that made me help Cinderella the night of the ball. It's this sense that made me force Agatha to look in the mirror her first year, when she'd given up on her Ever After. It's this sense that made me come to Camelot before the Snake's attack. My fellow teachers surely consider the last a mistake: a violation of the Storian's rules, beyond a fairy godmother's work. But I'd do it again. The King of Camelot will not die on my watch. Not just because he's king, but because he is, and will always be, my *student*.

Too many of my young wards have lost their lives: Chaddick, Tristan, Millicent . . .

No more.

And yet, what's my move now? I know there is one. I can feel my sixth sense burn even hotter. That familiar sting of hope and fear, telling me I can fix this fairy tale.

The fairy godmother's call.

There *is* a way out of this.

I wait for the answer, my nerves shredding. . . .

Nothing comes.

Tedros grunts near me as he jostles in frustration against his guards. He's realizing we've been beaten and there's nothing standing between him and the axe.

The breeze gusts harder from multiple sides, the smell of morning dew thickening, and for a moment I think we're outside the castle, death ever-near, only to realize there's still marble beneath my feet. The others aren't thinking clearly; I hear their panic—Willam's whimpers turning to sobs, Valentina hissing and cursing, Tedros' boots skidding, trying to stall—

Then it all stops.

My guard has let me go.

And from the silence around me, I know the others are free too.

I hear a sack pulled off someone's head.

Then Tedros' voice: "Huh?"

I whip the sack off myself, as do the others. We have the same dazed expressions, our hair laced with potato dust.

We are in the Blue Tower dining room, looking out over a veranda, the sky the color of amethysts, warning of dawn. The long dining table is made of glass mosaic, the shards of blue forming a Lion's head in the center. Laid out around it is a magnificent feast. Seared venison cut into pink hearts atop green broad beans. Marinated rabbit kidneys with emerald parsley. Hen's eggs perched on buttermilk biscuits. Chilled cucumber soup with sungold tomatoes. White caviar, sprinkled with chive blossoms. Chocolate mousse swimming in vanilla foam. A bloodred grapefruit consommé.

There are seven place settings at the table, each labeled with one of our names.

We stare at one another like we've detoured into a different story.

The guards are mostly gone too. Only a pair in full armor remain, one blocking each door.

Then like a kick to the gut, I understand.

So does Nicola.

"It's our last meal," she says, gazing over the balcony's stone rail.

We gather behind her, looking down at the execution stage atop a hill, burnished in the moonlight. There's a dark wooden block in the middle of it.

Tedros' throat bobs.

Two shadows suddenly glide overhead and Sophie passes on the catwalk above us. She's walking with Rhian, speaking to him in a whisper. I only glimpse her face for a moment: she looks calm and engaged, as if she's going with Rhian of her own accord. Her hand is on the king's bicep. She doesn't see us.

Then she's gone.

The room falls silent. Tedros looks at me. Seeing Sophie strolling with Rhian so intimately has shaken him further. As it has me. My young charges sense my unease.

"Come," I say, with a Dean's authority, taking my place at the table.

Not out of hunger or a desire to eat; my body feels weak beyond the possibility of replenishment. But I need them to keep their wits. And I need time to think.

No one follows me to the table at first. But Tedros isn't one to resist food and before he can help it, he's dumped himself at Bogden's place setting and is stuffing deer meat into his mouth, his eyes still brimming with fear.

Soon the rest are eating too, until their bellies are sated long enough for them to remember who served this meal and why.

"He's mocking us, isn't he?" Willam asks meekly.

"Fattening a pig before it's slaughtered," says Bogden.

"We can't just stuff our faces like it's a *quinceañera* and go die!" Valentina fumes.

"We have to do something," Aja seconds.

They instinctively look at Tedros, who glances between the pirates at the doors, inscrutable through their helmets, both wielding swords. We have no weapons. To attack them would lead to a faster death than the one already scheduled. Yet, they're listening to everything we say, as if Rhian's not only taunting us with food, but the hope of escape. The gears in Tedros' head are turning, knowing any plan he speaks out loud will be thwarted before it starts.

And then, as I'm looking at him, I feel it once more.

The sting of an answer.

Surfacing quickly . . . about to break through . . .

But again, nothing comes, like a ghost afraid to show itself.

"Do you have a fairy godmother, Professor?" Tedros asks, his face creased with stress. "Someone who saves *you* when you need it?"

I want to tell him to be quiet. That I'm close to something. That I need to think—

My sixth sense stirs once more.

But this time, it's pushing me to answer Tedros' question. To tell him my story.

Why?

Only one way to find out.

"Yes, even fairy godmothers have their own guides," I say, glancing out the window at the lightening sky. My tone is strained, my pace rushed. "I graduated from the School for Good as a leader, but I resisted my quest assignment: to kill a nasty witch who was luring children to her gingerbread house."

"Hester's mother?" Nicola asks.

"Indeed. If I had gone on my quest and succeeded, Hester never would have been born. Hester's mother didn't give birth to Hester until much later, thanks to dark magic that let her have a child at an unusually old age. But the reason I rejected my quest was simple: I had no instinct for violence, even against a child-eating witch. It was Merlin who changed my fortune. Merlin was a frequent guest teacher at the School for Good, and my fourth year, he'd been guest teaching Good Deeds after the original professor ran afoul of the Doom Room beast. Upon taking a shine to me as his student, Merlin told Dean Ajani that there was no reason for him to keep filling in when the Dean had a perfectly fine Good Deeds teacher in me. Because of Merlin, the Dean changed my quest and made me the youngest professor at the School for Good."

"So Merlin is your fairy godmother?" said Bogden. "Or father. Or whatever."

"No," I say, dipping deeper in my memory. "Because I wasn't fully fulfilled as a teacher, it turns out. Not even as a Dean, when I received that honor years later. A piece of me knew I was meant for more. I just didn't know what that was. Ironically, it was King Arthur who changed my fortune next."

Tedros gawks at me, mouth full of biscuit. "My father?"

I can feel myself settling into the story. As if the past will unlock the present.

"After you were born, your father commissioned a teacher from our school to paint your coronation portrait. Arthur loathed his own coronation portrait so much that he wanted to ensure you had one he approved of, since he wouldn't be alive when you became king. That teacher not only painted your portrait as Arthur asked, but also brought me along when he did."

"So King Arthur was your fairy godmother?" Willam says, agog.

"Wait a second," Tedros cuts in, heaping chocolate onto his plate. "Lady Gremlaine said a seer painted my portrait, which makes sense since he predicted exactly what I would look like as a teenager, but now you're saying it was a teacher—" His eyes startle like rippling pools. "Professor Sader. *He* was the seer who painted my portrait?"

"And your father and I watched every brushstroke," I add, remembering it had happened in this very room, spring flowers blowing in through the veranda. "Arthur had asked August to bring along the Dean who would one day teach his newborn son, no doubt to make me feel the burden of the future king's education. Guinevere kindly let me hold you, though you were fussing and giving me trouble, even then. Your steward, Lady Gremlaine, was there too, though she hardly said a word. When your mother left with you, I sensed a sadness in Lady Gremlaine and I found myself talking to her more than the king. Idle talk mostly, about how she missed seeing her sister's sons grow up and how I wished I'd had siblings of my own . . . but my attentions brightened her mood. Professor Sader noticed. On the way back to school, he mentioned that he was impressed with how I'd handled Gremlaine; that it took skill to connect with a person so forlorn. I had the sense he knew her well. Then August said he thought my talents as a teacher and Dean weren't being fully used. That I might consider being a fairy godmother to those in need. I dismissed the idea at first; I hadn't the slightest clue what it took to be a fairy godmother and it seemed like tedious work, chasing down sad saps and granting wishes. But August is persuasive and he made me a crystal ball, using a piece of his soul and mine. A crystal ball that showed me people in the Woods who needed help. *My* help. And I found myself answering the call. For the first time in a long while, I had a life beyond the School for Good and Evil."

"So it wasn't Merlin or my father. It was Professor Sader," Tedros realizes, so entranced he's finally stopped eating. "*He* was your fairy godmother."

"Professor Sader set me on my path," I answer. "It's his face that appears when I look in my crystal ball. At least until it broke. Now it's a glitching mess."

"Who broke it?" Aja prompts.

"August, believe it or not!" I shake my head. "You'd think a seer could see an accident coming, but he knocked it off my desk, chipping a big piece. Offered to make me a new one, but he died shortly thereafter. Merlin's repaired it as best he can, but it's changed. You saw its effects on me . . . my lungs haven't recovered. . . ."

"Then why were you still using it?" Nicola asks.

I ignore the question. That answer is between Merlin and me.

"Truth is, I didn't need a crystal ball to be a good fairy godmother," I say. "Seeing into people's hearts. That was always my strength. Not magic, which was Lady Lesso's. I'm sure she could have done wonders with a crystal ball. Indeed, I would have named Leonora my Second if August hadn't cautioned me against it."

I notice one of the pirates yawning. Something inside me sparks, as if I know at last why I'm telling this story. As if I know where it's headed. I stare intently at my frightened pupils.

"But now that I'm older, I realize that August wasn't my fairy godmother after all. Because fairy godmothers can't swoop in and change the story. Fairy godmothers only help you to be you. *More* you. I wasn't there when Agatha looked in the mirror and realized she was beautiful. I wasn't there when Cinderella danced with her prince. But each of them knew what to do at the time. Because I taught them the same lesson I'm teaching you now. When the real test comes, no one will be there to save you. No fairy godmother will hand you the answers. No fairy godmother will pull you from the fire. But you have something stronger than a fairy godmother inside of you. A power greater than Good or Evil. A power bigger than life and death. A power that already *knows* the answers, even when you've lost all hope."

I see my students looking at me now, their eyes unblinking, their breaths held. The pirates are listening too.

"There is no name for this power," I say. "It is the force that makes the sun rise. The force that makes the Storian write. The force that brings each of us into this world. The force that is bigger than all of us. It will be there to help you when the time is right. It will give you the answers only when you need it and not before. And whenever you lose it or doubt its existence, like I have again and again, all you have to do is look inside yourself and ask . . . *What makes my heart beat?*" I lean in. "That is who your real fairy godmother is. That is what will help you when you need it most."

The room is quiet.

I wait for a response. A sign that they understand.

Instead, most furrow and frown as if I'm speaking in tongues. The pirates go back to yawning, bored by an old woman's ravings.

But someone *does* understand.

Sitting at the other end of the table.

Tedros, who returns my gaze, his eyes twinkling like Cinderella's and Agatha's once did.

A prince awakened.

Nothing spoken after that could have possibly mattered.

WHEN THE TIME comes, none of us put up a fight.

The guards storm in, rip us from our feast and bind our hands with rope. The tattooed pirate in charge of Tedros cuffs a rusted collar around the prince like a dog and drags him by a leash. They shove us out of the dining room, through the hall, and across a catwalk to a staircase that leads down to the courtyard. From the courtyard, it's only a short walk to the executioner's stage, sitting atop a hill that slopes to the drawbridge and outer gates. A halo of gold rises behind the castle, the sun minutes from breaking through.

The first years are shivering, their eyes on the stage ahead, where a big-bellied, black-hooded man in a black leather vest and leather kilt takes practice swings with his axe. As we get closer, the hooded man sets his gaze on us and grins through his mask. The first years shrink into their skins.

But not Tedros.

There's something different in him now. Despite his slashed clothes, beaten-up body, and the tattooed pirate yoking him with his leash, the prince looks stronger, like he's more resolved in his fight. Our eyes meet, and I get that tingling feeling again: the conviction that I can fix this. That there is a way out of this death trap.

And then I realize . . .

Each time I've had the feeling, I've been looking at *Tedros*.

He gives me a curious glance, as if he knows I've figured something out.

In front of the stage, their backs facing the castle, a hundred leaders from around the Woods have gathered in their finest clothes. They must have traveled to Camelot for Rhian's wedding, only to see death added to the menu of festivities. We come from behind and for a moment, I see them before they see me. The first thing I notice is how haggard they look, as if they've been up all night. They speak in hushed tones, their faces grim beneath their crowns and diadems. The second thing I notice is that many are missing their rings: the silver bands that mark them as members of the Kingdom Council. Dread pits in my stomach. It's my instinct to look for these rings. The School Master taught Lady Lesso and me to check for them when a ruler asked to meet with us (usually about a relative they wanted admitted to the school). These rings, pledging loyalty to the Storian, are the best proof a king or queen is who they say they are. But now half of these rings are gone? Rings worn without exception for thousands of years?

I hear a scrap of conversation—

"My castle has been firebombed," says a woman I recognize as the Empress of Putsi, who pushed me to accept her son into Good. "As soon as I destroyed my ring, Rhian sent his men to Putsi and the attackers fled."

"I thought you and I agreed to *keep* our rings," the Duke of Hamelin retorts, still wearing his. "To protect the Storian. To protect the school."

"The school is *behind* these attacks. You heard the king," the Empress defends. "I didn't believe it before, but I do now. My people come first."

"Your *castle*, you mean," snipes the Duke.

The Empress is about to respond when she sees us coming. The other leaders spot us too, as we curl towards the steps leading up to the stage. From the looks on their faces, it's clear that they've either forgotten we were imprisoned or they didn't know it was more than Tedros who would die today. And when they see me—Dean of Good, fairy godmother of legend, protector of the pen that keeps our world alive—their eyes widen in recognition. . . .

And yet, none move.

They just stand there, tethered in place, as if the same reason they're not wearing their rings also precludes them from helping me and my charges.

I stare at the Princess of Altazarra, who once bawled in my arms when the boy she loved betrayed her to win a Trial by Tale her first year at school.

She looks away.

Sheep, I scorn. Rhian has the people's support and no ruler dares challenge him, even if they know better. Every one of these leaders lives in fear of what's about to happen to me happening to them, only at the hands of an angry mob instead of a king. Which means, even though I teach their sons and daughters, even though I've taught many of *them*, they won't stand up for me or my students.

We're dragged up creaking wooden steps to the stage, where the guards hold us in a line at the back, facing the chopping block and the audience below. A pirate is sharpening steel pikes and stacking them at the side of the stage.

I count seven.

"What are those for?" Aja murmurs on one side of me.

"Our heads," says Nicola on the other, her eyes on Lionsmane's message in the sky, ending with Rhian's promise to mount our skulls for the Woods to see.

Next come the maids, in their white dresses and bonnets, who roll out a long gold-trimmed carpet patterned with lions, leading up to the stage.

Guinevere is amongst them, one of Japeth's gruesome scims sealing her lips.

Tedros flushes red when he sees his mother in a maid's out-fit and the Snake's slithering worm on her face, but Guinevere looks right at her son, her eyes smoldering. The glare disarms him as it does me. It's the same look Lady Lesso used to give me before the Circus of Talents when Evil had a new trick up its sleeve.

Then I notice something in Guinevere's hair. Tucked behind the ear, standing out against the white strands . . . a stray purple petal, unusual in shape.

A lotus petal.

Strange. Lotus blossoms don't grow in Camelot. Nowhere near it. They only bloom in Sherwood Forest. . . .

But now the king approaches, his princess on his arm.

The crowd of leaders swivels to watch Rhian glide down the gold carpet, Excalibur on his belt, as he and Sophie make their way to the stage.

Rhian sees their faces, still stunned by the added execu-tions, and he calmly stares back. That's when I understand: this execution isn't about Tedros or his allies. Not really. This is about threatening every leader here: if Rhian can cut off the head of Arthur's son and Good's Dean . . . then he can cer-tainly cut off any of theirs.

The wind picks up, sweeping blades of grass across the hill. Sunlight spears past our shoulders, dawn anointing the copper-haired king and his princess with light.

Sophie grips Rhian like a crutch, her movement stooped and submissive. She's wearing a white ruffled gown, even more prim than the maids'; her hair is tied back in a staid bun; and her face is bare and humble, though as she ascends the stage on Rhian's arm and I get a closer look, I sense she's painted herself to look that way.

As she takes her place beside Rhian at the front of the stage, she glances back at me, but there's nothing in her eyes, as if the shell of her is here, but not her spirit.

I'm hit with déjà vu—

Not of Sophie, but Guinevere. That day I met her with her newborn son, when August was painting Tedros' portrait. While Lady Gremlaine fixed her attentions on Arthur, her eyes so soulful, Guinevere was dead-eyed and distracted. As if she was only playing the part of Arthur's wife.

Now Sophie has the same look as she holds on to a boy who is about to kill her friends and fellow Dean. Her gaze flits around the field, searching for someone. Someone she can't find. Rhian senses her inattention. Instantly, Sophie's demeanor changes: she gives him a doting smile, a caress of his arm.

I peer at her closely . . . then back at the lotus petal in Guinevere's hair.

No doubt about it.

Skullduggery's afoot.

Tedros studies me once more, knowing I've sleuthed something out—

Again that sting hits, telling me he's the key to a happy ending. Like the mirror was to Agatha or the pumpkin I used to send Cinderella to the ball. It's Tedros I need.

But for what! What am I supposed to do! What good is a

sixth sense if we have no heads! I hold in a scream, my chest imploding—

Rhian clutches Sophie tighter as he addresses his audience.

"For a brief moment, after the Council meeting, I couldn't find my princess." He gives Sophie a look; her eyes glue to her dull, flat, highly suspect slippers. "Then I saw her, sitting calmly by the window. She said that she'd needed a moment to think. That she'd had the same doubts all of you had at the meeting. Was the school the enemy? Should you destroy your rings? Must Tedros die? But she'd looked you in the eyes and answered yes for a reason. I'd pulled Excalibur from the stone and Tedros hadn't. That alone earned me the crown. For Tedros to no longer command the sword that he flaunted at school was proof that he was only a pretender."

I see Tedros' eyes flick to Sophie. He's glowering at her the way he used to in class. Back when she was trying to kill him.

"But there was more, my princess said," Rhian continues, Excalibur shining against his thigh. "She told me that Tedros was her friend. She'd even loved him once. But he'd been a poor king. He'd been the rot at Camelot's core. Arthur's will was clear: the one who pulls the sword is king. For Sophie to fight for Tedros even after I pulled the sword was to fight against Arthur's will. To fight against the truth. And without truth, our world is nothing."

The rulers of the Woods are quiet. The tension in their faces dissolves, as if Sophie's words have reminded them why they've traded their rings for a king.

"Now I know she's truly on my side," Rhian says, gazing at

his princess. "Because she's willing to sacrifice her old loyalties for what's right. She's willing to let go of the past and be the queen the Woods needs." He raises her hand and kisses it.

Sophie meekly meets his eyes, then steps to the side of the stage.

Glaring at her, Tedros is foaming at the mouth. He believes every word Rhian has said about Sophie. So do the other captives, judging from their expressions. They believe Sophie would trade our lives to save her own. I almost do too.

Almost.

Tedros looks at me once more, seeking a mirror for his rage, but his guard is dragging him forward now.

"Bring me the impostor king," Rhian declares.

Tedros is thrown to his knees, the prince's neck slammed over the wooden block, hands still bound, as Thiago tears off his metal collar. It happens so fast Tedros can't resist. Breath flies out of me. Time is slipping away. And I'm still frozen, like those sheep in the crowd.

Rhian bends down to Tedros.

"Coward. Traitor. Fraud. Any other king would kill you with pride," he says. "But I am not any other king. Which means I'll give you one chance, Tedros of Camelot."

Rhian lifts Tedros' chin.

"Swear your loyalty to me and I'll spare you," he says. "You and your friends can live out your days rotting in my dungeons. Speak your words of surrender and Lionsmane will write them for all to see."

Tedros searches Rhian's face.

The offer is real.

A humbled enemy is worth more to Rhian than a dead one. Sparing Tedros makes Rhian a merciful king. A Good king. Sparing Tedros makes Rhian a Lion instead of a Snake.

King and prince lock eyes.

Tedros spits on Rhian's shoe. "I'd rather give you my head."

Good boy.

The king goes a dark shade of red. He stands.

"Kill him," he says.

The executioner skulks forward, both fists on the axe handle, the leather flaps of his vest slapping against his hairy belly. I try to think harder, to will a plan into being, but I'm distracted by a young maid, shoving a basket beneath Tedros' head, before stepping back into line next to Guinevere and the other maids.

Tedros raises his eyes to his mother, who hardly looks at him, her gaze hollow. But the veins in her neck are pulsing, her body stiff as stone.

The executioner looms over Tedros, while Rhian speaks—

"Tedros of Camelot, you are hereby charged with the crimes of treason, usurpation, embezzlement of royal funds, conspiracy with the enemy, and impersonating a king."

"Those are *your* crimes," Tedros hisses.

Rhian kicks him in the mouth, crushing Tedros' cheek against the block.

"Each of these crimes carries a penalty of death," says the king. "Losing your head is only a fraction of what you deserve."

The leather-hooded man runs his fat fingers along Tedros'

neck, pulling down his collar and exposing his flesh to the sun. He touches his axe blade to the prince's skin as if to measure his stroke, all the while maintaining a lustful smile.

That's when Tedros looks back at me, petrified, realizing that I've lied. That there isn't a greater power within that can save him. That he's going to die.

My heart swoops like a diving hawk. I've failed him. I've failed us all.

The executioner leans back and swings the blade high over his shoulder. It comes crashing down towards Tedros' neck—

A crow skims his head, knocking him off-balance.

Screams rip through the crowd.

The executioner swivels, as does Rhian, but a demon's coming too fast, slamming through the crowd like a bullet, blasting leaders aside, before it bashes into Rhian's face, throwing the king off the stage and wrestling him downhill.

Time slows to a dream. As if Tedros is dead and my mind is masking it. I *must* be imagining this, because not only is a red-skinned demon biting and smacking Rhian like a rabid bat, but there's also a magic carpet floating down over the stage—less a carpet and more a sack, its billowing sides stitched up—with two figures standing atop, like marauding pirates. . . .

The Sheriff of Nottingham.

And . . . Robin Hood?

Together?

I see Robin grin down at me: the same bumptious grin he flashed when he wanted to avoid punishment at school. Then he raises his bow and lets an arrow fly—

It hits the executioner in the eye, who falls instantly, dropping his axe, missing Tedros' head by an inch.

Another arrow flies, stabbing the pirate holding me, spilling his blood onto my dress.

Time returns to full throttle.

From inside the sack comes an army—Agatha, Hort, Anadil, Hester, Dot, and more—who dive-bomb the pirates holding the captives onstage. All are armed for battle, like warrior angels, except Agatha, who has nothing but my old bag, the outline of my heavy crystal visible through the fabric. Within seconds, they subdue the pirates and sever their friends' binds, setting Nicola, Willam, Bogden, Aja, and Valentina free.

Meanwhile, Sophie's already hiking her dress and fleeing the stage into the frantic crowd, as if this is everyone else's battle but hers. I try to track her, but now I see the pirate Thiago lunging towards Tedros, who's still bound to the chopping block—

Agatha is on the pirate with a panther's speed, swinging the bag with my crystal ball like a mace and crushing Thiago in the ribs. Gasping, he kicks her in the chest, knocking her off the stage. Thiago collapses to his knees, reaches for his sword, and with his last dregs of strength, raises it above Tedros' spine, the prince still flailing against the block.

"*TEDROS!*" Agatha cries, too far to get to him—

Two pale hands grab Thiago from behind and break his neck with one twist.

Guinevere tosses his body aside. Then she seizes his sword, tears the scim off her lips and hacks it to shreds, crushing the remnants with her shoe. While she cuts Tedros loose with the goo-covered sword, she sees Agatha and her son gaping.

"I'm a knight's wife," she says.

Tedros grins at her, then spots Rhian in the grass, still thrashing at Hester's demon on his face. As his mother knifes into his binds, Tedros pins his eyes on the king, his face hardening, his muscles tensing, like a caged lion about to be unleashed. But now Tedros sees Agatha climbing to her feet, her eyes on Rhian too. The instant Tedros is free, he leaps off the stage, seizes his princess, and presses his lips hard against hers, before looking her in the eyes—

"Run. Somewhere safe. Understood?"

"Is that an order?" she says.

"You bet it is."

"Good, because I never listen to those."

Agatha's already sprinting towards Rhian, but my bag on her arm slows her down. Tedros cuts in front of her—

"He's mine!"

He flying-tackles the king, rips Hester's demon off him, and punches Rhian in the face. Reeling, Rhian goes for his sword but Agatha swipes it off his belt and flings it down the hill while Tedros keeps smashing the king's head into the ground.

I shake off my daze and realize my hands are still roped behind my back, preventing me from doing magic. Even so, we're on our way to victory, with Rhian's thugs outnumbered. I scan the stage around me—

Robin targets pirates' hands with arrows and the Sheriff wrangles their bodies into his enchanted sack. Nicola, meanwhile, conjures a storm cloud over Wesley's head, which zaps him with lightning, before Hort cuffs him with the rusted collar that leashed Tedros. A pirate comes barreling at Hester, swinging the axe; Hester levitates him into the air, while Anadil levitates the chopping block, before the two witches magically smash the block and pirate together (Dot turns the axe to chocolate). Kiko mogrifies into a skunk, sprays Beeba in the eyes, who writhes right into Beatrix and Reena's rope. Ravan and Mona hold up a wooden plank they've stripped off the stage, while Valentina climbs it like a tree and shoots spells at pirates from overhead. Even Willam and Bogden have somehow bagged a rogue of their own.

But I don't see Sophie fighting for us.

I don't see Sophie at all.

For a moment, I find myself wondering whether what Rhian said was true . . . whether she sold Tedros out to save her own skin . . . whether she switched sides after all. . . .

"*Watch out!*" Aja cries.

I wheel around and see bodies rushing the stage—leaders of the Woods, the strongest and most able, along with more guards from the castle and Camelot's gates—who launch into battle in defense of Rhian. If they needed proof the school is a menace, its students terrorists, we've given it to them. The Ice Giant of Frostplains sweeps Agatha and Tedros into his ice-blue fists and catapults them at the stage, knocking Robin and the Sheriff down like bowling pins. Beneath the giant, Rhian struggles to his knees in the grass, the king's face a mess of blood.

Like a second wave, Hester, Anadil, and Dot hurtle at him, fingerglows ready, but the Ice Giant spins towards them, hoisting Hester's demon up by a leg, poised to tear it apart. Hester blanches and stops short, Anadil and Dot too. The Ice Giant thrusts out a finger, magically freezing the witches into blocks of ice. He freezes the demon too, tossing it to the girls' side.

Rhian's recovering now . . . limping towards Excalibur. . . .

Onstage, the Fairy Queen of Gillikin slings off her crown, revealing a hive of whip-tailed fairies, who sting Robin and the Sheriff into submission before lifting them up and dropping them down the Sheriff's own sack. Pirates tie up Beatrix, Reena, and Kiko's skunk, while Hort lights up his fingerglow, about to morph into a man-wolf, only to be pummeled by the Elf King of Ladelflop, who shoves him to the ground next to Nicola, who he's already bound.

At the same time, I glimpse a pirate sword abandoned on the stage and duck to my knees, trying to cut myself loose—

A flurry of goose feathers and sweaty weight crushes me. "Your thugs attack my castle and you think you'll get away with it?" the Empress of Putsi bleats, squeezing my throat.

"Rhian's thugs . . . ," I wheeze, but she isn't listening, her face engorged red, her breath smelling of sausages.

As she strangles me, I see the sword close and inch my fingers onto its hilt, but I can't breathe with the Empress's buttocks on my chest, her nails jamming my windpipe. I scrape the swordblade against the rope cuffing my hands. My lungs, already weakened, are collapsing now. My mind fogs black, my field of vision shrinks. . . .

"You didn't take Peeta into your school," she boils. "Peeta, a real prince who would have challenged Tedros and warned us he was a fake! But you didn't take him. Because you wanted to protect Tedros. Just like you're protecting him now—"

The rope breaks over my wrists.

My eyes meet hers. "I didn't take your son . . . because he's . . . a . . . *fool*."

I stab a finger and shoot her off me with a blast of light, her shrieks resounding down the hill.

I try to stand, but I'm still choking for air. Around me, our team is beaten back as dozens more pirates surge into battle.

Where are they all coming from?

The enchanted sack, I realize.

Gillikin fairies are pulling them out from inside, biting their binds loose.

The Sheriff must have caught these pirates into his sack, only to now have them used against us.

One of these pirates—the captain, Kei—drags Robin and the Sheriff out of the Sheriff's sack too, where they'd just been held by the fairies. Both are tied at their hands and feet, and the captain shoves them down onto the stage with the rest of our defeated team, where guards and leaders assail them and my students with weapons and fists. Attacked from all sides, they shrink into the middle of the stage, collapsing on top of each other like lambs mauled by wolves. Agatha and Tedros are the only ones still standing, swinging desperately at Rhian's men—Agatha using the bag on her arm, Tedros brandishing his knuckles—but they're both felled in seconds, crashing backwards onto the heap of bodies. Robin, the Sheriff, Guinevere, Hort, the witches, our entire *fleet*: they're flailing on the ground, surrounded by the enemy, a pile of flesh being pounded into the stage.

No one bothers with me, the frail shrew who can't even get up.

Then I see Rhian, stalking towards the stage, blood caking his face like a mask, the Ice Giant at his side. Rhian's heading for my students, Agatha and Tedros in his crosshairs, Excalibur in his hands.

I will myself to my knees, still dizzy. I have to save them. I have to save the king . . . the *real* king. . . .

But as I plant my hands on the stage's planks, something glows through the gaps in the wood.

Green eyes flashing like a stowaway cat's.

"*Sophie*," I gasp.

"Shhh! Is it over yet? Is Rhian dead?"

"No, you spineless twit! We're all about to die! You have to help us!"

"I can't! Robin left me a message! He said to make Rhian think I'm on his si—"

She freezes. I do too.

The Queen of Jaunt Jolie is gaping at us from behind the stage, watching me and Sophie conspire like friends instead of enemies.

Sophie turns on me with fire. "You think you can trap me here under the stage while my king fights alone! You shriveled dragon! I'd rather die than abandon my love!" She raises a glowing finger and blasts me with a stun spell, shooting me backwards off the stage and crushing my flank against hard dirt.

Sophie tried to soften the blow, but magic follows emotion and her fear made the spell worse. The pain is red-hot, as if I've been impaled by a firebolt. My ribs are cracked, my lungs cast in iron. I try to suck air into my throat, but my ears are ringing with a tone so high and strident that I can only grit my teeth. My spirit dims like a dying candle, my heartbeat slackens, as if this is the last my body can take, as if there's no coming back from this.

But I have to fight. No matter what it costs.

I turn my head in the dirt and pry open my eyes, my head feeling like a melon that's been dropped from a tower. Water clouds my vision and I blink, struggling to see what's in front of me.

The Queen of Jaunt Jolie is gone.

But Rhian's storming towards Tedros now, the prince exposed at the top of the prisoner pile, pirates bludgeoning him. Rhian hurls his guards aside and, with a snarl, swings Excalibur at his rival's chest—

Sophie crashes into Rhian, acting as if she's been helplessly pushed in the mayhem, sending Rhian careening onto the mound of bodies. Pirates and leaders try to extricate the king from the pile, the Ice Giant leading the efforts, while Tedros, Agatha, Hort, Robin, and others try to wrest Rhian back, their only leverage against a sure death.

Meanwhile, Sophie keeps throwing pirates aside so she can pretend to help Rhian, mewling *"My king, my love!"*, only to let go anytime she has a firm grip, dropping him back into the cesspool of bodies. More pirates trying to save the king get pulled into this hellpit, including the Ice Giant, who topples like a tree, smashing into the stage. Wooden planks shatter and the platform implodes, sending every last soul, friend and foe, plunging to the grass and rolling down the hill. Flying wood obliterates the frozen blocks with Hester, Anadil, Dot, and the demon, who slide out of the ice and plummet down the slope with the rest. As bodies pile up at the base of the hill like a human bonfire, those defending the king meld with the students defending the school, fists and limbs flying, screams rising up like a smoke cloud, until I haven't the faintest clue who is who.

Except one.

A prince glowing in the sun, gold hair matted in sweat, blue eyes afire as he fights for his kingdom, his people, the way his father once did, a Lion amongst kings.

Then it comes.

The answer I've been waiting for.

Floating out of my soul, like a pearl.

Not an answer, but a spell.

A spell that Yuba uses for his Glass Coffin challenge. A

middling, magical gimmick, but now, as I watch Tedros fight, it comes to me like water in a desert. The spell pulses at my fingertips, demanding I intervene.

I know the Storian's rules. This is beyond a godmother's work. This is changing the course of a fairy tale.

But it must be done.

I see everything that is about to happen, as if my mind's eye is my real crystal ball. Yet there is no fear of what is to come. Only certainty that I'm on this field for a reason. That I came to Camelot to be here now. To do what I'm about to do.

Down the hill, Agatha and Tedros crawl for Excalibur, orphaned in the dirt, their friends and the pirates locked in muddy free-for-all around them. Sophie is racing alongside Tedros to get to the sword too, but he sideswipes her, knocking her into Agatha, taking both girls down and slowing his own progress. He realizes his mistake. Rhian lunges from the other side of the sword, his hand clasping the hilt—

I raise my shaking finger and with all the will I have left, I shoot a blast of white light into the sky, which rains down as sparkling dust, touching every friend and enemy, every pirate and prince and queen and witch, every single body on the battlefield, including mine.

The war stops.

No one moves.

Because I've turned us all into Tedros.

Fifty Tedroses, with the same bloodied mouth and black eye, the same shredded shirt, the same stunned expression.

No one can tell who's who.

But I can.

I know people's hearts.

And I also know that this spell will sustain for only a minute before we revert into our bodies.

Some of the Tedroses stir with recognition.

They remember this spell.

They remember how long it lasts.

Which is why they start to run.

Hort, Hester, Nicola, Beatrix, Kiko . . . My former students too: Guinevere, Robin, the Sheriff . . . All my Tedroses sprint for the drawbridge, baffling the pirates and leaders, who don't know whether to chase these Tedroses or escape with them. More of my Tedroses join the flight—Aja, Anadil, Dot, Valentina, Ravan, Mona—dashing for Camelot's gates and the freedom of the Woods.

Sophie is the last to run, dragged off by Robin, who she must recognize from his cap, because she doesn't fight. She peeks back anxiously as if panicked by the thought of being free . . . of saving herself while leaving so many Tedroses behind. . . .

Only two of my Tedroses don't flee, looking just as dazed as the enemy Tedroses around them. The two Tedroses I knew wouldn't run, not without finding each other first.

I'm already on my feet, stumbling downhill, my broken body masked by Tedros' form.

Thirty seconds left.

I push myself to run faster, even as I feel myself fading. I rush into the crowd of bewildered Tedroses and grab Agatha by her tattered shirt, the bag with my crystal still on her arm—

"It's me," I whisper, hearing my voice as Tedros', deep and assured.

Agatha's princely face softens. "Tedros?" she mouths.

I clasp her arm tightly. "Spell breaks in twenty seconds. Get Dovey. Take her into the Woods. She'll lead us to the Caves of Contempo. That's where Merlin is."

I can see the other Tedroses zeroing in on us. We're the only ones talking.

"What about you?" Agatha presses.

"If we run together, Rhian and his men will know it's us. I'll meet you at the old League hideout in one hour. Then we'll go to the caves."

"I can't leave you—"

"You will if you want me to stay alive," I say, my glare so sure it quiets her. "One hour. Go. *Now.*"

"Which one is Dovey?" Agatha breathes.

I point to the real Tedros.

"That one," I say, watching him claw out from under a pile of clones, scanning the field for his princess. "Get Dovey to the Woods. We need to rescue Merlin." I reach for her bag, determined to get my crystal away from her. "I'll take this."

"*No*," Agatha retorts, wrenching it back with more strength than I can challenge. Her steeliness burns through her prince's blue eyes. "One hour or I'm coming back for you."

And then she's running, diving for Tedros and seizing him

by the wrist and dragging him towards the Woods, thinking it's me. Tedros doesn't resist, either because he knows it's Agatha or because it happens too fast for him or anyone else to understand—

But Rhian sees them.

His Tedros knows exactly what's happening.

He won't let them get away.

His eyes fly to his sword on the ground.

He bolts for Excalibur—

I'm there first.

I hold up King Arthur's sword to the boy who claims to be his son, the boy who thinks he's king, the boy who pulled this sword out of the stone and who I could kill by its tip.

But I've only killed for one person in my life.

A friend I still haven't learned to live without.

Rhian doesn't deserve such a fate.

I have other ways.

"*This* is Tedros!" I declare to Rhian's men around me, pointing Excalibur at the king. "This is the impostor! This is *him*!"

An army of Tedroses converge on the king.

Rhian backs up. "No . . . wait . . . *he's* Tedros. He's him!" Then he gapes at me, his self-assurance cracking beneath Tedros' facade. "But if you're Tedros . . ." He looks back at Agatha and the prince, hurtling for the Woods. "Then who are—"

"Get him!" I cry.

"No!" Rhian screams.

But it's too late. The hyenas taste blood. His men besiege him.

I sink to my knees, Excalibur spilling out of my hands into the grass, my body drained of life despite its veneer of youth. Inside, my lungs wither. My heart falters. My eyes cloud as if I'm already far away.

As Rhian is crushed beneath his own mob, I look back at my two Tedroses, helping each other over the gatehouse wall that separates the castle from the Woods.

Suddenly they freeze, as if something in their touch has given it away. Agatha stares at the real Tedros in horror before she spins to me, the Tedros who tricked her, left behind on the battlefield—

The ground shudders, followed by the echo of hooves.

A dark horse streaks across the hill like a specter.

Its rider is blacked out by the sun as he crushes through the Tedroses assailing the king, shattering their bones and spraying them aside, before he swings off his saddle and sweeps the broken Tedros into his hands.

Crouched over the king, the shadow touches Rhian, as if he knows who he is beneath Tedros' face. His fingers run along Rhian's bruised, bloodied chest, feeling it rise and fall, alive with breath.

Gently, he lays the king down.

Then his cool blue eyes find me like sapphires in a cave.

He moves quickly, a black fog, like Death itself.

As he stands over me, his face comes into focus.

Japeth bares his teeth, his cheeks flecked with Rhian's

blood, his fists gnarled with murder.

He pulls Excalibur out of the grass, my princely face reflected in its steel.

Behind him, I see my two Tedroses sprinting to save me—

I give them a smile.

A smile that tells them I'm at peace.

This is what I've chosen.

This is what I want.

They run faster, harder towards me. But it's too late.

"Little boy who thinks he's a man. Little boy who thinks he's a king," Japeth seethes at me. "You tried to kill the one I love and now look at you. On your knees, bowing down to my brother. Bowing down to the *real* king."

I turn my smile on Japeth.

"No Snake will ever be king," I vow.

He puts his face to mine. *"Long live Tedros."*

With a roar, the Snake swings the sword for my neck.

I look boldly into his eyes, reverting to my true form.

His eyes flare in shock as the blade hits—

I shatter to a million crystals, spraying into the air, each filling up with a youth I've never known before they disperse, like seeds that will grow in a new time.

What's left of me rises like a mist, filling in stronger, deeper than ever before, higher, higher, the colors growing more vibrant around me like an aurora, until I'm awash in a swirl of celestial glow. . . .

And then, as I look up, I see someone waiting.

Someone who's waited patiently for me all this time.

Just a little bit higher.

There is no fear of flying. No temptation to turn back.

I lift into the light, my soul laid bare, as Leonora Lesso bends down and wraps me in her arms like the wings of a swan.

17

AGATHA

The Only Safe Place in the Woods

Two Tedroses jumped over the gatehouse wall, throttling for the Woods beyond the castle.

"Hurry!" the real Tedros panted, dragging his clone past the gatehouse, emptied of guards, who were still on the battlefield.

Tears streamed down Agatha's cheeks as she hugged the Dean's bag to her muscled flank, her thick thighs and broad shoulders hampering her run. Blood and welts streaked their bare chests, though her prince looked far worse. A strange déjà vu seeped into Agatha's grief, as if she'd lived this scene before—

All at once, the spell broke and she melted back into her own body, her tattered dress reappearing with a borrowed swan crest, her shoulders smaller, her legs more nimble.

But the crush of emotions was still the same.

"Dovey . . . ," she choked. "Tedros . . . she's . . . she's . . ."

"I know," he said, his voice rigid. He pulled her into the Woods, past the first line of trees, raining waves of red and yellow leaves. She could hear his heavy grunts, every part of his body wrecked. The only solace was that they'd left Rhian in far worse shape. Brambles hooked onto her dress and Tedros' breeches, their shoes slipping on heaps of dead autumn fronds.

Alarm bells pealed from Camelot's belfry, followed by a stampede of hooves.

"Run faster!" Tedros barked, his cheeks blotched red.

Agatha knew his anger wasn't for her. His anger was pain. His anger was guilt. The Snake had killed his best friend, his knight, and now his Dean, and Tedros had been powerless to stop him. He'd tried to save Dovey. Agatha had too. But Dovey hadn't intended to be saved.

Even so, they hadn't gotten away scot-free.

Japeth had seen the two Tedroses lunge for the Dean as she fell.

He'd known it was Agatha and her prince from the way they'd tried to save her . . . from the horror on their faces. . . .

Now the Snake and his men were coming for them.

"We can't outrun horses," Agatha fought, resisting Tedros' pull. "We need to hide!"

Hooves echoed over the drawbridge. They'd be here any second—

Agatha saw a steep downslope to the east, blanketed in fallen leaves. She wrenched Tedros towards it, who gleaned her plan, dashing for the hill and yanking Agatha behind him. Light faded around them, the treetops blocking out the sun.

Chasing her prince in the dark, Agatha felt despair overwhelm her.

Professor Dovey was dead.

Her fairy godmother.

The Dean who'd known Agatha was Good before she herself ever did. The voice that had lifted her from the darkness when she had no hope.

Dovey had given her life to let them survive. To let them fix this story and find its real end.

Just like Agatha's mother had, once upon a time.

All those she'd looked to as family: Callis, Professor Sader, Professor Dovey . . . One by one, they'd been felled by her story.

But not without purpose.

The thought hit Agatha like a wind to a sail, propelling her forward, even as the tears fell.

Dovey had sacrificed herself to save her students.

To save Camelot's true king.

To save the Woods.

She'd known her body was weak, her time coming to an

end. She'd known that Agatha would rise in her place. That her ward would never rest until the real Lion was returned to the throne.

Agatha's tears burned to fire.

Professor Dovey had known her too well.

Horses crashed into the Woods, their legs trampling leaves with staccato crackles. Agatha glanced back at a cavalry of men wielding torches and swords—

"There they are!" the King of Foxwood cried.

Horses veered in Agatha's direction, their riders' blades shining.

"Come on!" she gritted, surging ahead of Tedros and dragging him the way he'd dragged her, the hill ten yards ahead. Startled by her strength, Tedros tripped, losing his balance as the riders closed in, swords raised—

Agatha grabbed him by the waist and threw him off the slope, Dovey's bag cinched under her arm as she and her prince tumbled together, sucking in screams, before landing hard in a dune of dead leaves. Agatha hugged Tedros' sweat-soaked body, towing him beneath the red and gold pile, their bloodied skin camouflaged—

Horses soared over them, riders flashing torches like spotlights, before the steeds slammed down and galloped into the darkness.

The Woods went quiet.

For a long while, neither of them moved, their breaths puffing leaves into the air. Agatha clung to Tedros, her face in his neck, smelling that hot, minty scent her body knew so well.

Wet blood dampened her arm and she couldn't tell if it was hers or his. Slowly her breaths deepened, her nose to his skin, with every inhale remembering that she was still alive and so was her prince. Tedros' arm slid around her. She spooned closer, her hand tracing his stubbled chin and down to the cuts on his neck where the executioner had measured his blow. His throat quivered beneath her palm, tears pearling at his eyes.

"I love you," he whispered.

She kissed his bottom lip. "I love you too."

There was nothing else to say. They were together now. And despite everything that had happened, to be together even for a moment was an ember of light in the ashes.

Then she remembered something, so sharply it knocked the air out of her—

"Dovey told me where he is!"

"Who's he?" Tedros murmured.

"Merlin! She told me when she pretended to be you!"

Tedros jolted up. "Where is he?"

"The Caves of Contempo! We have to find him!"

"Caves of Contempo? Agatha, that's thousands of miles away! Past the frostplains, past the desert, past the man-eating hills. . . . It's a walled-off island in a poisonous ocean. We can't get to the caves, let alone inside them, and especially not with a million people hunting us!"

Agatha's hope withered. "But . . ."

A branch snapped.

Tedros launched out of the leaves, sweeping his gold finger-glow across the trees. "Who's there?"

Agatha leapt next to him, her glow lit.

A shadow stirred behind a tree.

"Make one move and I'll kill you!" Agatha spat.

"Oh, I doubt that," the shadow replied smoothly, prowling into the open. "Because we both know I'd kill you first."

A glow sparked in the dark, pink and hot as a sunset.

"And I really don't want to kill you after we've come all this way," said Sophie.

She grinned at Agatha.

Agatha gasped and ran towards her, Sophie practically buckling from the force of her embrace.

"I didn't think I would ever see you again . . . ," Sophie breathed. "You don't know what I've been through . . ."

"Never again," Agatha whispered. "Never again will we be apart. Swear to me."

"I swear," Sophie said back.

They held each other closer, welling tears at the same time. Sophie pulled away. "And Dovey?"

Agatha shook her head. A sob choked out of her.

Sophie's face lost its blood. "To let you get away."

Agatha nodded.

Her friend wiped her eyes with her ruffly white dress. "I knew. She was the only one who could have cast that spell. And when you three didn't show up in the Woods, I knew she'd stayed to help you . . . that she'd do what she had to for you to be free. That's why I came back . . . to find you . . . to find *her*. . . ." She looked at the bag on Agatha's arm. "That crystal must have weakened her more than we thought. She was dying and I think she knew." Sophie sniffled, tears lit pink by her glow. "She used every last drop of her life to save us."

"Dovey told me where Merlin is," Agatha said, composing herself. "But there's no way to get there. At least not yet. We need to find the others and search for a new hideout. Somewhere we can plot our next move. Last I saw, Robin was pulling you into the Woods. Where is he? Where are Robin and Guinevere and—"

But now Sophie was watching Tedros. The prince hadn't moved from the base of the hill, his arms folded over his bare chest.

"Hello, Teddy," said Sophie. "Strange saying that when just a moment ago I *was* you."

Tedros' eyes flashed like cut gems. "Now you come crawling back? After everything you said about me to that monster? That I'm a rot at Camelot's core? That I should *die*?"

Sophie's lips pressed into a line. "I'm here, aren't I?"

"Yeah, but whose side are you on?" Tedros spewed back.

Agatha turned on her prince. "Sophie pretended to be on Rhian's side. She said what she had to so he wouldn't suspect anything—"

"Don't bother, Aggie," Sophie said starkly. "A Dean is dead, *his* Dean, and he's thinking about himself as usual. And they say *I'm* Evil. I dove into that battle to save him. I stayed behind after the jailbreak to save him. I endured two monsters to save him, one of whom sucked my blood, and here he is, questioning my loyalty."

"You don't think I mourn for Dovey? You don't think I

feel responsible? Don't you dare make this about her!" Tedros retorted. "This is about the fact that no matter how Good you play, I still don't trust you, not with the things you said about me and not when you had a chance to free me from the dungeons and you freed Hort instead!"

"Freeing you would have led to you dying even faster than you almost did, you rock-brained oaf!" Sophie hissed.

Tedros looked confused. He stood up straighter.

"Then tell me it was all a lie," he insisted. "Everything you said about me to Rhian."

Sophie gazed at him keenly . . . then walked away. "I don't even remember what I said, to be honest. I was too focused on keeping you and your princess alive. But if you're this touchy, then there must have been a kernel of truth in it. Hurry, Aggie, before Rhian's men hear this buffoon shouting and come and kill us all. We still have miles to go and they're waiting for us."

"They?" Agatha asked. "Who's they?"

Sophie didn't answer.

Agatha hurried after her, leaving Tedros by the hill, still scowling.

She knew she should wait for him, that she should be the peacemaker between her friend and prince like always, but Agatha was already latching onto Sophie's arm, the two of them whispering and cuddling as if they'd never been apart. Sophie brushed the hair out of her best friend's face and smiled brilliantly at her, two girls forging through a dark wood.

It wasn't long before they heard Tedros' footsteps behind them.

"WHERE ARE WE going?" Agatha badgered.

"The only place in the Woods where we can be safe," Sophie replied, her voice low. "I need you to tell me everything that happened after you escaped."

Agatha thought they might be headed for the old League of Thirteen hideout, just like Professor Dovey urged, but then she remembered the League had disbanded and their den was nowhere near Camelot. Dovey had just wanted her and Tedros to get as far away as possible before the spell broke.

"Is your safe place the school?" Agatha nudged. "Because that's the first spot Rhian will look for us—"

"No," said Sophie tersely. "Now answer my question."

"Let me see your Quest Map. It'll show me where everyone is."

"No, it won't," said Sophie, pointing at the swan crest on Agatha's dress. "Not as long as it thinks you and the others are first years. When Robin and I escaped together, he told me you switched crests to fool the Snake's map."

"But his map will still show you and Tedros! You two don't have crests! That means Rhian can still see you! He can find us, wherever you're taking us! There *is* no safe place in the Woods—"

"Aggie, do you trust me?" Sophie said.

"Of course—"

"Then stop changing the subject. Have you learned anything new about Rhian and Japeth?"

Agatha's chest tightened. She needed to know what had happened to Robin, the Sheriff, and the rest of their team. She needed to know how she could possibly elude Rhian, with his map tracking her and Tedros' every move. . . .

But Sophie's stare was unyielding.

Agatha took a deep breath.

She told Sophie what she'd read in Sader's book while Sophie told her what she'd endured at Rhian's side, Agatha peeking back every so often at her prince. They moved stealthily, three silhouettes against the forest, taking cover at any sound of horses, but never seeing them appear. Agatha's gut gnarled with hunger and she needed water, but Sophie distracted her with more questions.

"So you're telling me that if a hundred rulers destroy their rings, Rhian will claim the Storian's powers," Sophie prompted. "Lionsmane will become the new Storian. Anything Rhian writes with it will come true, no matter how Evil. He can kill me with a penstroke. He can kill all of us. He'll be invincible."

"That's what Sader's prophecy says," Agatha replied.

"But plenty of leaders still have their rings," said Sophie. "They challenged Rhian at the Council meeting. Not everyone is ready to declare war on the school."

"After what we just did on the battlefield, that may change," Agatha muttered.

"Wait a second . . . *Robin* had a ring!" Sophie exclaimed. "At the meeting. He flashed it at me. That means we're safe. He'd never burn it!"

"Must have been a fake or you saw wrong. Sherwood Forest

isn't an official kingdom," Agatha dismissed. "First-year geography test in Sader's class, remember? Robin can't have a ring."

"But I swear I . . ." Sophie deflated, doubting her memory. "So there's no one we can count on? No leader who will hold the line?"

Agatha gave her an empty look.

"How badly was Rhian beaten by his men?" Sophie asked, trying to sound hopeful. "There were a lot of them. Maybe he's . . ."

"Snakes don't die that easy," said Agatha. "Speaking of snakes: you said Japeth used you for your blood. Your blood heals him, but not Rhian?"

Sophie shook her head.

"But they're twins," said Agatha. "How can you heal one and not the other?"

"The more important question is what they'll *do* with the Storian's powers if they get them," said Sophie. "I heard Rhian say there's something specific Japeth wants. Something they both want. And it can only happen when the last ring is destroyed."

Her eyes widened. "Wait. Rhian said something to me. The night I had dinner with him. That the day would come when the One True King would rule forever. That it would come sooner than I thought. That our wedding would bring everyone together."

"Your *wedding*?" said Agatha.

"He said it to the Mistral Sisters too. That they had to keep the kingdoms on his side until the wedding." Sophie paused.

"So I must be part of this also. Whatever Rhian's planning to do with the Storian's powers . . . He needs me as his queen."

Agatha mulled this over. "And he said a *'pen'* picked you?"

Sophie nodded. "Doesn't make the slightest sense."

"More riddles," Agatha agreed. "But if Rhian needs you for his plan, one thing's for sure." She looked at her best friend. "He's coming for you."

Sophie paled.

They didn't speak for a moment.

"No Dovey. No Lesso. No way to Merlin . . . ," said Agatha finally, almost to herself. "We need help, Sophie."

"Almost there," said Sophie vaguely.

Agatha peered at her. "You smell funny. Like you rolled around in dirt."

If Agatha expected a retort, it didn't come. Instead Sophie just sighed.

Agatha glanced back at Tedros, head bowed, listening to everything the girls had endured while he was in prison. Without a shirt, he trembled as a cold gust knifed through, his pained breaths thinning. . . .

An arm draped across his bruised back and he looked up as Agatha pulled him into her warmth. Then Sophie flanked Tedros from the other side, cozying him into her dress.

Tedros didn't resist, as if what he'd heard of their travails had humbled him.

Little by little, his body stopped shivering as the two girls sheltered him the rest of the way.

"The Storian has to survive. The *Woods* have to survive,"

Tedros said finally. "And the only way it'll survive is if I take back my throne. Rhian won't rest until every last ring is destroyed. I have to stop him myself. I have to defeat him once and for all."

"Tedros, you can barely walk," said Agatha. "You have no sword, no support in the Woods, and no way to get near Rhian without his brother or his men killing you first. You don't even have a *shirt*. Right now, we need a place to hide—"

"And here we are," said Sophie, stopping suddenly.

She stood over a tree stump swarming with fireflies, blinking orange in the dark.

"This is it," she said, relieved. "Only place in the Woods we'll be safe."

Agatha peered at the stump. "Um."

Horses thundered somewhere nearby, this time layered with voices.

"You're joking, I hope," said Tedros. "This was the old Gnomeland station for the Flowerground, when gnomes still had their home in Camelot. They disappeared after my father banished magic from the kingdom. Trains don't even run here anymore—"

He scrunched up his nose.

Agatha smelled it too: a familiar smoky scent, like the earthiest tea. Before she could place it, something peeped out of the stump, lit by the fireflies, staring right at her.

A turnip.

Or rather an upside-down turnip, with two blinking eyes and a mouth shaped like an O.

"Did you say *gnomes?*" asked the turnip. "No gnomes here. That would be illegal. No gnomes allowed in Camelot. But vegetables? Vegetables are definitely allowed. So kindly go on your way and—"

"Teapea," said Sophie.

The turnip's eyes darted to her. "Excuse me?"

"Teapea," she repeated.

"Well, then," said the turnip, clearing his throat.

He ducked out of sight and the top of the stump opened like a lid, revealing a wide hole.

The sound of horses grew louder.

"Follow me," said Sophie.

She put one foot on the edge of the stump and leapt inside.

Agatha looked back through the trees: a sea of torches rushed towards her atop sprinting stallions. Tedros was already lunging for the stump, pulling his princess in behind him—

Agatha careened headfirst through darkness and the top of the stump snapped shut above her. Clinging to her prince's hand, she plummeted until she couldn't hold him any longer and they ripped apart, twisting in free fall like sands through an hourglass. Then Agatha's foot snagged onto something and her pace slowed, her body floating like she'd lost gravity.

Tedros' gold glow illuminated, lighting up his own floating form. Agatha sparked her glow and cast it around them.

A lush green vine was caught around Tedros' waist like a lasso, another around Agatha's foot, drifting the prince and princess down through an abandoned Flowerground station, the carcasses of dead trains piled against the walls. Flowercars, once brilliant with the color of their respective lines, had rotted brown, molting petals and leaves into the hollow. A decayed stench stung Agatha's nostrils, cobwebs stringing onto her ears and legs. The vines around her and Tedros seemed like the only things still alive. An old, faded sign lay broken in the wreckage:

The vines towing Agatha and Tedros lit up with luminous glow, their green surfaces crackling with electric current, before they tightened around the prince and princess like safety belts. . . .

And started dropping them faster.

Agatha squinted down for Sophie, but all she saw was the

bottom of the pit rising. The vines unraveled like anchors, spinning the prince and princess towards hard, dark soil. Before Agatha or Tedros could react, the vines let go entirely.

"Tedros!" Agatha screamed.

"Ahhhhhh!" Tedros yelled.

They crashed into the earth, straight through to the other side, where they landed in the back of a rickshaw cart, Agatha in Tedros' lap, Sophie scrunched beside them.

"Now you know why I smell like dirt," Sophie said.

"This the rest of 'em?" piped a sprightly voice.

Agatha and Tedros looked up at a young gnome perched on a bicycle attached to the bright orange rickshaw, his eyes on Sophie. He had dark, ruddy skin, a sparkly, cone-shaped blue hat, and a spiffy matching suit.

"Thought ya said there'd be *three* more comin'," said the gnome.

Sophie swallowed. "No. This is it."

"Good. Can't keep the king waiting!" the gnome said, reaching back and handing Sophie a fold of fabric. "Kindly fasten your snakeskin."

Sophie unfurled a blanket of transparent scales and draped it over her and her friends' heads. Its cold, waxy surface crinkled against Agatha's cheeks and the bag on her arm.

"That'll keep you invisible till we get to the king's palace. Can't have anyone seein' ya on the way or you're dead, dead, dead," said the gnome, pedaling onto a lone track in the dark, which reminded Agatha of the roller coaster at the Gavaldon fair. "Non-gnomes are banned in Gnomeland, ever since King

Arthur expelled us. Any gnome catches ya and they have full right to put a knife through your eye. A squirrel wandered in the other day and got barbecued for Friday Feast."

Sophie yanked more of the snakeskin to her side.

"King Teapea sent me to fetch ya," the gnome prattled. "Teapea letting humans hide in Gnomeland?" He whistled skeptically. "Either he wants somethin' from ya or he'll kill ya to warn any other non-gnomes who get too close. Don't think ya have anything to worry about, though. It's not like you're King Arthur's family or anything."

Agatha's and Sophie's eyes shot to Tedros.

Tedros slid deeper under the snakeskin.

"To be honest, I didn't even know the king was home," the gnome rambled obliviously. "Comes and goes without warning, often for months at a time. But then I get word from the palace that there's humans roaming near the stump, lookin' for a hiding place, and I'm to bring them to him." He pedaled faster, approaching a steep drop—

"Met the blond one before when I found her with the Sheriff's group. Then she went back to look for you two," he said to Agatha and Tedros, gesturing at Sophie. "Meanwhile, I took the Sheriff's group to the palace. Sheriff crammed all his friends in that enchanted sack of his. Stuffed it in the back seat and none of the gnomes had a clue. You three, on the other hand, stick out like a hog in a henhouse, so keep your arms and legs in. This thing ain't meant for humans!" He hurtled down the dip, sending the snakeskin flying before Agatha and Sophie grabbed it down. The gnome tore around a curve, knocking Agatha aside and whacking Dovey's ball into Tedros, who almost fell out of the cart.

The gnome glanced at his passengers. "Should have introduced myself. I'm Subramanyam, page boy of Crown Royal Regis Teapea, king commander of Gnomeland. Well, not always page *boy*." In a puff of dust, he morphed into a girl gnome. "Get to choose if I'll be a boy or a girl forever on my thirteenth birthday. I'm thinking I want to be a boy, because most of my friends are choosing to be girls, so. . . ." He turned into a boy and grinned at his passengers. "Bet you're jealous we gnomes can do that."

"Not really," said Sophie, Agatha, and Tedros at once.

"Just call me Subby," said Subramanyam, turning around and pedaling hard. "Don't worry: whoever's chasin' ya can't track you here, no matter what kinda magic they got. Can't find a kingdom if ya don't know it exists! Best view in Gnomeland is coming up on the right. It's rush hour, though—stay under that skin!"

Agatha looked over the side of the cart and clutched Tedros' leg in surprise.

A colossal, swirling course of tracks funneled miles down into the depths of the earth, with hundreds of bright orange rickshaws and bicycles speeding through various dips and climbs, shuttling gnomes who honked their horns loudly, the horns mimicking cat meows. In the center of this meowing, madcap highway lay Gnome City: a massive neon metropolis held together by luminescent green vines, which not only strung all the gnome-sized buildings and cottages and towers in a giant pulley-system, but also seemed to power them like electric circuits.

Subby streaked into the traffic jam, veering up onto the edges of the track to bypass bicyclists and rickshaws piled with gnomes, angry meows blasting at him from every direction. Spiraling down through downtown Gnome City, they passed restaurants (Petite Pete's Puny Eats, The Elvish Maiden, Num Num Gnome), shops (Gnome Garden Grocery, Teeny Tots Daycare, The Beard Brothers' Barbershop), as well as the Slight & Mighty Gym, Smallview General Hospital, and the Fun Puddle, a pint-sized waterpark with slides so steep that a baby gnome rocketed off one, bounced onto the highway, ricocheted off their rickshaw, and landed in the lap of the driver next to them.

Every dwelling and edifice flashed the same sign—NON-GNOMES WILL BE KILLED—along with an icon painted in the corner, the official emblem of Gnomeland:

This same pawprint dominated the marquee of the Musée de Gnome, hosting the exhibition "The Golden Age of Teapea" with a long line of gnomes hanging off its vine, waiting to get in. Meanwhile, at the Temple of Teapea, pious gnomes raised their hands as a priestess gnome stamped their foreheads with a gold-dust paw. Signs pointed off vines to "Teapea Way," "Teapea Court," "Teapea Drive," "Teapea Park," and everywhere Agatha looked, gnomes greeted each other with smiles, raising their hands like paws, chiming "Blessed Be Teapea!"

Sophie whispered: "Whoever this Teapea is, he's a dictator."

"Says the girl who redecorated the School for Evil with murals of herself," Agatha replied.

Sophie pretended not to hear.

Down below, the king's palace came into view, shimmering bright blue against its vines like a fluorescent fortress, flanked at each corner by candlelit minarets. Gnome guards with sparkly blue hats like Subby's were perched on floating lily pads outside the royal gates, wielding scimitars bigger than their own heads.

But now the rickshaw was passing more wonders: a schoolhouse filled with itty-bitty gnomes learning the ancient history of Gnomeland . . . an open-air theater playing a matinee of *If I'd Only Gnome!* . . . a putt-putt course extending vertically down a vine, with golfing gnomes in gravity boots anchored to the greens . . . and the headquarters of the *Small Print News*, printing their latest edition: "FATIMA WINS GNOMELAND SPELLING BEE! WINNING WORD: 'BOUILLABAISE'!"

Agatha was so entranced that she'd forgotten everything they'd left behind.

"Totally in their own world," Tedros murmured. "Like they have no clue what's happening above ground."

"We don't," Subby chipped in. "After Arthur banished us, King Teapea said it was a blessing and made us build an underground colony. Some uppity gnomes stayed behind on land—hear one's even a teacher at that famous school—but the rest of us stuck with Teapea and cut ourselves off from all that happens up there. Not to be rude, but you humans think the Woods revolves around you. You divide up your land, create false borders, only to start fights, and before ya know it, you're declaring war on your own friends and brothers. Joke's on you, though. Not a single gnome has been bothered to use the Human World Observatory in the Musée de Gnome and see what's goin' on up in your Woods. Had to close the exhibit 'cause we couldn't care less. Imagine that. Gnomes who used to be your best allies, no longer the slightest bit interested in whether you live or die. And now that you know the secret of where we moved, not sure Teapea will let ya leave alive." Subby giggled. "Ah, here we are. . . ."

The royal gnome guards glared at Subby, scimitars gleaming, their eyes roving across Agatha and her friends, clearly seeing them beneath the snakeskin. They waved in the rickshaw and Subby pedaled onto a gold-paved track, approaching the blue-lit palace, the only structure in Gnomeland big enough to fit a full-sized human.

Nerves fluttered through Agatha's stomach, a reminder that she wasn't here as a tourist. Above ground, the whole Woods was hunting her and her friends. Now she was depending on a strange king's mercy to keep them safe. A king who despised her entire kind.

Two guards held open the palace doors as Subby wheeled inside. "You can take off your snakeskin," he said, coming to a stop.

Sophie was already fumbling from under the covering and ogling the opulent foyer, lined with blue-stone arches. Agatha climbed out of the rickshaw and inspected the stone closer, as thin drips of molten lava crisscrossed its surface, the lava switching directions at will, occasionally erupting in detonations of red smoke. Beneath her feet, blue stone sparkled with red glitterdust, rippling in paw patterns across the floor like constellations in a night sky.

Three lily pads floated from around a corner, topped with tall glasses of golden-rose milk and coconut cookies, which Agatha, Tedros, and Sophie devoured, the tangy drink mixing in their mouths with sweet coconut crumbles, before the milk and cookies magically replenished. Three more lily pads arrived with hot, peppermint-scented towels, which they used to wipe the dirt off their faces, along with a last lily pad toting a fresh shirt for Tedros.

"If this is our hideout, I don't see the need to go back above ground," Sophie quipped.

"Happy to leave you while this 'rot' returns to win his throne," said Tedros, putting on the shirt.

"The 'rot' can't win anything without my help, so the 'rot' should kiss my feet," said Sophie.

"Kissed you once and it was terrible," said Tedros.

That shut Sophie up.

"You two deserve each other," said Agatha.

That shut Tedros up too.

Subby's voice echoed: "This is where I leave ya."

All three turned to see the young gnome posed in front of a door at the end of the hall. He opened it, revealing a blue waterfall cascading over the threshold like a curtain, the water flowing up once it hit bottom, before raining down again.

"Go on, then," said Subby, nodding at the waterfall. "Kept the king waiting long enough."

Sophie humphed, as if she had no intention of getting wet, but Agatha was hugging Dovey's bag tighter and moving towards the door, her prince at her side.

"Think he'll help us? King Teapea?" Agatha asked Tedros, pausing at the waterfall.

Tedros' face clouded with doubt, no longer the boy who thought he could win this alone. "He has to."

They held hands and looked back at Subby.

"Good luck to ya," the gnome winked.

Agatha and Tedros leapt into the water and came out the other side, with Sophie bounding in after them, dress soaked, hair ragged, splashing her glass of milk: "Eeeee, I'm wet! I'm wet! I'm . . . wait a second . . ." She gawked at Agatha and Tedros, completely dry. Then she followed her friends' eyes.

A throne room made of velvet sprawled before them, with the walls, the floor, the ceiling blanketed in the same soft, midnight-blue fabric. The velvet on the walls was separated into panels, the columns between panels filled with glowing fireflies, which marched up and down in strict order like sentinels. A gold throne, big enough for a giant, lay at the front of the room, spotlit by a chandelier forged out of more fireflies, the words "**C.R.R. TEAPEA**" carved into the throne's head.

On the floor in front of the throne sat a full audience, their attention craned towards the three intruders.

Agatha exhaled.

Everyone was here: Hester, Anadil, Dot, Hort, Nicola, Robin, Guinevere, the Sheriff, and more . . . all her friends, who'd escaped from the battle at Camelot, now safe in Gnomeland. . . .

But not just them.

Those she'd left at school had also somehow made it to Teapea's palace: Professor Anemone, Professor Manley, Professor Sheeks, Princess Uma, Yuba, Castor, and all the first-year Evers and Nevers, quietly packed in on the floor.

They looked at Agatha, Sophie, and Tedros expectantly, then at the door, waiting for the Dean of Good to come through.

Then they saw Agatha's face.

And they knew.

"Wherever Dovey is, she's in peace now," Robin Hood said to Agatha. "She would have been proud of you."

Agatha met his eyes, holding down her grief.

But now her friends and teachers were on top of her, wrapping her in their arms, one after the other.

"I prayed you were still alive," Hester said breathlessly, unable to mask her emotion. "Dovey must have heard my wish. A fairy godmother until the end."

"We love you, Agatha," Kiko gushed.

"Even me, who doesn't really like you," said Hort.

Nicola shunted him aside, joining the hug. "We'd still be in the dungeons if it wasn't for you."

"It wasn't just me," said Agatha sheepishly. "All of us played a part."

She glanced at Tedros and Sophie, who were being smothered with their own hugs (Sophie was taking her time with the handsome Everboys).

Soon the buzz settled and everyone drifted to their seats again, huddled close, like a big, unlikely family. Even Agatha managed to feel some relief. They were together now. All of them. There was no one left to save.

But soon the seeds of fear bloomed once more.

Sophie was sitting next to Robin: "I could have sworn you had a ring at the meeting. Only now you're not wearing one."

"Wasn't my ring to wear," Robin piped.

Sophie frowned. "But—"

Agatha squished between them. "What do we do now, Robin? The whole Woods is hunting us. How do we fight back?"

"That's why we're here," said the Sheriff of Nottingham, seated behind.

"To ask King Teapea for help," said Guinevere, with the Sheriff.

"Wait a second. How did you and Robin get to Camelot in the first place? How did you have your sack?" Tedros asked the Sheriff as he sat with his mother. "That sack was destroyed! The Snake ripped it to shreds after he escaped the Sheriff's jail—"

"Can't destroy a magic sack," the Sheriff grouched, holding up the stitched-up bag. "Snake made the mistake of leaving the pieces of it behind. And Dot's mother is the best tailor in the Woods."

"My mother?" Dot called, poking her head from the back like a mole. "My mother died when I was a baby!"

Robin gave the Sheriff a look. "'Course she did!" the Sheriff called back.

Dot frowned. "Then how could she stitch up the—"

The Sheriff barreled on: "Sack divides friends from foes, so I used it to catch pirates and keep them trapped while getting our crew from place to place. Well, until those fairies let the pirates free during the battle. Must have smelled 'em in there."

"Given how you smell, surprised they didn't set you free with 'em," Robin quipped.

"Hold on." Agatha frowned at Robin. "You told me that you and the Merry Men wouldn't help me. And you and the Sheriff hate each other. How did *you* get here?"

"Tedros' mum has the answer to that," said Robin.

"Actually, Sophie does," said Guinevere.

"I do?" Sophie said, wringing out her hair into her empty milk glass.

"That night, when you had dinner with Rhian, you kicked me under the table," the old queen explained. "You said Tedros was on his own. That you weren't Tedros' mother. You were challenging me. Right there in front of that monster. You pushed me to keep fighting, even if it seemed impossible. Yet I had no way to send word out of Camelot, not with that scim on my face. But outside the queen's chamber is a tree with songbirds that I used to feed every day. In return, they acted as my little spies, singing louder whenever it was safe for me to sneak out and see Lance in the Woods. So after dinner, I slipped back into my old chamber, pretending to clean it, and there they were, my songbirds, singing outside the window like always. But when they saw me, with that disgusting eel on my face, their songs stopped. Their sad eyes asked how they could help. So while I cleaned, I hummed a song . . . a song every bird knows. . . ."

She hummed and Robin crooned along:

"Oh help us, Robin,
Dear dashing Robin,
Come save us Robin Hood!
Hear our song, the son of Good,
All the way through the Green Wood!"

"Hate that song," the Sheriff snarled.

"That's 'cause the only song people sing about you is 'Sheriff, Sheriff, Farty Sheriff,'" said Robin. "When the birds came singing of Gwen's ills, I told my Merry Men, but those lazy louts wouldn't ride for Agatha and they wouldn't ride for Gwen either, even though Arthur and I were mates. But then Sheriff, of all people, sends word he's riding to Camelot to save his daughter from the dungeons and begs me to help him."

"Bollocks," the Sheriff scorned. "I didn't beg you for anything. I said you're a pink-bellied chicken for letting the girl who saved you from jail rot in a cell and I hope the Storian would reopen our tale and tell the world what kind of man you really are."

"Sounds vaguely familiar," said Robin. "Anyway, then Marian piles on and asks what I'd do if it was my own daughter that Rhian had taken. And wasn't Dot the closest I had to a daughter? Marian knows how to push my buttons."

"You and me both," mumbled the Sheriff.

"Couldn't go back to putterin' away at the Arrow. Not after all that," Robin sighed. "So I joined the Sheriff and rode for Camelot. Sent Gwen a lotus so she'd know we were comin'."

"Wore it in my hair to give myself hope," sighed the old queen.

"Then while we're on our way, we hear that Dot and some others escaped the dungeons," said the Sheriff. "Even so, I wasn't lettin' this Rhian bastard win. Our Woods has a law and order and I ain't restin' until the pig's head is on a spike."

"Which is why we're all here now in King Teapea's palace, praying he'll help us," Robin Hood finished.

"And if he *doesn't*?" Agatha asked—

A trumpet blared, making her jump.

A guard gnome in a sparkly blue hat and stiff jacket appeared out of the darkness behind the throne. "Greetings, human enemies! You are here at the invitation of Crown Royal Regis Teapea. Please stand in honor of the king!"

Fireflies on the walls and chandelier beamed their orange glow at the throne.

Quickly Agatha and the rest of her friends rose to their feet.

"Listen to me," she whispered to Robin. "The gnomes have a vengeance against King Arthur for banishing them, which means they'll have a vengeance against—"

"*Me*," Tedros cut in, over their shoulders. "Agatha's right! What if King Teapea knows who I am? What if he sees us as enemies? What if we came to the one ruler who wants me and my friends dead even more than Rhian?"

"Then we're dead either way," said Robin grimly.

"In the meantime, stand in the back," the Sheriff grunted at Tedros.

Agatha's stomach lurched. The gold throne in front of her suddenly loomed larger. Here they were, preoccupied with their family reunion, when they'd willingly sealed themselves in a stranger's palace. A stranger who surely hated Tedros enough to kill him on sight. Her unease about this place exploded into panic. This was an ambush. She could feel it. They needed to get out of here *now*—

Before she could move, the gnome's trumpet blared again: "Presenting the Honorable, Exorable, Crown Royal Regis . . . Teapea!"

For a moment, nothing happened.

Then Agatha saw it.

A shadow slinking from the back of the room towards the throne, slowly, smoothly, like it was floating on air.

Agatha recoiled, doom impaling her heart.

The shadow drew closer . . . closer . . .

King Teapea came into the light, revealing himself.

Sophie dropped her milk.

Tedros toppled backwards.

All eyes in the room shot to Agatha.

She couldn't breathe.

There was no way.

No possible way.

Because the leader of the gnomes, their sole chance for survival, their only hope for help in all these Woods, just happened to be . . .

Her cat.

The Ultimate Mission

Tedros lifted his head blearily, quite sure he'd imagined the whole thing.

He hadn't.

Reaper sat on the gilded throne, his bald, shriveled skin looking especially sickly beneath his crooked crown, his one good eye glowering at the prince, while Agatha looked stultified, her mouth agape.

Two more gnome guards wielding scimitars emerged from the darkness behind the throne and flanked the cat from both sides, while the gnome with the trumpet manned the door. On the head of the throne, the carved letters **C. R. R. TEAPEA** rearranged to . . .

REAPER CAT

Tedros choked.

Reaper sat on his hind legs and meowed loudly into the silence.

Princess Uma stepped forward from her place amongst the first years. "Yes, Your, um . . . Highness?"

Reaper meowed again.

Princess Uma approached the throne.

Agatha's cat whispered to her.

Uma nodded and tapped a glowing fingertip to his throat.

"This is impossible," said Agatha, blinking like a fool. "There has to be some mistake—"

"No mistake," said her cat with a firm, deep voice. "You just haven't been paying attention."

Agatha rocked back on her heels. "You *talk*?"

"I find man's language a limited and ugly one, but thanks to Uma's spell, I can communicate for the purposes of our meeting," said Reaper, before turning his bold yellow eyes on Tedros. "And you're lucky I haven't spoken before today, given you've kicked me, called me Satan, and thrown me in a toilet, even though I've been a good friend to you when you've needed it." He looked at Agatha. "Both of you."

Agatha shook her head. "But . . . but . . . you're my *cat*!"

"Your *mother*'s cat," said Reaper, "which should have been your first clue that I'm a cat of the Woods, not Woods Beyond. As for my place here, gnomes believe that to be ruled by one of their own is to invite greed, self-interest, and corruption. If a gnome ruled Gnomeland, it would be just as broken as your human kingdoms. Since the beginning, then, gnomes have looked outside their kind for a king . . . a leader who could understand their way of life without abusing his power over it. The answer was obvious. Cats and gnomes are the same: at once friends to humans and indifferent to them. And yet cats are also solitary creatures, content with a bowl of milk and a warm bed. A cat king, then, would do what was best for the gnomes, while keeping apart and letting them live their lives."

"This is insane!" Agatha barked, finding her voice. "You lived with *me*! In my house!"

"And I was there!" Tedros touted, stepping next to his princess. "I spent weeks with you in that graveyard! This doesn't make sense—"

"I've been King of Gnomeland for five years and in those five years, I came and went from your side as I pleased," Reaper told Agatha. "I was with the gnomes when they needed me, just as I was with you when you needed me, with neither of you aware that I was living two lives. If I were a dog, you might have noticed my absences, since dogs are needy, odious beasts. But cats . . . we slip in and out of your life like old memories."

A gnome guard brought Reaper a goblet of spice-dusted cream, which he lapped at, before the gnome took it away.

Agatha went quiet, her face changing.

This is real, Tedros realized.

The cat is king.

"My father was ruler of Gnomeland before me. He, my mother, and my three brothers were beautiful, majestic black cats. I, on the other hand, was born like this," Reaper explained, nodding down at his scrawny, hairless frame. "My father was ashamed and had me exiled deep into the Woods, a defenseless kitten, where Callis found me and made her her pet." He smiled fondly at Agatha. "Sound familiar?"

"That's how my mother found me too," Agatha breathed.

"Your mother couldn't help loving those that others couldn't," said Reaper. "But even when she escaped from the School for Evil and hid in Gavaldon, Callis never kept me penned. I was free to return to the Endless Woods and venture back and forth as I pleased. Then your mother brought you home and I found myself feeling quite protective of you, despite my suspicion for humans. Meanwhile, I kept track of my father and brothers, the king and princes of Gnomeland, who had grown increasingly loyal to King Arthur, even going so far as to act as spies for Camelot. Wary, I returned to Gnomeland and appeared before my father's court. Cats should know not to serve humans, I told him, otherwise we are no better than dogs. I remember the way my father looked at me, perched on this very throne. He called me a traitor. If I ever returned to Gnomeland, he said, I'd be killed on the spot."

Reaper sighed. "Then Merlin deserted King Arthur and Arthur retaliated by banishing magic from the kingdom, including the fairies and gnomes who had been his steadfast allies. After Arthur expelled the gnomes and destroyed their kingdom, my father and brothers were run out of Gnomeland for aligning with a man who had betrayed the entire gnome race. My father's deposers found me and said I'd been right to warn my family about humans. Ironic, since my love for you and your mother had only deepened by then. Then the gnomes asked me to be their king."

He leaned back on his throne, his pink belly wrinkling like an accordion. "At first, I rejected the idea. I was happy on Graves Hill with you. But I realized I'd made the same mistake as the gnomes: I'd grown too trusting of humans, even ones I loved. Being king would let me live between worlds, belonging to neither. A selfish reason to take a crown, perhaps, but in the end, it's made me a better king. I've taught the gnomes self-reliance, for I'm never here very long. And the gnomes have never been happier. They idolize me, name streets after me, worship me at their temple, none of which matters to me, of course . . . but in truth, the illusion of a king is all they needed to govern themselves. Not so different from you," the cat said to Agatha. "I was your first friend, long before that other one knocked at your door. Without me, you might never have thought you even deserved a friend. Things have changed, of course. You don't need me the way you once did, and that makes me proud. But I'll always be with you, Agatha, even when you can't see me. Like Merlin to Tedros, I'm watching you every step of the way, coming in and out of your story like only the best wizards can." Reaper smiled. "Or the best cats."

Agatha wept into her sleeve.

Her pet's tale had moved her, Tedros sensed, but more than that, Agatha was relieved: they had a friend here in Gnomeland. A true friend. Tedros thought about all the times the cat had saved them: delivering Callis' message to the League of Thirteen . . . rescuing them from Graves Hill when guards came for them . . . helping Agatha find Excalibur in the war against Rafal . . . protecting Tedros at Camelot when Agatha left on her quest. . . .

"I'm sorry," the prince said, looking up at Reaper. "For the way I've treated you."

"I'm sorry too," the cat confessed. "I felt you were a poor match for Agatha. You reminded me of my father and brothers: too handsome and arrogant to ever see the world clearly. But you've grown more than you know. Most born into entitlement wither under adversity. You've admitted your faults and not only seek redemption, but are willing to put in the work to achieve it. You've earned the right to fight for your crown. How long and hard that fight will be, we cannot know. But I will help you in every way I can."

His eyes glowed like stars, bright enough to light the darkest night.

Tedros hugged Agatha to his side, wiping her tears.

"But I'm afraid storytime is over," said Reaper.

Out of the audience, two gnome guards ambushed Sophie, hoisted her off the ground by her hips, and held her upside down—

"EEEEEYYIII! WHAT ARE YOU DOING!" Sophie shrieked.

A gnome whipped off her shoe, pulled the necklace off her toe with its gold vial, and tossed it at Reaper, who caught it, before the guards dumped Sophie on her buttocks.

"I'd say I'm sorry that you were the only one to get wet as you came in," Reaper said to Sophie, twirling her Dean's necklace. "But that would be a lie."

Sophie gaped at him, soaked through. "You did it on purpose!"

"All hail the king," Tedros murmured.

The cat pulled open Sophie's vial and spread the golden liquid into midair, which congealed into the familiar Quest Map, floating over his throne.

Only one name and figurine still remained on the map, positioned over Camelot's castle, a name Tedros was surprised to see on the Quest Map at all. . . .

RHIAN

"Looks like the king's still alive, despite your best efforts," said Reaper. He brought the map down, spreading it in front of him. "Which means whatever we do next . . ."

His eyes lifted to his audience.

"It will have to be *better*."

THE STUDENTS AND teachers of the School for Good and Evil sat in a circle around the map, which floated in the center above the blue-velvet floor. Reaper paced back and forth across the levitating parchment, pondering everything Sophie, Agatha, and Tedros had just told him.

"So Rhian seeks the powers of the One True King," the cat said. "How close is he to securing them?"

Tedros could hear Yuba whispering to Agatha: "Why would Rhian's name be on a Dean's Quest Map? He wasn't a student at the school!"

"I had the same question," Agatha whispered back. "Speaking of students, how did you get the first years here?"

"After the Sheriff took you to Camelot, I received a message from King Teapea," said Yuba. "I'd never met the new Gnome King, so imagine my surprise! He said we must unite against Rhian and ordered me to bring the teachers and students here, with instructions how to use old Flowerground tunnels to arrive undetected."

Thup. Thup. Thup.

Tedros saw Reaper tapping his claw impatiently.

The prince cleared his throat. "Uh, what was the question?"

"How many leaders still possess their rings?" said Reaper, glaring. "Gnomeland never had a ring, since it was a domain of Camelot. And Camelot no longer has a ring, since your father is said to have destroyed it before he died. Which means we need to know how many rings are left that can prevent Rhian from claiming the Storian's powers."

Tedros and Agatha exchanged glances. "Not sure," the prince admitted.

"Only one ring needs to survive," the Sheriff grunted. "All that matters."

Reaper gazed at him thoughtfully. "Indeed."

Tedros waited for the cat to elaborate, but instead Reaper nibbled on gourmet mushrooms his guards had brought, his eyes still fixed on the Sheriff. Then he began pacing once more.

"To put Tedros back on the throne will be no easy task," said Reaper, padding past kingdoms on the map. "All of us will have to do our part." He stopped over the realm of Borna Coric. "Witches?"

The coven perked up.

"Yes, Your Highness," said Hester.

"Give us a mission," said Anadil.

"Anything you need," said Dot.

"You're to go to the Caves of Contempo and rescue Merlin," Reaper ordered.

"Anything but that," said Dot.

Hester and Anadil scowled at her.

"It's thousands of miles away and surrounded by a poisonous sea!" Dot argued. "There's no way to get to the caves!"

"*I'll* go," Tedros declared, puffing his chest. "Merlin is my friend—"

"Wait a minute," said Nicola, locked on Dot. "Aren't you part of the Coven of Room 66? Witches of legend, who've battled undead villains, murderous pirates, and were entrusted by the Dean of Good herself to find a new School Master?"

Dot twiddled her thumbs. "Yes, but—"

"Merlin needs your help," Nicola clapped back. "Merlin,

the greatest wizard of Good, who has saved you and your friends many times over. Merlin, who we need to win this war. Reaper could have chosen anyone here to rescue him. He chose *you*. But if you aren't up to the task, then maybe you aren't the witch I thought you were."

Dot was speechless.

"Maybe Nicola should be in our coven," said Hester.

"I like Nicola," said Anadil.

"I'll go," said Dot.

Tedros sprung to his feet. "Didn't you hear me? Merlin is too important to leave to anyone but me—"

The Sheriff of Nottingham cut him off. "Dot's right: the Caves of Contempo are no place for three girls to be traveling alone."

"Three girls who've thrashed you twice," said Robin.

"I should be the one to go to the caves," the Sheriff demanded.

"No," said Reaper, his eyes cutting through him. "You won't be going anywhere. You'll remain here in the palace under my guards' protection."

He said this so sharply Tedros wondered if Reaper and the Sheriff had a prior encounter: something that made the cat distrust him.

Reaper turned back to Hester. "The witches will travel to Borna Coric and find Merlin."

"And me?" Tedros pressured. "If I'm not going after Merlin, then I should lead the next mission—"

"Where are Hort and Nicola?" the cat said.

"Here!" said Hort, clasping Nicola's hand.

"You two will go to Foxwood, where Rhian claims to be from," said Reaper. "Find out what you can about him and his brother's history."

"Consider it done," Hort said, winking at Nicola. "History's what I do."

"God help us," said Nicola.

"Why is your cat ignoring me?" Tedros whispered to Agatha. "*I'm* the king. *I'm* the one he's trying to get back on the throne. And he's giving key missions to *Hort*?"

But his princess was listening to Reaper detail the next assignment—

"Bogden, Willam, you two will disguise yourselves to spy on Camelot. Willam knows the kingdom well, having grown up at its rectory. Use your wiles to discern Rhian's condition. Find out his next moves."

Bogden saluted him. "Aye-aye, King Pee Pee."

"Teapea, you dolt!" Willam hissed.

Reaper appraised them, stone-faced. "Beatrix, Reena, Kiko, you'll patrol the trees around the Gnomeland portal and ensure no one gets too close."

"Fitting, isn't it?" Kiko sighed. "Tristan died in a tree."

Willam gave her a look.

"Now that you've addressed everyone else, including first years and altar boys," Tedros stewed, "please tell me what—"

"As for the remaining students," said Reaper, pivoting

towards the young Evers and Nevers, "you will pair up, disperse throughout the kingdoms, and find those remaining rulers who have yet to burn their rings. Rhian will surely use any means necessary to turn them against the Storian and school. Do what you can to stop the leaders from destroying their rings without them spotting you. The teachers, meanwhile, will return to school and keep watch over the Storian in case it provides any further clues as to how we can defend it. Yuba, send me a secure message as soon as you count how many swans are left in the pen's carving. Hopefully more than a few kingdoms have held their ground against the king."

"Yes, King Teapea," said the old gnome.

Reaper surveyed the room. "Everyone understand their assignments?"

Tedros was about to explode—

"What would you like me and Gwen to do, Your Highness?" said Robin Hood.

"Return to Sherwood Forest and recruit your Merry Men. Their days of willful blindness are over," said the cat. "Guinevere will remain under my protection. The guards will take her and the Sheriff to their chambers in my palace so they can rest."

"Rest? Me? *Now?*" the Sheriff blustered. "I can understand Guinevere needin' a lie-down, but I should be up there fightin' the king!"

"Me too! Me *more!*" Tedros burst out—

"All teams will depart at once," Reaper commanded, ignoring the prince as the map under his paw evaporated. He leapt back onto his throne, dangling Sophie's necklace. "My page will escort you to the surface in the Sheriff's sack."

"Samarbati S. Subramanyam at your service!" Subby pipped, poking his ruddy face through the waterfall that curtained the throne room door. "Let's get ya sacked up!"

A gnome guard blew a trumpet next to him so loudly Subramanyam fell back through the waterfall—

"The Honorable Crown Royal Regis Teapea hereby dismisses you from his presence!" the gnome proclaimed. "Depart for missions!"

"DEPART FOR MISSIONS!" two more guards yelped.

Before Tedros could move, his friends, teachers, mentors, and the whole first-year class bounded up, tittering about their new quests and grabbing at their teammates as they blew past the prince and streamed through the waterfall in groups.

"Wait . . . hold on . . . ," Tedros stammered, lost in the stampede—

"I'm with Priyanka!" Bodhi claimed.

"Can't leave your best mate for a girl!" Laithan carped.

"It's like Sophie and Agatha but with boys," Bossam sniggered.

Castor grabbed all three—"I'LL ASSIGN TEAMS 'CAUSE I KNOW WHO'S GOT BRAINS AND WHO'S A DONKEY"—before the dog herded more first years into the water and leapt through behind them.

More faculty followed: "Suppose Rhian sends his men to the school again?" Professor Sheeks asked.

"Without the students present, we'll have full license from

the Storian to defend ourselves," Professor Manley growled. "Uma, any word from the fairies? You sent them to find help days ago."

"Been scouring the Woods for the League of Thirteen," Princess Uma replied. "Won't rest until they find one of the old League members who can help. . . ."

Hort nudged Beatrix on the way out. "How do we share information while we're in different places?"

"Professor Anemone has Agatha's old courier crow from Camelot. We can use it to send messages," said Beatrix.

"Not secure enough," said Hort. "What we need is a squirrelly nut."

"For all we know, squirrels are on Rhian's side too," Kiko pipped.

"What's a squirrelly nut?" Nicola butted in.

More first years vanished into the waterfall with them— Aja, Valentina, Bossam, Bert, Beckett—with Ravan, Vex, Mona, Dot, Anadil, and others surging through the exit too, until there was no one left in the throne room except the cat king and the three who knew him best: Tedros, his princess, and his nemesis.

The last of the three yawned. "Lovely, everything's settled," Sophie sighed against the velvet wall, forcing fireflies to march around her. "I'm going to have a cucumber salad, draw myself a foam bath, and take a long, warm nap."

"That won't be happening," said Reaper, slipping Sophie's necklace around his own neck. "You three have the most difficult assignment of all. That's why I saved it for when we could be alone. Because it is the *ultimate* mission. The mission that supersedes all the others. The mission that must be accomplished if Tedros is to reclaim his crown."

Sophie pursed her lips, eyeing Agatha.

But the cat was only looking at the prince.

"You must find out why Excalibur wouldn't pull out of the stone for you," he said.

Reaper turned to Agatha and Sophie. "And both of you must help him."

"That isn't a mission. That's a dead end," said Tedros, shaking his head. "I tried to pull the sword. I tried everything. And then a stranger pulls it in one go. I asked Merlin and he didn't have answers either, except for some crackpot riddle telling me to 'unbury' my father. I've racked my brain to understand it, *any* of it, but there's nothing to understand. Because none of it makes sense! How am I supposed to know what Excalibur was thinking? How am I supposed to learn a sword's state of mind?"

"The same way Merlin and Professor Dovey did before their work was interrupted," said Reaper.

His eyes glowed—instantly, the bag on Agatha's shoulder yanked open and the crystal ball flew out, landing snugly in the cat's paws.

"Because while you were on your fourth-year quests, Merlin and Clarissa Dovey were on a quest of their own," the cat explained, holding up the glass orb. "Namely, using Dovey's crystal ball to find out why Tedros failed his coronation test. Turns out breaking a crystal ball allows you to do things that a normal crystal ball does not. A working crystal ball is a window to time. But Merlin and Dovey discovered quite accidentally that a broken crystal ball is more than a window . . ." Reaper leaned forward. "It's a *portal*."

"A *portal*?" Sophie and Agatha said.

"A portal you three will now enter together," Reaper clarified. "The risks are steep. We've seen its effects on Good's Dean." He looked at Tedros. "But entering the crystal world is the only way you'll ever learn the truth about your father, your sword, and your fate."

"What do you mean, 'crystal world'?" Agatha said, flummoxed. "There's a world . . . *inside* the crystal ball?"

"A world bigger than you could possibly know," Reaper said.

Tedros frowned. "This doesn't make sense. How do you know what's inside Dovey's crystal?"

"How do you know what Merlin and Dovey saw?" Sophie asked.

"How *could* you know what they saw?" Agatha pressed.

Reaper grinned. "Isn't it obvious?" he said, his voice a teasing drawl.

The cat's pupils deepened like black holes.

"I went with them."

Into the Crystal World

Agatha watched the crystal ball sink into the water.

"Nothing's happening," said Tedros, next to her.

"Good, because if you expect me to get wet *again* . . . ," Sophie huffed, still soggy in her white dress.

Agatha turned to her cat. "You said the portal opens when the crystal is underwater—"

"And turned *on*," said Reaper.

Their voices echoed through the Crown Royal Regis' bathroom, appointed with a grooming station of jeweled brushes, fragrant oils, and milky creams, along with a sparkle-dusted sand litterbox and a heated blue-stone bathing tub, big enough for an army of cats, the steamy water sprinkled with orange blossoms. When Reaper had shown them into the room, lit by panels made of blue and orange fireflies, Agatha had been mystified. The Reaper she knew itched with fleas, peed exclusively on gravestones, and nearly killed her the one time she'd tried to clean him.

"It's my father's old bathroom," Reaper explained, seeing her face. He climbed onto the edge of the tub. "This is the first time I've been in here."

Now Agatha watched as her cat finished sinking Dovey's crystal into the hot bath, mist rising off the surface. The orb drifted down and settled on the blue-stone floor, the crack in its glass refracting through water, seeming bigger than its actual size.

Agatha, meanwhile, felt like she had a crack in her head. *Dovey dead . . . Reaper, a king . . . the crystal ball a portal into a secret world . . .* Tension pounded through her skull, her lungs sucked of air as if she was already underwater—

Tedros touched her arm. "You okay?"

She gazed up at him, then at Sophie and Reaper, both assessing her.

Agatha wanted to say no . . . that it was all moving too fast . . . that she wanted to turn the story back to a time when life had no magic, no secrets . . . to a time when she had a home . . . a mother . . .

But then, as she took in her best friend, her prince, and

her cat, Agatha realized she had another family now. A family she'd *chosen*. And after all they'd been through, to be with that family again, no matter how daunting the challenges ahead . . . it was all Agatha needed to wrench out of the past and find the present.

"You said the crystal is a portal," said Agatha, composing herself. "A portal into *what*?"

"Merlin called it a 'crystal of time,'" said Reaper vaguely, skirting the edge of the tub. "We must get started—"

"How did Merlin and Dovey discover the portal?" Tedros cut in.

"I told you. By accident," said Reaper impatiently. "After you failed to pull Excalibur, Merlin and Dovey tried to use her crystal ball to understand why. Given how poorly you were treating Agatha after your botched coronation, I wanted you to pull the sword soon, for her sake, so I joined Merlin and Clarissa in their efforts. At first we had little luck. But during the summer, Professor Dovey's office grows insufferably hot. Studying the ball one night before Dovey activated it, Merlin left a sweaty handprint on the crack in the glass. The crack grew softer, the glass spongy. The change made Merlin curious. So he and Dovey put the ball in the Groom Room pool to see what would happen when the Dean turned it on. Now, if there are no more questions, it's time to get into the bath."

Agatha studied the dull orb, motionless underwater. *What happened when Dovey turned it on?* Her heart drummed. *What happens when I turn it on?*

"That's what they were up to this whole time. Merlin and

Dovey," Tedros realized, peering into the water. "They were going inside her crystal ball. It's what was making Dovey sick."

"*Deathly* sick. And now you want us to do the same thing?" Sophie challenged Reaper.

"It's too dangerous," Tedros agreed.

"The secret of why Tedros couldn't pull Excalibur is inside that crystal. Then again, maybe there is no secret. Maybe Rhian is the real king," said Reaper, holding up his paw when Tedros started to protest. "But the only way we'll know for sure is to cross the portal. Too much is at stake to leave the question of why the sword recognized Rhian instead of Tedros unanswered. The fate of Camelot, the Storian, and our world *depend* on that answer. Merlin and Dovey were close to finding it, but they ran out of time. Since Agatha is Dovey's Second, it is our duty to finish their work. No matter the risks."

Agatha looked at Tedros.

He was quiet now.

"Once Agatha submerges and activates the ball, the portal will open," said Reaper, before turning to Sophie and the prince. "Both of you will be submerged with her and ready to enter."

Agatha was already climbing into the steam bath, the sweet-scented water flooding under her dress, warming the sore spots on her skin. Sweat beaded her temples, the bath feeling hotter by the second. She immersed her head and soaked her face and hair, her foot sliding along the stone floor until it touched the crystal.

A bomb of water detonated near her, tan muscles peeking

through liquid clouds. Agatha resurfaced and through the mist, she saw Tedros, eyes closed and gritting his teeth as the heat burned at wounds on his bare chest. His breeches ballooned with water, his legs stretching out and grazing Agatha's thigh. He opened his eyes and caught her watching. He flicked foamy water at her. Agatha splashed him back hard. Tedros grabbed her puckishly and pulled her to his chest, her body smushed against his bubbling breeches. He whipped his hair back and held her tighter, dripping sweat onto his princess as steam walled them in.

Slowly the steam broke apart and they saw Sophie gaping at them.

"I have to get in with *them?*" she said.

"You took a steam bath with Hort," said Tedros.

"That was espionage," Sophie defended.

"And this is to save the world," Agatha retorted. "Get in."

Muttering to herself, Sophie hiked up her ruffly dress and dipped her toe into the edge of the tub. . . .

She pulled back. "You know, I can't swim and I'm feeling a bit feverish. Might be jaundice or diphtheria. All that over-salted food at the castle. And now that I think about it, this is Aggie and Teddy's mission. They should be the ones to find out why Rhian pulled the sword instead of Teddy. I hardly know Rhian at all—"

"You're still wearing his ring," said Agatha dryly.

Sophie glanced down at the diamond on her finger. "I'm perfectly capable of divorcing fine jewelry from its symbolism."

"Rhian picked you to be his *wife*," Reaper pointed out. "He chose you to stand by his side, even though he has a brother far more loyal to him than you'll ever be. So why would Rhian take a queen at all? A queen he certainly doesn't love? He chose you for a *reason*. You are as much a part of this story as Tedros and Agatha and we need to find out why. Though if you insist you serve no purpose, I'm happy to leave you to the gnomes and see what they do with a friend of King Arthur's *son*."

"I liked it better when you didn't talk," Sophie growled, shoving into the tub, her white dress pooling with orange blossoms. She drew into a corner, away from Agatha and her prince, still cozied together on the opposite side. "What now?"

From the edge of the tub, Reaper clawed down Agatha's shoulder and clasped onto her dress. "On the count of three, we'll all go under. Agatha will trigger the crystal. The portal will open for a split second. Touch the crystal in that moment and you'll be transported inside. This is important. You must *touch* the crystal. If you don't, you'll be shut out from the portal and so disoriented you will likely drown."

"Meanwhile, Beatrix gets to patrol a tree," Sophie murmured.

Reaper's shriveled body clung tighter to Agatha's collar, the cat trying not to let his tail touch the water until it had to. "On your count, Agatha."

Agatha pulled away from Tedros and slid across the stone rim of the tub until the crystal was under her toes again. Gone was her sense of being overwhelmed, replaced by trust in where her story had led her. If this was Dovey's and Merlin's unfinished quest, then she would do everything to finish it.

She looked at her prince, then her best friend. "Ready?"

"Anything that gets me to the truth," Tedros steeled.

"Anything that gets me to a new dress," said Sophie.

Agatha took a deep breath. "3 . . . 2 . . . 1 . . ."

She plunged into the tub with Reaper, the twin splashes of Sophie and Tedros blooming underneath. Agatha thrust her head downwards, tangling in her friends' limbs as she flattened her body against the stone floor so she was level with the orb. She gazed through the cracked glass into the center of the ball, the silence of the water stilling her mind.

The crack split open like a doorway and blinding blue light burst through like a tsunami, slamming Agatha against the wall of the tub and blasting Reaper away from her. The assault of light paralyzed her brain and weighed on her chest, her lungs pinned under the force of a boulder. She couldn't think anymore, as if she'd lost the top of her head and any thoughts were flying away before she could catch them. Her hands and feet seemed to move where her eyes and mouth were, her eyes and mouth now down by her knees. She didn't know where she was or how she'd gotten there. She didn't know her own name or if this was happening in past or present, in forward or reverse. Two other bodies flailed near her, but she didn't know whose they were or if they were human or monster.

Touch the crystal, a voice echoed.

Crystal?

What crystal?

Touch the crystal.

Pummeled by the light, she stabbed out her hand, two

other hands thrashing into hers at the same time, all of them finding nothing but water. Agatha tore herself off the wall, reaching further, further, running out of breath—

Her hand scraped glass.

Instantly her body shattered, like she was made of glass too, any last shreds of awareness shattering with it.

For a moment, there was nothing: just light inhaling her, then crumpling to darkness like a sheet of paper charring in at the edges.

Slowly, she reassembled, body, soul, self.

When she opened her eyes, Agatha was no longer in Gnomeland.

She was standing in a glass room, the transparent walls and floor glowing wintry blue, the inside of the room swirling with thin, silvery smoke. A faint ache throbbed at her temples, but her chest had gotten worse; every breath felt like it was packing her lungs with rocks.

"Where are we?" someone wheezed.

Agatha turned to Tedros and Sophie, their wet bodies framed by a rounded, luminous glass wall. Both looked shaky. Tedros rubbed at his bare chest.

"We're inside the crystal ball," said Agatha. "Look."

She pointed at the wall behind them. Outside the glass, water rippled and foamed, contained by a blue-stone bathtub.

"I feel like I got clubbed by a troll," Sophie choked, clutching at her flank. "No wonder Dovey was such a mess."

"For once, I agree with Sophie," Tedros said, still breathing hard. "Whatever we just went through beat the living hell out of me. How could Merlin survive it?"

"Merlin is a skilled enough wizard to defuse the power of the ball," said a voice from the corner. "Most of it, at least."

They turned to see Reaper stagger up, a gnarled, drippy mess, looking less like a cat and more a mashed banana. "And while cats don't actually have nine lives, we are much hardier than humans. Now stay alert. Our time inside the crystal is limited. Twenty or thirty minutes at most. The sooner we find answers, the fewer trips we have to make. The fewer trips we make, the less chance we suffer the same fate as your Dean."

Agatha's neck smoldered red, her body's sign that she was out of her depth. She gulped for air. "So what do we do now?"

The silvery smoke whooshed past her head from all sides, crystallizing into the same phantom mask she'd seen at school. The mask glitched again between the features of Professor Dovey and the face of someone familiar, someone Agatha was so sure that she knew. . . . But there was no time to study it further because the phantom was diving towards her, primed to ask her who she wanted to see—

Except this time, it blew right past her and pressed against the back of the glass, facing the empty bathwater as if Agatha was still *outside* the ball. Agatha watched from behind the mask as it spoke to no one, its voice echoing.

"Clear as crystal, hard as bone,
My wisdom is Clarissa's and Clarissa's alone.

But she named you her Second, so I'll speak to you too.
So tell me dear Second, whose life shall I cue?

A friend or an enemy, any name I'll allow,
Say it loud and I'll show you them now."

"Hurry! Start examining crystals!" Reaper exhorted, standing on tiptoes and inspecting the back edges of the mask.

"What crystals?" Tedros said, confused.

Agatha approached her cat, watching him paw the beads of smoke that formed the phantom—

Her eyes widened.

It *wasn't* smoke.

Each bead of mist was a crystal. Thousands of these little glass orbs, the size of teardrops, floated in the mask's shape like pearls held together without a string. And within every one, a scene played out, like its own miniature crystal ball.

Agatha pulled a handful of these crystals towards her, their surfaces cool and bubbly to the touch. She peered into the small glass droplets, replaying key moments from her own life: as a toddler, chasing her mother across Graves Hill . . . walking with Sophie for the first time through Gavaldon's square . . . falling from the stymph into the School for Good. . . .

But now she was finding crystals that played moments

from *Sophie's* life: Sophie as a baby with her mother . . . Sophie singing to animals in Gavaldon . . . Sophie battling Hester in an Evil classroom. . . .

Then, suddenly, Agatha was seeing scenes from *Tedros'* life—

And *Reaper's* too, she realized, peering into a crystal that showed her cat bullied by his handsome brothers.

"It's showing all of our pasts," Agatha said, thrown.

"Because all four of us are *inside* the ball. The crystal absorbs our collective souls," said Reaper quickly, studying various crystals before discarding them to the floor. "That's where Merlin and Dovey were limited in finding answers to why Excalibur rejected Tedros. Inside the ball, they only had access to their own lives. I told them to bring you three in—Tedros at the very least—but Merlin had vast experience at Camelot and Dovey a deep knowledge of the Woods, and they thought they could find what they needed in themselves without putting the prince at risk. They were wrong." The cat batted more crystals away. "Enough talking. Look for anything that might shed light on why Excalibur favored Rhian over Tedros. Anything that has the slightest connection."

"You said we only have twenty or thirty minutes. These are our whole lives, Reaper. All four of us," Agatha argued, still battling the pain in her lungs. "We don't have time to ransack every moment from our pasts!"

"Um, this *isn't* my past," Sophie sniffed, wielding a crystal that showed her climbing a tree in a ghastly black dress with shiny spikes that made it look like a porcupine hide. "I've never worn that dress, I never will wear that dress, and I don't climb trees."

"Well, it must have happened at some point . . . ," Agatha started, then stopped. In her hand was a crystal playing out a moment she'd seen before. A scene of two Tedroses running shirtless through a forest. She'd observed this very same scene back at school, when she was in the library, using the crystal ball to break into Camelot's dungeons. The ball had glitched to this image . . . an image that made no sense at the time . . .

Because it hadn't *happened* yet.

The crystal had first shown it to her days before she and Tedros would live out the scene in real life, two Tedroses escaping the execution after Dovey's spell.

Which meant . . .

"This wasn't the past. This was the *future*," said Agatha, turning to her friends. "The crystals must show the past *and* future. Sophie, that's why you're seeing that dress."

"There is no future in which I will wear *quills*," Sophie snapped.

"That's what I would have said about two Tedroses running through a forest," said Agatha. "But you wearing that dress *will* happen—"

"Wait a second. Something's wrong with this one," Tedros cut in, holding up a new crystal.

Agatha and Sophie peered into it from both sides and watched a scene of a young Tedros, nine or ten years old, chasing after his mother as she scurried through the Woods.

"This is the dress my mother wore when she left Camelot to be with Lancelot. I remember that night so clearly," said Tedros. "She escaped the castle without saying goodbye. But I never saw her go into the Woods. I never chased her. This is what I *wished* happened. I wished I'd gone after her like this." He stared at the crystal, perplexed. "But it isn't the truth."

Agatha and Sophie were just as puzzled.

All three turned to Reaper, immersed in scanning scenes and knocking them away.

"Must I remind you: the ball is *broken*," the cat said, not looking at them. "A working crystal ball only shows the present. This one has a crack in it and that crack altered its sense of time, mixing up the present with the past and future. But not only that: the crack added the dimension of space, turning the ball into a *portal*. Now that we're inside that portal, it's up to you to sort through the ball's broken time and determine which scenes happened when."

"But this scene never happened at all!" Tedros emphasized, holding up the crystal of his mother.

"Because human souls aren't as reliable as cats'," said Reaper, still studying crystals. "Humans store their memories, regrets, hopes, and wishes all in the same messy vault. Merlin may have called this a crystal of time. But that was wrong. This is a crystal of *mind*. The ball is cracked: it no longer shows us objective reality. It shows us reality as perceived by each of our minds. And the human mind is as cracked as this ball, clouded with error and revision. With each crystal, you must try to see clearly and determine what is true and what is illusion."

Agatha couldn't believe what she was hearing. "So it's not just time we have to filter, but we also don't know if these scenes are actually real?"

"Like this monstrosity of a dress," Sophie said, holding up the crystal with the offending gown. "It could be the past . . . or the future . . . or a false memory like Tedros chasing his mother?"

"Reaper, we can't find answers when we don't even know if the answers are true!" Tedros assailed.

The cat finally looked at them. "If it were easy, Merlin and Clarissa would have solved it."

Agatha looked at Tedros and Sophie. Without saying a word, all three began sifting through crystals.

Most of the scenes Agatha found were from her own life, as if the crystal ball was privileging her soul over the others since she was Dovey's Second. But a few scenes seemed dodgy: one where she and Tedros were in Reaper's throne room, with Tedros rifling through Dovey's bag (that didn't happen) . . . another where Agatha kneeled in a dark cemetery and laid a flower in front of a headstone marked "THE SNAKE" (that would *never* happen) . . . and one where she was hugging the bald, decrepit Lady of the Lake (she hadn't hugged her when she'd gone back to Avalon . . . or had she? She'd been so sleepless and scared. Who knows what she'd done?).

Sophie's scenes, meanwhile, were rife with mistakes: in Sophie's memory, she'd saved Tedros in the Trial by Tale (it'd been Agatha), won the Circus of Talents with a beautiful song (it'd been a murderous scream), and slain Evelyn Sader and her wicked blue butterflies (it'd been the School Master). But most of the crystals from Sophie's past featured Agatha in them, with Sophie again attempting to right wrongs: letting Agatha and Tedros go to the Evers Ball together; holding back the spell that made Tedros mistrust Agatha at the School for Boys; staying with Agatha and Tedros in Avalon instead of going back to Rafal. . . . But whether all these moments were truth or lies (mostly lies), Agatha still found comfort in being as much a part of Sophie's soul as Sophie was hers.

Tedros' crystals, on the other hand, tended to reflect scenes of him pranking stewards and nannies, feasting on steak and pheasant, and winning rugby games and swordfights, as if he'd repressed any part of his life that involved real emotion.

"It'd be nice to find one crystal of yours with me in it," Agatha muttered to him, batting down a scene of her prince and his Everboy friends doing daredevil dives into the Groom Room pool. "The only things your soul is concerned with are meat and sports."

"You're one to talk," said Tedros, rifling through crystals. "All you and Sophie seem to think about is each other."

"Hold on. Here's one of Teddy and King Arthur," said Sophie, pulling down a crystal.

Agatha, Tedros, and Reaper gathered around.

Inside the crystal played a scene of Tedros as a squirmy three-year-old, climbing his father like a tree while King Arthur sat at a desk in his bedchamber, putting a feathered quill to a gold card of parchment. A waning candle dripped red wax onto the edge of the card, splattering it with thick gobs.

"That's it!" said Tedros, stiffening. "That's the card from my father's will! The one he wrote the coronation test on. I remember holding it during the ceremony. It had red wax on it and the same crescent-shaped tear at one of the corners. . . ."

Reaper's eyes flared. "Agatha, touch the crystal and look inside the center, as if you were trying to activate a new crystal ball. Sophie and Tedros: hold Agatha's hand. Quickly! This might be the one!"

Agatha felt Tedros, Sophie, and Reaper grab on to her as she gazed directly into the glass droplet—

Another storm of blue light attacked her, turning her mind to glue. This time it took longer for her to recover, as if she'd been severed into parts that she couldn't put back together. Straining to focus, she saw she was *inside* King Arthur's bed-chamber, her friends and cat at her side. Her chest throbbed harder than before, as if it'd been whacked with a hammer. But there was no time to wallow in pain.

Tedros was already approaching his father, who was calmly writing at the desk in his nightclothes, floppy blond hair falling over his eyes the way his son's often did. The Tedros of the present waved his hand in front of his father but Arthur didn't see him. Tedros tried to touch his younger self, who was squirreling around in his father's lap, playing with a gold Lion locket around the king's neck, trying to get it open . . . but Tedros' hand went straight through the boy's clothes, through his father's chest, and through the frame of the chair like a ghost's.

"We are merely observers," Reaper explained. "The Present

cannot interfere with the Past. It is one of the five Rules of Time."

"What are the other four?" Agatha asked.

But now King Arthur was speaking to his young son nestled in his lap.

"This will be your coronation test when it's your turn to be king," Arthur said, finishing writing on the card. "And you will not fail, my boy." He blew the ink dry, his face darkening. "No matter *what* that woman says."

The king sat there quietly, staring at the card, as young Tedros fussed harder with the locket, trying to open it with his mouth.

Then Arthur pulled out a second card from the drawer, this one blank.

He began writing.

The scene went dark, as if someone had blown the candle out. Agatha had the sensation of yanking backwards, like a misfired slingshot—

When she opened her eyes, they had reappeared inside Dovey's ball, surrounded by the floating mini-crystals and the ones they'd discarded on the floor. Only now, the entire room seemed more translucent, the blue glow in the walls dimmer.

They were running out of time.

"What did your father mean?" Agatha asked Tedros, who was lost in thought. "'No matter what that woman says'?"

"I have no idea," said her prince.

"And what was he writing on the other card?" Agatha wondered. "Did he have second thoughts and alter the coronation test? Did he plan for something else and then change it to you pulling Excalibur from the stone?"

"There was only one card included in the will or the priest would have told me," said Tedros. "Likely the second card had nothing to do with my coronation test. Those cards were reserved for official proclamations. It could have been for anything."

"Or it could be a false memory," said Sophie.

"Maybe," said Tedros. "But I feel like I was too young to store false memories."

"*You will not fail*,'" Agatha repeated, reliving Arthur's words to his son. "'*No matter what that woman says . . .*'" She chewed on her lip. "Could he have meant Guinevere?"

"But why would my mother have thought I'd fail my test?" said Tedros, scratching at his rippled stomach. "She was so confident I'd pass it the morning of the coronation. . . . No, it couldn't have been her."

"We need to bring Guinevere inside the crystal ball," said Agatha, despite feeling sick over the thought of making Tedros' mother endure the portal. "Surely her memories can help us—"

"No," said Reaper. "Merlin was clear about leaving Guinevere in the dark about the crystal's powers. That's why I sent her up with the Sheriff instead of bringing her here. Merlin believed her soul unreliable when it came to her life with Arthur. Leaving Tedros behind to pursue a life with Lancelot made her more apt to paint her husband as a villain to relieve her guilt. Bringing her into the crystal would open up too many tainted memories that would yield more trouble than answers."

"Tedros, wasn't this your steward? That Gremlin woman?" Sophie asked from the other side of the room, brandishing a crystal.

Tedros and Agatha turned.

It was a scene of Chaddick outside Camelot's castle, climbing onto a gray horse dappled with white spots as Lady Gremlaine, robed and turbaned in lavender, saddled the horse with a satchel of provisions and fussed over Tedros' knight, smoothing Chaddick's jacket and brushing it of leaves and dirt. She squeezed Chaddick's hand and smiled at him, before Tedros moved into the frame and wished Chaddick off. Lady Gremlaine stepped back, giving the king and his knight space to say goodbye.

"I remember this," Agatha said, looking at Tedros.

"I do too. We don't need to go inside," Tedros preempted, clearly skittish about jumping into another crystal. "Chaddick stayed at Camelot a few days before he left on his quest to find knights to join my Round Table. This was the last time I ever saw him."

"Lady Gremlaine took a shine to Chaddick," Agatha recalled. "One of the only times I ever saw her smile."

"Because Chaddick respected and listened to her, unlike me," said Tedros. "Until I got to know her better, at least."

"Lady Gremlaine," Sophie mulled. "She's the one who had a long past with your father, isn't she? The one who the Snake killed before she could tell you her secret and the one who

Rhian and Japeth told me you treated poorly. Which means Lady Gremlaine could be Rhian and Japeth's mother and King Arthur their father. Which means Rhian could actually be the real . . ."

She looked at Tedros. Tedros didn't meet her eyes.

Agatha took her prince's hand as they watched the scene again and again.

"Reaper, we need to send a crow to Hort and Nicola," Tedros said finally, his eyes still on the crystal. "We need to tell them to find everything they can about Grisella Gremlaine."

Agatha's skin prickled. That name. *Grisella*. She knew that name. Someone she'd met? Or learned about at school . . . ?

The blue glow in the walls around them faded lighter, Dovey's ball losing connection fast.

"What happens when we run out of time?" Agatha asked, swiveling to her cat.

But Reaper hadn't heard Tedros' order or Agatha's question, his attention locked on a tiny crystal between his paws.

"Wait a second. That's *me*," said Sophie, kneeling towards it before Agatha and Tedros did the same.

Inside the crystal, Sophie was waiting by the Gnomeland stump in the same white dress she wore now. The sky was dark, the Woods blacked out around her.

Sophie glanced at Agatha and Tedros. "This must be when I first came with Robin and then went back to look for you—"

"No. It's not," said Tedros sharply.

Because in the crystal's scene, Sophie wasn't going to look for her friends. She was pacing by the stump, her eyes darting around the Woods, making sure no one had seen her. Then her body froze, suddenly bathed in flamelight, which grew brighter and brighter. . . .

A blue-and-gold carriage, lit by torches and carved with Camelot's crest, entered the crystal's frame, slowing down as it approached Sophie. There was a boy inside the carriage, his face shadowed as the driver pulled the horses to a stop.

The carriage door opened.

Sophie climbed in next to the boy.

The driver whipped the horses and the carriage reversed direction, back towards Camelot, as the shadowy boy and Sophie rode away, the leaves of the Woods dusting up behind them.

The scene went dark, before it began to replay.

Slowly, three pairs of eyes, two friends' and a cat's, all shifted to Sophie. Agatha's heart pumped harder, her neck on fire. She looked at Sophie as if she were a stranger.

"You think I'd go *back* to the castle? To . . . *him*?" Sophie spluttered.

"You went back to Rafal the same way!" Tedros attacked. "The same exact way. Leaving Agatha and me behind, in the middle of the night, in secret."

"But I loved Rafal!" Sophie bit back, her cheeks pink. "I'd never go back to Rhian! Rhian's a monster! He tried to kill both of you!"

"While you stood by his side!" Tedros pounced. "While you fought for him!"

"*Pretended* to fight for him!" Sophie shouted. "Everything I've done has been to put you back on the throne—"

"Yes, me, the rot. The rot you said should have been *killed*," Tedros lashed.

"You can't think this is real. You can't think it's true," Sophie said, her mouth trembling. She turned to Agatha and clasped her shoulders. "Aggie, please . . ."

Tedros glowered at Sophie, so sure it was the truth. And for the briefest of moments, so did her best friend. . . .

Then Agatha's heart slowed, the heat seeping out of her.

"No," she exhaled. "It's not true."

Sophie let go of her, caving in relief.

Tedros shook his head. "You always trust her, Agatha. Always. And it's nearly killed us a thousand times."

"But it *hasn't* killed us," said Agatha calmly. "And the reason why is staring at us, crystal clear. I've been searching through Sophie's memories, just like I have yours and mine. And the difference between Sophie's memories and ours is that she wishes she'd done the right thing all those times she didn't. She wishes she'd been Good again and again and again. That's why she's my friend. Because I know what's in her heart, beneath all her mistakes. And this future here? To return to a boy she doesn't love and destroy everything she's been fighting for? To throw away the friendships she's given her life to build? It's the darkest kind of Evil. And that kind of Evil . . . That's not Sophie."

She squeezed Sophie's clammy hand. Sophie smeared away tears.

Tedros tensed, veins straining against skin. "Agatha, if you're wrong . . . imagine if you're wrong . . ."

"She's not wrong," Sophie rasped. "I swear on my own life. She's not wrong."

But Agatha wasn't looking at them anymore.

Her eyes were on a single crystal, suspended in midair at the bottom corner of the phantom, where Reaper had batted down all the others.

It caught her eye because this crystal was different.

It wasn't a scene of her, Sophie, or Tedros.

It wasn't a scene of her cat.

It was a scene of someone else.

Someone whose soul the ball shouldn't have recognized at all.

"Huh?" said Tedros, examining it over his shoulder. "Definitely a mistake—"

"I'm going inside," Agatha declared, touching the crystal.

"No! Dovey's ball will go dark any second!" Reaper warned. "You're the only one who can *reopen* it, Agatha! If you're inside a crystal when the ball loses connection, you'll be trapped inside the scene forever!"

But Agatha was gazing firmly into her crystal's center.

"No, you don't!" Sophie hissed, seizing her hand. "You're staying right here—"

Blue light clobbered both of them and again Agatha's chest suffered the blow, her lungs crumpling like parchment, before solid ground appeared under her feet. Blinded by light, she couldn't see, her mind a globby puddle, too weak to revive. As the blue glow dulled, she peeled her eyelids open and found Sophie by her side, just as battered and gripping onto her.

Pallid and shaking, Sophie glared at Agatha, about to chastise her for putting them both at risk—

Sophie stopped cold.

They were in a room Agatha knew: the walls covered in gold and crimson silkprint, matching the rug on the dark wood floor; the chairs refinished with Lion crests woven into the gold cushions; a bed curtained in red and gold.

I've been here, she thought, still disoriented.

Her mind locked in.

Of course.

Camelot.

The king's bedroom.

Agatha and Sophie craned their heads out from behind a standing lamp—

Rhian lay on the bed, his body cased in plaster, his face mummified by bloody towels so only his blackened eyes and gashed lips were visible.

His brother was feeding him broth, his gold-and-blue suit soaked in Rhian's blood.

"I should have stayed behind," said Japeth softly. "I never should have left you here alone with that . . . *she-wolf.*"

Rhian's voice came out gritty and weak. "No. She fought for me. She was on our side. They must have taken her hostage. Agatha and the rebels—"

"You fool. You don't think she was in on it?" the Snake blistered. "She conspired with the rebels before the execution. To pretend to be on your side. To act your loyal princess. She played you like the sweetest harp."

Blood oozed out of Rhian's lips. "If that's true, then why did the pen choose her? Why did the pen choose her to be my queen?"

Japeth didn't answer.

"She's meant to be with me, brother," Rhian rasped. "She's meant to help us get what we want. What *you* want. To bring the one we love back from the dead."

Agatha's heart stopped.

Sophie's hand clamped hers like a vise.

The one we love?

Back from the dead?

Between the gap in the bed-curtains, the two boys were still, Rhian's pained breaths the only sound in the room.

Japeth touched his brother's lips. "There's only one way to find out the truth. I'll ride to find Sophie. If the pen is right, then she'll be trying to find her way back to you. She'll be on her own. But if she's with Agatha and Tedros, the three of them thick as thieves, then the pen was wrong. And I'll bring her heart back in a box." His jaw sharpened. "I'll bring you all *three* of their hearts."

Rhian struggled for air. "And . . . and . . . if you don't find her?"

"Oh, I'll find her." His brother morphed into his shiny black suit of eels. "Because my scims will search every crevice and cave and hole in the Woods until they do."

Agatha and Sophie turned to each other, panicked—

They knocked heads, sending Agatha reeling into the lamp, which rattled against the wall.

Agatha rubbed her skull. "I thought we couldn't affect things inside the crystals," she said, eyeing the lamp askew. "I thought we were ghosts—"

"Aggie," Sophie croaked.

"Mmm?" Agatha said, turning.

Sophie wasn't looking at her. She was looking ahead, her face milk-white.

Through the slit in the bed's curtains, Rhian was staring right at them.

So was Japeth.

"They see us," said Sophie.

"Don't be an idiot. They can't see us," Agatha scoffed.

Japeth bolted to his feet, teeth bared.

"They see us," Agatha gasped.

Hundreds of scims flew off the Snake's body, ripping straight for the two girls' heads—

But Agatha was already falling backwards into darkness, her best friend screaming and holding on for dear life.

The House at Number 63

ort tried to ignore the posters, but it was impossible when there was one pinned to every single orange tree lining the Rue du Palais.

WANTED

All Current
Students & Teachers
of The School for
Good and Evil

REWARD:

60 Gold Pieces for
Each Soul,
Dead or Alive

BY ORDER OF

KING DUTRA OF
FOXWOOD

Kids their age in prim Foxwood School uniforms loitered by the trees, just out of school, guzzling glass bottles of orange soda and sharing gummy chews and sugar sticks.

"How we supposed to tell one of those School of Good and Evil stiffs from a sorry sop on the street?" asked a red-haired boy, inspecting the poster.

"They got that glowing finger," said a girl, reapplying lipstick in a pocket mirror. "The one they use for spells."

"For sixty gold smacks, I'll make my own finger glow and turn myself in," a dark-skinned boy said, eyeing Hort as he passed.

Hort picked up his pace. The boy was right. For sixty gold pieces, Hort would turn in his own mother. (If he knew who his mother was. Anytime he'd asked his dad, he'd got a grumble or a slap.) Hort glanced at his girlfriend, walking with him, expecting her to be just as alarmed by the high price on their heads.

"The boys in this kingdom are all so handsome," Nicola marveled at the well-dressed crowd on the Rue du Palais, Foxwood's tree-lined thoroughfare of shops, inns, and pubs, leading up to the king's palace. There seemed to be a uniform here, even for non-students: women wore solid dresses in a spectrum of colors, while men wore tailored suits in the same unpatterned shades. The sum effect made Hort feel like he was at a paint shop, trying to pick the perfect hue. Nicola ogled two passing boys, muscles barely contained by their suits. "Seriously, every single one looks like a prince."

"You can have 'em," Hort grumbled, picking at his new

blue pants, wedged up his bottom. "Foxwood is known for good-looking blokes, who are boring, brownnosing, and can't think for themselves. Just take Kei and Chaddick. Both from Foxwood, both pretty-faced sidekicks, working for twits. Nic, there's a lot of people here. Maybe we should wait until dark—"

"Tedros is not a twit and Chaddick is *dead*. Have some respect," Nicola chided, walking faster in her new beige dress. "And we can't wait until dark because we need to get inside the Foxwood School for Boys and look for Rhian's files. Rhian told Tedros he was a student there."

"But Merlin tried already and couldn't find any files for Rhian," Hort pointed out, itching at his hair. "I say we poison the Foxwood king instead. Robin said he was the first coward to burn his ring, plus if we kill him, no one can pay the sixty gold pieces for our heads."

"We are not killing a king who has nothing to do with our mission," Nicola retorted. "Reaper told us to find out about Rhian and his brother's past. And Rhian told Tedros he was a student in Arbed House. We have to at least check it out."

"I thought Rhian went to the Foxwood School for Boys."

"Arbed House is *in* the Foxwood School for Boys. It's a dormitory," Nicola said impatiently. "Didn't Tedros explain all this to you?"

"Tedros and I had a conversation once," said Hort. "I spent the whole time farting silently, hoping it might suffocate him."

Nicola side-eyed him. "Arbed House is where parents in Foxwood hide their children who they fear are Evil. So Evil they're afraid the School Master might kidnap them. No parent here wants a famous *villain* as a child. So Dean Brunhilde magically conceals these wayward children from the School Master so he never knows they exist. The Dean doesn't tell her Arbed kids they're Evil, though. Does her best to turn their souls Good." Nicola paused. "Clearly she failed with Rhian."

"*If* Rhian was her student at all," Hort reminded. "No files, remember?"

"Kei was a student in Arbed House too. So was Aric. And we know Japeth and Aric were close friends," said Nicola. "Look, I know it's a stretch, but it's worth a shot. All we have to do is find Dean Brunhilde and ask if she knows Rhian."

"Can we trust her?"

"Merlin and I talked before he was captured. He told me Dean Brunhilde was a friend of his. If she's a friend of Merlin, then she's a friend of ours—"

A gorgeous black boy reading the latest edition of the *Foxwood Forum* grinned at Nicola as she passed. Nicola smiled back.

"This is why Nevers only date Nevers," Hort crabbed, scratching his hair harder. "Nevers don't flirt with boys on the street and they don't turn down the chance to kill a king."

"Ten minutes ago, you were kissing me in the fitting room of Le Bon Marché and now you're acting like I forced you to be my boyfriend," said Nicola, noticing Hort clawing at his head. "Ugh, I told you not to mess with it. The point was to *blend in*. Robin gave each group ten gold pieces to spend and I used less than one to buy this dress so I'd look like a Foxwood girl. And you not only choose a suit that costs *nine* gold pieces, but then you go and do . . ." She pointed at his hair. ". . . *that*."

"Well, you're a first-year Reader who no one knows, but I'm *famous*," Hort insisted, itching his dyed, bright blond hair and walking tall in a spiffy prince-blue suit. "Everyone knows me from Sophie and Agatha's storybook. I had to change my look."

"You look like vampire Tedros," said Nicola. "Vampire Tedros with *lice*."

Hort scowled. "I look like a Foxwood boy and I blend in here better than you!"

A group of kids sidled up to him. The same ones he'd seen by the tree.

"What are you like?" Lipstick Girl sniggered, pawing his suit.

"Like a cream puff gone bad," said the redheaded boy, ruffling Hort's hair.

"Or one of those knobs from that school . . . ," said the dark boy, peering at him.

Someone kicked Hort in the backside.

Hort's finger glowed blue, about to fire at their heads—

Nicola seized Hort's hand, obscuring it. "Excuse me, is this the right way to the palace?" she asked the bullies. "We have an appointment with the king. My father's his Minister of . . . Poutine. What are your names? I'll be sure to mention your kindness to him."

The kids gave each other anxious looks and dispersed like flies.

Hort exhaled, knowing he'd been one second from giving

himself away and ending up back in Rhian's hands.

"Thanks," he sighed to Nicola. "You saved me."

"Saved *us*. Because that's what Evers do," she said, tugging at his blond bangs. "Even if their Never boyfriend looks like a cockatoo."

Hort puffed at his hair. "What's a Minister of Poutine?"

Nicola nodded at a sign, hanging outside a shop.

POUTINE PUB
Best Cheesy Potatoes in Town!

"Can we stop inside?" Hort asked.

"No," said Nicola.

Hort took her hand.

With her ebony skin and festoon of curls, Nicola didn't resemble Sophie in the slightest, the only girl Hort had ever loved before, but Nic and Sophie both had a supreme confidence and wicked humor, neither of which Hort possessed. Is that why he liked them? Is that why you like anybody? Because they have what you don't? Or was it that Nicola appreciated him when he was scrawny or pimply or in a bad mood, while other girls—girls like Sophie—only paid attention when he was pumped with muscle and playing the rebel to Tedros' prince? Maybe that was it, Hort thought: Nicola reminded him of Sophie, with her wit and moxie and charm, without all the bad parts of Sophie. And yet, the bad parts of Sophie were why he'd liked Sophie in the first place, just like Nicola didn't mind the bad parts of him. . . .

"We turn left on Rue de l'École, right before the palace gates," said Nicola.

Ahead of them, more students in Foxwood School uniforms came onto Rue du Palais, buzzing and dispersing into cliques. A few joined the packed crowd at a tent selling Lion merchandise: coins, pins, mugs, hats in tribute to King Rhian. Hort remembered the same Lion mementos worn by the people outside the Blessing, from kingdoms around the Woods. *They must be selling this stuff everywhere*, he thought.

"School just got out. Hurry!" said Nicola, pushing Hort past the tent. "We need to find Dean Brunhilde."

A smatter of young schoolboys pooled in front of the palace gates, tossing candy crumbs at pigeons idling on gold-paved stone inside. A palace guard butted the boys aside with the hilt of his sword and they ran off, whimpering.

"Turn here," said Nicola, hooking left at a corner.

But Hort's eyes were still on the guard, manning the gates with a second one, the two of them in shiny new armor, swords at the ready.

"Nic, look at their armor," Hort whispered.

Nicola peered at a familiar Lion crest carved into the guards' steel breastplates. "Odd. Why would Foxwood guards be wearing Camelot armo—"

Hort yanked her behind a wall.

"What?" Nicola gasped. "What is it?"

Hort peeked an eye out and Nicola peeped over his shoulder

at the two guards' faces, sunlit through their open helmets.

Not guards.

Pirates.

And one of them was glaring right at the corner they'd just turned from.

"Ya see somethin'?" Aran asked, a pigeon pecking at his boot.

"Coulda sworn I saw one of 'em Tedros-lovin' freaks. The weasel-face," said Beeba. "But his hair's gone yellow."

"Mush fer brains, you got. Even that twit's smarter than to show his face 'round 'ere with a bounty on his head," Aran grouched. "I hate bein' in the same place all day like a pile-a-bones. Can't we go back to sackin' kingdoms with Japeth?"

"Fancy King Foxwood melted his ring, so now we have to protect 'im," said Beeba, yawning.

The pigeon pecked at Aran again. He stabbed it with his sword. "Protect 'im from what? We're the ones who attack—"

"Shhh! Don't 'cha remember what Japeth said? Everyone's gotta think that Agatha 'n her mates are the ones tearin' up kingdoms so their leaders'll beg Camelot for protection. All they gotta do to *get* protection is burn their rings," said Beeba. "That's why Japeth sent men to sack Hamelin, Ginnymill, and Maidenvale—'cause their kings still wearin' theirs. Wish we could be doin' the sackin'. Love the feelin' of an Ever's face under my boot." She glanced behind her. "King Melty-Ring's comin'. Quick, act proper-like."

She and Aran lowered their helmets, leaving only their eyes

visible, as a procession of carriages topped with Foxwood flags rode up the driveway from the castle, stopping just inside the gates. The window of one of the carriages slid down and King Dutra of Foxwood appeared, his face still battered from the battle at Camelot.

"Duke of Hamelin sent a dove. His daughter was killed by masked rebels," he said breathlessly. "Any sign of trouble?"

"No, and there won't be, Your Highness," Aran assured. "As long as we're here, you're safe."

"Duke has since burned his ring and sworn loyalty to King Rhian. Should have done it sooner. Now he's lost his daughter," the king said, shaking his head. "How's King Rhian?"

"Recovering, sire," said Beeba, her vowels crisp. "His brother is at his side and helping with the kingdom's business."

The king nodded soberly. "Long live the Lion!"

"Long live the Lion!" the guards echoed.

They pulled opened the gates and the king's convoy rode down the Rue du Palais and out of sight.

"They're killing people, Hort. They're killing *princesses* and blaming it on us," Nicola breathed as Hort dragged her away from the palace and down Rue de l'École, weaving through groups of school children. "Rhian's willing to murder innocent people to make rulers destroy their rings!"

"We need proof that Rhian isn't who he says he is. And we need it *now*," Hort fumed. "Proof we can show the people. Which means we're not leaving this kingdom until we find it."

He pulled Nicola along, trying to convince himself that

they could succeed where Merlin had failed . . . that they could expose Rhian and take him down . . . that they could save this fairy tale from a very wrong end. . . .

But as the Foxwood School for Boys came into view, a gray stone cathedral draped in silhouette, Hort saw a tall woman in a turban blocking its doors, her arms crossed, the whites of her eyes glowing through the shadows, locking on the two strangers walking towards her . . .

And suddenly Hort didn't feel very convinced at all.

Up close, the woman in a rose-pink turban and robes had tan skin with deep lines around the mouth, chilly brown eyes, and brows so thin and arched it gave her a permanently suspicious expression.

"We're looking for Dean Brunhilde," said Hort, lowering his voice to sound more imposing. "Is she in?"

The woman crossed her arms tighter. The only sounds were the *snip, snip* of a gardener, pruning the hedges next to the stairs, and the *slup, slup* of a cleaner on a ladder, scrubbing the school's gray stone.

"Dean Brunhilde of Arbed House," Nicola clarified.

Snip, snip. Slup, slup.

Hort cleared his throat. "Um . . ."

"Do you have an appointment?" the woman asked.

"Well—" Nicola started.

"I'm the Headmistress of this school and seeing a Dean requires an appointment," the woman cut in. "Particularly for children from other kingdoms, pretending to look like they belong in this one. What school do you attend? Are you even Evers?"

Hort and Nicola exchanged glances, unsure whose turn it was to lie.

"We've had a string of attacks in Foxwood. The whole Woods is under assault by rebels. Good people have *died*," the woman said, hot with emotion. "The king has ordered all citizens to report suspicious activity to the Camelot guards—"

"Mother, I'm taking Caleb to play rugby in the park," a voice breezed, and Hort lifted his eyes to a strapping boy with curly brown hair in a Foxwood school uniform, sixteen or seventeen, ushering his younger brother, also in uniform, past the woman and out of the school. He whispered into his mother's ear. "Started crying during his history class. They were learning about Camelot's knights and well, you know . . ."

"I can hear you," sniffled Caleb, his cheeks pink.

"Be home before seven, Cedric," said the woman tightly. "Your father's making supper and I don't want you and Caleb out when it's dark."

"Now you're sounding like Aunt Grisella," Cedric sighed, brushing by Hort and Nicola, hugging his brother to his side. "Maybe we'll pick up a meat pie on the way home." He peeked back at his mother. "If Father's making supper."

A smile cracked through the woman's hard features as

she watched her two sons go, her eyes softening, then turning mournful. She noticed Hort and Nicola still standing there and her imperious stiffness returned. "The school is closed for the day. You may write my office to schedule an appointment with Dean Brunhilde for a future date. Now please leave before I call the king's guards," she said, scuttling past them and down the stairs. Hort watched her accost the gardener—

"Caleb and Cedric went to the park. Keep an eye on them," she told him quietly, handing the gardener a few silver coins.

"Cedric's a grown man, Mistress Gremlaine," he said. "He don't need me over his shoulder—"

She squeezed his arm. *"Please."*

The man searched her face. "Of course, miss," he said, gently. He slipped the coins back in her hand. "If I was in your shoes, I'm sure I'd do the same."

He put down his shears and hustled after the boys, while Mistress Gremlaine stayed behind, that mournful gaze returning. . . .

She frowned suddenly and swiveled towards the school steps, the door still open at the top, just as she'd left it.

But Hort and Nicola were no longer there.

"DID YOU HEAR what that man said? He called her Mistress *Gremlaine*," Nicola whispered as they scurried through the entrance hall of the school, Hort peeping back nervously to make sure the woman wasn't following them.

"So what?" Hort said, lost in the maze of musty corridors and spiral staircases. "How do we know which one goes to the dorms—"

"So *what*? Lady Gremlaine was Tedros' steward at Camelot!" Nicola reminded him. "Suppose this Gremlaine's related to her!"

"Doesn't help us get Rhian off the throne, so stop playing Detective Nic and start looking for a way to Arbed House," said Hort, peering into deserted classrooms, reeking of sweat and mildew. He sneezed, his eyes watering from the veils of dust. On the outside, the Foxwood School for Boys looked like an elegant cathedral, the hedges pruned, the gray stone polished, but on the inside it felt like a decrepit church, the floorboards creaking, the walls covered in mold, and cracked plaques offering dubious advice: "HEADS UP AND FALL IN LINE"; "FOLLOW THE LEADER"; "RULES ARE THE SPICE OF LIFE." Growing up, he'd thought of Foxwood as obscenely rich, given its steel trade, but clearly none of that wealth was going towards boys' education. Even the old schoolhouse in Bloodbrook, the poorest realm in the Woods, was in better shape. It's what he hated about Evers, Hort thought, recalling the workers sprucing up the school's facade: so much of being Good was a show. You had to rip away the surface, past the Beautification lessons and noble intentions, to find out who an Ever really was. At least Nic wasn't like that, he thought, as his girlfriend towed him to the end of the hall. Nic was more like a Never: too much herself to ever be able to hide it.

Turning a corner, they were hit with sunlight from a

scummy stained glass window, illuminating another plaque over their heads: "Loyalty over Boldness."

"No wonder every boy in this town becomes a sidekick," Hort muttered.

A door slammed somewhere close.

Sharp heels clacked on stone.

Hort's stomach flipped. He pulled at Nicola's arm, guiding her towards a staircase ahead, but Nic resisted, her eyes pinned through the stained glass.

A redbrick, two-story cottage lay in the yard outside, apart from the rest of the school, surrounded by clean, neat grass. Hort glimpsed a sign on a stake in front of it:

PERMITTED STUDENTS ONLY

And in the corner of the sign, a signature . . .

"Let me do the talking," Nicola whispered as Hort followed her into the foyer.

"You're a Reader. I know how to talk to *real* people," Hort rebuffed.

"And I'm the one who knows how to get what we need, so just smile and look pretty like the blond prince you are,"

Nicola ordered. "And don't touch anything."

Hort was certainly temped to. From the moment they'd come into the cottage, met with a clean breeze through the open windows, it was as if they'd left the school and stepped into Mother Goose's den. Cozy patterned rugs covered the floor, appointed with rocking chairs and soft couches. Potted lilies and fiddle trees bloomed near a spiral staircase, the bookcases behind it teeming with storybooks. Hort fingered a heavy blanket on the couch, furry and soft. He could feel his eyes closing. All he wanted to do was gorge on cheesy potatoes and hide under the blanket. The lighting wasn't helping: a sleepy orange glow seeping from dozens of glass-cased candles.

Then Hort noticed the picture frames, peppered across the tables and mantel. In every portrait, there was a stout, dark-skinned woman with beehive hair posed with a group of boys. Hort bent over, peering at more of these portraits. In each one, the boys changed but the woman remained, presiding over a new group.

Dean Brunhilde, Hort thought, moving to the last portrait on the mantel. . . .

His stomach dropped.

He picked up the frame—

Nicola slapped his hand. Then she saw what he was looking at and snatched it from him.

In the picture, Dean Brunhilde stood with a class of eight boys, all teenagers.

Four weren't familiar. But the other four were, huddled in the corner with mischievous grins, like a band of thieves.

A boy with angled eyes and a square jaw.

Kei.

A boy with violet eyes, spiky black hair, and sculpted muscles.

Aric.

A boy with copper hair, pale skin, and cold blue eyes.

Japeth.

And next to him . . . a boy with the same face.

Rhian.

Slowly Hort and Nicola looked at each other.

Rhian had told the truth.

He'd been here.

They'd all been here.

In this house.

This is where it began.

Chills swept up Hort's spine—

"You must be lost," said a voice, and Hort jumped out of his skin.

A boy in a school uniform came out of the next room, fourteen or fifteen with black hair, sunken eyes, and misshapen teeth, wielding a fistful of steak knives.

Nicola recoiled, bumping into Hort, who shoved the portrait behind his back.

"No one comes to Arbed House unless they're lost," said a younger boy, emerging next to the first, clutching forks and spoons. "Or if they want to steal our tea. We have the best tea: mint, assam, rose, tulsi, eucalyptus, licorice, cardamom, chamomile. . . ."

"Arjun and I are setting the table for dinner before the rest of the boys get back," the older one cut in. "I can show you to Mistress Gremlaine's office—"

"NO," blurted their two guests.

Nicola cleared her throat. "We have an appointment with Dean Brunhilde."

"It's important," Hort added.

Nicola gave him a look. *Let me handle it*, it said.

But Hort was on edge. That portrait spooked him. Something happened in this house. Something that made Rhian, Japeth, Kei, and Aric band together and become killers. The answer was here. And they had to find it.

"The Dean isn't in," said the older boy.

"Took the others to buy pins from the market," the younger boy prattled, a ball of baby fat. "She loves those pins. Been giving them to us as a reward. To keep us doing good deeds. Emilio and I already got ours."

"Our guests don't need every detail of our lives, Arjun," Emilio sighed, looking back at Hort and Nicola. "I'll tell the Dean you came by."

"We'll wait for her outside," said Hort, heading for the door, anxious to talk to his girlfriend alone—

Nicola yanked him back by his collar and Hort squawked. "Actually, we'll wait for her here," she said.

Hort looked at Nicola, confused.

Emilio frowned. "I'm not sure when she'll be ba—"

"Oooh, they can help us make supper!" Arjun said excitedly. "Girls are good at cooking!"

Hort could see Nicola gritting her teeth.

"Arjun, that wouldn't be appropriate," said Emilio.

"But we never get company! Rest of the school thinks we're Evil!" Arjun insisted, turning to Hort. "You know, cause we're separate from 'em and live at the school instead of going home to our parents. But we know the truth: that we're the best souls. That's why our parents sent us to Dean Brunhilde for training—"

"Mind if I ask your names?" Emilio asked, appraising his guests.

Hort answered: "Oh, we're two friends of Merl—"

Nicola pinched him and Hort bit back a yelp.

Then he saw it.

On the two boys' lapels.

Their pins for doing good deeds.

Lion pins.

Hort's heart stopped. Nicola's clammy hand grazed his.

"She loves those pins . . ."

Dean Brunhilde might have been a friend of Merlin's once.

But not anymore.

Because Dean Brunhilde was clearly on King Rhian's side.

"So?" Emilio asked, his eyes sharpening.

"Yes?" Hort squeaked like a rat.

"Who are you?" Emilio repeated, colder this time.

"Oh, my boyfriend's a former student of the Dean's," said

Nicola smoothly, nodding at Hort. "Must have graduated just before you started. Now working as a guard for King Rhian. We've come to surprise her with the news."

"I thought you said you had an appointment," Arjun pipped.

"We do," said Nicola, smoothing her dress, "but the news is a surprise. Apologies, but it's been a long journey and I need to sit down. We'll just wait in the Dean's office until she returns."

Emilio bristled. "I don't think that's—"

"She'll be thankful you took good care of us. Don't worry, keep on with supper duty and we'll show ourselves there," said Nicola, scooting past the staircase towards the hall.

"But her office is on the second floor!" said Arjun.

"Of course it is," said Nicola, turning on her heel, Hort scurrying up the steps behind her.

"FOUND THEM," HORT breathed, scavenging through a cabinet, pulling out stacks of leather-bound files and spreading them on the floor, soot spiking off the covers. "Labeled by name, but not in any order."

"Rhian would have been a student recently. Maybe he's at the top," said Nicola, seated at the Dean's desk, picking through her papers.

They'd found Dean Brunhilde's office at the end of the hall, but they hadn't anticipated what a mess it would be: books and notes everywhere, drained mugs with soggy tea bags, vases of flowers that had been dead for years, and a pervasive layer of dust that fogged up the room. *How can a Dean be so squalid?* Then Hort remembered his own dad, who was so busy taking care of other pirates that his personal quarters were a wreck. Kneeling on the floor, Hort rifled through the files, searching the labels for Rhian's name: ATTICUS . . . GAEL . . . THANASI . . . LUCAS . . . MISCHA . . . KEI . . .

"DEAR MERLIN—"

Hort wheeled in shock and saw Nicola leap at a brown chestnut bouncing around the desk like a jumping bean, the two sides of the nut flapping open as it spoke: "I'VE TRIED TO SEND THIS MESSAGE SEVERAL TIMES—"

Hort lunged for the nut, swiped it into one hand, and crushed the two sides shut, silencing it.

He and Nic stood frozen, listening to the hallway through the closed door.

It remained quiet.

"What is *that*?" Nic whispered, pointing at Hort's hand.

"A squirrelly nut," said Hort. "Safer than a letter, because there's no paper trail. Squirrel delivers the message and eats the nut, so there's no evidence it was ever sent. My dad got them from Hook all the time."

"That message was for Merlin. We need to hear it!" Nicola insisted. "How do we play it softer?"

"Whole point of a squirrelly nut is the message can't be preserved," said Hort. "If you try to open it with your hands, it plays at twenty times the volume, which lets everyone know the recipient is a cheat. Only way to open the message without a squirrel is to do it the way a squirrel does. Like this."

He raised the chestnut like a magician about to do a magic trick and popped it in his mouth. The woody edges chafed against his cheeks, but the nut slid open and a warm bubble of air floated out and pressed against his throat. He closed his eyes and someone else's words and voice came out of him in a low, hushed tone.

"*Dear Merlin, I've tried to send this message several times, but even Mistress Gremlaine's squirrel can't find you and hers is the best in Foxwood. I'm aware King Rhian, my once-student, has you in captivity as a traitor for supporting Tedros' claim to the throne. And though I hate to admit it, Merlin, I believe Rhian's actions justified. I didn't know he was Arthur's heir, but I was his Dean for years and I know his soul. You might think him Evil for all that has transpired, but that is because you and your ward, Tedros, believe you are on the side of Good. Yet Excalibur chose Rhian and Excalibur does not lie. It knows, as I do, that Rhian will make a great king. Just look at how he's handled the behavior of his own brother. That alone proves the Goodness of Rhian's soul.*

As for Rhian's files, I know you sent a snoop spell to my office to find them. My students' files are secret, as you know, since you were the one who helped me brew the teas that kept their souls invisible from the School Master. (I still make them drink the tea, even with him dead; you can never be too careful.) But regard-less of our friendship, you have no right to snoop in my office, which you well know, otherwise you wouldn't have resorted to criminal means. The reason you didn't find Rhian's files, however, is because I keep them with his brother's, which I've now moved to a secure location, untouchable by your magic.

I do wish you the best, Merlin, whatever your condition, but the sooner you align with the king and swear your loyalty to him, the sooner you will be on the side of Good. True Good.

Best wishes . . . Brunhilde."

The nut went spongy in Hort's mouth and dissolved down his throat, sweet and earthy.

He opened his eyes.

"His files aren't here, then," said Nicola, panicked. "She moved them. Somewhere we won't find them." She grabbed Hort's wrist. "We have to leave before she comes back!"

"Wait," said Hort, kneeling down to the files on the floor. He picked up the one labeled: KEI. "Just because Rhian's files aren't here, doesn't mean we can't find something in one of his friends'."

He pulled open the leather folder as Nicola dropped next to him. Hort read the first page of notes.

> Father: Footman for King Dutra
> Mother: Kei is disturbed; cold, emotionless,
>   no love towards sisters
> Father thinks it's a phase: says Kei loves Camelot
>   & King Arthur; wants to be a Camelot guard
> Agree on 1-year trial in Arbed House

Hort flipped to the next page.

Rhian & Kei: constant Camelot role-play (Kei
  believes R's delusions that he's king); Others,
  incl. RJ, bully Kei for believing R

Separate Kei & R?

Hort moved to the next page.

Kei: chosen for Ever Guard Trials

Then—

Kei & R no longer speaking

The rest of Kei's file tracked his performance in the Trials, leading up to his selection by Camelot as a guard at the royal castle.

Hort bit his lip. So Rhian had known that he was Camelot's king when he was at school. Only no one at school believed him, except Kei. So why had Kei and Rhian become estranged? Had Kei stopped believing Rhian? Only to later return to Rhian's side? That would explain Rhian's comment to his captain at the castle, when Kei failed to catch Agatha: *"But if you're going to be the weak link, especially after I took you back . . ."*

Was that also why Dean Brunhilde believed Rhian's soul was Good? Because she'd ignored his "delusions," only to be proven wrong?

Maybe that's why Rhian was sent to Arbed House in the first place. Because he insisted to his parents that he was King Arthur's heir . . . Because they thought him delusional, like the Dean did . . . But then where was Japeth in all this?

"Hort," Nicola said.

He turned and saw her holding a file labeled: **ARIC**.

The first page had more notes.

> Found starving & alone in Woods (age: 8? 9?)
> Raised by Mahut family (Aric attacked their
>   daughter; murdered pets; burned down house)
> Brought to Arbed House for full rehabilitation

Hort moved to the next page, the writing more scratchy and frantic.

> Spending too much time with RJ

Then—

> Attempts to separate them failing

There were no more pages in the file.

"Who's RJ?" Hort asked. "I thought you said Aric was friends with Japeth."

"Japeth is RJ's middle name," said Nicola.

"How do you know?" said Hort.

Nicola held up a faded envelope.

R. JAPETH OF FOXWOOD
62 STROPSHIRE ROAD

It had already been opened. They read the letter inside.

DEAR JAPETH,

TRIED TO WRITE YOU AT SCHOOL. THAT WITCH
DEAN PROBABLY KEPT MY LETTERS FROM YOU.
BECAUSE I ATTACKED YOUR BROTHER. EVEN
THOUGH I HAD FULL RIGHT. YOU KNOW I HAD
FULL RIGHT. NOW I'M EXPELLED FROM THE ONLY
HOME I HAD. AND THE ONLY FRIEND.
    DEAN TRIED TO GET THAT FAMILY I LIVED WITH
TO COME GET ME BUT THEY'D SOONER KILL
THEMSELVES. SO THE SCHOOL DUMPED ME IN
THE WOODS LIKE AN ANIMAL. LIKE MY MOTHER
DID. WHAT'D I TELL YOU. PAST IS PRESENT AND
PRESENT IS PAST.
    I'M AT THE SCHOOL FOR BOYS NOW. THE OLD
SCHOOL FOR EVIL.
    IT'S NOT THE SAME WITHOUT YOU.
    I'M NOT THE SAME.
    COME FIND ME.
    PLEASE.
    PLEASE.

ARIC

Hort's palms dampened the parchment. He didn't know why Aric's letter bothered him. Maybe it was a sadistic monster sounding like he had feelings. Or maybe it was that line—"I attacked your brother"—and its suggestion that Rhian's and Japeth's history was about more than the two twins; that there'd been a boy between them, a boy who was now a ghost. Hort glanced edgily at his girlfriend.

"Told you they were friends," said Nicola.

"This sounds a whole lot closer than friends," said Hort.

Voices echoed outside. The sounds of boys laughing, singing.

Hort sprung up. From the Dean's window, he could see them walking across the grass towards the cottage: eight boys, led by Dean Brunhilde.

All of them wearing Lion pins.

The Dean sang—"*First we go to hoe our garden!*"—and the boys chanted back: "*Ya, ya, ya!*" "*Next we carry jugs of water!*" "*Ya, ya, ya!*"

Hort and Nicola gaped at each other, then at the mess they'd made on the floor. No time to clean it up. And no way to get out of this house without being caught.

"Come on!" Nicola said, pulling Hort out of the room and into the hall.

"*Then we pound the yellow corn!*" "*Ya, ya, ya!*"

The door opened downstairs and the song cut off, Emilio's and Arjun's voices overlapping. . . .

A third voice boomed, matching the one from the nut: "IN MY *OFFICE*?"

Footsteps slammed up the stairs.

Nicola shoved Hort into a dark bathroom, the two of them barreling for the window as boots surged onto their floor. Hort counted to three with his fingers: on cue, both his and Nicola's fingertips glowed, so brightly it spilled into the hall. Dean Brunhilde swung into the bathroom, steak knife raised—

The last thing she saw was a black sparrow and a blond-headed squirrel leap out of the window, two pairs of colorful clothes floating down behind them.

THE HOUSE WAS easy enough to find, once Nicola's sparrow swiped a map of Foxwood from a market stall on the Rue du Palais, while Hort's squirrel bounded along the street beneath.

"62 Stropshire Road. That's the same address Rhian gave Dovey when she asked where he lived," Hort called to the sparrow after they'd made it to a quiet street. "Remember? Dovey questioned him when we were on the *Igraine*. He told us his parents' names too. Levya and Rosalie."

"Rosa*mund*," said Nicola.

"Even as a bird, you're a know-it-all," Hort sighed.

Stropshire Road was on the outer bands of the Foxwood Vales, so peaceful and still that Hort could hear Nicola's wings flutter as she drifted down to meet him in front of Rhian and Japeth's old home. There was nothing special about the one-level cottage, perched in between other cottages that looked exactly the same. Shadows moved across the closed curtains, suggesting someone was inside. But first there was the matter of clothes, a problem that was solved by the squirrel and sparrow probing houses on an adjacent road until they found an unlocked window, snuck inside, and raided the closets. A few minutes later, dressed like average Foxwood folk, Hort and Nicola knocked on the door of House 62, and flashed polite smiles when it opened.

A sweet-looking lady peeked out with gold-rimmed glasses. She had a Lion coin on a necklace around her neck. "Can I help you?"

"You must be Rosamund?" said Nicola.

"Y-y-yes," the lady answered, surprised.

"Lovely to meet you," said Nicola. "We're from the *Foxwood Forum*."

"Doing a story on King Rhian's childhood," said Hort.

"Since you're his mother, we thought we'd start with you," said Nicola.

"You must be very proud," Hort smiled. "Mind if we come in?"

Rosamund blinked. "Oh . . . I'm a-a-afraid there must be a mistake? I'm not King Rhian's mother."

Hort stared at her. "But King Rhian gave us your address—"

"Oh. He did?" Rosamund hesitated. "Well . . . it was a long time ago. I suppose there's no harm in telling you now. Especially if the king gave permission. This was back when he was a boy. We had an arrangement with Rhian's mother when Elle lived across the street. In House Number 63. She told Levya and I that she'd come to Foxwood to hide from the boys' father. We could save her life by telling anyone who might ask that her boys were ours instead. Clearly Elle didn't want the boys' father to find her or his sons. Understandable, of course, now that I know she was raising the future king and liege of Camelot."

"You said her name was Elle?" Hort asked.

"That's the name she gave me," said Rosamund. "But she was very private. I wouldn't be surprised if it wasn't her real name."

"How long did she live here?" Nicola pressed.

"Ten years, maybe? From the last months of her pregnancy until she sent the boys off to school. Then she left and I never saw her again. It's been ages."

"And what did Elle look like?" Hort hounded.

"Tall, thin, dark hair. Lovely mouth and eyebrows. The last time I saw her at least," said Rosamund. "Wish I could help, but she told me hardly anything about herself or the boys and they rarely left the house."

Hort glanced at Nicola, reading her face. Tall, thin, dark hair . . . Elle sounded a lot like Tedros' steward. *Lady Gremlaine*, Hort remembered.

He suddenly thought of something Mistress Gremlaine's son said to her before he took his brother to the park: "*Now you're sounding like Aunt Grisella . . .*"

Grisella, Hort thought.

Ella.

Elle.

Lady Gremlaine must have raised the boys here in secret

and put them in Arbed House before she returned to work in Camelot's castle.

"You said Elle lived in Number 63?" Nicola asked, turning back to Rosamund.

"Right there," the woman nodded, pointing at a house across the street. "Been empty for a long time now. Nothing to see at all."

A FEW MINUTES later, once Rosamund had gone back into her house, Hort and Nicola were already inside Number 63.

It had been easy to break in, given the state of the house's doors: waterlogged and splintered, the locks long broken. But the mission was a futile one. There was little left inside: no furniture, no clothes, no junk or trash or crumbs of food. The walls and floors had been bleached or repainted, even the ceiling, as if Grisella Gremlaine had wanted to leave no trace of her or the family that lived there.

"She was right," Hort sighed, leaning against a closet door. "Nothing here."

They heard voices outside and Nicola peered out the window to see three Foxwood guards in red uniforms coming down the road, knocking on each house, holding up crude sketches of her and Hort to the occupants.

Nicola's finger glowed. "Let's go," she said, mogrifying into a sparrow and hopping out of her puddle of clothes, towards the door.

Hort closed his eyes, fingertip glowing blue, about to morph back into a squirrel and follow Nic out—

But then he heard something.

A strange sound.

Coming from the closet in front of him.

Rat-a-tat-tat.

Rat-a-tat-tat.

Hort opened his eyes.

More rustling. More tapping.

Against the back of the door.

His skin went cold.

Leave, his body told him. *Leave now.*

Hort moved towards the closet.

"What are you doing?" Nic's sparrow hissed. "They'll catch us!"

But Hort's hand was already reaching out, his heart vibrating in his chest, as his sweaty palm curled around the knob and pulled it open—

A single blue butterfly flung out from inside, skeletal, dried up, flying madly around Hort's head with one last rush of life . . .

Then it fell at his feet, dead.

Blood Crystal

For a moment, Agatha thought she was on a cloud.

She raised her head, her body sprawled on a sea of white pillows across the floor of an elegant chamber. Through a window above her, the blue glow of King Teapea's palace mixed with the distant lights of Gnomeland's metropolis. She didn't know how long she'd been asleep or who had put her in warm pajamas or in this bed, but she saw now that she hadn't been sleeping alone.

There was the imprint of a body in the pillows next to her, a few long blond hairs snaking around the silk.

Sophie's ruffled white lace dress lay dumped in a corner.

Suddenly Agatha remembered everything: she and Sophie in the crystal . . . Rhian believing Sophie was on his side . . . Japeth promising his brother he'd find her . . . and if he found Sophie with Agatha and Tedros, he'd murder all three . . .

That's when Japeth had seen them.

Inside the crystal.

He and his brother had seen Sophie with Agatha.

Which could only mean one thing.

The Snake was coming.

Agatha flung out of the bed and found her black dress hanging in the closet, steamed and clean.

She could hear voices from another room.

Sophie, Tedros, and Reaper were sitting on a blanket, breakfast spread out around them as bleary-eyed gnome servants refilled the trays: almond-stuffed croissants, cinnamon toast, grilled cheese and tomato squares, broccoli and egg frittatas, buttercream pancakes. Tedros was already on his second plate of food, his hair wet from a bath. Sophie wore a stylish blue-and-red dress that seemed oddly familiar, but she wasn't eating, her face tense.

"His scims will find us," Sophie insisted. "It's a matter of time."

"Beatrix's team is on the lookout in the Woods. She, Reena, and Kiko are capable Evers," said Reaper. "Plus, we'll know when Gnomeland's defenses have been breached—" A meow squeaked out of him and he rubbed at his throat. "Uma's spell won't last much longer. Once it wears off, I'll no longer be able to speak to you."

"Rhian still thought I was loyal to him. I had him fooled," said Sophie, giving Tedros a satisfied look. Then her face tightened. "He said something about wanting to bring someone back from the dead. Someone he and his brother loved."

"Back from the *dead*?" Tedros said, stunned. *"Who?"*

"Never got the chance to find out," Sophie admitted. "We knocked over a lamp and they saw us. Rhian and Japeth saw me with Agatha."

"But how? And why was there a scene of Rhian and his brother at all?" Tedros pushed. "The crystal only reads the souls of the people inside it. And they weren't inside the ball with us."

"I had the same question," said Agatha.

They turned to her, standing under the archway.

"Why didn't you wake me up?" Agatha directed at Sophie.

"You looked so peaceful for once," Sophie said, smelling of fresh lavender. "Besides, I'm perfectly capable of briefing your cat and your boyfriend without you."

"You and Sophie emerged from the crystal barely conscious, just as the ball lost connection," Reaper explained to Agatha. "Tedros pulled you both from the portal and he and my guards put you to bed."

"Tried to sleep too, but couldn't really. Not without knowing what you two saw," Tedros said to Agatha, his eyes haggard. "My mum and the Sheriff are sleeping. Been here stuffing my face, before Sophie came down."

Sophie noticed Agatha still glaring at her. "Like my dress, darling? Made it out of the rug in Reaper's toilet, after I took a long lavender bath. Needed to extinguish the scent of that cursed white frock."

Agatha plopped onto the blanket. "Scims are coming for us. Kings are burning their rings. Reaper won't speak much longer. We don't have time to be sleeping or eating pancakes or taking lavender baths. We should be going back into the crystal and looking for answers."

"Or going back to the castle and killing Rhian while he's down," Tedros intoned, swiping another pancake.

"The castle is surrounded by guards and the crystal needs more time to recharge, as I learned firsthand with Clarissa," Reaper rebuffed. "If you were to go back in now, the connection would only last minutes. And it would be pointless until we understand: How could Rhian and his brother see you when they are at Camelot and you are *here*? And how could you knock over a lamp? It goes against the Rules of Time."

He raised a paw and yellow glow seeped out of it, casting words onto the blue wall.

1. The Past is *fiction*. The Present is *fact*.

2. The Past is *memory*. The Present is *the moment*.

3. The Past is *there*. The Present is *here*.

4. The Past is *retained*. The Present is *released*.

5. The Past is *weakness*. The Present is *power*.

"Rule #3," said the cat. "If they saw you, then you were physically in the king's bedroom. And you cannot physically be in Gnomeland and in Camelot at the same time." He paused, his wrinkled lips twitching. "Unless . . . *unless* . . ."

"What?" Agatha, Sophie, and Tedros hounded.

"Unless the ball recognizes Rhian's or Japeth's soul . . . even a sliver of it," Reaper proposed. "If the ball recognizes one or both of their souls, then maybe the crystal believed *them* the ball's rightful Second instead of Agatha. When you tried to enter their scene, it made your presence known. Like a defense system or an alarm. That's what bent the Rules of Time—" His voice caught, another burp of meows floating out before he regained control. "It would also explain why the crystal had a scene of them inside: they might be far away from the ball, but their souls are always connected to it."

"Utter dog crap," Tedros blustered, prompting a curdled expression from the cat. "There's no way Rhian's or Japeth's soul is connected to Professor *Dovey's* crystal ball—"

"Unless they are related to her," Reaper said coolly. "Past is Present and Present is Past. Lady Lesso used to say that to Agatha's mother, when Callis was a teacher of Uglification at the School for Evil. Callis had recently found me in the Woods as a hungry kitten and nurtured me back to health. It unlocked something in her. She openly wondered to Lesso what it might be like to have a baby of her own one day. The Dean warned her: the sins of the parent can live on in the child. The soul lives on through the blood. It's why Nevers make terrible parents."

"Past is Present and Present is Past. . . ." Sophie spoke softly, almost to herself. "Rhian said that to me."

Dread fluttered in Agatha's stomach, as if her own soul had figured something out. Something it wasn't telling her. "You're saying Rhian and Japeth could be related to Professor Dovey? But Dovey didn't have children."

"Dovey's siblings may have, though," said Reaper, his voice faint and scratchy. "And any children in Clarissa Dovey's bloodline—*meow, meow, meow*—would also be recognized by—*meow, meow*—Dovey's crystal."

"Dovey was an only child. She mentioned it at our last meal," Tedros countered. "There were no siblings to carry on the bloodline. So it's impossible that Rhian and Japeth's souls are part of the crystal."

"Only it's not just a fairy godmother's soul that goes into her crystal ball," Agatha realized, looking up at Tedros and Sophie.

Her two friends stared back at her. "*Professor Sader*," Sophie breathed. "A crystal ball has the soul of a fairy godmother and the seer who made it for her. And Sader made the crystal for Dovey."

"That phantom in the ball," Agatha said. "It glitches between Professor Dovey's face and a second face. I couldn't place it at first but now I know. . . . It's *Sader's*."

"But that still doesn't get us anywhere," Tedros groused. "Why would Sader's soul have anything to do with Rhian's or Japeth's? It's not like he could have been their father—"

He dropped his pancake.

"Except Professor Sader knew Lady Gremlaine! Dovey told me!" the prince exclaimed. "Sader was the seer that painted my coronation portrait and Dovey went with Sader to Camelot when he did it. Something Sader said to Dovey made Dovey think that he and Lady Gremlaine had a history."

"Hold on," Agatha said, agape. "You think Rhian and Japeth could be the sons of Lady Gremlaine and *August Sader*?"

"I thought August Sader didn't like women," Sophie volunteered.

"He didn't like *you*," said Tedros.

"Let's think about this," Agatha said. "Rhian and Japeth both have light eyes like Sader. The same good looks and thick hair. And if Sader is their father, that explains how Japeth would have magic in his blood, since Sader is a seer." She paused. "That always bothered me. That Arthur wasn't magical. So if Japeth was Arthur and Gremlaine's son, where would Japeth's scims and magic have come from? But having Sader as a father explains that . . ."

"Could a son of Sader and Gremlaine really be so Evil, though?" Sophie wondered.

"Could a son of *Arthur* and Gremlaine?" Agatha returned. "Lady Gremlaine was cruel at times. At least to me. Maybe it was *her* soul that infected the boys."

"Past is Present and Present is Past . . . ," Sophie mulled.

"Look, all I care is that if Rhian and Japeth are the sons of Sader and Gremlaine, then they're not my father's sons and Rhian isn't my father's blood," Tedros spewed. "And if Rhian isn't his blood, then he isn't the heir and he isn't king and the people of the Woods have to know they've been duped by a lying, filthy scum."

"And to think: all we have to do is prove it before magic eels kill us," Sophie chimed.

Reaper tried to say something, but strained meows came out instead, Uma's spell at an end.

Agatha cuddled her cat to her side. "But why would Excalibur pull from the stone for a son of Sader and Gremlaine? It still doesn't make sense . . ."

"Unless there's something about Lady Gremlaine we don't know," Tedros guessed. "What *do* we know about Grisella Gremlaine? She was a childhood friend of my father's, then came to work as his steward when he became king. Then my mother fires her after I'm born and she goes to her home in Nottingham until the Mistral Sisters bring her back. . . ."

That name again, Agatha thought.

Grisella.

She'd heard it before. *Where?*

Grisella.

Grisella.

Grisella.

"Wait," she gasped.

Agatha bounded up from the blanket and raced out of the room. She could hear Tedros scampering after her and Sophie stumble with a yelp, dishes clattering, before exclaiming, "Oh, no one should eat croissants anyway!" and chasing Agatha too.

"Where are we going!" Sophie yelled.

"Throne Room!" Agatha shouted.

"It's the other way!" Tedros barked.

Agatha spun on her heel and now Tedros led the group, sprinting around blue-stone columns as red pawprints lit up on the floor under their feet, before they hurtled between two gnome guards, jumped through the waterfall, and landed breathlessly in the familiar blue velvet room.

Dovey's bag lay limp in a corner. The bag that once held the Dean's crystal ball.

Agatha ripped it open.

"What are we looking for?" Tedros panted, thrusting his hands into the bag.

Watching him, Agatha had another bout of déjà vu. She'd seen this before . . . in one of the crystals . . . Tedros scrounging through Dovey's bag in the throne room. At the time she'd thought it was a lie. But it wasn't. It was the future. What else had she thought was a lie that would bear out to be true?

"Hey, this is my coat," Tedros said, pulling out his black jacket, spotted with dried blood, which Agatha had used to cushion Dovey's crystal ball. He opened the coat up and a stack of letters fell out, banded together, onto the velvet floor.

"*Grisella*," Agatha said, grabbing them. "That's the name these letters are addressed to!"

"The letters from Lady Gremlaine to my *father*?" Tedros blurted, accosting her. "Where did you find them!"

"Never mind that," Agatha said, spreading the letters on the floor, putting aside the stray card she'd found for the Bank of Putsi. "I read a few of them already. Arthur confesses a lot of his feelings to Lady Gremlaine. Maybe there's something here . . . something that tells us whether Lady Gremlaine was Rhian and Japeth's mother!"

"And if so, who the *father* was," said Sophie, picking croissant flakes off her shoe.

Tedros and Agatha looked at her.

Alarms exploded through the room: a fusillade of high-pitched meows, like a helium-drunk cat being stung by bees.

All the fireflies in the throne room poured out from between the velvet panels and the tiers of the chandelier, thousands and thousands of them, blanketing the walls from floor to ceiling, the flies jammed together and wings spread in a glowing orange matrix. Instantly, these lit walls morphed into magic screens, surveilling the various areas of Gnomeland. One of these screens was flashing, with grainy footage of the Woods outside the tree stump marking Gnomeland's entrance, the fireflies on the stump magically beaming back their field of view.

From what Agatha could tell, Beatrix, Reena, and Kiko were in full combat, shooting spells at something. . . .

A *scim*.

The eel stabbed Reena in the shoulder and gashed Beatrix's leg, before Kiko smashed it down with a rock. Kiko raised the rock again, but the scim had recovered, shooting out from underneath it, the shining, scaly tip spinning straight for Kiko's eye.

Agatha screamed futilely—

Beatrix tomahawked the scim with both fists, wrestling the eel to the ground. The eel ripped at her dress, slashing cuts in her hands and arms. Beatrix lost grip, the scim stabbing up for her throat—

Reena impaled it with a sharp branch, leaking goo all over her dress. Kiko stomped on the eel furiously, long after it stopped shrieking, then set it on fire with her fingerglow.

The three girls collapsed, heaving quietly, covered in dirt and blood.

Agatha slackened against the wall, just as drained.

"More will come," a gruff voice said.

Agatha turned to a firefly wall showing the palace dining room: the Sheriff, Guinevere, and Reaper together in frame, clearly monitoring the same surveillance. They could see Agatha, Sophie, and Tedros like the young trio could see them.

"Japeth will sense a scim is dead," the Sheriff warned. "We don't have much time. Gwen, Reaper, and I will man the tunnel above Gnomeland."

"*Meow meow meow. Meeeow!*" Reaper hectored at Tedros.

"Learned a bit of Cat under Uma's mother at school," said Guinevere. "Whatever mission Reaper gave you . . . he's telling you to do it *fast*."

Screens around the room went dark, fireflies floating back to their stations.

"We need proof Rhian isn't King Arthur's son," Sophie said, eyeing the mound of letters on the floor. "Before Japeth comes and kills us all. We need proof we can escape with and take into the Woods."

"We need proof even if we *can't* escape," Tedros said soberly. "Proof we can send out to the Woods before we die. The fate of our world is far bigger than the three of us."

Agatha and Sophie looked at him.

Fireflies gleamed in his hair like a crown.

"Uh . . ." Tedros shifted under the girls' stares. "Something on my face?"

"Come on," Agatha said, dragging Sophie to the floor.

The prince joined them as they ransacked King Arthur's letters for clues . . . something that would prove who the true father was to Lady Gremlaine's sons . . . something that would prove who Rhian and Japeth *really* were. . . .

Ten minutes later, Tedros said he found it.

It was in a letter from Arthur to Lady Gremlaine.

DEAR GRISELLA,

I KNOW YOU'VE GONE TO STAY WITH YOUR SISTER GEMMA IN FOXWOOD; I REMEMBER YOU SAYING SHE RUNS THE SCHOOL FOR BOYS, SO I'VE SENT THIS LETTER THERE, HOPING IT WILL REACH YOU.

PLEASE COME BACK TO CAMELOT, GRISELLA. I KNOW YOU AND GUINEVERE DIDN'T SEE EYE TO EYE WHEN SHE FIRST CAME TO THE CASTLE. I SHOULD HAVE EXPECTED THIS. IT MUST HAVE BEEN DIFFICULT TO BE MY DEAREST FRIEND MOST OF MY LIFE, AND THEN TO SEE ME RETURN FROM SCHOOL WITH BOTH A NEW FRIEND IN LANCELOT AND

A SOON-TO-BE WIFE. BUT I STILL VALUE YOUR FRIENDSHIP AS MUCH AS I EVER DID. AND I KNOW, DEEP IN MY HEART, THAT WE CAN MAKE IT ALL WORK. GWEN, YOU, AND ME TOGETHER.

PLEASE COME BACK.

I NEED YOU.

CAMELOT NEEDS YOU.

WITH LOVE,
ARTHUR

P.S. CAUGHT YOUR FRIEND SADER SNEAKING AROUND THE OUTSIDE OF THE CASTLE, TOSSING PEBBLES AT YOUR WINDOW. (CLEARLY WASN'T AWARE YOU WERE GONE.) QUITE CHARMING, DESPITE THE TRESPASSING! I EXTENDED AN INVITATION TO DINE WITH US AS SOON AS YOU RETURN.

"So Sader and Gremlaine were friends. More than friends, since he was prowling around her room at night," said Tedros, relieved. "Here's our proof that Rhian is their son."

Agatha reread it. "This isn't proof that Rhian is Gremlaine's son, let alone Sader's. It's compelling evidence. But we need more."

"Agatha, this letter proves August Sader and Lady Gremlaine were sneaking around at Camelot together, and we know from Lady Gremlaine's own admission that she had a secret child," the prince argued. "Any reasonable person in the

Woods would look at this letter and come to the conclusion Rhian is Sader and Gremlaine's son."

"But we're not dealing with reasonable people, Teddy. We're dealing with a Woods blindly loyal to Rhian," said Sophie. "Aggie's right. The letter's not enough. Sader and Gremlaine are both dead. They can't confirm it. And the Woods' newspapers are under Rhian's control. None of them will print it, let alone peddle a story that Rhian isn't King Arthur's heir. Only newspaper that might is the *Courier* and they're on the run. Not like anyone would believe them anyway."

Agatha was still gazing at Arthur's letter. That prickly dread pitched through her stomach again. The one that told her she'd missed something—

Alarms blared once more. Fireflies surged to the walls, lighting them up like screens.

On one of these, Agatha watched as above ground, in the Woods, a thousand scims assaulted the stump outside Gnomeland, while the stump sprayed back an array of magic shields and spells. Beatrix, Reena, and Kiko were nowhere to be seen.

On an adjacent screen, an army of armored gnomes, wielding swords, clubs, and scimitars, climbed up the abandoned Flowerground tunnel and stood on each other's shoulders to blockade the entrance under the stump. The gnome pyramid filled the vast hollow, a lattice of a thousand tiny bodies, determined to prevent any scims from breaching the stump and penetrating Gnomeland's metropolis.

Above ground, the eels smashed the stump with more

force, coming from all directions, but they still couldn't find a way in.

"I need to be up there, you meddlin' bag of bones!" Agatha heard the Sheriff growl from another screen. She turned and spotted him, Reaper, and Guinevere on the dirt floor of the Flowerground hollow, beneath the massive gnome blockade. The Sheriff spat at the cat: "You hear me? I'm a *man*. I should be first line of defense. Not a buncha *gnomes*!"

Reaper shook his head, meowing.

"What'd the damned thing say?" the Sheriff snarled at Guinevere.

"Too dangerous," said Guinevere.

The screens in the throne room went dark.

"Why is the cat keeping the Sheriff from fighting?" Tedros asked, lunging to his feet. "All I know is he can't stop *me*. Come on, let's go!" He dashed for the waterfall and leapt out of the room.

Sophie scurried after him—

Agatha yanked her back. "This isn't enough, Sophie, and you know it!" she said, holding up Arthur's letter. "We need Rhian to *tell* us who his parents are. We need him to *confess*!"

Sophie paled. "What?"

"Japeth is attacking us, which means Japeth *isn't* in the castle," said Agatha. "We need to go back inside that crystal. The one with Rhian, wounded in his room. He'll be able to see us like last time. We'll show him this letter. We'll make him tell us the truth! All we have to do is magically record it and send it to the entire Kingdom Council!"

"Have you lost your mind!" Sophie hissed. "First of all, Rhian will kill us!"

"He's mummified in bed—"

"His guards, then!"

"Not if we gag him—"

"Second of all, the crystal hasn't recharged! You heard Reaper. The connection will only last minutes!"

"We'll move quickly—"

"And thirdly, if Tedros knew what we were doing, he'd kill us himself!"

"Why do you think I waited until he left?" Agatha said.

Sophie gawked at her.

But Agatha was already hustling out of the room, dragging her best friend behind her.

"IF RHIAN'S TRAPPED in bed, why can't we just kill him!" Sophie hassled as she followed Agatha into Reaper's bathroom.

"Because killing Rhian won't put Tedros back on the throne. We need proof Tedros is the real king," Agatha declared.

"Rhian confessing Arthur isn't his dad won't give us that proof. Nor does it solve the fact Tedros can't pull Excalibur from the stone. Or the fact people hate him—"

"But it gets Rhian off the throne and gives Tedros a chance to redeem himself," said Agatha, finding Dovey's crystal wrapped in towels near the tub, still smelling of lavender. "Maybe once Tedros proves Rhian's a fraud, Tedros will be able to pull

Excalibur. Maybe it was his real coronation test all along."

"A lot of 'maybes' to risk our lives for," Sophie grumbled.

Agatha turned to her sharply. "Unless you have something better, it's the best plan we have. The connection won't last long. I'll show Rhian the letter, make him admit Arthur isn't his father, and we jump out before the portal closes." She snatched one of the vials off Reaper's vanity, emptied it of cream, and folded Arthur's letter inside, before sealing it and hiding it in her dress. She slipped into the tub, gripping the crystal ball against her chest, the steamy water making her heart thump faster than it already was. "Just do the spell to record everything he says."

"*Spell?* I don't know a spell to do that!" Sophie flung back. "I figured *you* knew a spell since this was your rattle-brained idea!"

"You're a *witch*!" Agatha retorted. "Supposedly a good one!"

Sophie blushed as if Agatha had questioned her very core. She climbed into the tub, her rug dress absorbing water like a sponge. "Well, there is a mimic spell to parrot back anything someone says, but it's so elementary, I can barely remember it—"

"Mimic what I'm about to say," Agatha ordered.

"Oh. Hum." Sophie bit her lip, before she tapped her thumbs together in a pattern, and her fingertip glowed pink.

Agatha dictated: "I will not waste time in the crystal, I will let Agatha do the talking, and I will leave when Agatha tells me to."

Sophie opened her mouth and Agatha's voice came out, but

slow motion and an octave too low: "I will not waste time in the crystal, I will let Agatha do the talking, and I will . . ." She squawked like a parrot. ". . . me to."

Agatha frowned.

"I'll work out the kinks by the time he confesses," Sophie clipped, submerging in the bath.

Agatha's splash unfurled next to her and the two girls held their breaths as Agatha laid the ball on the floor of the basin and gazed into its center. Agatha prepared for the assault—

Blue light pummeled her, but less brutally than the last time, as if the portal didn't have the same power. Even so, her chest felt packed with concrete and she could see Sophie quailing in the water, beaten by the force. Shielding her eyes from the light, Agatha clasped her friend's wrist and dove forward, pushing past the spike in pain and slamming her and Sophie's hands against the ball. A supernova of white light exploded, tearing the girls apart, leaving Agatha falling into a void, her awareness fractured.

Slowly her breaths settled, the glass bubble blurring into view around her.

They were inside now, two soggy heaps.

"Connection's weak," Agatha panted, pointing at the dim blue glow casing the walls. She pulled the vial out of her dress and unsealed Arthur's letter to Lady Gremlaine, clean and dry. "We need to move fast—"

Silver mist whooshed over their heads and the phantom face pressed against the glass: *"Clear as crystal, hard as bone, my wisdom is Clarissa's and Clarissa's alone . . . But she named you her*

Second, so I'll speak to you too. . . ."

"Hurry, Sophie," Agatha said, kneeling at the phantom's edge and searching the crystals comprising its mist. "Find the one with Rhian. It was in this corner last time."

Rubbing her chest, Agatha brushed aside familiar scenes: her and Reaper on Graves Hill, when a cat was just a cat . . . Sophie trying to kill her at the No Ball their first year . . . Sophie in the lacy, ruffled white dress, pacing by the Gnomeland stump, before getting into a royal carriage with that shadowy boy. . . .

Agatha paused, rewatching this last scene that Sophie and Tedros had fought about earlier. The scene so obviously a fake. For one thing, Sophie had already dumped that white dress and was wearing a new one. For another, Sophie was here with Agatha, helping her fight for Tedros. She would *never* go back to Rhian! Yet here the scene was again, Sophie whisked off in the king's carriage, repeating on loop as if it were real . . .

Then Agatha spotted it. Out of the corner of her eye.

A glass droplet with Rhian inside.

He was asleep in the king's bedroom, wrapped in blood-stained bandages, the sky pitch-dark through the windows.

"Sophie, I found it," she said, holding up the crystal—

But Sophie was staring into another small crystal, her body stiff, as she watched the scene inside replay over and over.

"What is it?" Agatha asked, the ball darkening around them.

Sophie snapped out of her trance. "Nothing. Junk crystal. That's the one? The crystal with Rhian?"

"If it's junk, why did you just slip it in your pocket—" Agatha started.

"So I don't mix it up with the others! Stop wasting time we don't have!" Sophie berated, pointing at the crystal in Agatha's palm. "Hurry! Open it!"

Sophie grabbed on to her friend's hand as Agatha stilled her breath and peered into the glass—

Blue light poured forth and the two girls leapt inside.

Their feet hit ground in the king's bedroom, humid and smelling of a thousand flowers, well-wishing bouquets from other kingdoms piled into corners. A slit of blue light hovered vertically behind the two girls, their portal to escape.

King Rhian lay motionless on the bed, his body trapped in plaster, his bruised eyelids closed and gashed lips oozing blood onto the pillow.

Agatha took a step towards him.

His eyes flew open, the blue-green pools locked on the two girls. Before he could scream, Sophie ripped the letter out of Agatha's hands and jumped onto the bed, covering Rhian's mouth with her palm, pinning him under the weight of her chest. He writhed beneath her blue-and-red dress, his blood smearing her fingers.

"Listen, darling. Listen to me," she said, fumbling at the letter in her lap, losing hold of it a few times before thrusting it in front of his face. "I need you to read this. Do you see what it says?"

Agatha saw Rhian startle with shock, his cheeks drain color.

Sophie pulled the letter down. "The situation is clear now, isn't it?"

Rhian lay stiff as a corpse.

"Good," said Sophie. "Agatha seems to think King Arthur isn't your father. This letter is her proof." She leaned in, her nose almost to the king's. "So I need you to tell me who your real father is. The truth, this time. I'm going to move my hand and you're going to tell me. Understood?"

She's moving too fast, Agatha thought. *She's forcing it—*

Sophie glared into Rhian's eyes. "3 . . . 2 . . . 1 . . ."

"Sophie, wait!" Agatha gasped.

Sophie lifted her hand—

"HELP! HELP ME!" Rhian yelled. *"HELP!"*

Guards burst through the doors, armor gleaming and swords raised, but Agatha was already swooping Sophie off the bed and throwing both their bodies through the blue portal.

Agatha landed hard on the glass of Dovey's crystal ball, her body radiating pain. She lurched up and seized Sophie by the arm: "You idiot! You fool! You acted like his friend instead of threatening him! You should have held your fingerglow to his throat or suffocated him with a pillow! Something to make him tell the truth! *I* could have gotten the truth out of him! That's why I made you swear to let me handle it!"

"You were too slow," Sophie croaked, clutching at her chest, her hand still streaked with Rhian's blood. "I did what had to be done. I did what was right."

"What was '*right*'? What are you talking about! That was

our one chance!" Agatha cried. "Our one chance to get the truth—"

She stopped cold.

Sophie backed up in shock.

Because the spatter of Rhian's blood was magically peeling off Sophie's hand.

The girls watched the pattern of blood lift off Sophie's skin and float upwards, the blood thickening and deepening in color. Slowly the pattern began to collapse, the drops of blood pooling together into a tiny sphere, swelling like a seed, the surface hardening, the edges sharpening, until at last its shape was complete. . . .

A crystal.

A *blood* crystal.

It drifted higher, towards the phantom mask, and took its place at the center of the mask, between the two eyeless holes.

Agatha reached up into the phantom and pulled the crystal down into her palm.

She and Sophie hunched forward and peered inside the smooth red glass, watching the beginning of a scene unfold.

The two girls exchanged tense looks.

"We need to go in," Agatha said.

Sophie didn't argue.

The glow of Dovey's ball faded, the connection barely holding on. . . .

But Agatha was already grasping Sophie's hand and glaring into the red center.

A storm of light later, they were inside the crystal of the king's blood.

THE SCENE HAD a red tint to it, as if taking place in the haze of a blood sun.

They were inside Lady Gremlaine's old bedroom in the White Tower of Camelot, watching Tedros' former steward pace back and forth, glancing anxiously out her window.

Agatha almost hadn't recognized her. Grisella Gremlaine still wore her signature lavender robes, but she was younger, *much* younger, hardly twenty years old, her tan face supple and radiant, her eyebrows thick and lips full, her brown hair loose to her shoulders. Lady Gremlaine stopped and put her nose to the window, searching the dark garden outside. . . . Then she went on pacing.

The glass of her window didn't reflect the two intruders from another time nor the faint portal of light behind them.

Agatha's hand squeezed Sophie's harder. Not just from the eeriness of traveling back in time or witnessing a woman she'd seen murdered back from the grave, but also having proof, right here, that Lady Gremlaine was linked to King Rhian's blood. Proof that Lady Gremlaine was indeed King Rhian's mother.

And Agatha was quite sure that whoever Grisella Gremlaine was waiting for was King Rhian's real father.

"You sure she can't see us?" Sophie whispered.

"She's *dead*," Agatha said loudly.

And indeed, Lady Gremlaine didn't break a step, pacing even faster now, her eyes darting again and again to the window.

A pebble hit the glass.

Instantly the steward surged forward and threw open the window—

A hooded figure climbed in, shrouded in a black cloak.

Agatha couldn't see the face.

Professor Sader?

"Do you have it?" Lady Gremlaine asked, breathless.

The hooded figure held up a piece of knotted rope.

Agatha peered at the rope, her insides turning.

It looked like it was made out of human flesh.

"Where is he?" came the stranger's low, soft voice.

Agatha reached out to lift the person's hood, but her hand went straight through.

"In here," said Lady Gremlaine.

Quickly the steward ran her hands along the wall and found the edge of what appeared to be a secret door. She pulled it open and the hooded figure followed her inside, through a bathroom, and into an adjoining room. So did Agatha and Sophie—

Agatha froze.

It was the strange guest room that Agatha had been in once before. Back then, she'd been struck by how out of place the room seemed, far away from the other guest rooms and poorly decorated, with a small bed pressed against the wall.

Only there was someone *on* the bed now.

King Arthur.

He was asleep, hands folded over his chest.

Light brown stubble coated his golden skin, his cheeks rosy and smooth. He was eighteen or nineteen, in the prime of his youth. But there was a gangly softness to him . . . a delicacy that Agatha hadn't seen in her magical encounters with elder versions of Arthur. He snuffled serenely, undisturbed by Lady Gremlaine and the stranger.

"I don't understand," Sophie whispered. "What's happening?"

Agatha was just as confused.

"I put hemp oil in his drink like you told me to," Lady Gremlaine said to the stranger. "Fell straight to sleep."

"We must move quickly, then," said the stranger, holding out the rope. "Place this spansel around his neck."

Lady Gremlaine swallowed. "And then I'll have his child?"

"That is the power of the spansel," the hooded figure whispered. "Use it and you will be pregnant with King Arthur's heir before Guinevere marries him."

Agatha's stomach dropped like a stone.

"He'll have to marry me instead," Lady Gremlaine realized quietly.

"You'll be his queen," said the stranger.

Lady Gremlaine looked at the hooded figure. "But will he love me?"

"You didn't pay me for love. You paid me to help you marry

him instead of Guinevere," replied the stranger. "And this spansel will do that."

Lady Gremlaine watched King Arthur sleep, her throat twitching.

With a rushed breath, she turned to the stranger and took the rope into her hands. Lady Gremlaine stepped forward, holding the spansel out, her shadow stretching over the sleeping king, until she stood over young Arthur. She gazed down at him, so enamored, so possessed, that her entire body seemed to blush. Hands trembling, she reached the spansel around his neck. . . .

Agatha shook her head, tears fogging her eyes. Sophie, too, was stricken. *This* was how Rhian and Japeth came to be. By cold, calculated sorcery. Devoid of love.

Which meant Rhian was King Arthur's son, after all.

His eldest son.

Rhian was the true heir.

All was lost.

Agatha pulled Sophie towards the door. She'd seen enough. They couldn't watch what followed—

"I can't," a voice gasped.

Agatha and Sophie both turned.

"I can't do it," Lady Gremlaine sobbed. "I can't betray him like this."

Tears ran down her face as she faced the stranger.

"I love him too much," she whispered.

She dropped the rope and fled the room.

Agatha and Sophie stared at each other.

They were alone in the room with the hooded figure and the sleeping king.

The stranger exhaled. Retrieving the spansel, the hooded figure traipsed towards the door to follow Lady Gremlaine out—

The stranger halted.

Time seemed to stop, the only sounds in the room the deep breaths of the king.

Slowly, the visitor looked back at young Arthur.

Smooth hands reached up and pulled away the hood, revealing the stranger's face and forest-green eyes.

Agatha and Sophie jolted.

Impossible, Agatha thought. *This is impossible.*

But the figure was skulking back into the room now, step by step, towards the bed until the stranger loomed over the sleeper. The figure smiled down at the powerless king, green eyes twinkling like a snake's. Then calmly, deliberately, the stranger hooked the spansel around Arthur's neck. . . .

Agatha was about to be sick—

The scene stalled. Bolts of red and blue static ripped through the room. Arthur and his seducer glitched into blurry clouds. The floor under Agatha's feet strobed and fractured, vanishing piece by piece. . . .

The crystal ball.

It was disconnecting.

Sophie was already hightailing towards Lady Gremlaine's room.

"Wait!" Agatha choked, tripping in the slippery bathroom

between the two rooms, but Sophie took a running start and dove into the portal as it started to close up. Agatha stumbled to her feet, the portal obscured by strobing static. She flailed towards it, the portal shrinking fast, the size of a plate . . . a marble . . . a pea. . . . With a flying leap, Agatha launched herself at the light—

Hot water engulfed her, filling her mouth and nose, as she sank to the bottom of Reaper's bath. Any relief at escaping the crystal was drowned out by what she'd just seen. Panic speared her like arrows, her heart taking slingshots against her chest. It all made sense now: the twins' evil . . . the Snake's magic . . . the suit of spying eels . . .

"Caught your friend Sader sneaking around the castle . . ."

"Your friend Sader."

"Sader."

The wrong Sader.

Agatha burst out of the water, wheezing. "Her . . . It was *her. . . .*"

Tedros crashed through the bathroom door. "What are you doing! Scims might get through any second and you and Sophie are . . ." He took in the scene. His cheeks went scarlet. "Have you lost your mind! You went into the crystal withou—"

"Evelyn Sader," Agatha gasped. "Evelyn Sader is Rhian and Japeth's mother. She hexed your father. She had his child. Rhian is the son of King Arthur and Evelyn Sader. Rhian is your father's eldest child. His rightful heir. Tedros . . . Rhian is *king.*"

Her prince looked at her. For a second, he smiled stupidly,

as if he thought this was all a joke, a ruse to distract him from being angry with her.

But then he saw it in her eyes. In the way she was shivering despite the steam.

She was telling the truth.

Tedros shook his head. "You're talking nonsense. My father didn't even know Evelyn S-S-Sad . . ." He backed against the wall. "You didn't see it right. . . . Whatever it was, you misunderstood. . . ."

"I wish I did. I wish it was a lie," Agatha said, anguished. "I saw everything, Tedros." She lifted out of the bath to touch him, to hold him—

"Wait," Agatha said, stopping stiff. A new panic ripped through her. "Sophie," she breathed, searching the room. "Did she make it back . . ."

Her voice trailed off.

Small, wet footprints led out of the bathroom into the hall.

Agatha raised her eyes to Tedros. "Did you see her?"

Tedros was still shell-shocked. "You're wrong. You have to be wrong. She has nothing to do with my father! E-E-Evelyn? The Dean?"

But now he caught the fear in Agatha's eyes.

The fear about something else entirely.

"Sophie," Agatha rasped. "Did you see her?"

Tedros gazed at her blankly.

Then his face went cold.

He was already running. Agatha chased him, water flying off her as she and her prince hurtled down the hall, checking each chamber, following the trail of footprints until they ended in the last room, the one sprayed with white pillows across the floor, where she and Sophie had slept—

Sophie wasn't there.

The window was open, two wet footprints gleaming on the windowsill.

Agatha's scream reverberated through the palace.

Because it wasn't just Sophie who was missing.

Her white dress was gone too.

Script of a Murder

Evelyn Sader, Sophie thought, steering the rickshaw up the spiral track.

A name from the past. Now a curse in the present.

Evelyn Sader: imperious and milky-smooth, with that wicked dress made out of butterflies. Evelyn Sader, Dean of the School for Girls, who'd brought the School Master back from the dead to show her love for him. But Rafal never loved Evelyn. He'd loved Sophie. He wanted Sophie as his bride. So he'd killed Evelyn Sader to get her out of the way. That was supposed to be the end of Evelyn's story. Her dark, devious schemes of love had borne no fruit.

But somewhere earlier in Evelyn's story, those dark schemes *had* borne fruit.

Because Evelyn had hexed King Arthur to have his sons. That much was clear. (Unless the scene was a fake . . . *Not possible*, thought Sophie. It had come from Rhian's *blood*, not his mind.)

But there were still so many questions. How had Evelyn Sader met Lady Gremlaine? Did Gremlaine know Evelyn had used the spansel she herself had disavowed? Did Gremlaine know Evelyn had borne Arthur's sons? Was that Lady Gremlaine's terrible "secret"? And had the School Master, Evelyn's true love, learned of it?

Sophie was so distracted, she was driving the rickshaw straight towards the side of the track—

She corrected course, holding down her panic.

She'd stolen the rickshaw from that noisy page boy (Snubby? Smarmy? Sauron?), who had parked his cart outside the window of the bedroom where she'd slept. She'd tiptoed past his snoring body, slumped against a tree, and found the snakeskin in the rickshaw's front seat. Wheels screeched against stone, and the gnome bolted awake to see his cart scuttling away, no driver in sight. "*Bhoot!*" he brayed. "*Bhooooot! There's a ghost in my cart! Bhoooooot!*" Sophie guessed that *bhoot* meant ghost in Gnome, so she did her best to play the part, swerving menacingly as the page boy chased. Soon his rickshaw was long gone, cruising upwards into the bright lights of the city.

She pedaled harder now, past Teapea's Temple and the Musée de Gnome, stress wrenching at her ribs. Tedros would hate her for leaving. He'd think Evelyn Sader being revealed as Rhian's mother and Arthur as his father had sent Sophie running back into the king's arms. Because now Sophie knew that Rhian was the true heir. Rhian was king. Which meant Sophie could be queen of Camelot. The *real* queen. And Tedros knew nothing came between Sophie and a crown.

Agatha would try to defend her, of course. Agatha would search for some kind of sign that her best friend was still on their side.

But Aggie wouldn't find any. Not just because Sophie had no time to leave one . . . but because if she'd let Agatha in on her plan, her best friend would have come after her, right back into Rhian's hands.

Which meant Tedros would win for now. Sophie would be branded a soulless, two-faced fink. The same girl who left them for Rafal and had played them for fools once more. Sophie, who had no loyalty. Sophie, who only cared about herself.

She didn't blame Tedros. If she were him, she would think the same things.

But losing her friends' trust was the price she had to pay.

Because this had nothing to do with Evelyn Sader.

This had to do with what Sophie had seen in a crystal.

Not the blood crystal.

Another crystal.

A crystal she'd found on her own.

The crystal Agatha had caught her staring at before she'd pretended it was junk and slipped it into her pocket.

But it wasn't junk.

That crystal was the reason she was abandoning her friends in the middle of the night.

And this is what she'd seen inside . . .

Her own self.

Cowering in the corner of the king's bedroom, her cheek gashed, her white, ruffled dress soaked with blood.

Rhian was across the room, in his blue-and-gold king's suit.

So was Japeth, in his gold-and-blue liege's suit.

They were fighting.

More than fighting.

A Lion and Snake, going for the kill.

Hands clawed at eyes and hair. Teeth sank into skin. Punches landed, spewing blood from mouths, their faces mangled to crimson pulps. The twins battled onto the bed, each straining to get to Excalibur—

Rhian got there first.

The blade swung through the air, the edge catching the light like a sunflare—

It impaled Japeth's chest.

Clean through the heart.

Rhian drew the sword out and his brother fell.

Slowly, Rhian kneeled over Japeth's body, watching him take his last breath. The king bowed his head, holding his brother's corpse.

Excalibur lay abandoned behind him.

Rhian didn't see Sophie move from the corner.

The fear was gone from her face.

Replaced with intent.

She raised the sword over Rhian's back—

The crystal went dark.

Sophie had watched this scene play out silently in the glass droplet, again and again and again.

Rhian kills Japeth.

Sophie kills Rhian.

That's how this fairy tale ended.

Or it's how she *wished* this fairy tale ended.

The crystals were unreliable, Reaper had warned.

Especially hers.

But it didn't matter.

This was her future.

She'd *make* it her future.

She drove the rickshaw faster, her teeth grinding hard.

Dovey said something to her once: "*This is about whether you are capable of growing from the snake of your own story into the hero of someone else's.*"

Deep down, Sophie never thought it possible.

At her core, she was a villain, not a hero.

Agatha and Tedros were the heroes.

The best she could do was to help them.

The witch turned sidekick.

And yet, joining forces with Good hadn't worked.

The son of Evelyn Sader sat on Camelot's throne.

Evelyn Sader! Sophie thought, still stunned.

Her bastard son from Arthur, born of black magic.

It didn't matter what Agatha and Tedros did.

This Evil was one step ahead.

This Evil was beyond Good's reach, a two-headed dragon scorching every shield.

This Evil was seeded so deep in the past that only Evil in the present could undo it.

Agatha and Tedros were the wrong heroes for this war.

But Sophie?

Evil was her blood.

She was the hero to slay this dragon.

And she had the crystal in her pocket to prove it.

Not that she could watch it again, since only Agatha had the power to make a crystal work. But just having it on her body gave her a cold-blooded resolve. All she had to do was follow the script of what she'd seen. The script of a murder. It's why she'd changed back into this repellent white dress. The future told her to.

As Sophie ascended through Gnome City, the lights of the kingdom blinked and beamed, but it was quiet now, not a gnome in sight, except a toothless grandma filling street lanterns with glowing fireflies and sweeping out the dead ones. Grandma Gnome glanced up at the ghost rickshaw, then shrugged and went back to work. Sophie heard a buzz growing as she pedaled higher, towards the top of the track, like she was a bee outside the hive.

With one steep push, she found the track's end, a landing pad beneath the ceiling of dirt that she, Teddy, and Aggie had fallen through to arrive in Gnomeland. Sophie climbed out of the rickshaw, the snakeskin cloaked tightly around her, and raised her palm into the dirt. Like quicksand, it grew wet and thick around her fingers, sucking up her hand, then her arm, then her hair, then her face. . . .

She pulled herself out the other side.

The din of war detonated through the abandoned Flowerground tunnel, shrieks and screams and thunderous slams reverberating. Lit green by glowing vines, the gnome blockade rose as far as she could see into the hollow, male and female gnomes of every age balancing on each other's shoulders and locking arms to withstand the shattering smashes of Japeth's scims against the pit.

But the gnomes' defense had started to crack. Two scims had broken into the tunnel, scudding around the lattice of bodies, stabbing at will, as the gnomes tried to fend them off without losing grip on each other and collapsing the blockade.

Sophie pushed the rest of her body through the dirt, sliding between the legs of a big, muscled gnome—and almost knocked straight into Guinevere and the Sheriff. Agatha's cat was clinging to the Sheriff's sack, tied around the Sheriff's bicep, the group of them hidden in the shadows of the blockade.

"I'm gonna fight those eely maggots and you can't stop me," the Sheriff growled at Reaper, but the cat knifed his claws into the Sheriff's shoulder, baring his teeth.

"*Meow*," the Gnome King commanded.

The Sheriff shoved his nose to the cat's. "You rat-faced, skunk-smelling troll—"

Reaper's body stiffened, his yellow eyes flaring.

"*Meow!*" he blurted suddenly. "*Meow meow!*"

He jumped off the Sheriff's shoulder and sprinted for the dirt patch Sophie had just come through.

"Agatha! He says she's in trouble!" Guinevere conveyed, dragging the Sheriff after Reaper. "And Tedros is *with* Agatha! If she's in trouble, so is he—"

Agatha's cat was about to dive through the dirt, back into Gnomeland, when he froze sharply. He glanced in Sophie's direction, her body hidden beneath the snakeskin, and she ducked on all fours behind the hulking gnome. The cat peered harder. . . .

"Let's go, then," the Sheriff barked, shoving Reaper down through the dirt and helping Guinevere too, until both had disappeared.

Except the Sheriff didn't follow.

The moment the cat was gone, the Sheriff flung his enchanted sack over the dirt pit, so that if anyone came back for him, they'd go flying into the sack instead. Then the Sheriff stormed towards the gnome Sophie was hiding behind and put his dirty boot on the gnome's shoulder. The gnome yelped in surprise, but the Sheriff had already started to climb. More gnomes shrieked, alarmed by the massive, hairy human scaling them like a mountain, but they were arranged too precariously to fight, reduced to wayward slaps at the Sheriff's head and bops at his nose. The Sheriff gritted his teeth, his boots digging into gnomes' backs, their shouts and smacks getting louder and harder, until he was high enough to spot one of the two free-flying scims, puncturing gnome after gnome, about to collapse the center of the pyramid and send half the kingdom tumbling to its death. The loose scim shot towards the strongest gnome, who'd already been stabbed twice and was struggling to hold the blockade together. The scim's sharp tip lined straight for the gnome's neck—

The Sheriff swiped the eel into his bare hand. He bit off the scim's head and spat it out, pulverized the rest with his fist, and dripped the goo into the darkness of the pit.

A thousand gnomes gaped at him.

They exploded into cheers, drowning out the rumbles of the scims outside.

Suddenly man's best friend, the gnomes helped the Sheriff climb higher, chanting *"GO SMELLY! GO SMELLY!"* in reedy chorus. Taking advantage of their distraction, Sophie hopped up gnomes in the Sheriff's wake, the dwarfish creatures grunting at her weight and swiveling their heads, only to see nothing there. As she scaled higher, Sophie heard more boisterous cheers and glimpsed the Sheriff crushing the second scim, sending its leaky guts spattering down and spraying onto Sophie's snakeskin. The gnome she was climbing gawked at the seemingly levitating goo, but Sophie was already past him, chasing the Sheriff, who was headed for the lid of the tree stump.

Outside, the scim assault on the stump ceased, the vibration of the thunderous blasts against the pit petering out to nothing. Gnomes erupted in celebration, thinking the battle won, but the Sheriff only climbed faster, as if the real villain was about to get away. Sophie struggled to keep up, losing ground. The Sheriff was clawing up the last group of gnomes, reaching out his meaty palms and forcing open the heavy stump, the chill of the forest flooding the hollow. With a snarl, he thrust his big belly and hips out the hole, letting the lid fly closed. Gasping, Sophie swung between gnomes, her soft slippers dancing on their shoulders. She dove for the last sliver of moonlight—

Brisk night air kissed her face before she yanked her last leg through and the stump slammed shut.

THE WOODS WAS silent.

Sophie lay only a few inches from the Sheriff, flat on her stomach, but he couldn't see her with the snakeskin coating her body. She stayed dead still as the Sheriff rose to his feet.

"I know you're out there," he growled, his eyes roaming the darkness, weakly lit by the stump's fireflies. "Hiding like the coward you are."

A leaf crackled—

The Sheriff spun.

Kiko froze, her rosy face and pigtailed hair painted in moonlight. "Beatrix and Reena heard noises and went to investigate and left me on guard, but I had to pee so I did it over there because those fireflies on the stump watch everyth—" She stopped.

The Sheriff had a finger to his lips.

"*Hide*," he mouthed.

Kiko ducked behind a tree.

The Sheriff listened closer, the silence widening around him. He prowled forward, his boot about to crush Sophie—

Then his eyes chilled.

Slowly, he turned around.

Japeth snaked out of the shadows, the orange glow of the stump reflecting in his scaly black suit like flames.

"Clever, clever. Giving Robin Hood your ring so he could sneak into the Council meeting undetected," the Snake said, face unmasked. "But why? What did he do there? Leave a message for a *princess*, perhaps?"

He held up his eel-covered hand, the scims pulling apart over his milky skin like ants fleeing a nest, revealing a blank card in his palm. Japeth bit hard into his own lip, drawing blood. Then he dipped the tip of his finger in the blood and streaked it across the parchment, the blood countering the magic, making words visible.

MAKE HIM THINK YOU'RE ON HIS SIDE

The Sheriff didn't flinch.

"It had to be your ring that Robin used, because Robin doesn't have a ring," Japeth pointed out. "Sherwood Forest left those duties to Nottingham, where the forest lives. Ironic, isn't it? Robin Hood, a subject of his mortal Nemesis? Which means it's not Robin who can save the day this time. It's the dear, misunderstood Sheriff."

The Sheriff snorted. "So that's why your brother sent his half-wit pirates to kill me in Nottingham. Thought they could get my ring. Got some smashed bones instead."

Sophie's heart shuddered so hard under the snakeskin she thought it'd fly off. *So I was right about Robin having a ring*, she thought. *Only it wasn't Robin's. That's why Reaper wouldn't let the Sheriff fight. He was protecting the Sheriff. He was protecting his ring.*

"Only three rulers still wear their rings. Three out of a hundred," said Japeth crisply. "And when tonight's attacks on two of those kingdoms are over, those three will be down to one. You, the last man standing."

"And so here you are to kill me," the Sheriff grinned.

"Didn't think it'd be so simple, to be honest," said the Snake. "I thought I'd have to kill Agatha, Tedros, and all the rebels to get my chance at you. Figured once you knew my brother was onto you, your friends would hide you well—"

He saw the Sheriff's face twitch.

"Ah, I see. They don't know you're here. They don't know you left your hiding place to come and fight *me*," Japeth mused. "Pride is the deadliest sin."

"Oh, there are deadlier ones," said the Sheriff. "Killin' a fairy godmother. Stealin' the Lady of the Lake's powers. Playin' henchman for a lying mongrel."

Japeth's eyes slashed through him. "And yet, the Lady of the Lake kissed *me*. The Lady of the Lake wanted *me*. That's how I stole her powers. Would Good's greatest defender fall in love with a *henchman*?"

The Sheriff had no answer. Neither did Sophie, trapped on the ground.

"Let's see it, then," Japeth ordered. "Show me your ring."

"Robin still has it. You'll have to fight him for it," the Sheriff replied calmly. "Good luck surviving in Sherwood Forest. Bet my boots you won't."

"I see," Japeth cooed. "It's just . . . I don't believe you. I'd bet my boots, as you say, that you wouldn't let that ring out of your hands, now that you know my brother's after it. You wouldn't trust anyone to protect it but yourself. Especially not Robin Hood."

The Sheriff met Japeth's eyes. Sophie waited for the Sheriff to laugh . . . to show he'd outwitted his opponent . . . to prove Robin still had the ring, like he'd said. . . .

"Think you're smart little arses," the Sheriff spewed, reddening. "You and your brother. You'll never win. Killin' me won't do a thing. Only the *ruler* of Nottingham can burn the ring. If I die, it goes to the next in line, and Dot ain't burnin' it, no matter what you do. Her friends will protect her—"

"I'm afraid your memory fails you," said the Snake. "If you die, that ring transfers to your successor, who according to Nottingham law should have been your daughter, until you *changed* the law so that your successor would be Bertie, your jail attendant, instead. According to the *Nottingham News*, you did it in quite the fit of rage after Dot rescued Robin from jail. I take it you and your daughter have a spotted history? In any case, Bertie's been basking at a new estate in Camelot, paid for by my brother. Which means Bertie will gladly burn your ring before your body makes it to a grave." Japeth's eyes flashed. "Betraying your own blood has costs, it turns out."

The Sheriff roared and charged the Snake like a battering ram. The Sheriff hit him so hard that Japeth went flying to the ground, knocked out cold. In an instant, the Sheriff was on him, beating him with both fists, gashing open the Snake's ghost-white cheeks, the Sheriff's punches fueled by a fire so deep Sophie wasn't sure he would ever stop. But something was moving on Japeth's thigh: a single scim still wiggling . . . struggling to peel itself off the Snake's suit. . . .

Sophie lunged too late—

The eel stabbed into the Sheriff's ear.

The Sheriff screamed in pain, writhing onto his back and mauling at his ear spouting blood, before he finally yanked out the scim and tore it to shreds. He crawled to get up, but Japeth kicked him in the chest, then delivered a hammer blow to the Sheriff's head with both fists, crushing him to his knees.

A blast of yellow light shot past the Snake's head.

Japeth turned to see Kiko sprinting towards him.

Scims shot off his suit, aimed for Kiko's face—

Sophie sprang to her knees. She fired a flare of hot pink glow that bashed into Kiko's chest, blasting her like a cannon-ball into the darkness of trees.

It was the strongest stun spell Sophie could muster, powered with the resolve to keep Kiko alive. Wherever Kiko was, she'd be slow to recover, but hopefully Beatrix and Reena would find her before any of Rhian's men did.

Meanwhile, the Snake had glimpsed the spell hitting Kiko

and wheeled in Sophie's direction, but he couldn't see anyone there—

The Sheriff took advantage of Japeth's distraction and clubbed him in the neck, throttling him to the ground. The Snake flipped over and kneed him in the groin, climbing on top of the Sheriff with lightning speed and pressing his hands to his throat.

Wrapped in snakeskin, Sophie scrambled to her feet, rushing for Japeth, another stun spell at her fingertips—

Then she stopped.

Or rather, something stopped Sophie.

Her *dress*.

It flayed at her body, the white lace hardening like a corset, tighter, tighter against her skin, burning hotter, hotter, until beneath the snakeskin, her white dress began to turn *black*.

What's happening? she gasped, stuck in place.

The entire dress morphed as shiny and dark as obsidian, hugging her body like a second skin, the once white ruffles hardening, elongating, sharper, sharper, into spiny, needling . . . *quills*.

Sophie's stomach dropped.

This dress.

She'd seen it before.

In a crystal.

The first time she went inside the ball: a vision of her clad in this porcupine dress as she climbed a tree.

She'd pooh-poohed the scene back then. The thought that she'd wear such a travesty. And not just that, but to wear this spiny-quilled dress in the middle of the Woods and then to start climbing trees—

Sophie's eyes quivered.

Oh no.

Like a gale wind, the dress began moving Sophie towards the nearest tree, an invisible force so strong she couldn't fight it. The dress dragged her up the trunk, so she wasn't climbing as much as ascending, being pulled past branches to the top, where the quills of the dress gouged into the thick bark, securing Sophie in place like a straitjacket, far away from the Snake and the Sheriff, still warring on the ground.

Sophie thrashed against the tree, the snakeskin shrouding her. Why couldn't she get the dress off like she could before? Japeth didn't even know she was here. How could a dress have a mind of its own? How could it come alive *now*? She should have known not to trust it: from the way Japeth insisted she wear it . . . to the way it itched when he'd been close . . . to the way it'd reappeared after she'd burned it to ash. . . .

It was his beloved mother's dress.

Evelyn Sader's dress.

And like the butterfly dress Evelyn once wore and her son's suit of eels, this was alive too.

Down on the ground, Japeth was strangling the Sheriff so hard that the Sheriff's face had gone cherry-red, the veins of his throat shearing at his skin.

The Sheriff raised a big, trembling palm—

And slapped Japeth in the face with all his strength.

Japeth let loose a startled shout, drowned out by a primal

war cry, the Sheriff bounding off the ground and snaring the Snake like a lion. A blade-sharp scim shot off Japeth's suit but the Sheriff caught it midair and stabbed Japeth in the rib. The eels on Japeth's body shrieked in terrible chorus, before they all launched from the Snake's suit like a thousand black knives and impaled the Sheriff's wrists and ankles, crucifying him into dirt. The Sheriff grunted in shock, then stared upwards, his black eyes big, his lips wheezing panicked breaths.

Bolted to the tree, Sophie floundered to make her finger glow, but was thwarted by the dress. She'd never felt so beaten, so scared. This was Dot's father. A villain who'd redeemed himself. A man of Evil who'd sided with Good when it mattered. He didn't deserve to die. Not now. And yet, she couldn't help him. She couldn't do anything.

Japeth stood up, face bludgeoned to an ugly shade of purple, rivers of blood flowing down his naked form.

He picked up a heavy stick off the ground and broke it over his knee, the end of it sharp as a stake.

The Snake approached the Sheriff and straddled his helpless body, his eyes empty and cold.

"You'll . . . never . . . win. . . . ," the Sheriff rasped.

"Isn't that what you said before this started?" Japeth replied.

Sophie let out a silent cry—

The stake ripped through the Sheriff's heart.

Sophie turned away, tears spilling onto her hands, leaves and branches scratching at her cheeks. She could hear Japeth ransacking the Sheriff's body for the ring. The Snake's breaths grew louder, his movements more frantic. He couldn't find it. . . .

Then it went quiet.

Sophie looked down at Japeth kneeled over the Sheriff's body.

He was frozen still.

Thinking.

"Bet my boots . . . ," Japeth murmured.

His eyes floated to the Sheriff's shoe.

He pulled off the dirty leather boot.

Then the other.

The silver ring glinted around a blackened toe, almost as bright as the Snake's smile.

Japeth sauntered into the Endless Woods, whistling a tune, his bare snow-white skin glowing through the darkness, before he glanced back at his minions. The eels released the Sheriff's body to the dirt and chased after their master.

Up in the tree, Sophie's dress melted back to white lace, gently unlocking her from the bark as if the dress was suddenly her friend. In a flash, she was sliding down branches, diving onto the ground, falling onto the Sheriff's body—

His eyes were still open, blood foaming from his mouth.

"Tell . . . Dot . . ."

"Shhh! I'll get the gnomes! I'll get help!" Sophie said, spinning for the stump—

The Sheriff seized her hand. "Tell Dot . . . me and her mother . . ." He choked out blood. "It was . . . love."

His heart stopped.

Slowly his eyes closed.

His hand let go of Sophie's, the skin ice-cold.

"No . . . ," Sophie whispered. She sobbed over the Sheriff, soaked with his blood. She would have saved him. She would have stopped this. She was the Witch of Woods Beyond. She would have torn out Japeth's heart and fed it to his eels. She'd have given her life to protect that ring, to protect the Woods and her friends. If only she'd been given the chance.

Enraged, she ripped at the white dress, shredding its layers and flinging them into the wind, but the dress instantly repaired and erased the Sheriff's blood, its magic sealing her in tighter, like a suit of armor.

Sophie hunched there, wet with sweat and tears, as dawn threatened the dark.

Something cut against her thigh. Inside her pocket.

The crystal.

The one that made her leave her friends and escape here in the first place.

The one that showed her a way to fight back.

A thick rumble echoed in the forest—

Sophie turned.

Seeds of flames flickered through the trees, gliding in her direction.

Sophie's eyes knifed to green glass.

Follow the crystal, she thought.

Follow the script.

The Sheriff would be avenged.

Payback was coming.

For Japeth *and* his brother.

Quickly, Sophie pulled the Sheriff's body into the trees,

away from the haze of sunrise bleeding onto the forest floor.

She paced by the stump, her eyes darting around the Woods.

No sign of Kiko, Beatrix, Reena.

No sign of Reaper or the gnomes.

She needed to contact Agatha . . . to ask her a question she needed answered . . .

But how?

Something Kiko said floated back to her: *"Those fireflies on the stump watch everything . . ."*

The rumbling grew closer . . . the torches brighter. . . .

A blue-and-gold carriage approached, carved with Camelot's crest, bathing Sophie in flamelight as the driver slowed the horses.

Through the window, Sophie spotted a boy inside the carriage, his face shadowed.

The door opened.

Using her pink glow to light her steps, Sophie climbed in next to the boy and shut the door.

He turned towards Sophie, his square jaw and thin eyes sculpted in silhouette.

"Rhian saw your message," said Kei.

He held up a familiar piece of parchment.

The letter from Arthur to Lady Gremlaine.

"Dear Grisella, I know you've gone to stay with your sister Gemma . . ."

The letter Sophie had shoved in Rhian's face as he fought her in his bed.

The letter that had made the king's eyes go wide, his bloody hands limp against hers.

But it wasn't the letter that had done it.

It was the words Sophie had painted over the letter, out of Agatha's sight.

The words she'd secretly scrawled with Rhian's blood.

She'd lied to Agatha, pretending to go along with her plan.

She'd betrayed her friends and the forces of Good.

But only Sophie had seen the crystal now hidden in her pocket.

Only she had witnessed how this tale really ended.

Soon the Lion and the Snake would be dead.

Sophie looked up at Kei. "He knows I'm on his side, doesn't he? The king?"

The captain didn't answer. He faced forward as the driver whipped the horses and the carriage veered on its wheel, back towards Camelot.

Cat in a Museum

Agatha stood at the center of the earth, her body coated with sweat, an endless pit of blue lava swelling beneath her like a luminescent sea.

Slowly, a glowing green vine lowered the Sheriff's body towards the lava.

Behind Agatha, hundreds of gnomes gathered on Lands End, a grassy slab suspended by vines, dominated by a golden obelisk, carved with the names of gnomes come and gone. Beneath the levitating field of grass, an ocean of fluorescing lava roiled, where the dead had been cremated. The audience of gnomes held

their hats and bowed heads as the lava welcomed its first ever human, molten waves storming and splashing over the Sheriff's body, before devouring it in a hiss of smoke.

Agatha didn't shed any tears. The Sheriff was dead by the time she, Tedros, Reaper, and Guinevere had made it past the enchanted sack the Sheriff had left as a trap. They'd tried to gather the fireflies from the stump and extract everything they'd seen, but the scims had decimated nearly all of them, corrupting the footage. But they'd watched enough to know that Japeth had killed the Sheriff in cold blood and stripped him of his ring. The one ring that could stand between Rhian and infinite power.

Agatha's soul raged like the inferno below.

Japeth killed Chaddick.

Japeth killed Millicent.

Japeth killed Lancelot, Dovey, the Sheriff.

All this time, she'd been obsessed with a lying king and his throne.

Meanwhile, his brother was murdering her friends without mercy.

Tedros and Guinevere flanked her, their eyes reflecting bright lava and dark thoughts.

"Your Highness?" a voice said.

They all turned.

Subby, the king's page boy, stepped forward. "Someone stole my rickshaw," he puled, gnomes watching. "Took it right from the palace!"

"*Meow, meow,*" Reaper exhaled, with no patience for this.

"I thought it was a *bhoot*!" Subby insisted. "But it was a human *bhoot*!"

"Meow! Meow!" the cat assailed—

"A human who was up there!" Subby blurted. "Up there when the Sheriff died!"

Reaper's face changed.

"I found this near his body," his page explained.

Subby held up something, catching the light of the graveyard.

All the gnomes let out a startled *oooooh*.

Tedros turned on his princess with a glare.

So did Reaper.

Agatha gritted her teeth.

Even from here, she could smell it.

The snakeskin in Subby's hands.

Stinking of dirt and mulch . . .

And lavender.

A TOOTHLESS GRANDMA gnome sat cross-legged on the floor, tapping her fingers across the bellies of a hundred dead fireflies like they were piano keys.

"Stop there," said Agatha.

Grandma Gnome stopped her tapping, pausing the distorted footage playing out on a glowing wall in the throne room.

Tedros, Guinevere, Agatha, and Reaper all leaned in, studying the scene on the wall.

"Any way to fill it in a bit more?" Agatha asked the old gnome.

The toothless grandma fussed with the dead fireflies, repairing broken carcasses and wings with her fingertip, which seemed to fill in the corrupted frame. *"A birdie doo doo on you,"* Granny Gnome warbled as she worked. *"A birdie doo doo on you . . . A birdie doo doo—"*

"Can you work any faster?" Tedros said, exasperated.

The grandma gave him a fetid look, punctuated by a fart. Then she went back to fussing and singing, exactly as before.

Tedros appealed to Reaper.

The cat mumbled as if to say, "Try ruling a kingdom full of them."

"Look! That's her!" Agatha exclaimed, studying the filled-in frame of Kiko bum-rushing the Snake, derailed by a blast of pink light to her chest. Agatha pointed at the disembodied glow. "It's Sophie's spell. She must have been hiding nearby."

"There's your proof, then. Your supposed best friend attacked Kiko to stop her from fighting the Snake," Tedros seethed. "Your supposed best friend was helping Dovey's and the Sheriff's murderer."

"Or she was trying to save Kiko from being killed," said Agatha reflexively.

"Still defending her! Still defending that witch!" Tedros spat, angrier than she'd ever seen him. "I never thought you could be so stupid!"

Agatha fought with Tedros often. Her prince was well

aware that she was as tough as he was and he loved her for it. But this time, Agatha had no ground to stand on. Sophie had deserted her friends and crawled back to the enemy. Not only that, but now Agatha recalled the way Sophie pinned Rhian to the bed when they went into the crystal . . . the rushed way she'd confronted him . . . as if trying to play out a different script than the one she and Agatha had agreed on. . . .

"*I did what had to be done*," Sophie had defended after. "*I did what was right*."

She botched the plan on purpose, Agatha realized.

But why?

That crystal, she thought.

The one she'd caught Sophie staring at and sneaking into her pocket.

Sophie had seen something inside of it.

Something that made her want to go back to Camelot.

"Hmm . . . if this is Sophie's spell, then *this* must be Sophie," Guinevere deduced, pointing to a wrinkle of glow in the corner of the frame. "The stump's fireflies picked up the presence of the snakeskin. Is there any way to track this spot of light through the rest of the footage?"

Granny Gnome strummed her fingers across firefly bellies once more, scanning through images and dexterously filling in scenes, following the blip of glow as it scaled a tree, where it remained until the end of the Snake and Sheriff's battle, when Sophie doffed the snakeskin and dragged the Sheriff into the darkness, before climbing into the royal carriage with a shadowed boy. Agatha watched as Sophie used her pink glow to light her steps into the carriage and close the door, before the footage froze on a final frame: the carriage driving off, dust kicking up from its wheels.

Tedros was about to combust. "So Sophie watches the entire fight from the safety of a tree, then cries over the Sheriff's body like a bad actress, then dumps him in the bushes and returns to the castle to be with those two monsters. If I get back my throne—*when* I get back my throne—that devil minx will lose her head with them."

He's right, Agatha thought, still at a loss. Everything Tedros was saying about Sophie was indisputable fact.

But why couldn't she accept it, then?

Why was her heart still defending her best friend?

Out of the corner of her eye, she noticed Guinevere chewing on her lip, just as conflicted.

"What is it?" Tedros growled.

"When Sophie was at the castle, she played Rhian's side so convincingly that I *believed* she'd betrayed you," said Guinevere. "But even under Rhian's thumb, she found a way to show me her loyalty. She found a way to tell me the truth. Suppose we're missing something?"

"Well, that was when she thought I was the real king," Tedros retorted. "But now that she thinks—" He clammed up.

Guinevere frowned. "What do you mean '*when*'? What's changed?"

Reaper, too, looked suspicious.

Agatha and Tedros shared a harsh glance. Her prince still seemed in denial about what his princess had seen in the blood crystal. And now the thought of him sharing the possibility with his mother that he might not be the true heir . . . that her husband had been hexed to father someone else's sons . . . that Excalibur had been correct to spurn him. . . .

Tedros turned back to Guinevere. "N-n-nothing. Nothing's changed."

"But why would you say Sophie doesn't think you're the real king—"

As Tedros deflected, Agatha found herself pondering something Guinevere said.

"She found a way to show me her loyalty."

"She found a way to tell me the truth."

Agatha's eyes floated back to the final frame, paused on the wall.

"There's something you're not telling me, Tedros," Guinevere strong-armed.

"Mother, I promise you—"

"Don't promise, if it's a lie."

Tedros swallowed.

His mother and Reaper stared him down.

Tedros began to sweat. "Uh . . . the name Evelyn Sader doesn't mean anything to you, does it?"

Guinevere's eyes flickered. "Evelyn Sader?"

"August Sader's sister?" Tedros said quickly. "Took over as Dean our second year at school? You and Dad wouldn't have known her. I'm just making sure—"

"Wait," said Agatha, cutting off mother and son.

She gestured towards the screen and the cloud of dust,

stirred up by the carriage. "Can we zoom in on this?"

The old gnome brushed her fingers across the heap of dead fireflies, back and forth, widening the image on the wall until Agatha held up her hand.

"Right there," she said.

Amongst the dust, something didn't fit.

A small cloud of mist.

Pink mist.

"Go closer," Agatha ordered.

The gnome obeyed, honing in on the pink dust with increasing detail, clearer, clearer—

"Stop," said Agatha.

Tedros held his breath, peering at the wall.

Reaper and Guinevere had gone quiet too.

Agatha ran her fingers over the frozen frame . . . over the smoky pink words that Sophie had cast as she'd lit her steps into the carriage . . . . an unmistakable message she'd left for her friends to find . . .

WHY DID THE LADY KISS HIM?

Behind the words, in extreme close-up, Sophie was glaring through the carriage's window, right at the screen, right at Agatha, her emerald eyes shining like stars in the dark.

"What does it mean?" Tedros asked, mystified.

Agatha gazed at the message, her own eyes reflecting Sophie's.

She turned to her prince. "It means your Devil Minx left us some homework."

AGATHA FACED TEDROS, Guinevere, and her cat as they sat on the velvet floor of the throne room, snacking from bowls of yogurt-covered almonds, caramel-soaked figs, and sweet potato chips. She hadn't the faintest clue what time it was, with several hours gone since Sophie escaped.

"Here's what we know," Agatha started. "Sophie is still on our side—"

"We don't know that," Tedros argued, mouth full of nuts.

"King Teapea, there's a stranger trying to enter the palace," a gnome guard announced from the door. "A highly *suspicious* stranger."

Reaper flashed a perturbed look and followed the guard out.

Agatha still hadn't gotten used to her cat having kingly duties, but she had bigger things to worry about. She leveled a stare at Tedros. "We know Sophie's on our side because she left that message."

"Agatha's right, Tedros," Guinevere confirmed. "Sophie's playing a dangerous game. Just like she did when she pushed me to save you from losing your head."

Her son scowled. "So she went back to Rhian and his monster brother . . . for *me*? Sophie, the saint? Sophie, the selfless? Wonder why she wasn't in the School for Good. Oh, I remember. She was too busy trying to kill us all."

"Sophie is unpredictable," Agatha conceded. "And we don't know why she went back or what she's up to. But we know she's trying to help us. That's why she gave us that question. It's the mission she wants us to focus on while she focuses on hers."

"You got all that from a dusty riddle? Wish you could read my mind the way you read hers," Tedros groused, grabbing a fistful of chips. "That message doesn't mean anything. *'Why did the Lady kiss him'*? Who's 'the Lady'? Who's 'him'?"

"The Lady of the Lake and the Snake," Agatha replied calmly. "Sophie wants us to figure out why the Lady kissed Japeth."

"The kiss that stripped the nymph of her powers. Merlin told Tedros and me about it when he came to Camelot," Guinevere remembered. "It was after the Snake killed Chaddick. The Lady of the Lake kissed him, thinking he was the true king."

"And thinking the Snake would make her his queen," Agatha added.

"But if that's true, why would she kiss Japeth instead of Rhian?" Tedros puffed. "Rhian is the heir. Not his brother."

"*Exactly.* Hence Sophie's question," Agatha pounced. "And it's the same question I had for the Lady when I went back to Avalon. She'd told Sophie and me that Japeth had King Arthur's blood. But not just that. She'd claimed Japeth had the blood of Arthur's *eldest* son. Only we know that's untrue, because Rhian was the one to free Excalibur from the stone. Which means Rhian is the eldest son, not Japeth. I told the Lady she'd made a mistake. She hadn't kissed the real king.

But she insisted that *I* was wrong. That whoever she'd kissed had the heir's blood and whoever she'd kissed was the one who pulled Excalibur. Which means something is still wrong here. *Magically* wrong. And now Sophie is asking us to find out why."

"But we already know the answer. Rhian and Japeth don't *have* Arthur's blood!" Guinevere snapped, losing patience. "Either one of them. They're liars. They're frauds. They found black magic that helped Rhian pull Excalibur and it's that same magic that made the Lady kiss his brother. That's the only explanation. Because they're not Arthur's sons! So it doesn't matter who the Lady kissed! It's all a big bluff! My son is the heir! My son is the king!"

Agatha and Tedros went mum.

Guinevere glanced between them, her face drawing in. "What's happened?" Her eyes clouded. "Does this have anything to do with that Sader woman?"

"It has *everything* to do with that Sader woman," said a weaselly voice behind them.

They turned to see two gnome guards and Reaper usher in a shock-blond boy Agatha didn't recognize—

Her eyes flared.

Hort.

But that wasn't the surprise.

He was holding something in his open palm.

A butterfly.

A *blue* butterfly.

Agatha glimpsed Tedros' face, denial giving way to horror.

And right then and there, Agatha knew it was time to tell his mother the truth.

BY THE TIME Agatha had finished speaking, Guinevere was pale as a ghost and Tedros was no longer in the room.

Agatha, Hort, and the former queen sat in pained silence, the prince's absence palpable.

"The woman in the butterfly dress. I met her once, a long time ago," Guinevere rasped finally, wiping away tears. "I didn't know her as Evelyn. Lady Gremlaine called her 'Elle.'"

"Elle was the name she used in Foxwood, when she raised Rhian and Japeth in secret," said Hort, eyeing the bowls of snacks but dissuaded by the moment. "I thought Elle was for the 'el' in Gris*el*la Gremlaine. Thought it was proof Lady Gremlaine was Rhian and Japeth's mother. Except there's an 'el' in Ev*el*yn too."

Hort looked uneasy without his girlfriend there, but Nicola and Reaper had gone with two gnome guards to retrieve Kiko, who Nicola and Hort had found badly stunned in the Woods.

Hort looked at Agatha. "Do you think Tedros will come back?"

Agatha didn't answer, lost in her own thoughts.

She'd told Tedros and his mother the truth about the blood crystal.

She'd told them the truth about Arthur's heir.

At first, mother and son had looked incredulous. The idea

that King Arthur could be linked to the half-sister of August Sader, the seer who painted Tedros' coronation portrait, wasn't just preposterous, but daft. Yet as Agatha relived each moment—the way Lady Gremlaine had enlisted Evelyn and her spansel to seduce Arthur and have his child; the way Gremlaine abandoned her plan and fled the room; the way Evelyn had retrieved the spansel, her snake-colored eyes dancing with Evil—Guinevere's face had seemingly aged in minutes, her hand grasping at her throat as if suffocated from the inside. When Agatha reached the moment where Evelyn hooked the spansel around sleeping Arthur's neck, Tedros thrust out his palm, stopping her, and fled the room without a word, leaving Agatha alone with his mother and Hort.

The silence thickened now, Guinevere's face a death mask. Hort peeked at Agatha, expecting her to comfort the old queen. But the truth left no room for comfort.

"Elle came to dine at Camelot at Arthur's invitation. That was the only time I met her," Guinevere went on, still shaken. "The dinner was a peace offering. After Arthur and I graduated from the School for Good, he'd brought me back to the castle to meet the staff, led by Lady Gremlaine. Arthur told them we were to be married." Guinevere paused. "Gremlaine was caught off guard. She treated me snidely and I chastised her for it in front of her staff. If I had known she was in love with Arthur, I would have handled it better, but the damage was done. She went to stay with her sister in Foxwood and refused to return, ignoring Arthur's pleas. That is, until Arthur met a friend of Gremlaine's prowling around the castle: a woman named Elle Sader. He invited Elle to dine with us as a way of letting Gremlaine return with an ally at her side. He thought it would help her save face and come home."

"What happened at dinner?" Hort asked.

Guinevere choked up. "I'm sorry. It's just . . . the whole idea of it!" she cried, face in her hands. "That Arthur's steward conspired with a witch to make him have children he didn't want . . . and then for the witch to take them for herself . . ." She shook her head. "Did Arthur know about this? Did he know a stranger had his *heirs*? Could he really have kept such a secret from me? From *everyone*?"

Agatha looked down. "I don't know. I only know what I saw."

Guinevere's eyes suddenly widened. "It must have happened after that night. There were signs at the dinner. Between Gremlaine and that snake—"

"What signs?" said Tedros' voice.

The prince came back into the room, his eyes stained red, his shirt wet with snot. He sat beside Guinevere and took her hand. All the defiance had melted out of his face, replaced with vulnerability and fear, as if in accepting that he might not be a king, he'd found permission to be a son.

Tedros' touch settled the old queen. "What signs?" he repeated.

His mother took a deep breath. "The way they whispered and snickered anytime Arthur spoke about our impending wedding. As if they knew something we didn't. And when Arthur mentioned that he wanted a seer to one day paint his child's coronation portrait, Elle's mood darkened. She said her brother August was a seer, but that his powers paled beside hers. That he might see the future, but she could *hear* the present— people's desires, fears, darkest secrets—and that the present had far more force to change lives than the future or past. I suggested that she use her powers to be a fairy godmother. She cackled like a witch. That's what her brother had told her. Use your powers to help people, he'd insisted. As if she would spend her life flitting around the Woods, making dresses for homely girls and reforming selfish princes, Elle mocked. Meanwhile, her brother grew more and more famous amongst kings and wizards, even coming to the attention of the School Master himself. A woman didn't have the same opportunities a man had, Elle said bitterly. A woman had to rely on her wiles. But that's what made her befriend women like Grisella, Elle added, grinning at Lady Gremlaine. To help other women use their wiles to their advantage . . . For a price, of course."

Guinevere wrung her hands. "She'd cackled again as she said this, and Arthur took it as a joke, laughing with her. He found Elle harmless. He liked that Lady Gremlaine had made a new friend. But I'd found Elle strange and unsettling. I remember feeling great relief when dinner was over and she'd left the castle. Later, that night, I found a blue butterfly in my room as I drew a bath." She looked into Agatha's eyes. "I killed it on the spot."

Guinevere sobbed into her son's shoulder. Tedros held her and caressed her ash-white hair. His eyes met Agatha's, any residue from their fights erased, the two resolved to battle through this somehow, to not let this be the end of the story.

"Evil may have won in the Past, but it will not win in the *Present*," the prince simmered, the veins in his neck pulsing. "Rhian might be my father's heir by birth. But that doesn't make him King of Camelot. Camelot is the great defender of Good. The leader of these Woods. And Evil will not sit upon its throne. Not while I'm alive. I'll protect my father's legacy. Whether I'm king or not, I'm still his son. I'll protect his right to rest in peace."

"Whatever we do, it has to be soon," Hort warned. "When Reaper let us in, a message arrived for him from Yuba, coded in Gnome. The first years and teachers are safe. But there's only three swans left in the Storian's carving. Or was it four. My Gnome is awful. Just a few rings that haven't been burned, then. And Japeth has the Sheriff's . . ."

Agatha was lost in her head, Tedros' words replaying.

"I'll protect his right to rest in peace."

Rest in peace.

Rest in peace.

Agatha jolted, as if a butterfly had taken wing in her chest. "Tedros?"

Her prince looked at her.

"You mentioned something earlier," she said. "When Reaper gave us our mission. Something about a riddle from the Lady of the Lake. A riddle about 'unburying' your father. What did you mean?"

Guinevere raised her head, suddenly alert.

"After she lost her powers, the Lady of the Lake let Merlin

ask her a question," Tedros replied, feeling the weight of his princess's stare. "One question and then he could never return to Avalon again."

Agatha remembered what the Lady told her about the wizard: "*We made a deal.*" The same deal she'd made with Agatha. One question and one question only. Except in the stress of the moment, Agatha hadn't thought to ask her what Merlin's question was.

"Merlin wanted to know if my father's sword had a message for me. The Lady wrote the answer to Merlin's question on a slip of parchment," the prince went on. "'*Unbury Me.*' That's all it said. Except I recognized those words. They were the same ones my father said to me in my dreams. It's *his* message." He looked at his mother. "But I don't understand it. It can't mean to literally unbury *him*—"

"Of course not," Guinevere agreed. "But it has to mean something!"

Tedros shifted anxiously. "Maybe it meant Dad has secrets. Secrets we've now found. Dad wanted me to know the truth about his real heir."

"And so la-di-da The End? Leave a pig on the throne?" Hort scorned. "If your dad gave you that message, it wasn't to stop you from fighting! It was to make you fight back!"

"But *how*?" Tedros asked. "What am I supposed to unbury?"

"Maybe he hid something in Excalibur's hilt?" said his mother.

"Or in his statue in King's Cove?" said Tedros.

"Or maybe the message means exactly what it says," said his princess.

They all turned to her.

Agatha raised her gaze from the floor.

"What if he did mean it literally?" she said. "What if 'Unbury Me' means unbury King Arthur from his grave?"

The throne room was so quiet, Agatha could hear the thumps of Tedros' heart.

"Dig up my father?" he breathed.

"But Arthur's been dead for years," said Guinevere, her voice cold. "There's nothing left but bones and dust."

"No. Merlin enchanted his tomb," Tedros countered tentatively. "He's preserved exactly as he was."

His mother tensed, her years absent from Tedros' and Arthur's lives suddenly obvious.

"Even so, disturbing his grave is out of the question," the prince assailed, stronger now. "I'm not dragging my father's body out of the ground."

"Even if it's what your father would have wanted?" Agatha asked. "Even if it was his *command*?"

Hort cleared his throat. "Look, not that I'm afraid to dig up a grave, since Nevers do that kinda thing on Friday nights, but having waited my whole life for my dad to get a proper grave, shoveling up Tedros' doesn't seem right to me. Plus, there's no way we can *get* to Avalon to unbury him. Whole Woods is hunting us and the Snake is on the loose. Nic and I barely escaped Foxwood alive."

"And, even if we did get to Avalon, we can't reach Arthur's

grave," Guinevere added quickly. "The Lady of the Lake has to give us permission to enter her waters and from what you've told me, we're not welcome anymore."

"On top of all that, my father's coffin is guarded by Merlin's spell to prevent people like us from desecrating it. Only Merlin can unlock it," said Tedros, relieved by all these obstacles. His mother and Hort murmured their agreement.

Agatha didn't have the heart to argue. They were right: the risks were too steep. And more than that, she was asking her prince to raid his own father's grave. Would she do the same to her mother's? With no assurance of the outcome?

A shadow flew across the waterfall veiling the entrance to the throne room, and a body leapt through, hands aflutter.

"Come quick!" Nicola gasped at Agatha. "It's Reaper!"

"What happened!" Hort asked, but his girlfriend was already diving back through the waterfall. Hort chased after her, and Agatha and Tedros followed close behind with Guinevere, all of them bounding through the magical curtain, into the foyer, where Subby and his banged-up rickshaw awaited, its cart now stamped with dozens of stickers of Sophie's face, X'ed out with the warning: "*BAD BHOOT!*"

"Hurry!" Subby jabbed. "King's waiting!"

Poof! The page boy morphed into a girl gnome—

"Girl Subby drives faster!" he/she pipped. "Let's go! No time to waste!"

Agatha and the rest crammed in, sitting in each other's laps, bottoms barely settled before Subby was off and careening up the spiral tracks, twisting around the thick glowing vines that connected the different levels of Gnomeland. She drove past gnomes haggardly returning to their houses after the all-night blockade and funeral, past shopkeepers pulling down their anti-human posters, past gnome doctors wheeling Kiko flat on a gurney into Smallview General Hospital . . . before Subby and her cart headed straight for the Musée de Gnome. She screeched to a halt at the entrance.

"Follow me!" Nicola ordered, hopping out.

"Why is the cat in a *museum*?" Tedros asked, but Agatha was already sprinting at full pace next to Nicola, through the Musée's doors—

Agatha banged her head on molding. "Ow!"

"Keep your head down!" Nicola said. "It's made for *gnomes*!"

Agatha rubbed her skull as she crouch-walked into the pint-sized hall, an ornate banner with "THE GOLDEN AGE OF TEAPEA" grazing her head, while Tedros and the others stooped down behind her. She tried to keep up with Nicola, passing regal portraits of her cat along with scenes of Reaper's history, including the banishing of his father and brothers from Gnomeland, and his spectacular coronation, complete with a confetti-filled parade, a royal feast, and a city square jammed with dancing gnomes. Agatha hustled through more exhibits: a chronicle of the underground construction of Gnomeland . . . the biology of the luminescent vines wiring through the kingdom . . . a celebration of the years without human interference . . . until at last they reached a narrow, twisting staircase at the back of the museum, with a sign overhead:

HUMAN WORLD OBSERVATORY

A chain barred the stairs. *"Permanently Closed."*

"He's waiting up there," Nicola said, face fraught.

"What is it? What's wrong?" Agatha pressed.

Nicola nodded towards the steps. "Hurry."

Agatha jumped over the chain, as did Tedros and the others, and they scuttled up the stairs, with Hort tripping on the tiny, cobwebbed planks, nearly taking down the entire group before they reached the top—

Agatha froze on the landing, the others crowding behind her.

They were on an open-air platform, looking up into the bright-lit tracks of Gnomeland city spiraling above them like glowing snakes. In the middle of the observing platform rose a colossal telescope, the size of a grown gnome, with a wide circular eyepiece and a long white tube that disappeared into the hollow of a glowing green vine that stretched up towards the top of the kingdom.

Reaper was clasped onto this telescope like a koala to a tree, his body a quarter the size of the contraption, his pink, hairless head bowed as he peered into the eyepiece.

The cat looked up at the group.

Agatha, Tedros, Hort, and Guinevere gathered around him, each taking a sliver of the eyepiece.

The telescope magnified a long, deep view: up through Gnomeland city, up through the abandoned Flowerground tunnel, up through the stump, up through the dense treetops of the Woods . . . all the way into wide, red-lit sky and a magnificent view of the Woods at sunset, the expanse of kingdoms extending in every direction.

For a moment, Agatha was mesmerized by how beautiful it was.

Then she saw it.

Glittering in gold.

Lionsmane's latest screed, emblazoned against the evening sky.

The wedding of King Rhian and Princess Sophie will take place as scheduled, this Saturday, at sundown, at Camelot Castle. All citizens of the Woods are invited to attend.

Slowly, Agatha raised her head.

Reaper glowered back at her. So did Tedros.

"Still think she's on our *side*?" he said.

Agatha's heart went up in smoke.

Was I wrong?

After all this?

Was I wrong about Sophie this whole time?

"But . . . her message . . . the way she looked right at us . . . ," Agatha said. "I don't understand. . . ."

Tedros just shook his head, less with anger than with pity, at his princess who couldn't help but trust the one person who couldn't be trusted.

"Saturday at sundown," Guinevere spoke. "That's two days."

"And now he has Nottingham's ring," said Nicola, near the staircase. "Which means, unless the remaining kingdoms stop him . . ."

"Rhian becomes the One True King," said Hort. "Rhian becomes the Storian. Sophie said it would happen at the wedding. Which means in two days, he has the power to write anything he wants and make it come true. In two days—"

"We all die," said Agatha.

Everyone fell quiet.

"And all I have is a message from my father that I'm too afraid to obey," said a voice.

Tedros'.

"Agatha's right," the prince said, looking up at the group. "Rhian is my father's son. He is my father's heir, I accept that. But then why is my father reaching out to me from his grave? Why did the Lady of the Lake give me that message? There has to be a reason. There has to be something we don't know yet. When I was king, I let others take the lead too often. But either I lead now or our story is at an end. We're beaten from all sides and this isn't the time to hold back. Not against an enemy that will kill us all and erase everything we stand for. We have to go to Avalon and unbury my father. We have to dig up the Past if we're going to save the Present. We have to step into the belly of the Lion. There is no other choice. It doesn't matter if people in the Woods want to kill us or if the Lady isn't on our side or if the coffin is hexed with a thousand locks. It's what Merlin would have wanted us to do. It's what Dovey and Lesso would have wanted us to do. It's what *my father* would have wanted us to do. They're our guides now, even if they're not here. They've left behind a path." Tears hovered in Tedros' eyes, his jaw clenched. "And like my princess, I must have the courage to follow it."

He gazed hard at Agatha. "Now . . . who's coming with us?"

Agatha held his stare, prince and princess united.

"Guess I should put on my grave-robbin' boots," she heard Hort murmur.

The Garden of Truth and Lies

Sophie watched the towers of the castle loom closer as her carriage trundled through Camelot's village, the streets dappled with red and gold light. Kei posed like a statue in the seat next to her, spine stiff, jaw tight, eyes cold and fixed ahead.

In Maker's Market, wind blew dust off cobblestones onto bakers opening their shops, butchers unloading carcasses, and young children sleepily herding towards Camelot's school. Every shop seemed to have a gold Lion painted in its window, while schoolchildren flashed Lion pins on their lapels to two pirates in Camelot armor checking for evidence of loyalty to the king. Amidst the market stalls, a dark gap caught Sophie's eye: a shop burnt to the ground and a notice nailed to a stake in the ashes.

CONDEMNED
FOR SUSPECTED SYMPATHY TO REBELS

There was no mention what became of the shopkeeper.

The carriage rolled past a newsstand, an old humpbacked man laying out the new edition of the *Royal Rot*, the stand's marquee once labeled CAMELOT COURIER now poorly etched over with a Lion crest. Sophie scanned the morning's headlines.

TEDROS STILL ON THE LOOSE!
King Raises Bounty for Rebels' Heads!

PRINCESS SOPHIE MISSING!
Kidnapped by Tedros? Or in League with Rebels?

MORE ATTACKS IN THE WOODS!
Rebels Sack Bloodbrook and Ladelflop!

The Snake had said only three rings were left. And Nottingham's was one of them. . . .

So Bloodbrook and Ladelflop must be the other two.

Had these new attacks convinced their rulers they needed Camelot's protection, like the others who'd destroyed their rings? Had these attacks bullied the two holdouts into siding with Man against the Pen?

Sophie's throat went dry.

Is the Sheriff's ring the last one left?

Sophie pictured Japeth striding into the forest, his scims laminating his body as he flipped the carved ring on his thumb like a coin.

He'd bring it back to his brother, Rhian's faith in him affirmed. Bertie, the Sheriff's old jail attendant, would burn it on the king's command. Man would become Pen, just like August Sader warned.

Nothing could stop Rhian now.

Nothing could stop him from infinite power.

Except her.

Doves in formation circled Camelot's castle, standing tall against cloudless blue, the stains and nicks that tarnished the towers under Tedros' reign since smoothed away. Sophie thought of the fairy-tale castles she'd read about in story-books back in Gavaldon . . . castles that made her dream of Ever After . . . castles that looked just like this one. She sighed mordantly. Mooning over those storybook castles, she'd never bothered to ask herself what was happening inside.

High in the Gold Tower, the windows to the king's

bedroom stretched wide open.

Rhian must be up and moving.

Nerves punctured Sophie's stomach. If Rhian was on his feet again, he was dangerous. But if he was feeling well enough to roam around, he was also able to fight . . . and if he could fight . . .

She touched the crystal in her pocket, squeezing its sharp edges between her fingers. *Rhian kills Japeth. I kill Rhian.* That's what the crystal promised. Which meant first, she had to turn the two brothers against each other. *But how?* She'd have to make Rhian trust her . . . which meant she'd need time alone with him, away from his brother . . . But suppose Japeth had gotten back with the ring already?

In her window's reflection, she noticed Kei yawn.

The statue lives.

Studying his reflection, Sophie considered his sensuous lips, his high cheekbones and structured jaw. Until now, she'd never thought of Kei as human, let alone as a boy. She suddenly remembered the ogling look he'd given her that first night at dinner, practically drooling with lust. . . .

So he was a boy, after all.

Well, then. A witch could do her work.

She turned to him, pulling her dress tighter. "Kei, darling. I heard Rhian mention something about 'taking you back.' What did he mean?"

Kei didn't look at her.

"You answer to me, you know," Sophie pointed out.

"I answer to the king," Kei corrected.

"Who you apparently crawled back to like a dog," Sophie snipped.

The captain stared forward.

"Certainly treats you like one," she added.

Kei swiveled. "You don't know what you're talking about. He took me back even though I was a traitor. Even though I'd gone and worked for *him*."

Sophie blinked. "Tedros, you mean?"

Kei ignored her.

Sophie moved closer. "How do you think I feel? Being friends with Tedros but knowing in my heart that Rhian is the better king. How do you think I feel betraying Agatha so I can do what I think is right?" she said, shifting in her white dress, just happening to show more of her leg. "Playing both sides isn't easy."

Kei tried hard not to look. "Maybe you're still playing both sides."

"I'm on Rhian's side, just like you," Sophie vowed, cozying in, her lavender scent drifting towards him. "But Tedros and Agatha won't give up. This is war now, between a real king and a false one. We need to work together, Kei. To protect *our* king. But you've known him longer." Her hand brushed his. "Which means I can only protect him if I understand him like you do." She caressed her throat, delicately biting at her lip. . . .

"Look, what do you want to know?" Kei blurted, pink spots on his cheeks.

"How did you meet Rhian?" Sophie questioned.

"We were friends at school. Best friends."

"And then you helped him become king," said Sophie, all business now. "When did he tell you he was Arthur's son?"

"Rhian told everyone when we were at school," Kei said, still piqued. "No one believed him. Not even his own brother. But I did. Even when Japeth and the others mocked me, I defended him. Not just because I loved Rhian like a brother or because I loved Camelot and fantasized about my best friend being its king. But because I hated the idea of *Tedros* as king. All of us in Arbed House did. We knew your fairy tale and we knew Tedros was unfit to lead a horse, let alone a kingdom. But then the Ever Guard trials started . . ."

"And you chose to be in Tedros' guard," said Sophie.

"As much as I'd loved Rhian, I'd despised his brother. I wanted to be away from Japeth," Kei admitted. "Plus, there was the lure of serving Arthur's kingdom, which I'd dreamed about since I was a boy. . . . So I gave Tedros a chance."

"No shame in that," said Sophie.

"Yes there is, when you betray your best friend and when the king you chose turns out to be more of a coward than you thought. All Tedros had to do was stand up and fight Japeth's attacks. Rhian never would have become the Lion."

"You knew Rhian's brother was behind the attacks?" Sophie asked.

"I tried to tell Tedros when he was king," said Kei ruefully. "The one time he and I spoke. He needed to ride out and fight the Snake . . . to kill him like Arthur would have . . . to be a *leader*. He would have become the Lion instead. He would have stayed king. Even with Excalibur trapped in that stone.

The people would have stood by him. *I* would have stood by him. No one else would have gotten hurt. But he didn't listen." Kei shook his head. "That's when I knew I'd chosen the wrong king."

She waited for him to go on, but his gaze went back out the window.

"What about Rhian? Do you think he's a good king?" Sophie guided, trying to keep him talking.

"Better than Tedros," said the captain. "But that's not what makes him Good."

"What do you mean?" Sophie asked.

Kei turned, meeting her eyes. "He's loyal to people, despite their flaws. Like his brother. Or me. Or you. Isn't loyalty a mark of Good?"

For a moment, Sophie actually believed him.

"Except you don't just serve Rhian," she pointed out. "You serve the Lion *and* the Snake now. The Snake who you wanted to be away from."

"I don't serve the Snake," Kei said, ice-cool.

"Pshh. You rescued him from Nottingham's prison—"

"Because Rhian ordered me to and I'm loyal to Rhian. And because as king, Rhian assures me he has his brother under his firm control. I have no loyalty to Japeth. We weren't friends at school. *Rhian* was barely friends with him at school. Japeth had his own best friend. A monster, if you ask me."

"Aric," Sophie said, out loud.

Kei froze. "How do you—"

She'd said too much.

His eyes glassed over and his spine straightened.

The rest of the ride was silent.

As the carriage barreled through the gates, a team of twelve black-masked pirates were dismounting their horses in front of the stables and hosing the blood off their black suits, having returned from a night of attacks. One of the Mistral Sisters lurked amongst them, handing out satchels of gold. Through the pirates' masks, they watched the carriage drive by, their cold, hollow eyes tracking Sophie like a fox let into the chicken coop.

Rhian kills Japeth.

I kill Rhian.

Pirates kill me.

Sophie shuddered.

The carriage stopped in front of the castle doors. She followed the captain up the Blue Tower stairs, Evelyn Sader's white dress tingling at her skin again, as if fully aware of her murderous plot and warning her not to go through with it.

Sophie bit down her fear and climbed faster. This time, a dress wouldn't stop her.

She trailed Kei across the catwalk towards the Throne Room, with a view into the Blue Tower dining hall.

Someone was at its table.

Sophie bucked up, a forced smile on her face, anticipating her enemy. . . .

It wasn't Rhian.

An old, filthy man slurped messily from plates of parsnip soup, salmon pie, roast chicken with applesauce, stuffed eggs, stewed yams, and butterscotch pudding.

Another Mistral Sister sat across the table. "Now, Bertie, if something were to befall the Sheriff—highly unlikely, of course—that would turn Nottingham's ring over to you. And you'll burn that ring on the king's command, just as we discussed—"

"We discussed you freein' me brutther frum Bloodbrook jail," Bertie growled, fisting pudding into his mouth. "And a house for me mum."

"Your mother will stay in Stink Swamp and your brother in jail until you burn the ring," the Mistral woman said curtly.

Bertie gave her a dead-eyed glare. "Better be a big house for me mum. With a tub—"

Kei was well ahead of Sophie now and she hurried to keep up, her dress stinging threateningly at her skin.

They passed the Map Room, where Wesley and a second pirate, in their black marauding suits, hovered in front of a floating map of the Woods, every kingdom X'ed out except Bloodbrook, Ladelflop, and Nottingham.

"A good night's work," said the dark pirate.

"Bloody good night's work," Wesley smirked.

He dipped his middle finger in black ink and slashed it across Bloodbrook and Ladelflop, leaving only Nottingham untouched.

Sophie fended off a wave of nausea.

Japeth has the last ring.

A ring that Bertie would burn on Rhian's order.

She had to move quickly.

Kei was skirting past the Treasury Master's office now, where Sophie noticed the third Mistral Sister seated opposite the bald, egg-shaped Treasury Master, pug-nosed and pink-skinned, surrounded by piles of ledgers on his desk. She tried to eavesdrop—

"The *Camelot Courier* has been making inquiries into our accounts, Bethna," said the Treasury Master. "They've sent reporters to the Bank of Putsi."

"Warrants are out for the *Courier*'s staff," said Bethna. "They'll never make it to Putsi."

"Even so, the manager of the bank has a mind of his own," the Treasury Master observed. "If he begins investigating our accounts, he could alert the Kingdom Council before the last ring is burned. . . ."

Bethna weighed his words. "I'll go to Putsi at once," she said, turning for the door.

Sophie ducked out of view, scuttling after Kei.

What is in that bank? she wondered. *What are they hiding?*

But there was no more time to think, for Kei was already walking through the doors of the Throne Room.

Sophie hesitated as she entered, dark shadows crisscrossing the long, vast hall. For a moment, it was so dark she couldn't see anything, the thick carpet rustling beneath her slippers.

A ray of light cut through the shadows.

Sophie looked up.

A boy stood at the window, his back to her, a crown nestled in his coppery hair. Sun haloed him as two seamstresses cinched a belt of gilded Lion heads around his high-collared white fur cape.

A wedding cape.

As if in response, Sophie's dress began to morph on her skin. She flung up her arms in shock as the dress tightened around her ribs, the fabric hardening from lace to crepe and sealing her chest in a creamy-boned bodice. The sleeves spouted wings and ruffled cuffs while the hem unraveled to the floor, pooling behind her in a rich, white train. Along the edges of the bodice, gold thread wove a pattern of Lion heads, matching the boy's belt. The back of Sophie's neck tickled as the collar extended up her nape, higher, higher, then pulled down over her face in diaphanous silk, like a hood or a mask or a . . .

Veil.

Sophie started shaking.

A wedding dress.

She was trapped in her own wedding dress.

The boy turned from the window.

Rhian smiled, his face battered and bruised.

"Yes, Mother," he said, blue-green eyes twinkling. "I think that'll do nicely."

"YOUR MOTHER IS *inside* the dress?" Sophie asked, morning dew dripping off a rosebush onto her white lace, restored to its prim, ruffled form.

"A piece of her, perhaps," said Rhian, walking with her through the royal gardens. Clad in his blue-and-gold suit, he limped gingerly, Excalibur on his belt. In the sunlight, Sophie could see the mess of welts on his tan face and neck, still healing. As he bent to inspect a tulip, she glimpsed a scar at the top of his skull, jagged and faded. A scar from long ago.

"My mother left that dress to us when she died," he went on. "It's shown signs of life. Even given my brother and me answers. But fashioning you a wedding dress . . . ? That was a surprise." He peered at Sophie. "Has it done anything else?"

Sophie tightened. "No," she lied. "What do you mean it gave you and your brother 'answers'? How can a dress give answers?"

"How can two girls magically appear in a king's bedroom? Each of us has questions, it seems," said Rhian dryly. "Want to see the Orangerie?" He moved towards a short staircase ahead. "It's almost finished."

Workers clustered on the level below, tending to perfectly square plots of orange trees, planted in the pattern of a giant chessboard, a titanic stone fountain of a Lion at its center, occasionally shooting jets of mist over the grove. Rhian struggled down the steps and Sophie took his arm, feeling his muscles resist hers, then slowly soften. At the bottom she let go, and they walked in silence between the squares of trees, the mist from the fountain lacquering their faces.

"The crystal . . . the one that let Agatha break into my dungeons," said the king, a low branch brushing his crown. "That's how you broke into my bedroom too, isn't it?"

"Why don't you ask my dress?" Sophie cooed.

Rhian chuckled. "They don't make girls like you in Foxwood. At least not the ones I met when I was in school."

"Because girls like me go to the school you want to tear down," Sophie remarked. "I'm sure you had your share of girls anyway."

"I had other priorities."

"Like trying to convince your classmates you were King Arthur's son, when even your own brother didn't believe you?"

Rhian side-eyed his princess. "And here I thought Kei was impenetrable to a girl's wiles. I'll have to have a talk with him."

"Do it tomorrow," Sophie smiled.

There would be no tomorrow, of course.

She plucked an orange from a tree and peeled open its skin, extracting a slice and holding it out to the king.

"Is it poisoned?" Rhian asked.

"Naturally," said Sophie.

She slipped it into his mouth and he bit into it, the juice dripping off his gashed lips. Their eyes locked. Sophie thought about how, in just a short while, the boy standing in front of her would plunge his sword into his own brother's heart. And how she would rise from behind, in his moment of shock and mourning, and cut it short with a single blow. She'd feel no remorse. The killing would come easy.

"You're smiling," said Rhian. "What are you thinking about?"

"You," Sophie replied.

She lifted onto her toes and kissed him, sugary wetness coating her tongue and mixing with the cool mint of his mouth. For the briefest of moments, she thought of Rafal. Their lips parted, sticky and sweet. Rhian looked dazed, like she'd stabbed him, before he glanced away and padded forward, trying to steady his limp.

"I knew you would come back. I *knew* it. Even when Japeth told me I was a fool. I knew that we were meant to be together. King and queen."

"Ah. The boy who said that he'd never love me. That love made people into foggy-eyed fools," Sophie hazed, fully in control now. Her emerald eyes glimmered with mischief. "Suddenly, he isn't seeing so clearly."

"No, that's not it." Rhian rubbed at his close-shorn skull. "It's just . . . You could have stayed with your friends. But you were loyal to me instead. When you didn't need to be. And loyalty is something I haven't had much of in my life."

"You have the loyalty of your men and the rulers around you," Sophie pointed out. "You have Kei's loyalty. And your brother's."

"All of them want something from me, my brother included," the king said, glancing at her. "Maybe you want something too."

Sophie twinged with guilt and almost laughed. Guilt for a monster!

"Oh? What do you think I want?" she asked, playing with fire.

Rhian stopped on the path. He studied her carefully. "I think you want to make a difference in these Woods. That's why you were unhappy as Dean. You said it yourself when we had dinner: you want a bigger life. It's why you were drawn to me when we met." He brushed aside a stray lock of her hair. "Think about it this way. The Pen put Tedros on the throne and he couldn't keep these Woods safe. If the Pen can no longer be trusted to protect the Woods, then it's up to a Man to take its place. Not just any Man. A King. The One True King. That's why you came back to me. Your friends will think it's because you're Evil, of course. That you want to be a queen for the sake of a crown. But we both know the truth. It's not enough to be queen for you. You want to be a *good* queen. And you can only do that with me."

Sophie frowned, thrown by his earnestness. She kept walking. "I would be a good queen. That is true. But where's the proof you would be a good *king*? You don't believe in the Pen and yet the Pen keeps the balance between Good and Evil. That's why the Storian has lasted all these years. If a king had the Storian's power, he would destroy that balance. *You* would destroy that balance. You would wipe out all those who rebel against you. You would rule with Evil in a way the Pen never would."

"Quite the opposite, in fact," said the king, trying to keep up with her. "I would use the power of the Pen to do *Good*. To bring down that worthless school and reward ordinary people doing right in these Woods. Just like Lionsmane's messages tried to do, before you hijacked them."

"Oh please. Those messages were filled with lies—" Sophie argued.

"In the service of Good. To raise people up," said Rhian. "But Lionsmane's messages are just the beginning. A Good king protects his people. A Good king protects the Woods. What better way to protect the Woods than to wipe out Evil completely."

"Impossible," Sophie pooh-poohed, facing him. "Evil has always existed. You could never wipe it out."

"I can and I will." Rhian stared at her, his eyes glazed and hot. "Everything I've done in my life has been to get me here. I didn't get into your lofty school. I wasn't kidnapped from reality and dropped into a magic castle like you and your self-righteous friends. While you basked in the privileges of your school, bright, young 'lords' of the Woods, I was with real people. In the *real* Woods. And here's what I learned. The Storian isn't the keeper of balance. It isn't a peacemaker at all. The Storian thrives on the *war* between the two sides. On pitting Good and Evil against the other and letting that war drag on for eternity. That's why my pen made a show of twisting the Storian's tales: to prove that every one of its villains can be a hero and every hero a villain. And yet, we cling to the Pen's every word, reacting to each victory and loss as if it was our own, the balance swinging between Good and Evil, back and forth, back and forth, while the real people of the Woods are forgotten. Their lives left out of our storybooks, lost in the fog of a pointless war."

The king's face softened. "But the Pen has the power to end that war if it chooses. It knows that every villain has something they want. Something they've turned Evil to get. Give them what they want and it can *stop* them. Before they cross the point of no return. Evil preempted by the hand of fate. The Pen would never do such a thing, of course; it needs the two sides at war to preserve its power. So it binds them together like twins, so that Good can't live without Evil and Evil without Good. . . . But I know better. If *I* had the Pen's power, I'd wipe Evil out. Neutralize it. Cut it off at the root. Take my brother, for instance. His soul skews to the worst kind of wickedness. But with the Pen's power, I can bring back to life the only person Japeth has ever loved. I can give him the only Ever After he's ever wanted. His Evil would be cured. Imagine if I could do that with *every* threat, extinguishing every villain, every spark of darkness. If I could use Lionsmane to give them love or fortune or even just a friend: whatever it takes to restore their souls to Good. I could prevent attacks like the Snake's from ever *actually* happening. The war between Good and Evil would end. The spotlight stripped from a Pen and a School and returned to the people. Peace, true peace forever. That's why I need to be king. The One True King. I can do what the Storian could never do. I can erase Evil from these Woods permanently. *I* can be the balance."

Clammy coldness clawed at Sophie's core. The boy in front of her suddenly felt like the knight she once fell in love with, his aqua-green gaze clear, honest . . . *real*.

"But you can't stop Evil. Look at you! *You're* Evil!" Sophie resisted, snapping from her trance. "You ordered the attacks on kingdoms! You set the Snake loose just so you could be king! You're responsible for people's *deaths*! And so much more. You enslaved Guinevere: a *queen*. You blackmailed leaders. You've tortured Merlin and sent pirates to attack schoolchildren and stabbed me to give my blood to your brother. You told lies about Tedros to get leaders to burn their rings. Lies about Agatha. Lies about me. Lies about *everything*!"

"Yes, I have told lies," the king replied evenly. "I have done things that are ruthless and vile. I've let my brother attack the Woods at will. At times, I've hated myself for it, but like a good king, I know how to do what needs to be done. Even if it means I have blood on my hands. Because unlike Tedros, I spent my life in the shadows, where Good and Evil are never so simple. Every day in my world requires sacrifices. Sacrifices that can be awful and ugly. But I want a better future for people like me, where even a baker or bricklayer has the chance to tell his story. To know that they matter. To be proud of their lives. For that to happen, the Storian must be replaced. The School must fall. And a King of the *People* must rise. Any Evil I've done, any lie I've told, it's to make that future possible. Because only I can lead these Woods to a real peace, a real Ever After, for everyone. Beyond the legacy of my father. Beyond Good and Evil. I can save the Woods from *all* Evil, forever. I can be the One True King, the immortal Lion, cutting the head off every Snake. Anything is worth that. *Anything.* So look me in the eye and tell me I'm not as Good as my father. Look me in the eye and tell me I'm Evil, when everything I've done has been to save these Woods from it."

Sophie's lungs turned inside out.

This was lies.

This had to be lies.

This was the villain!

The boy she needed to kill!

The boy who was pure Evil, except now he was telling her *he* was the Good one . . . the one who could keep the Snake contained, the Snake living inside *every* villain . . . the one who could *erase* Evil forever. . . .

What if it was true?

What if it were possible?

Her head spun, like she'd been bashed by a crystal's blue light and dropped in another dimension.

"Your mother," she breathed. "She's the one you want to bring back to life?"

Rhian nodded. "My mother's the only person Japeth ever loved. If he had her back . . . he would be happy and at peace. His Evil would be gone. I could be the king I want to be, the Lion the people need, without a Snake breathing down my neck."

Sophie was so addled that she found herself trundling ahead, leaving him hobbling behind her. All this time, she'd believed Rhian a savage intent on the Storian's infinite power, his brother his loyal henchman. That was her version of the story. The one she and her friends agreed on. But in Rhian's version, Rhian wanted the Pen's power for another reason: to keep his brother happy. To kill the monster inside of him. To kill the monsters inside *all* the villains of the Woods. To bring peace to the people. Forever.

Sophie pictured the eel-covered pen she'd first met in the Snake's hands, changing the Storian's tales to make the heroes villains and the villains heroes, twisting known stories into something darker and untrue. Lionsmane, the messenger of lies.

But when it came to Rhian's tale . . . had *she* become the messenger of lies? Had she failed to see the real story, while clinging to a warped version of it?

Impossible, she thought.

And yet the way he'd looked at her, so pure-eyed and sure—

"How did you escape?" he asked, appearing at her side again. His forehead shined with sweat. She hadn't realized how far she'd gotten ahead of him.

"Escape what?"

"Agatha and Tedros. You escaped them and their rebels. Where are they? Where are all of them?"

Sophie blinked at him. "On the run, of course. That's how I got out. In the chaos of moving between hideouts."

Rhian searched her face. His knuckles twitched near Excalibur's hilt.

Sophie's finger glowed strong behind her back—

"Doesn't matter," the king groused, moving towards the last patch of trees. "Once my brother claims Nottingham's ring, their days are numbered."

"I thought you said you were Good," Sophie retorted, tailing him.

"I am Good," said Rhian. "My father's sword choosing me is the proof. Your friends are the ones who are Evil. They deny the will of the people who want me as King. They arrogantly stand in the way of a better Woods. A more peaceful Woods. A Woods that King Arthur would have been proud of. Your friends aren't just rebels against what's right. They're my *Nemesis*. They won't stop attacking me until I'm dead. Which means I need to defend myself. First rule of Good."

Sophie opened her mouth to argue. Nothing came out.

Rhian pulled up his shirt to inspect a deep laceration between two ribs, a pinprick of blood oozing between two stitches. He exhaled and kept walking. "Wish your blood healed me."

"Why doesn't it?" Sophie prompted. "Strange that my blood would heal one twin and not the other."

He didn't answer for a moment.

"Rhian?"

"It's the pen's prophecy," he said, pausing on the path. "*Only* with you as a wedded queen can the Storian's powers be claimed. One brother weds you and becomes the One True King. The second brother is restored by your blood. Sophie, the Queen for one. Sophie, the Healer for the other. You, the bond between brothers, each with an incentive to protect you."

Like the Storian, Sophie thought. Kept by two brothers, each safeguarding it for their side.

Something needled at her. Something that didn't make sense.

"*One* brother weds me and becomes king?" Sophie said.

"You meant when *you* wed me. You're the elder. You're the heir."

Rhian cleared his throat. "Yes. Obviously."

Sophie walked ahead. "But *which* pen? You've spoken of this mystery pen again and again. The pen that supposedly told you all these things. Which pen was it? The Storian or Lionsmane? Which pen knew I would be your queen? Which pen knew I could heal your brother?"

She looked back at Rhian and to her surprise, she saw him grinning. "Found a way to magically break into my room. Found a way to get me a message under your friend's nose. And yet, you still don't know why you're here. Maybe you're not as smart as I thought."

If there was one thing Sophie despised, it was being called stupid.

"Oh?" she said cuttingly. "I know who your mother is. I know all about her. I know how you came to be born. Do you?"

Rhian snorted. "You don't know the slightest thing about my mother."

Sophie gave him a cold stare. And suddenly, as if her thoughts were making it happen, her dress shape-shifted again. This time, the lace ruffled tighter, tighter, pinching in at every corner, before the ruffles began to quiver in unison, like a thousand gossamer wings. The white wings flapped harder, a little head poking out between every pair, as if about to take flight. A shot of color appeared at Sophie's breast, like a stab wound, which bled outwards, covering these tiny winged creatures in rich, brilliant blue, the dress on her body now transformed into a dress so familiar, a dress once worn by her enemy, a dress made out of . . . *butterflies*. An army of them, blue as sapphires, rippled and flowed as she breathed in and out, their heads rising and falling with her heartbeat, as if the dress was no longer fighting her or binding her, but *obeying* her.

Rhian's eyes went big, his skin as pale as his brother's.

Then in an instant . . . the butterflies vanished.

The dress melted back to white lace.

Sophie arched a brow at the king.

"Oh, I know more than you think," she said.

25

SOPHIE

Rhian and the Real Thing

"My mother was a secretive woman," said Rhian, taking off his shirt. "I know very little about her time as your Dean."

With cloud cover cooling the garden and the king increasingly limp, they'd returned to the veranda. Maids brought Rhian fresh bandages and creams for his wounds, which he now applied to his bare torso, grimacing and struggling to reach.

Sophie sat next to him.

Do I kill him?

Do I not kill him?

After everything Rhian had just told her, she didn't know if he was Good or Evil anymore. If he was lying or telling the truth. If he should live or die.

But one thing was still true.

His brother had to die.

Kill Japeth and the worst Evil would be gone.

Kill Japeth and Rhian might leave Evelyn Sader in her grave.

Kill Japeth and maybe she could let Rhian live.

Maybe.

But what about Tedros?

Rhian had to die or Tedros couldn't retake the throne.

Presuming Tedros *should* retake the throne.

But what if Rhian was right?

What if Rhian would be the better king?

He was the *real* heir, after all.

And just because Agatha and Tedros were Sophie's friends didn't mean Tedros should rule Camelot. Nor had Tedros ever talked about his people or why he should be king with the same passion that Rhian showed her.

What if being the One True King is Rhian's destiny? Sophie thought, stiffening. What if his having the Storian's powers could bring lasting peace to the Woods? What if it could stop Evil forever, just as he promised?

Then killing Rhian wasn't the Good thing to do.

Killing Rhian would be Evil.

Sophie's heart shriveled.

And I'm Evil.

Is that why the crystal showed her murdering him?

Because her soul wanted her to do an Evil deed?

Because it wanted her to be a witch?

Rhian wrestled awkwardly with a bandage—

"Oh, I'll do it," Sophie sighed.

Rhian eyed her tentatively . . . then lay back. She kneeled by his side and wrapped the cloth around his ribs. He flinched at the coldness of her touch.

First things first, she told herself.

Rhian kills Japeth.

That part of the script hadn't changed.

Which meant she had to find their weak spot.

That thread of mistrust she could unravel.

"Tell me about her," she said, rubbing cream into a bruise on his shoulder. "Your mother."

"Japeth inherited her magic, unlike me," said Rhian, eyes closed, trying not to wince. "I must be like my father. Who my mother never, ever brought up. We knew not to ask. But I had my suspicions."

"Such as?"

"There was the old card with Camelot's seal I found in my mother's room, inviting her to dine at the castle. *'Looking forward to seeing you,'* it said, in the king's own hand. I was obsessed with Camelot like every young Everboy, so imagine my excitement. My own mother knew King Arthur? My own mother once *dined* with the king? But when I asked her about the card, she punished me for snooping in her things. Then there was the way she hid us in Foxwood, not allowing us to leave the house or go to school, as if she was afraid someone might find us out. Then one day, a woman showed up at our door: a woman I recognized from the *Camelot Courier* as King

Arthur's steward. I couldn't hear her and Mother's conversation, but why would King Arthur's steward come see *our* mother? Yet if I tried to ask questions about the king, Mother would shut me down. And any mention of Queen Guinevere would draw a black glare and mumbles about 'that uppity shrew.' It was obvious my mother and King Arthur had a history. That something happened between them. And both Japeth and I seemed to have Arthur's looks . . . or at least I did. A little bit of sun and I match his complexion. Put Japeth in the sun and he looks like burnt ham."

"But that's absurd! Why wouldn't your mother tell you who you were? Why not tell the whole Woods she'd borne Arthur's sons?" Sophie asked. She thought of the way Evelyn's eyes gleamed triumphantly before she looped the spansel around the king's neck. "That was the *point*. To claim Arthur's heirs—"

Rhian opened his eyes, peering at her.

He doesn't know, Sophie realized. *He doesn't know how he was made.*

"I think she tried," said Rhian. "I heard her crying once, cursing my uncle August for siding with '*him*.' She must have told Arthur she was pregnant with his child. But Arthur had a queen by then. He had Guinevere. Maybe he threatened my mother to keep her quiet. Maybe my uncle August helped him. That's why she was hiding us."

"But what about *after* Arthur died?" Sophie pushed. "Surely then she would have told people—"

"Who would have believed her?" said Rhian. "What proof did she have?"

"And your brother? Did he suspect that King Arthur was your father?"

Rhian batted away a fly. "Tried to talk to him about it, but he wouldn't listen. He said he was quite sure who our father was."

"Who?" Sophie pushed.

"'*Not King Arthur*,'" said Rhian, mimicking Japeth's hard tone. "He thought I was a fool about all of it, so enamored with the king that I'd convinced myself I was his long-lost son. But truth be told, Japeth and I never really saw eye to eye about anything. We're twins, but total opposites. Two halves of a whole."

Sophie resisted a smile. Rhian and his brother weren't so different from she and Agatha. Finding the wedge between brothers might be easier than she thought. . . .

"So your mother was closer to Japeth?" she asked. "He seems quite attached to her."

"*Too* attached," said Rhian crisply. "It's why Mother loved me more."

Sophie looked at him. "Go on."

"Japeth couldn't share my mother with anyone. Including me. If my mother showed me even the slightest bit of attention, he'd have terrible rages. When I made her a cake for her birthday, he put something in it that made her ill. When she showed our cat too much love, it disappeared. After every incident, he'd be sorry; he'd cry and vow it would never happen again. But it always did. And worse each time. Mother and I were prisoners of his rage. It's what made us so close."

Sophie tensed, still unused to feeling sympathy for the boy she'd come to kill. "And there was nothing you could do? You couldn't send him away or . . ."

"My brother?" Rhian said, stone-cold. "My *twin*?"

"But from what you've said—"

"Every family has problems. Every single one. You find a way to right the wrong. To heal the rot at the core."

"You speak about family the same way you speak about the Woods," Sophie said cynically. "But Evil can't just be erased."

"Well, here I am, still at my brother's side, our relationship stronger than ever. Tells you what I'll be like as king, doesn't it?" Rhian boasted. "I never gave up on him. Unlike my mother."

Sophie raised her brows, but Rhian anticipated her question.

"The rages got worse," he explained. "Nearly killed my mother and me a few times. She used her butterflies to spy on him. To pin him down during his fits. Thankfully she was more skilled with her magic than he was with his. That's how we stayed alive." Rhian paused. "Then she wrote the School Master about him."

"The School Master? Why?"

"My mother taught there once. My uncle August had gotten her a job as Professor of History. She and the School Master grew close—too close, I hear, since he ended up expelling her from the school. My mother believed that women didn't have the same advantages that men like her brother had. That her only chance at glory was to cozy up to powerful men. Like Arthur. Like the School Master. Both attempts backfired.

Clearly Arthur wanted nothing to do with her. And the School Master didn't just banish her; he cut off contact entirely. My mother sent him letters, begging him to accept Japeth to the School for Evil, to take him off her hands. He owed it to her, she said. But he never answered. Nor was Japeth claimed by the stymphs when the time came."

"Did your brother know any of this?" Sophie asked, treating another bruise. "That your mother was trying to get rid of him?"

Rhian shifted uncomfortably. "No. We were out of money by that time too, barely having anything to eat. Finally my mother told us she was going to see our father. If she could just face him in person, she had hope he'd help her. She'd *make* him help her. In the meantime, my brother and I would be enrolled at Arbed House. She'd had a talk with Dean Brunhilde, who, after meeting my brother, assured my mother she could handle Japeth, or 'RJ' as the Dean affectionately nicknamed him. She seemed to relish lost causes. Even so, my mother insisted I be there to help keep an eye on him. Until she came back, of course."

Rhian took a shallow breath.

"Never heard from my mother again. My guess is Arthur rejected her. This was around the time the king died. Something in her must have broken after that. She never came back for us. Didn't send a single letter. The love I thought she and I shared . . . the bond I thought we had . . . None of it mattered. She wanted to get away from Japeth. She wanted to get away so badly she was willing to leave me behind too."

A tear hovered at the corner of his closed eye.

"For a long time, we didn't know where she was. We heard rumors. That she met the Mistral Sisters and became interested in the theory of the One True King. That she joined a colony of women, intent on enslaving men. That she killed King Arthur herself. All we knew for sure is that she ended up at the School for Good and Evil as its Dean, with a vendetta against Arthur's son. It only gave me more proof that Arthur was our father. Clearly she wanted to take revenge on Tedros for his father's betrayal. For taking everything *her* sons deserved. She even tried to bring the School Master back from the dead to kill Tedros. But in the end, it was the School Master who killed her." Rhian exhaled. "My brother and I were on our own for good."

A warm gust curled through the veranda as they sat in silence, Rhian's heart pumping under Sophie's palm. For him, this was digging into the darkness of the Past; for her, it shined new light on the Present. Evelyn's dress softened against her body, like a loving embrace, as if at last she knew all its secrets. For a moment, any agenda, any plan she'd had evaporated in the wind.

"She abandoned you," Sophie said quietly. "She abandoned you because of your brother."

Rhian didn't answer.

"Does he know?" Sophie asked.

Rhian opened his eyes and the tear fell. "He thinks she went to see our father because she still loved him and was proud to tell him about her sons. That when he rejected her, she died of a broken heart. I could never tell Japeth the truth. That it was *him* that drove her away. That it was *him* that broke her heart. It's the curse of being Evil. It makes you torment the ones you love. And Japeth loved my mother too much."

Sophie went quiet, thinking of all the times love made her a monster.

"Not long after my mother died, the Mistral Sisters came to us," said Rhian. "They told us King Arthur was our father, just like I'd always known. When Japeth mocked them, they gave us that dress you're wearing now. My mother's dress that came alive before our eyes. It led us to the pen that showed us our futures. The pen that picked you as my queen. The pen you think is a mystery . . . but that dress knew where to find it. The pen told us our mother's wishes. That the future queen be given her dress. That her son seize his rightful throne. And if we did as she said, there was a way to bring a soul back from the dead. To bring *her* back from the dead. All the Evils of our past would be erased. The story would have a new ending: me, the One True King . . . Japeth, Mother, and I, reunited at Camelot's helm . . . Our family restored, as it was meant to be."

Sophie thought about Lionsmane's storybook at the Blessing; the one that told Rhian's fairy tale. It had left out the secrets. The shades that mattered. Like all storybooks.

"What did Japeth say?" Sophie asked.

"Well, he went from mocking them to suddenly believing I was the One True King. He made me promise that if he helped me become that king, I would bring the one he loved back to life. It took time for us to work out our plan, of course . . . but Japeth never flagged. He was as invested as I was, now that he had my mother at stake. I could see the hope in his eyes," Rhian recalled.

Sophie pictured Evelyn Sader, with her milky skin and bee-stung lips . . . with her manipulative ways and vengeance against men . . . with her nefarious butterflies and revisionist histories worthy of her son's pen. . . .

But Evelyn Sader had been a mother too.

A mother, like Sophie's own, who'd made mistakes.

A mother who'd died, wishing for another chance.

Sophie's skin goose-pimpled under the white lace, caressing her like someone's touch. She let out a breath of disbelief.

"What is it?" he asked.

"Your mother's dress," Sophie said, brushing her hands across the downy corset. "I know it sounds absurd, but all of a sudden, I feel like it . . . *likes* me."

She raised her eyes. Rhian was watching her through clear, blue-green pools. A Lion's deep, assessing gaze.

"I see why every boy falls in love with you," he said.

"Before, you saw why every boy dumped me," Sophie replied. "Which is it?"

Rhian leaned over his chair and took her hand. "I thought I knew your fairy tale. But no story can do you justice. It took me time to see deeper. Beneath the beauty and wit and games. I know you now, Sophie. The real you. Petals *and* thorns. And I love you for them both."

Sophie couldn't find air, blood pounding through her. She hadn't been spoken to with such passion. Not since Rafal.

"You have your brother," she said weakly, trying to keep

her wits. "You have Japeth. You can't have me too."

"After what happened with my mother, I was afraid to ever love someone," he said, sliding off his chair. "I couldn't let Japeth do to them what he'd done to her. I had to put him first. But I can't give you up, Sophie. I need you too much. I can be myself with you like I can't be with anyone else, even my own twin. I love you in a way I can never love him." He put his lips to her neck. "Because this is love that I *choose*."

He slipped his hands around her throat and lifted his mouth to hers. His hands ran over her dress and the lace turned to white butterflies beneath his fingers, rippling and flapping in waves, the sound of their wings beating, the symphony of a kiss.

Then, as their lips tangled and danced . . . a chill swept through the room.

Rhian didn't notice, his hands sifting through Sophie's hair.

But Sophie noticed, along with the shadow creeping over the veranda.

She kissed Rhian harder. "What do we do about Japeth?"

"Mmmmm?" Rhian said, in a hot fog.

"I don't want to end up like your mother," Sophie breathed. "I want us to be happy. Just the two of us. We could be alone. We could be free."

"What do you mean?" Rhian asked, between kisses.

Sophie let the words come. "If he was . . . gone."

Rhian stopped kissing her.

He pulled back, his face hard.

"I told you. He's my *brother*. He's my *blood*."

Sophie gripped his shoulders. "You think your mother will

be happy to see him when you bring her back? He'll drive her away, like he did the first time! 'Past is Present and Present is Past. The story goes round and round again.' *Your* words. And you said she wanted to get rid of him . . . that she left because of him . . . that she loved you more—"

"*Did* she?" said a voice.

Rhian stopped cold.

Slowly he turned to see his twin standing against the wall of the corridor, bloody and beaten in his tattered suit of scims.

"Well, then. Give Mother my regards," said Japeth, walking away.

He tossed something at Rhian's feet.

A silver ring, stained with blood.

The king stared at it, his eyes wide and frozen, before they rose to Sophie. . . .

Then he went after his brother.

SOPHIE HAD ORCHESTRATED this, of course.

The moment she'd seen Japeth's shadow and sensed that chill. She'd chosen her words to Rhian and made sure his brother overheard.

Witches knew how to start wars.

If all went well, Japeth would soon be dead.

Whether she let Rhian live or die, on the other hand . . .

Maybe that's why the scene in the crystal cut off before she killed him. Before she buried Excalibur in his back. Because even the future didn't yet know what would become of Camelot's king.

Clouds brewed darker overhead. Sophie followed the boys' voices to the catwalk between towers. She peeked around a stone column.

"I told you she's dangerous," Japeth boiled, his cheeks bruised in violet hues. "She's the *real* snake."

"I didn't mean those things. Not in the way she said," Rhian defended as he threw on a shirt, the two boys separated by a long length of stone. "Mother loved you. I love you—"

"You think I'm stupid. You think I didn't know our own *mother*? I know she loved you more. I know what I am," Japeth lashed. "What I didn't know is that you'd trade me, your own blood, for the kisses of a *wench*."

"You don't know Sophie. Not like I do," Rhian battled. "I told you she'd come back. She's my queen, just like the pen said. That's why she escaped the rebels. That's why she betrayed her friends. She believes in me. She's *loyal!*"

"Did you ask *how* she escaped?" Japeth attacked. "Or where the rebels are?"

"She doesn't know," Rhian returned fervently. "They're always on the move. . . ."

Japeth smirked, letting him hear the echo of his own words. Doubt shadowed Rhian's face.

"Your 'queen' is a liar," said the Snake. "She won't be happy until we're both *dead*."

A scim began to shriek, squirming over his mangled shoulder. Japeth lifted it off his suit like a butterfly, letting it softly babble in his ear.

The Snake's eyes floated up to Rhian . . . then past the king's shoulder.

"Come out, come out, little spy," Japeth cooed.

Sophie's heart leapt into her throat.

She knew better than to disobey.

Without a word, she stepped onto the catwalk.

"Brother?" Japeth said calmly.

The king glanced at Sophie, then at the Snake.

"Bring me her blood," said Japeth.

Rhian returned an empty stare.

"You speak of *loyalty*? Look at my wounds! Look at what I've endured to get the last ring! For you!" Japeth scorched. "That was the pen's promise. You get a queen and I get her blood. *Forever.* Now, *bring* it to me."

Rhian flexed his jaw.

He didn't move.

A scim launched off Japeth's suit, tore across the catwalk, and slashed Sophie in the cheek, spilling blood onto her white dress.

Sophie screamed, repelling into the stone column and hitting her head. She grabbed at her cheek, her skull exploding with pain, blood slipping through her fingers.

Across the catwalk, the eel had returned to its master, dripping Sophie's blood onto him, healing the Snake's face to a smooth, flawless white and breeding new scims to sew up his suit. He gave his brother a venomous look.

"Now, if you'll excuse me, Your Highness. I'm going to go

sit in your bath and by the time I get out of it, either that witch is gone from this castle or I'll kill her myself. Magic blood be *damned*."

He shot Sophie a lethal glare, then strode into the Gold Tower.

Rhian watched him go.

Slowly the king's eyes moved back to Sophie, splotched with blood, flattened against the stone column.

"He's the devil," she gasped. "You have to fight him! You have to *kill* him!"

Rhian shook his head. "I told you. He's my family. *My* family," he gritted. "I can cure him. I can *make* him Good."

"Good is about standing up to Evil!" Sophie blasted. "Real Evil, even if it's your own brother! He drove your mother away from you. And now he wants to drive me away too. Past is Present and Present is Past. The story repeats until *you* change it. That's what a hero does. That's what a *king* does. You say you love me? You say you're Good? Well, until you fight back, all I see is a coward. All I see is a *fool*."

Rhian's mouth trembled, his whole body slacking under the weight of his emotions. For a moment, he looked like a little boy. A little boy who'd had to make this choice many times before.

He steeled himself, his face a hollow mask.

"Take the carriage," he said. "Leave here and never come back."

He limped off the catwalk, Excalibur askew at his hip.

Then he was gone.

Sophie stood there, tasting her own blood in her mouth.

Waves of fury crashed and foamed through her.

To think she almost let that coward live.

No.

Rhian would die.

They would *both* die.

But how?

Japeth was taking a bath.

Rhian had surrendered to him.

The promised fight would never happen.

And she had nothing to replace it, no weapons, no plan, except a crystal in her pocket—

She held still.

Across her gashed face crept a wicked smile.

A crystal and a bath.

They were all the weapons she would need.

By the time Sophie neared the king's bedroom, she could hear the bath running.

From behind a column in the dim hallway, she spied two pirate guards outside the doors, swords on belts.

Her eyes roved to the other end of the hall . . . and a massive chandelier over the foyer to the king's wing.

Sophie's finger seared pink—

She shot a flare, shattering the chandelier, spraying crystals in every direction.

"Whawazzat?" one guard pealed.

The two of them abandoned their post, sprinting for the foyer.

Quickly Sophie darted from behind the column and kneeled at the doors to the king's chamber. Her cheek throbbed with pain, still dribbling blood onto her dress. Through the crack, she saw the bedroom empty, the door to the bath half-closed, the sounds of the tub filling behind it. She caught a glimpse of Japeth through the bathroom door. No sign of Rhian anywhere.

She slipped into the king's chamber.

Pearl-gray skies glowed through the windows, illuminating the gold-and-crimson silkprint walls, the chairs carved with Lion crests, and the perfectly made bed, the gold-and-red curtains drawn back. She heard Japeth's footsteps padding behind the half-closed door in the corner.

Treading lightly, Sophie crawled under the bed. She had to get Japeth out of the bathroom, long enough for her to sneak inside.

She'd only get one shot.

Raising her lit finger, she launched a flare into the closet, which detonated like a firecracker, collapsing all the racks of clothes.

Instantly, Japeth bolted out, still in his suit of scims. While he inspected the closet, Sophie slithered on her stomach through the door.

The king's bathroom shimmered like a gilded mausoleum, with mirrors reflecting mirrors and Lion crests carved into every tile and tap. Steaming water gushed into a vast tub, perched on gold-sculpted lion claws, the bath nearly overflowing now. A separate nook for the toilet lay dark and tucked away in the corner.

Sophie glanced into the bedroom as Japeth emerged from the closet, frowning, and pulled open the doors of the king's chambers, only to see the two guards missing.

"Idiots," he murmured.

He headed back to the bath.

Heart rattling, Sophie seized the crystal from her dress pocket, said a silent prayer . . . and dropped it into the tub.

She ducked into the toilet nook as Japeth entered.

His suit of scims magically receded, revealing his frost-white flesh as he approached the tub and disappeared into the thick steam.

Without his spying eels able to detect her, Sophie breathed easier, safely concealed. Evelyn Sader's dress swaddled tighter, nuzzling her reassuringly. As Japeth climbed into the bath, Sophie was surprised at how vulnerable he looked, the savage who'd murdered her friends nothing more than a slim teenage boy. Little by little, the Snake submerged into scalding water, letting out an ordinary gasp of pleasure and pain.

Sophie peeped out of the nook, waiting for it to happen.

Because if Rhian's and Japeth's souls were recognized by Dovey's crystal, then they had the same powers as Dovey or her Second . . . which meant the moment Japeth sank into the bath, fished the crystal out from under him and looked into its center . . . all of which unfolded now as Sophie watched, her stomach in knots . . . then in 3 . . . 2 . . . 1 . . .

Blue light beamed through the bath and Japeth sprung back in surprise, splashing water everywhere.

Slowly Japeth extracted the glowing crystal from the water and held it up to inspect it. Then he noticed there was something inside . . . a scene playing out within its glass edges. . . . He peered closer as Sophie held her breath. . . .

"Japeth?" a voice called.

Rhian's.

Japeth squeezed the crystal in his fist, snuffing its light.

"Get out," he ordered.

"She's gone."

Japeth's face changed. "How gone?"

"Gone."

Silence passed between brothers.

"I made you tea," said Rhian's voice. "Just the way you like it."

Japeth slipped the fist with the crystal back underwater. "Come in."

Sophie cursed to herself.

Rhian pushed through the door. He was in his blue-and-gold suit and carrying a mug.

"Poisoned, I assume?" said Japeth.

"Naturally," said the king, his crown catching gilded light. "What was that noise?"

"Avalanche in your closet. Shoddy work."

"Evidently. A chandelier just crashed outside. Could be Sophie's parting gift, though. Guards are searching the castle to make sure she's left."

The twins eyed each other.

"No wedding, then?" Japeth asked.

Rhian smiled limply. "Not sure what we'll do with all the gifts. Apparently the Sultan of Shazabah is sending a magic camel."

Japeth exhaled. "You won't miss her, brother. In a few days, you won't even remember her name."

The king smoothed his blue-and-gold suit, as if brushing away this part of the conversation. "We'll summon the Kingdom Council tomorrow and burn the last ring."

"Then the Pen's magic will be yours," his brother said eagerly. "Lionsmane, the new Storian. You, the One True King with infinite power."

"With infinite power comes the burden to do right by that power," said the king. "A responsibility I hope I'm worthy of."

"As if that's in question," Japeth flattered. "You've always been the Good brother. The one everyone loves. That's why *you're* the king."

Rhian cleared his throat. "Where should I put your tea?"

"What will you do first?" Japeth pushed. "What will be the first thing you write with Lionsmane?"

"To abolish the Kingdom Council and that wretched school forever," Rhian replied. "Time to return these Woods to the people."

"Never got over that you weren't taken to be an Ever, did you?" Japeth baited. "Or maybe it was that *I* wasn't taken away, leaving you and Mother in peace."

Rhian stiffened. "Japeth—"

"What will you do with the school?" Japeth asked sweetly.

"Burn it to the ground," the king said, relieved by the change in subject. *"A conflagration so fierce and high that it can be seen all across the Woods.'* Something like that. Words to be written. Words you and I will watch come true."

"And Agatha and Tedros and all the rebels? What of them?"

"They'll be dead with a penstroke. Erased into thin air."

"No Harpies to skin their flesh or trolls to eat their brains? No cataclysm of pain?"

"Only the pain of a footnote," said Rhian.

Japeth snorted. "I knew there was a reason I helped you become king."

Rhian turned serious. "We both know the real reason, Japeth."

His twin suddenly looked unsettled.

"You helped me fulfill my wish, Japeth," said Rhian. "And once we burn the last ring, it'll be my turn to fulfill yours."

Blush spots rose on Japeth's cheeks.

"A wish I promised you, for your loyalty and faith," said Rhian intensely. "You vowed to help me become king if I vowed to bring the one you love back to life with the Pen's powers. You've kept your word. Tomorrow I'll keep mine."

Japeth choked up with emotion, hardly able to speak.

"Thank you, brother," he whispered.

Rhian rested the tea on the tiled edge of the tub. "First day back on my feet has been more than I can handle," he sighed. "No magic healing blood for me, I'm afraid."

"Go lie down," Japeth said, with tenderness Sophie had never heard from him before.

Rhian nodded, loosening his belt and sword. He turned for the door—

"Rhian?" Japeth said.

The king looked back.

"Mother would be proud of you," said the Snake. "For putting family first."

Rhian smiled faintly. "We'll see, won't we?"

He shut the door behind him.

Japeth leaned back in his bath. He closed his eyes, as if drained by the exchange, only to open them when he realized he still had something in his fist.

He raised the glowing blue crystal out of the water, honing in on the scene inside.

Sophie held her breath.

This time there were no interruptions.

The Snake watched the scene replay, again and again and again.

Slowly his muscles tensed, his body curling upright, his knuckles gnarled around the glass droplet. Ice-blue veins popped out on his neck; his teeth clenched, coated with saliva; his eyes narrowed to murderous slits.

Slowly, the Snake looked up at the door.

He rose out of the water, eels materializing on his skin, black scaly strips crisscrossing the smooth white flesh, re-forming his suit. Then he stepped out of the bath, his wet feet shrieking softly against the tile.

He pulled open the bedroom door.

"Where is she?" he asked.

"Mmmm?" Rhian answered sleepily, Sophie unable to see the king from her hiding spot.

Japeth stepped into the room, out of Sophie's view. "The girl. Where is she."

"I told you. Gone—"

"*Liar.* Your little she-wolf never left. You made me think that you gave her up. That you chose me. But she's been here all along. Waiting for you to get rid of me."

"What are you going on about—"

"*WHERE IS SHE!*" Sophie heard Japeth roar. "You think she'll love you? You think she'll be your beloved queen when I'm gone? She'll murder you in cold blood the second you kill me."

"*Kill* you? Did a scim cut a hole in your brain?"

"I see through you. I've *always* seen through you. I'll find her myself!"

Sophie heard the familiar *shhhppp!* of scims scudding off Japeth's suit and the sound receding as they sprayed into the castle, hunting her.

"You really think she's here?" Rhian retorted angrily. "That I'm *hiding* her?"

"I know what I saw."

"Saw what? Saw *where*? Search the castle all you want. She's in a carriage, halfway to Gillikin—"

Sophie slid out from her nook, crawled along the bathtub, and scrunched into the tiny triangle of space behind the door. She peeked between the hinges.

"You've always chosen others over me. *Me*, your own *blood*," Japeth hissed at the king, who was on the bed in his rumpled blue-and-gold suit, the belt with Excalibur strewn aside. "And yet, I choose you over and over and over. I kill for you. I lie for you. I sack and pillage kingdoms for you. I do *everything* for you. Rhian, the Good. And me, the Evil monster. Me, who can never love. And yet, when I did have love, the one and only time in my life, you *destroyed* it."

"Here we go," Rhian moaned.

"I had a friend. The only friend I ever had," Japeth said, quivering with emotion. "A friend who made me believe I wasn't so Evil after all. And *you* took that friend away."

Rhian sprung to his feet, scowling. "That's not true—"

"You voted with the others to banish him! You voted to dump him in the Woods like a dog!"

"He tried to *kill* me!" Rhian thrashed, clutching at the scar on his skull. "He put a dagger in my *head*!"

"'Cause you said things about him! About him and me! About our friendship!"

"Because he was a monster! A sadist with no soul! And you were too blind to see it. Cozying up to him and following him around like a dog. Siding with him over me. Like *he* was your brother. Or *more* than a brother—"

"He was my *friend*! My best friend!" Japeth screamed. "And the Dean put his expulsion to a vote and if you'd voted for him to stay, if you'd forgiven him, everyone else would have too! They would have listened to you! The Good forgive. And they thought you were Good. *I* thought you were Good."

Tears soaked Japeth's eyes, his voice a child's. "You made my friend leave. Just like you say I made Mother leave. But Mother left by choice. You had my friend *banished*. I never saw him again. Because of *you*."

"You think he deserved forgiveness? Your brother's would-be murderer?" Rhian blasted. "He wouldn't have rested until I was dead! I saw it in his eyes. Those hateful, violet eyes. He wanted you all to himself. Disgusting animal. Deserved what happened to him. And I never said you made Mother leave—"

"Lies. *More* lies. I know what you think of me. The same thing she did. That I can't love. That *I'm* a disgusting animal," Japeth wept. "You were just waiting for an excuse to get rid of me. And now you found it in a girl. A girl you think loves you, when I can see the truth in *her* eyes. The truth that she wants you dead." Japeth smeared at his face. "It's the same way you and Mother looked at me."

"Don't say things you can't take back," Rhian assailed. "You're my brother. My family. I love you. And Mother loved you too. That's why I'm bringing her back to life. For you. Because you want a second chance. Because we *all* want a second chance."

"Right," said Japeth quietly. "Funny that."

The tears stopped.

He raised his eyes, red-veined and raw.

"You assumed it would be her. All this time. But you never asked me who I would bring back to life with my wish. You just presumed. That she was the one I loved. That she was the one I wanted back. But that's who *you* wanted back. Not me."

Rhian went cold. "What?"

"It was obvious if you just thought about it," his brother said, fully composed now. "But you only think of me as something to be used. A liege, a henchman, who would get you a crown and also get you Mother back in the process. You made your wish into mine. But I wish for someone else. I've always wished for someone else."

Behind the door, Sophie paled. She'd understood. She knew who Japeth wished for.

"The only person who ever truly loved me," said the snow-white twin. "The only person willing to *kill* for me. The only person I trust more than my own brother. My *real* family."

Rhian stepped back. "A-A-Aric?"

Sophie couldn't breathe.

"And now you'll help me bring him back, brother. Just like you *promised*," the Snake said to Rhian, his gaze smoldering. "Right?"

The king froze. His eyes darted to Excalibur on the table—

"I'll take that as a no," said the Snake.

He went for the sword.

Rhian got there first. He grabbed Excalibur by the blade and swung the jeweled hilt, smashing the handle into his brother's neck. Japeth crashed onto the night table, shattering the glass top, before scims rocketed off his black suit and pinned his brother to the wall, knocking Excalibur out of Rhian's hand and onto the floor. Rhian tore at the scims with all his strength, ripping his body from the wall and bludgeoning eels with his fists, just before Japeth came swinging again. The two boys launched at each other wildly, punches and kicks landing with bone-crushing cracks, sprays of blood flying, before they locked arms viciously and hurled each other to the ground.

"You think I'd bring him back? To run rampant in my castle? My own death sentence?" Rhian snarled. "Never. *Never!*"

Japeth bashed the king's head against the wall. Rhian kneed him in the face—

Sophie watched, her heart in a knot, the scene following the crystal's script.

Only not quite.

Because in the crystal, *she'd* been in the room with them, cowering in plain sight.

Something tapped her shoulder. Sophie spun. Three eels screeched with discovery, snaring her in a tight collar and dragging her from the bathroom into the bedroom, throwing her into a corner.

Japeth jolted upon seeing her, his bloodied face contorting with rage, before he turned on his brother. "Halfway to *Gillikin*, I see."

Rhian gaped at Sophie. "But I . . . I didn't . . . I . . ."

Japeth pummeled him, spurting Rhian's blood onto the Snake's own face. "Thought you could kill me! Your own *brother*! Thought you could replace me with *her*!"

Choking, spitting, the king flailed towards Sophie. "Call the guards! Now!"

Sophie swiveled to the door, but the scims collaring her jumped off, re-forming into a thick spike before they bolted the doors to the chamber from inside. Sophie cowered against the wall, trapped. *Trust the crystal*, she told herself. Rhian would win in the end. And yet, he was losing *now*. . . . Should she help? Should she stay put? Had she missed something in the crystal's scene? But she didn't have the crystal to look at anymore. Nor did Evelyn's dress intervene, suddenly dormant, as if it had never been alive at all.

Japeth seized the advantage, the king too weak to fend off his brother's assault. The Snake savaged him with a punch to the eye, swelling Rhian's face beyond recognition, sending the king crumpling to the ground, his crown knocked off his head.

Japeth stood up, breathing heavily, covered in blood.

Then his eyes went to Sophie.

He prowled towards her. Sophie blanched. This wasn't in the crystal! This wasn't in the script—

Rhian snagged his twin by the ankle and pulled him to the ground. The king scraped to his feet and kicked his brother in the face, harder, harder, until the Snake wasn't moving.

Rhian wheeled to Sophie, masked with blood. "I told you to leave. I *told* you," he wheezed, staggering towards her. He reached a wounded palm and touched the wet blood on her cheek, her blood mixing with his. "Now look what you've don—"

He stopped, his arm still in the air.

Because his hand was repairing before his and Sophie's eyes.

Sophie's blood snaked along the lines of Rhian's palm, magically sealing up the open cuts, restoring his tan, perfect flesh.

Her blood was *healing* him.

The same way her blood had healed Japeth.

Slowly, Rhian and Sophie met eyes, both shell-shocked.

"Well, well," said a glacial voice behind them.

Sophie and Rhian turned as Japeth rose from the ground, his face as bloodied as his brother's, his hair matted tight against his skull. The Snake had Excalibur in one hand. With the other, he reached up and placed Camelot's crown on his head.

"The pen said one of us would be king, the other healed by her blood," the Snake spoke, leering at his brother. "But it never said *which* of us would wear the crown. It never said the elder. Two brothers. Two possible kings. And yet I let *you* be king. Not because I thought you deserved the crown. But because you promised me a wish. You promised to bring back the one person I loved. A love that is worth more to me than a crown. Ironic, isn't it? The Good brother wishes for power. The Evil brother wishes for love. But that was the deal we made, bonded by a promise. A promise you no longer are willing to keep. So I propose a new deal. *You* can be the one healed by your new love's blood. And *I'll* be the king. A king with the power to fulfill your promise *myself.*"

Japeth's black suit of scims morphed into Rhian's blue-and-gold suit. The king's suit. One of the newly gilded scims flew off Japeth and, like a paintbrush, magically swept across Rhian and turned Rhian's suit gold and blue. Japeth's old liege's suit.

The Snake grinned. "I like this arrangement better."

Rhian charged at him, ramming his head into Japeth's

chest, spraying the king's crown into the wall and Excalibur onto the bed. The twins grappled for the sword, blood obscuring their faces, as the Snake magically transformed their suits, from blue to gold, gold to blue, back and forth, until Sophie couldn't tell who was who anymore.

"Who's the king, who's the king," Japeth chanted, their suits changing faster, their blood-covered hands straining for Excalibur, closer, closer . . .

Sophie suddenly questioned what she'd seen in the crystal. Two brothers dead. Herself, still standing. Had it been the truth? The *real* future? Or had it been a crystal of mind? A script of wishful thinking?

She couldn't leave it to chance. Witches won wars themselves.

Lunging out of the corner, she dove for the sword—

The king threw her out of the way, his blue-and-gold suit spattered red. Sophie rebounded, but she was too late. Rhian swiped the hilt into one hand, double-fisting with the other. His blade swung through the air, the edge catching the light like a sunflare—

It impaled Japeth's chest.

Clean through the heart.

Japeth closed his eyes in shock, stumbling backwards, his face slick with blood.

Rhian drew the sword out and his brother fell.

Sophie put a hand to her mouth, watching the scene play out as it had in the crystal. Only this time it was real, the smell of blood and sweat suffocating her.

Rhian kneeled over Japeth's body, watching his twin take his last breath.

The king bowed his head, holding the Snake's corpse.

Excalibur lay abandoned behind him.

Rhian didn't see Sophie move from the corner.

The fear was gone from her face.

Replaced with intent.

She picked up the sword, her slippered feet creeping along the carpet.

Without a sound, she raised the sword over Rhian's back.

Then she froze.

Rhian was crying.

Sobbing.

Like a little boy.

Crying for his dead brother.

Crying for his other half.

Something in Sophie's heart stirred.

A bond of blood she understood.

"Rhian?" she whispered.

He didn't look at her.

"You can bring him back," Sophie breathed. "You can use the pen. You can bring him back to life."

His sobs went softer.

"Rhian?"

Then his cries changed. Louder, wilder, pealing through the silent room. Until Sophie realized they weren't cries at all.

They were laughs.

He turned around, his ice-blue eyes slashing through her. As he stood, he wiped the blood off his face, revealing his milk-white skin.

A scream caught in Sophie's throat.

"Not Rhian," she choked.

Not Rhian!

Not Rhian!

"Oh?" said the Snake.

A gold scim floated off his king's suit and sheared the wet, matted locks of his hair to a close-skulled crop. Then it stroked the Snake's face like a pen, magically tanning him to a burnished amber.

"More Rhian than the real thing," he smiled.

He stabbed a finger at the hovering scim and it shot through the window like a knife, surged into the sky, and inked a golden message against the slate of gray.

The wedding of King Rhian and Princess Sophie will take place as scheduled. . . .

Sophie dashed for the door, but it was still bolted by scims. She recoiled in horror, watching Japeth move towards her, his grin dark and unhinged.

Agatha!

Agatha, help me!

Sophie backed against a wall.

The Snake put his cold lips to her ear.

"Ready for a wedding?"

She belted him in the face and leapt for the sword, her hands finding the hilt—

But the eels were already coming. As they speared into her ears from both sides, her consciousness fading, the last thing she thought of was her best friend, the other half of her soul, the Lion of her heart.

26

A Grave Mistake

Agatha dreamt of her own coffin.

She was trapped inside, water filling it as she pounded and kicked against steel walls, carved with strange symbols, her shouts choked by the liquid coating her face. Tiny black-and-white swans floated past, the size of seahorses, oblivious to her plight. A few seconds more and she was fully underwater, holding her breath and thrashing harder against her coffin . . . but now she felt a deep pain in her ears and then something warm and thick leaking out into the water, turning it red. *Blood*. Agatha screamed out any air she had left. Around her, swans began to sink like stones. Agatha bashed at the walls, but she was losing consciousness, the coffin's sides closing in. She clawed at her own tomb, her last breaths leaving, her face reflected in the murderous steel.

Only it wasn't her reflection.

It was Sophie's.

Agatha threw herself awake. "Sophie," she gasped, lunging through pitch-dark—

She hit her face on a hard wood beam and ricocheted backwards into more wooden beams, arranged in a lattice around her like a cage. A *bird*cage. For a moment, she thought she was still dreaming. Then she looked through her cage at two other birdcages, hooked to a thick blanket over a camel's rump, each cage filled: Tedros and Guinevere in one, Hort and Nicola in the other. The camel teetered downhill in the moonlight, kicking up dust around gravestones.

"Sultan of Shazabah gives me gold. Tells me: 'bring camel across Savage Sea to King Rhian,'" said the camel's rider as the birdcages jostled, sending the prisoners tumbling. "Wedding gift for king."

The rider looked back: a balding beaver with yellow-stained teeth.

"Extra wedding gifts now," he said, grinning at his prisoners. "Extra gold for Ajubaju."

That's when Agatha remembered everything.

As HER CAGE tossed her around, Dovey's bag under her arm, Agatha watched Tedros probe at his cage bars with his fingerglow, only to see his gold spell burn out. Either the cages were cased in magic or the wood was too dense to penetrate.

"Told you we should have gone through the Stymph Forest," Hort groused to Nicola in their coop. "Fastest way to Avalon. And we wouldn't have gotten caught!"

"Skirting the coastline was the safest plan," Nicola argued, her voice masked by the camel's grunts as Ajubaju smacked it with a stick. "We were nearly to the Lady of the Lake. If we hadn't passed those docks just as the Shazabah ship came in…"

"Or if Tedros' mother hadn't barreled straight into the *beaver,*" Hort whispered.

"It was dark," Guinevere sighed.

The camel tripped over a headstone, launching the old queen across her cage—

Tedros caught her in his arms. He glowered at Hort. "You're looking for someone to blame. I'm looking for a way out. Difference between a boy and a man."

Hort grumbled, glancing away.

Tedros gripped his bars, trying to snap them, his face red, muscles swollen, battling his cage the way he once battled his father's sword in the stone. He failed now as he did then. Agatha and her prince locked eyes through their cages. Tedros' father had given him a message: *Unbury Me.* Now they needed to follow that command and dig up the old king. *Something is in that grave*, Agatha thought. Something that could give them a chance against Rhian even when all seemed lost. But after a full day of sneaking up the coast from Gnomeland, with only a few miles to go, they'd been snared by Ajubaju, a goon for hire, who'd nearly killed Agatha in Avalon once before. Now with the beaver towing them back to Camelot, they were passing through a different gravesite altogether: the Garden of Good and Evil, where Evers and Nevers of the Woods were buried.

A glass coffin with a fair princess resting beside her prince mirrored blurs of gold overhead, and Agatha glanced up to see Lionsmane's announcement of King Rhian and Sophie's wedding glowing against a star-filled sky. Residues of her dream fluttered in her chest: the black-and-white swans . . . the blood coming out of her ears . . . Sophie's reflection as her own. . . . Her soul was trying to tell her something. *But what?* They'd been on the road more than a day since Lionsmane's message had branded in the sky and there'd been no change to it. No sign that it was anything other than the truth. Which meant there was less than a day left until Rhian and Sophie were married. Until Rhian had the Storian's powers. Until Agatha, Tedros, and all their friends were dead. And their only hope was in a king's coffin that they were riding farther and farther away from.

"That's where my dad's buried. Vulture Vale," Agatha heard Hort whisper to Nicola. "Not Necro Ridge or anything, but decent enough. School Master got my dad a proper burial. Only nice thing that bastard ever did."

"Must have wanted something from you in return," said his girlfriend.

"Not even. Said he understood the bond between father and son. That one day he'd have a son with his true love," Hort replied. "Gave me the creeps. His true love was *Sophie*."

Agatha shuddered.

"Wait. Look there," said Tedros, pointing ahead. "On Necro Ridge."

Atop a hill with the most lavish villain memorials— menacing statues, obsidian obelisks, thorn-wrapped tombs— rose a polished slab of stone, freshly laid and bigger than any other, lit by torches on both sides. Agatha could read it clearly.

HERE LIES THE SNAKE
Terror of the Woods
Slain by the Lion of Camelot
As Witnessed by the People

Agatha thought of the newspapers Devan and Laralisa had shown her when she'd first returned to school. The *Camelot Courier* had questioned the Snake's death, claiming the Crypt-keeper had never buried him, only to have other kingdoms' papers confirm the Snake's burial in Necro Ridge. No doubt Rhian took matters into his own hands after the Cryptkeeper spoke to the *Courier* and had this showy grave made to avert further queries. A grave Agatha knew must be empty. As for the

Cryptkeeper . . . it was telling that he was nowhere to be seen.

They were nearing the outskirts of the cemetery now. In hours, they'd be back at Camelot.

"We have to do something," Agatha said to Tedros. *"Fast."*

"Magic won't work. Can't break the cage. No one's coming to save us," the prince gritted, shielding his mother from the rough ride. He pointed at the bag under Agatha's arm. "What about Dovey's crystal?"

"You want me to throw it at the beaver's head?" asked Agatha sarcastically. "It's not a weapon!"

"Then why did you bring it?"

"Dovey told me not to let it out of my sight!"

"Well, she wouldn't know, would she?" Tedros said, frustrated. "I refuse to die on a camel—"

A fireball streaked over Tedros' head, singeing his hair. They spun to see the camel spit a new flamebomb at Agatha, who ducked just in time.

"No more talking," Ajubaju warned.

The beaver turned back around.

"Not an ordinary camel," Guinevere whispered to the others, undaunted. "*Spitfire* camel. Invincible killers, like gargoyles. Sultan of Shazabah has an army of them. Arthur was wary; thought those camels gave Shazabah too much power. King must really trust Rhian to be giving him one as a gift. . . ."

Agatha's mind snagged on one of the old queen's words.

Gargoyles.

"Invincible killers."

Only Agatha had beaten a gargoyle once. Her first year at

school. . . . She'd used her special talent to stop it from eating her. A talent she wasn't sure she still had.

Somewhere in the cave of her heart, an old spark kindled.

Agatha hoisted herself onto her knees, clutching Dovey's bag tighter. For her talent to work, she needed to look in the camel's eyes, but from her cage, all she could see was Ajubaju's big buttocks obscuring the creature's head.

She closed her eyes.

Can you hear me?

No answer.

Maybe talents dried up like unnourished fruit.

Maybe talents had a life and death of their own.

Agatha focused harder.

Tell me if you can hear me.

Give me a sign.

A breeze cooled her face.

She opened her eyes to see the camel raise its tail and poo, just missing her.

Agatha smiled.

So you can hear me.

I'm your friend here, not the beaver.

I know what you've left behind.

The camel's steps stuttered, sending the prisoners toppling against their bars. Ajubaju lashed the camel harder and the animal moaned. Agatha struggled back onto her knees.

I can help you.

This time, the camel subtly peeked back.

You're in a cage, came its voice. A female's. *You're in no position to help anyone.*

Agatha met its eyes. In the camel's dark pools, she saw Present and Past. Agatha's heart throbbed harder, as if pumping for two.

I hear wishes. That is my gift, she said to the camel. *And I know your wish is to return home. To your two daughters. To the rest of your herd.*

The camel stalled in surprise, then faced forward, withstanding more blows from Ajubaju's stick.

I am a soldier of Shazabah, the animal spoke coldly, moving faster. *I do as ordered.*

No one is a soldier first, said Agatha. *You are a mother first. A sister. A daughter. A friend.*

You'll say anything to be free, the camel scoffed.

We can both be free if you help me, Agatha replied.

I'm a gift for King Rhian, said the camel. *If I reject my duty and return to Shazabah, I'll be killed.*

King Rhian's reign will soon be at an end, Agatha replied. *The sultan will be relieved you never made it to Camelot. Hide in the Woods until that time comes. Then you will be reunited with your family.*

The camel marched ahead silently.

Why should I trust you? it said.

For the same reason I trust you, Agatha answered. *Because I have to.*

The camel glanced back at her. Then it faced forward.

What they say about you is true, Agatha of Woods Beyond.

Who's "they"? Agatha asked.

The camel didn't answer.

Sharply, it began to turn.

Get ready, the camel said.

Then it was running, back into the graveyard, towards the densest patch of tombs.

"What's happening!" Ajubaju blurted, beating the camel—

Agatha spun to her friends. "Take cover!"

Tedros, Hort, Nicola, and Guinevere gaped at her.

"Now!" Agatha cried—

At full sprint, the camel threw itself against a tomb's obelisk, shattering Agatha's birdcage and spraying her to the dirt in a hail of wood. The camel bashed Tedros' cage against a headstone, then Hort's cage against another, freeing the prisoners. Shell-shocked, Ajubaju seized the camel's throat, trying to strangle it—

The camel reared like a horse, bucking the beaver off and pinning him to the ground with its hoof. Gobs of fire spewed from the camel's mouth, burning an outline in the dirt around the beaver's body. The ground imploded. With a scream, Ajubaju plunged into the hole, disappearing into darkness.

The camel shook out its fur, as if it had hardly broken a sweat, before surveying the stunned prisoners strewn across graves. It found the one it was looking for. Gently, it nosed Agatha out of her cage's wreckage and pressed its warm, scratchy cheek to hers.

Thank you, princess.

The camel bowed to Tedros and her friends . . . then pranced into the forest.

Flat on her back, hugging Dovey's bag, Agatha stared into the sky, stars winking down at her. None of her friends moved. It was so quiet Agatha could hear the embers crackling around Ajubaju's new grave.

"What just happened?" Hort rasped, shaking wood out of his pants.

Tedros pulled Agatha up. "Whatever happened, I'm pretty sure I know who was responsible."

Agatha blushed, holding tight to her prince's hand.

Then her face changed.

"Someone's here," she breathed.

Tedros and the others tracked her eyes down the slope.

On Necro Ridge, shadows were coming out of a carriage.

Agatha recognized the carriage at once.

It was the same one that had taken away her best friend.

FIVE SHADOWS TIPTOED between graves until they got close enough to see. They hunched behind a tomb crowned with a wreath of flowers. Agatha peeked out first.

Two pirates in Camelot armor were digging up the Snake's grave. Kei watched over these pirates, his arms crossed, the captain's face a cold mask. Soon, they'd dug enough for Agatha to confirm what she'd already known: the grave was empty.

Kei opened the carriage and the pirates reached inside,

Agatha expecting them to bring out the king.

Instead, the pirates brought out something else.

A *body*.

Quickly, they lowered the corpse into the Snake's grave and began refilling it.

"Who is it?" Nicola asked. "Who are they burying?"

"I can't see," said Hort, leaning further over the tomb—

He knocked into the wreath and it spun away, smacking into an adjacent headstone.

Kei swiveled in their direction—

Hort plastered to the ground.

"He saw me," the weasel croaked. "Definitely saw me."

"They're coming for us, then," said Guinevere.

"Light your glows," Agatha ordered.

They waited behind the tomb, fingertips lit, prepared to defend themselves. . . .

Minutes passed.

No one came.

Slowly Agatha peered out.

The Snake's grave was filled in. Down the ridge, the pirates were climbing back into their carriage.

Agatha crawled out from behind the tomb. . . .

Tedros squeezed her hand. "Wait for me."

The prince followed her into the moonlight—

Both of them froze.

Kei was watching them.

He stood on the Snake's grave, his face half-lit by the

torches, his eyes pinned on the prince and princess.

Panicked, Agatha shielded Tedros, her fingerglow aimed at the captain.

But Kei didn't attack.

He just gazed at her. Not with anger or threat . . . but with something softer. Sadness. *Mourning.*

The captain kneeled down and laid a rose on top of the Snake's grave.

Then he glanced back at Agatha and Tedros one last time, before he hustled to join his men. Agatha watched the horses quietly pull the royal carriage back into the night, stars moving against the horizon as if to make way for it.

Tedros, meanwhile, was already scrambling downhill. He flung himself to the Snake's grave and started scraping away dirt with both hands.

"What is he doing?" Guinevere asked Agatha, as Hort and Nicola rose from the ground with them. But now, Agatha was running too, Dovey's bag pounding her flank. By the time she got to the Snake's grave, Tedros had lurched back in surprise—

Rhian's tan face lay uncovered. Blood coated the king's hairline. Deep, needle-like wounds flecked with black scales dotted the sides of his neck.

Agatha's heart plunged.

"He's d-d-dead," Tedros stammered. "Rhian . . . how can he be dead . . ."

"And looks like he's been dead awhile. At least a day," said Agatha, studying the corpse. She drew back, her body stiff. "Tedros . . . on his neck . . . those are *scim* wounds." She looked at her prince. "Japeth killed him. His *brother* killed him."

"None of this makes sense. Sophie's *marrying* Rhian . . . that's what Lionsmane says. . . ." Tedros insisted, checking the announcement in the sky, still beaming bright. "If he's been dead for a day, that means the message went up around the same time. Which means Sophie's marrying—"

"*Japeth*," said Agatha. "She's marrying Japeth. Sophie's marrying the *Snake*. That's the only reason they would be burying Rhian in *this* grave, secretly, in the middle of the night. Japeth's going to pretend to be his brother. He's going to wear his crown."

"The Snake?" Tedros said, a choked whisper. "The Snake's . . . *king*?"

His throat bobbed, his eyes fixed on the king's lifeless face. Rhian had been his mortal nemesis. Tedros had wished nothing more than to see him dead. But that's the problem with wishes: they need to be specific. Now Tedros was faced with an enemy far more deadly and deranged. A Snake masquerading as a Lion. A Snake on his father's throne.

Agatha clasped his arm. "Whatever Sophie went back to Camelot to do . . . it's gone wrong. She's in trouble, Tedros."

"And Kei wanted us to know," Tedros realized. "That's why he didn't attack us. He was Rhian's best friend. Kei was telling us to check the grave. He wanted us to know the Snake is king."

A gust blew the rose off Rhian's grave. Agatha carefully put it back where Kei had left it. As the petals rippled in the wind, Agatha remembered this—laying a rose on the Snake's grave—as if it had already happened in the past. . . .

A crystal.

She'd seen it in a crystal.

At the time, she'd thought it a lie. But like all the other crystals she'd taken for lies, this one had come true too. Nothing in her fairy tale was as it appeared to be: good or evil, truth or lies, past or present. She always had the story wrong. Even the stars seemed to be mocking her, free-falling in her direction, as if her world was turning upside down.

Hort, Guinevere, and Nicola caught up and jolted at the sight of Rhian in the Snake's grave.

"Um, this can't be good," said Hort.

"We need to get to Avalon," Tedros commanded, starting to move. "Before the wedding. *Everything* depends on it."

"We won't get there in time," said his mother, standing still. "Took us more than a day to get here from Avalon. By *camel.*"

"She's right," said Nicola. "On foot, we don't stand a chance. Sophie and Japeth are getting married at sunset. There's no way—"

Agatha wasn't listening.

Her eyes were on the falling stars, plummeting even quicker now, hundreds of them, thousands, aiming straight at her and her friends.

"That's the thing about Good . . . ," Agatha marveled. "It always finds a way."

Tedros and the others looked up at the army of fairies ripping through the night sky, swooping towards them. And leading the light brigade: a pear-shaped fairy with poofy gray hair, a green dress far too small, and ragged gold wings.

Flashing a mischievous smile, Tinkerbell flung a cloud of sooty dust—

Before Agatha could brace herself, she and her friends were off their feet and flying high into the dark, as fairies clustered around each one, hiding them in starry cocoons. Then they whisked them back towards Avalon, five comets against the night.

27

TEDROS

The Unburied King

In the mists of dawn, the gates of Avalon, two mangled heaps, resembled twin jaws about to swallow them up.

Tedros heard the others in a pack behind him, the grunts of their frozen breaths, their feet crushing fresh-fallen snow. The

fairies from school flocked around Tinkerbell like their queen, the only member of the League of Thirteen they'd managed to find. Peter Pan's favorite nymph landed on Tedros' shoulder, awaiting instructions—

"Keep watch for us outside the gates, Tink," said the prince.

Tinkerbell replied with twinkly gibberish. Alongside her fairies, she burrowed for warmth into the bright green apples hanging off vines, the one sign of life in Avalon's endless winter. Tedros, meanwhile, led his group through the gates, crossing into the Lady of the Lake's domain. The crash of the Savage Sea against rock echoed like a slow-beating drum. Over his head, Lionsmane's promise of Sophie's wedding glinted in the sunrise, a dead man her supposed groom. All this time, he'd been so obsessed with Rhian, thinking him the real threat, instead of paying attention to what was actually happening. Rhian had been a pig. But Japeth was a *monster*. A boy of no conscience, the murderer of his friends, a black hole of Evil. If Japeth could kill his own brother, his own blood, then with the Storian's powers, he'd tear the Woods apart without mercy. He'd bring back the worst Evil from the dead and write Good out of existence. He'd watch the world burn with a smile.

The prince took a deep breath, trying to settle himself. The End wasn't written yet. They'd gotten here alive. That was the first challenge. Now they had to convince the Lady of the Lake to let them cross her magical waters and dig up King Arthur's grave. Tedros could feel oily nausea filling up his stomach. When he was a boy, he'd leaned in and kissed his father goodbye before they'd closed his coffin. To open that coffin back up like a graverobber . . . to ransack his father's body and disturb his peace . . . His hand clamped at his throat. He couldn't do it. He couldn't. And yet . . . he had to. He tried to focus on the next obstacle, on getting to his father's tomb, step by step—

A hand stroked beneath his shirtsleeve in just the right way.

"You're brave to do this, Tedros," said Agatha. "Your father would have done the same to protect his people. It's why you're his son. The son he *raised* to be king."

Tedros wanted to hold her and never let go. He knew what she'd said was the truth. Agatha never lied. That's why he loved her. Because she didn't just want him to be king. She wanted him to be a *good* king. And he wanted to be a good king for her. One day he hoped to tell her all this, when this moment was just a memory. . . . But for now, he could only nod, unable to speak anything in return. He glanced back at his mother, walking with Hort and Nicola. She, too, looked stricken, but more self-conscious and meek, as if questioning this entire endeavor or whether she should be here at all.

Still, she followed as Tedros walked the path around Avalon's castle. The bone-white spires were connected in a circular palace, overlooking a maze of staircases leading down to the lake. Snow fell harder, covering the prince's bootprints the second they formed. Somewhere here, Chaddick had died, killed by the animal who'd just taken the throne. Now his friend's body lay in the grove beside his father, a grove Tedros wanted to desecrate. Emotions reared like a tidal wave, too high for the prince to wall in. He couldn't do this. Not even with Agatha at his side. He needed Merlin. He needed a father.

"Shouldn't we have heard from the witches by now?" he rasped to Agatha. "Shouldn't we know if they've found Merlin?"

His princess heard his desperation, because she clutched his palm gently. "The Caves of Contempo are difficult to get to. That's why Reaper trusted the witches for the job," she said, guiding him down the steps towards the lake. "But they will get there. They're probably closing in as we speak."

"Or they're dead," murmured Hort.

"Unlikely," said Nicola. "If we're still alive, then Hester's alive, because she's smarter and tougher than all of us, including you."

Agatha pulled Tedros faster down the steps. "Look, we don't know where anyone is or if they're safe: witches, Beatrix, Willam, teachers, first years, even Anadil's two rats. But it doesn't matter unless we stop the Snake from becoming the One True King and killing us all. That's why we're here. To find a way to put Tedros back on the throne."

"Except there is no way," said Guinevere's voice. She stood at the top of the stairs. "Rhian might be dead, but Japeth is as much Arthur's son as Rhian was. You witnessed the past with your own eyes, Agatha. You saw Evelyn Sader bewitch Arthur into giving her his sons. His *heirs*. Japeth is king, then. Nothing in the Past can change the Present. Nothing in Arthur's grave can make Tedros king again."

Everyone fell quiet. Agatha included.

"Then why did Father's sword give Merlin that message for

me?" Tedros appealed to his mother. "Why did Father send me here?"

"Did he?" said Guinevere. "Or was it the Lady of the Lake who gave Merlin that message? The Lady, whose loyalties we're not even sure of?"

Tedros' breath caught in his chest.

He looked at Agatha, doubting himself, doubting everything—

But it was too late.

Down below, the waters had started to churn.

THE LADY ROSE like a dragon, her bald head reflecting the fire of the sunrise. Black pits grooved beneath her eyes, her face more shriveled and deathly than Tedros had imagined it. No longer did she seem Good's great defender, but instead a Witch of the Woods, haunted and bitter and enraged. She locked on Agatha, her low, deep voice hissing across the water.

"You *promised*. You promised to leave me in peace." She flew across the lake, her tattered gray robes like shredded wings, and thrust her face in Agatha's. "You're a liar. A *liar*—"

"Don't talk to her that way," Tedros retorted, shielding his princess. "You're one to talk about promises. You broke your own vow. To protect Good. To protect Camelot. You've put our entire world at risk by kissing a *Snake*."

"He had the heir's blood. The *king's* blood," the Lady spat at him, her breath salty and old. "And yet you come here, acting like I serve you. Like *you're* the king."

"We're not here for you," said Tedros firmly. "We've come to visit my father's grave. I have that right."

The Lady laughed. "You're not king. You have no rights here. *None.* This is my domain. I could kill you all if I wish. I still have enough powers left for that."

Tedros felt Agatha back up behind him, Dovey's bag to her chest, as if she took this threat seriously. The prince stood his ground. "Excalibur gave you a message for me. A command from my father. The king you served faithfully his entire life. I've come to obey that command. And if you loved my father, you'll let me into your waters."

"You're a fool," the nymph lashed. "I loved your father because he was a good king. Better than any other that came before. That's why I made Excalibur for him. A sword that *rejected* you. A sword that his heir, the *true* king, pulled from the stone."

"*Wrong*," said Tedros. "Rhian pulled the sword from the stone and now he's dead. His brother, his *murderer*, sits on the throne. The boy *you* kissed. Excalibur thought one brother was king; you thought the other brother was king. Both can't be right. Even a *fool* would know that."

The Lady glared at him, her whole body starting to quake, her eyes steaming furious tears. "Go. Now. Before I fill these waters with your blood."

Tedros could see Agatha fiddling with Dovey's bag. Why wasn't she saying anything? He turned his ire on the Lady. "You made a mistake. A mistake that will destroy the Storian and end our world unless I save it. Take me to my father's grave."

"You trespass here and accuse *me*?" the Lady seethed.

"I order you to let me pass," the prince charged.

"This is your last warning!"

"And this is *yours*. Let me pass."

"I'll tear you apart!"

"Let me pass!"

"You liar! You *snake*!" the Lady screamed.

"*LET ME PASS!*" Tedros bellowed.

The Lady snatched him into her taloned fists and hammered him down towards the water with such force he'd tear into pieces the instant he hit the surface. Tedros thrashed against her, bracing for his death—

—just as he saw his princess sprint across the shore, a crystal ball in her arms. With a flying leap, Agatha rammed her head into the Lady of the Lake's chest. The nymph dropped Tedros into the lake, as the Lady and Agatha plunged underwater, knotted in each other's limbs.

Before Tedros could take a breath, the lake around him exploded with blue light.

Guinevere pulled Hort and Nicola away from the shore; Tedros could hear his mother screaming his name, but he was sucking in a wad of breath and dunking underwater, glimpsing Agatha as she seized the Lady of the Lake's hand and touched it to the glowing crystal ball, the two of them evaporating inside the portal. Already the bright blue light was fading, the portal starting to close; Tedros flung forward, kicking his legs like a dolphin tail, stabbing out his fingers as the crystal darkened—

Pain exploded through his chest and he fell backwards, splayed in the blinding light, before he felt cold glass catch him from beneath, puddling with the water off his skin.

In the wet reflection, he watched his princess kneel down and help him to his feet inside Dovey's ball. She grimaced, still unsteady herself, neither of them recovered from the crystal's assault. But Agatha's eyes weren't on him. They were on the Lady of the Lake, posed silently on the other side of the ball, her hands caressing the thousands of tiny glass droplets arranged in the phantom's mask, as if she was instinctively versed in the crystal's magic.

Tedros and Agatha moved towards her, but the Lady paid no attention, the old crone hunched over as she studied scenes inside the crystals, brushing past any with the prince and princess and fixing instead on her own. . . . Forging Excalibur from her own silvery blood. Bestowing the sword on Tedros' father. Talking intimately with Arthur on the shores of her lake. Surging across a battlefield at Arthur's side like his warrior angel, obliterating the king's enemies . . . In all of these she was beautiful, powerful, so rich with powers that Tedros could see her eyes sparkle, gazing into these magic mirrors of time. There were no scenes of her present or future. Her soul only knew the past.

Then the Lady froze.

It was a crystal near the phantom's edge.

She backed away from it, her hands starting to shake.

"That's it, isn't it?" Tedros realized. "The moment you lost your powers."

The Lady of the Lake didn't move.

"We need to go inside," said Agatha.

The Lady turned, the fever of rage broken, replaced by anguish and grief. "No. *Please*."

"It's the only way we'll know the truth," said Agatha.

The Lady appealed to Tedros. "Leave it be."

Tedros looked back at the haggard old witch who had just tried to kill him, a witch who had let his knight die and protected a Snake. A witch whose sword had rejected him. He wanted to feel anger. He wanted to feel hate. But deep in her eyes, all he could see was someone as flawed as he. Both their stories had taken detours into darkness. Both their futures were unclear. He reached out and clasped her decrepit palm.

"He is my father's son. The boy you kissed," Tedros spoke. "But I am Arthur's son too. So if you see my father in me, even a trace of that king you served so loyally, then help us. We need you, even without your powers. *Good* needs you."

The Lady searched Tedros' face. Tears streamed down her cheeks, her lips quivering, but no sound came out.

Slowly she reached up and pulled down the crystal.

She held it out to Agatha, the Lady's breaths shallow, her fingers tremoring.

Without a word, Agatha took the glass droplet into one hand, then Tedros' palm into the other.

Raising the crystal, Agatha stared calm and still into its center.

Light broke through like a sword.

Hard, wet snow pelted Tedros' cheek.

He glanced down and saw his boots floating on top of clear water, Agatha with him at the edge of the lake, his princess still holding his hand. Behind them, the portal's gash of blue light glowed strong. They were inside the Lady's crystal, two ghosts revisiting the past.

Sounds came from the shore: metal into skin . . . a wheeze of breath . . . a sword hitting snow . . .

Slowly Tedros and Agatha looked up.

The Snake rose from Chaddick's dead body, his scaly black suit and green mask flecked with blood. He walked towards the Lady of the Lake, who floated over her shores, her silver hair thick and flowing, her dark eyes pinned on Chaddick's killer.

"A king stands before me," said the Lady. "I smell it. The blood of Arthur's eldest son."

"A son still alive thanks to your protection," said the Snake. "The usurper's knight is dead."

"A usurper your father believed would be king," the Lady remarked. "Arthur never spoke of you to me. And yet, Excalibur remains trapped in stone. A coronation test unfulfilled. Waiting for you, it seems. Arthur had his secrets. . . ."

The Snake moved closer, stepping into the Lady's waters.

"As do you," he said. "The kind of secrets only a king could know."

"Oh? Then why wear a mask, King of Secrets?" the Lady asked him. "I smell the blood of a Good soul, the blood of a Lion. Why wear the guise of a Snake and attack your fellow kingdoms? Kingdoms you are meant to rule?"

"For the same reason you wish to be a queen instead of the Lady," the Snake replied. "For *love*."

"You know nothing of my wishes," the Lady scoffed.

The Snake removed his mask, revealing Japeth's ice-blue eyes and smooth, sculpted face. The Lady gazed at him, transfixed.

Watching from the shore, Tedros' blood boiled, his body ready to attack, unable to discern Present from Past.

"Come with me," Japeth said to the Lady. "Come to Camelot. Leave this lonely cave behind."

"Precious boy," she cooed. "Many a king has flattered me with promises of love. Your father included. Perhaps to make me even more devoted and passionate in my service. But none ever meant it. How could they? None could accept the costs. To love me means I must relinquish my powers. No king would abide that. I'm more valuable here. Good's greatest weapon."

"I can protect myself," said Japeth.

"Says the boy who just admitted he's alive because of my *protection*," the Lady replied, glancing at Chaddick's corpse on the shore.

"And yet here I remain," said Japeth. "Why? I don't need anything more from you. I can walk away right now. But I sense a kindred heart, imprisoned by magic. A heart that can give us both what we want."

He stepped deeper into her water, his breath misting

towards her, their bodies so close. The Lady leaned in, inhaling him. "Sweet, sweet blood of Arthur . . . ," she sighed softly. "And what of my duties to Good? My duties to defend Camelot beyond your reign?"

"Good has grown arrogant and weak," said Japeth. "You've defended it for too long. At the expense of your soul."

"My soul," the Lady bantered, touching his cheek. "A boy claims to see my soul. . . ."

"I know you are lonely," said the Snake. "So lonely you've started to feel bitterness over your place here. You feel yourself changing. No longer do you hold the purity of Good within your heart. You dip into darkness and desolation, the fuels of Evil. All because you won't give yourself what you want. Stay here any longer and you'll begin to make mistakes. Instead of protecting Good, you'll come to harm it. Evil will stake its seed in your heart. If it hasn't already."

The Lady looked at him. All playfulness was gone.

"You yearn for love as much as I," said the Snake. "And yet, neither of us can attain that love without another's help. Someone who can bring that love to life. Otherwise, that love will remain a ghost, a phantom, beyond the rules of the living. I will do anything to find that love. *Anything.* As will you."

The Lady's skin flushed. "How do you know? How do you know I would do anything for love?"

The Snake met her eyes. "Because you already have."

He kissed her, his hands pulling her down, as the Lady fell into the Snake's embrace, the lake's waters curling up around them like the petals of a flower in full bloom.

But then something in the Lady's face changed. Her body went rigid, resisting her new love's. Her mouth pulled away, the veils of water collapsing. She stared at the boy who'd kissed her, her big black pupils jolting with surprise, panic . . . *fear*.

Japeth grinned.

Instantly, the Lady began to dwindle, her body blighting, desiccating. Her hair fell out in clumps; her spine contorted and crackled . . .

All as the Snake calmly walked away.

Tedros felt Agatha's hands on him, pulling him back into the portal.

The instant the glass of Dovey's ball appeared beneath Tedros, he was on his feet, pointing at the old crone—

"Your face . . . I saw your face . . . ," he panted. "You knew something was wrong. . . . You *knew* it!"

The Lady was cowering in the corner, head in her hands.

"It was the king . . . the heir . . . ," she defended. "Arthur's blood . . ."

"You felt something when you kissed him!" Tedros cried, charging for her. Agatha held him back. "What was it!"

"Let me out," the Lady begged.

"Tell me what you felt!" Tedros assailed.

The Lady pounded on the glass. *"Let me out!"*

She bludgeoned the crystal with both fists—

"Tell me!" Tedros yelled.

The Lady slammed the walls, tapping the last of her powers, her fists bashing Dovey's crystal harder, harder, until it cracked.

"No!" Agatha shrieked, she and Tedros dashing for the Lady too late as she raised her fists one last time—

Glass exploded.

Tedros and Agatha launched backwards, the lake rushing in and filling their shocked mouths. Choking, they thrust out hands for each other, Tedros hanging on to Agatha's dress, Agatha gripping his thin white shirt. Then came the storm: thousands of glass shards crashing down on them, plunging them into the deep. Thrashing in vain, they sank under the mass of crystals, screams unheard. The Lady of the Lake watched them, robes floating over her head like a reaper's, her silver tears clouding the sea.

"Forgive me," she whispered, her voice resounding. "Forgive me!"

She thrust out her hand—

Dark water swirled around Tedros and Agatha, a chasm ripping open in the lake's center like the mouth of a snake, before it swallowed them both inside.

Dew coated Tedros' lips, the rich, fresh smell of grass mixing with the scent of Agatha's hair, his princess spooned in his arms. He opened his eyes to see a lush green heath, sparkling under the sunrise. Agatha stirred, her prince helping her up.

"We're . . . here," she breathed.

Tedros still felt like he was underwater, the Lady's last words reverberating. . . . *"Forgive me!"*

She had nearly killed them.

Dovey's crystal was destroyed.

And yet, she'd let them pass.

She'd stayed true to Good.

He thought of the way she'd embraced the Snake . . . the way she inhaled Arthur's blood in his veins . . . the way her face darkened once their lips touched. . . .

What does she know? he asked himself. *What does she know that we don't?*

Across the moors, the old farmhouse where Lancelot and Guinevere once lived lay dormant and overgrown. Sheep, cows, and horses grazed unbounded on the hills.

"It's like we never left," Agatha sighed.

For a brief moment, Tedros wished he and Agatha could hide here, like his mother and her true love once had. *Past is Present and Present is Past*, he thought. . . .

"Tedros?"

He looked at his princess.

She squeezed his hand.

There would be no hiding today.

THE GRAVE LAY in shadow, sheltered by a small oak grove. A shining glass cross rose out of the ground between two trees, marking King Arthur's tomb. Garlands of white roses draped the cross, along with a glowing five-pointed star resting against the base. There were more of these stars strewn nearby, ashy and burnt out, as if Merlin returned to lay a new one whenever the old had grown cold.

But there was a second grave now, Tedros realized, only a short distance from his father's, deeper in the shadows. A grave he hadn't seen before, marked with a second glass cross.

"Chaddick," said Agatha quietly. "This is where the Lady buried him."

Tedros nodded. "It's where he belongs."

His knight. His friend, valiant and true. *He shouldn't be here at all,* Tedros wanted to say. Chaddick was too young, too Good to die. He never should have tried to take on the Snake. He never should have tried to do a king's work.

Tedros swallowed the knot in his throat.

Work still left to be done.

His eyes roved back to his father's plot.

"Merlin enchanted the tomb to preserve him," he said. "Whatever we find, there'll be hexes and curses to break through. A test I have to pass." His voice thinned, his palms sweating. "But first, we have to dig him up."

He raised his fingerglow to his dad's grave, his heart jittery, his stomach lurching. His finger started to shake, his gold glow unsteady—

Agatha stepped in front of him, her own gold glow lit.

"Look away," she said.

She began burning through the dirt.

Tedros kept his eyes on the glass cross at the head of the grave, reflecting Agatha's calm face as she worked. At the base of the cross, Merlin's glowing white star mirrored Tedros' fidgeting shadow, his square jaw and sweep of curls. He was thankful for his princess, thankful it was just him and Agatha that had made it this far. As much as he loved his mother, his father wouldn't have wanted her here—

He broke out of his thoughts.

Merlin's white star. His shadow in it.

It was still moving.

Only he *wasn't*.

He glanced back at Agatha, her glow burning away more and more earth.

"They must have buried the coffin deep," Agatha murmured, tense with concentration.

Tedros turned back to the star and leaned closer, the shadow inside receding from him, as if to lead him somewhere.

"This doesn't make sense . . . ," Agatha's voice rasped.

The prince reached for the star. His fingers brushed the warm white surface and sank right through—

"Tedros, the grave is *empty*. There's nothing here."

By the time Agatha turned to her prince, he was halfway in.

She lunged in horror, grasping her hand for him, but all she found was a cold star, the light snuffed out, like a sun fallen into a sea.

TEDROS TASTED CLOUDS in his mouth, feather-soft, dissolving like spun sugar, with the sweet tang of blueberry cream. He lifted his eyes to see a silvery five-pointed star shoot past him across a purple night sky, lit by a thousand more of these stars. The air was toasty and thick, the silence of the Celestium so vast that he could hear the drum of his own heart, like it was the beat of the universe.

A rustle of movement . . . then an intake of breath.

Tedros grew very still.

Someone else was on the cloud.

He looked up.

King Arthur sat on the edge of the cloud in his royal robes, his hair thick and gold, his beard flecked with gray, a Lion locket sparkling around his neck.

"Hello, son," said his father.

Tedros was ghost-white. "Dad?"

"Merlin kept this place a secret from me when I was king," said his father, gazing up at the sky. "I understand why now."

"This . . . this is i-i-impossible. . . ." Tedros reached out a shaking hand towards the king. "This isn't real . . . this *can't* be real. . . ." His palm touched his father's face, quivering against Arthur's soft beard. The king smiled and pressed his son's hand into his.

Tedros stiffened. "But you're . . . you're supposed to be . . ."

"Here. With you, just as you need me to be," said his father, his voice soothing and deep. "In the way I wish I'd been for all the days I had with you, up to the very last. Our story didn't have the ending we wanted." Gently, he brushed Tedros' hair out of his face. "But I knew long ago that there might come a time when you needed me. A time beyond the Present and your memories of our Past. Yet how can a father see his son beyond the Rules of Time? That's where it helps to have a wizard as your dearest friend."

"So you're a . . . ghost?" Tedros asked.

"When most kings die, they embalm the body to preserve it," King Arthur replied. "But no one can truly preserve a body against time. In the end, all graves are raided or neglected or forgotten. It is the nature of things. Leave it to Merlin, then, to suggest getting rid of my body entirely. To preserve the soul instead. This way you could find me when the time came. The magic was limited, of course. My soul could only reappear to the living once, for the briefest of meetings, before it dispersed forever to the source from which it came. Until then, I would live amongst the stars, waiting patiently for the Present to catch up with the Past."

Tears grew in Tedros' eyes. "How brief a meeting?"

His father smiled. "Long enough for you to know how much I love you."

Tedros panicked. "You can't go! Not after I've found you! Please, Dad . . . You don't know the things I've done . . . the mess I've made. . . . A Snake sits on the throne. A Snake that's your *son*." His voice cracked, his posture sinking like he was weighed down by a stone. "I failed your test. I never became king. Not the king you wanted me to be." Sobs choked out of him. "Only I didn't just fail the test. I failed Camelot. I failed Good. I failed *you*—"

"And yet, you're here," said King Arthur. "Just as I asked you to be."

Tedros lifted his wet eyes.

"You passed a test far greater than pulling a sword," said his father. "A test that is only the beginning of many more."

Tedros swallowed, barely able to speak. "But what do I do? I need to know what to do. I need to know how to fix this."

King Arthur reached out his hand. He put it to his son's heart, pressing firm and strong, its warmth filling Tedros' chest.

"A Lion roars within," he said.

Tears slid down Tedros' cheeks. "Don't leave me. I'm begging you. I can't do this alone. I *can't*."

"I love you, son," his father whispered, kissing his head.

"No . . . wait . . . don't go . . . ," Tedros gasped, reaching for him—

But the prince was already falling through clouds.

"Tedros?" a voice said.

The prince roused to the smell of rich, dense earth and the comfort of a deep bed.

He opened his eyes.

Agatha looked down from high, oak branches swaying above her, dappled by the sun.

Then Tedros understood.

He was in his father's grave.

He was *in* his father's grave.

Instantly he was on his knees, scrambling out of the hole Agatha had dug, dirt crumbling beneath his hands and boots, crashing him back down, before he finally managed to claw himself out. He collapsed against his father's glass cross, the white star cold against his cheek as he heaved for air.

"What happened?" Agatha hounded, dropping to his side.

He couldn't answer. How could he answer? He'd seen his father. He'd smelled him and touched him and felt his dad's hand upon his heart. Tedros thrust his palm under his shirt, where his father had left his mark. But now the moment was gone, his father lost forever. And Tedros was left with only the memor—

The prince paused.

Beneath his shirt, something brushed against his hand. Something that wasn't there before.

"Where were you?" Agatha asked, her arm around him. "Where did you go?"

The prince rose to his knees and pulled down his shirt. A Lion locket hung around his neck, lit by a stream of sun.

Agatha let go of him. "But that's . . . that's your father's . . ."

Tedros fingered the gold Lion head at the end of the chain, its two sides fused together. All those years as a child, he'd tried to get it open, day after day, testing any trick he could think of, failing every time, until one day . . . he *didn't* fail. His dad had given him the most assured of smiles, as if he'd known it was only a matter of time.

Slowly Arthur's son slipped the Lion's head into his mouth like he had that day, a long time ago. . . .

"I don't understand," Agatha pressed—

He felt the gold magically soften, his teeth prying at the

crease between the two sides at just the right angle . . . until the locket popped open. Bit by bit, his tongue probed the inside of its case, searching for something from his father, a note or a card or—

His eyes froze.

Or that.

He lifted it onto his tongue, tasting the cold, hard surface, savoring the deep grooves along its side, holding it in place as he let the locket slip out of his mouth.

"Only three swans left," Hort's voice echoed. *"Or was it four."*

"Tedros?" Agatha asked, seeing his face. "What is—"

He kissed her.

So softly, so delicately, he saw her eyes widen as it moved from his mouth to hers. A glow sparked like a flame in her big brown gaze, the two of them silent and still, sharing this moment as one.

Carefully Tedros drew his lips from hers. Agatha kept his stare as she reached shaking fingers and pulled it out.

The ring.

The ring with the Storian's symbols.

The ring that had never been burned, but instead gifted across time.

A king's true coronation test for his son.

"Tedros . . . ," Agatha whispered, her eyes aflame. *"Tedros . . ."*

Blood rumbled through the prince's veins, from the forgotten corners of his soul, pounding at the door to his heart, harder, harder, demanding to be let in.

His princess held out the ring, shining like a sword.

"Now it begins," Agatha vowed.

The prince's eyes reflected her steel. "Now it begins."

He took the ring onto his finger, the door to his heart ripping open, a Lion awakened, a Lion reborn, before Tedros gnashed his teeth to the sky and unleashed a roar that shook heaven and earth.